D1135402

H03

Slough Library Services

Please return this book on or before the date shown on your receipt.

To renew go to:
Website: **www.slough.gov.uk/libraries**
Phone: **01753 535166**

THE WOOLWORTHS GIRLS

It's 1938 and as the threat of war hangs over the country, Sarah Caselton is preparing for her new job at Woolworths. Before long, she forms a tight bond with two of her colleagues: the glamorous Maisie and shy Freda. The trio immediately form a close-knit friendship, sharing their hopes and dreams for the future. But with war clouding the horizon, the young men and women of Woolworths realize that there are bigger battles ahead. It's a dangerous time for the nation, and an even more perilous time to fall in love...

THE WOOLWORTHS GIRLS

THE WOOLWORTHS GIRLS

by

Elaine Everest

Magna Large Print Books
Long Preston, North Yorkshire,
BD23 4ND, England.

British Library Cataloguing in Publication Data.

A catalogue record of this book is
available from the British Library

ISBN   978-0-7505-4316-3

First published in Great Britain 2016 by Pan Books,
an imprint of Pan Macmillan

Published in Large Print 2017 by arrangement with
Macmillan Publishers

Magna Large Print is an imprint of Library Magna Books Ltd.

Printed and bound in Great Britain by
T.J. (International) Ltd., Cornwall, PL28 8RW

To my husband, Michael,
for having the patience to live with a writer xx

Prologue

Sarah Caselton reached into her handbag and pulled out a small leather purse. Ignoring the biting-cold wind from the river, she searched for a couple of pennies, then dropped them into the carol singers' collection tin. 'Silent Night' had always been her favourite Christmas song. For a few moments she stood with her eyes closed and let the rich tones of the choir wash over her, taking her back to when she had performed this much-loved carol at her school's nativity play. Without thinking, she joined in with the final chorus, her sweet voice soaring high and clear above the bass tones of the men: '...*sleep in heavenly peace.*'

'God bless you, love – and a merry Christmas.'

Sarah thought the choir were very brave to stand outside singing on such a chilly day. The sky was threatening snow too. If it hadn't been for an interview for a sales assistant position at Woolworths, she'd have stayed home with Nan. A weather-worn man, a row of medals across the chest of his overcoat, patted her arm. He was the one who'd held the collection tin in front of her as she stopped amid the bustle of Christmas shoppers.

'For melting an old man's heart on such a bitter day, you can pick the next carol. What do you fancy?'

Sarah considered his question, warming her hands by a brazier set in front of the motley collection of choir members. The glowing embers were most inviting on that cold December day. The snow was now falling steadily, starting to deaden the footsteps of passing shoppers in the busy riverside town of Erith. Sarah shuddered and pulled her knitted scarf closer to her ears. Erith was such a pretty place in the summer, with the gardens down by the river where you could sit and watch the world go by. Who'd have thought that just up the River Thames was the bustling city of London and the other way down the river were the seaside towns of north Kent? No wonder her dear old nan never wanted to move away from her beloved Erith.

As Sarah thought about which carol to choose, she noticed that the choir was made up only of men: one in a wheelchair, another leaning heavily on a wooden crutch and a few in old overcoats that had seen much better days. A sign propped against the tobacconist's shop showed them to be from the Seamen's Mission. Her granddad had loved his life at sea and had been a merchant sea-man in the Great War. He may even have known some of these ex-sailors. A tear threatened to fall on her cheek. This wouldn't do, she thought to herself. Nan Ruby was always saying he'd had a good innings and went without too much pain. And after all, if Nan hadn't been alone, Sarah might not have had the chance to escape her life in Devon to come and live with her here in Erith.

'Why the glum face, love? You look as though you've lost a shilling and found a penny. You've gotta make the most of life and be happy. After all, we could be at war by next year, going by

12

what the papers keep telling us. No one believes all that talk from Chamberlain and his "peace in our time" nonsense.'

Sarah shrugged her shoulders. She couldn't tell this brave old sailor why she was sad. 'I'm fine. Just a bit cold.' She grinned.

'So how about that song? What'll it be?'

'Oh, I don't know. How about "The Twelve Days of Christmas"?'

The old sailor turned to a comrade who was holding an accordion. ''Ere, Ernie, can you play "The Twelve Days of Christmas"?'

His mate pulled a face and laughed. Resting the musical instrument on his knee, he delved into the pocket of his coat and fished out a hip flask with his free hand. 'I might have been able to a while ago, but after knocking back this to keep out the cold, I ain't so sure I can remember all the words.'

Sarah laughed. They were certainly a cheerful bunch. She checked her watch. 'My goodness, just look at the time. I must dash.'

'Going somewhere nice, love?' he asked, taking another swig from the flask.

Sarah gave a nervous smile. 'An interview for a sales assistant job.' She nodded towards the glass-fronted shop nearby. 'In Woolworths.'

'Where everything costs a tanner,' Ernie called out.

Sarah was puzzled. Whatever was he talking about? 'I'm sorry – I don't understand.'

'It's a fact. You tell her, Fred.'

The man with the collection tin nodded. 'He's right. There was a time when everything cost thruppence or a tanner in all their shops – and there are plenty of them. Come from America they did. They've got shops the length and breadth of the land.' He nodded wisely.

'A tanner?'

'Sixpence to you, love.'

'Ah yes, that's what Nan calls a sixpence, come to think of it.'

'Mind you, prices are not so good now. They started charging sixpence a shoe when prices went up. So you remember that if they put you on the shoe counter,' Fred said, giving her a nudge with his elbow.

Sarah giggled. It sounded so funny. 'I'll try to remember it, but I have to get the job first.'

'Well, you just give them one of your lovely smiles and you'll be running the place before the day is out.'

She laughed and waved goodbye to the carol singers. She stopped for a moment to gaze at the building where hopefully she would soon be working. Gleaming windows set either side of dark mahogany double doors were crammed full of toys and gifts, enticing customers to enter and stock up for Christmas. Through the doors she could see female sales staff busy serving customers from behind high counters. Each was dressed identically in a smart maroon overall that buttoned up to the neck and had full sleeves with tiny cuffs. It looked like a lovely place to work, Sarah thought, filled with excitement, as she headed towards a side door marked, 'Staff only', following a group of women into the dark interior of the F. W. Woolworth Company. As the heavy wooden door closed behind her, Sarah could hear Fred and his mates burst into 'We Wish You a Merry Christmas'.

Sarah removed her woolly hat. Pulling a comb from her handbag, she ran it quickly through her shoulder-length dark brown hair before checking her face in a small powder compact. I'm as ready as I'll ever be, she thought.

1

Freda shivered, pulling her coat close to her body. The well-worn fabric did nothing to keep out the chill. If only she'd been able to wear her better coat, but then her stepfather would have known she was up to something. Not that the other coat was much better. It had only cost two bob on the second-hand stall down the market, but it was a little more presentable than the threadbare rag she was wearing now. At least she'd been able to put a few clothes in a battered suitcase she'd picked up cheap and hidden in the coal bunker until she made her getaway from home.

She shuddered as she thought of the past week, trying to pretend that nothing was amiss. The morning the coppers came knocking on their door, she'd almost fainted with the shock. To be told her sixteen-year-old brother had run away from borstal was bad enough, but when the police asked if she knew where he was, it put the fear of God into her. She'd never been in trouble in her life and there they were asking her about her brother and if she knew a chap called Jed Jones who had got away with him. As if she'd tell them anything!

Thank goodness Lenny's letter had arrived in the early post and her stepfather was still sleeping off the excesses of the night before. Freda pulled the letter from her pocket and scrutinized his words, looking for more clues as to where he could be. Lenny hadn't said where he was, but the postmark on the letter said as clear as day, 'Erith'. Freda had to go into the library and ask for help to find out where it was. The librarian had been very kind, pulling out a map of England and a couple of books that listed towns. She could see that it was on the shores of the Thames in Kent and was a busy area, with factories, pubs and lots of shops. It was when she saw how many pubs there were that she remembered him mentioning a cellmate named Jed whose father was the landlord of a pub called the Ship by the side of the Thames. If only Lenny had served his sentence of eight years, he could have started life anew.

Freda and Lenny had always looked out for each other, so she had to find him. He was her junior by just thirteen months. Her mum still cursed that he'd taken her by surprise arriving so soon after his sister. Not that she bothered much with either of them once they could fend for themselves. She was soon off down the pub carrying on with her job as a barmaid. Her dad had always had time for them, even though he worked long hours at the foundry. She knew she shouldn't think such things, but sometimes she wished that her mum had perished in the flu outbreak and not her dad. He wasn't cold in his grave before Mum took up with the man they now called their stepfather. She couldn't remember the wedding. Being only ten at the time, her memory was a little sketchy about things back then. In fact, she could hardly recall her dad's features at all. If she closed her eyes and emptied her mind of her life as it was now, she could just about remember him. The oily smell of the overalls he wore home from work each night and the distinctive pipe tobacco that he used. Yes, she could remember them if she tried hard. She only had to sniff a bar of carbolic soap to be reminded of times he'd dragged the tin bath in from outside and had his bath in front of the fire. Her dad liked to be alone then, reading the racing news while he had a good soak. It was always fun to help him empty the bath water in the backyard afterwards. Freda smiled to herself. They were good times.

Freda wondered if Lenny was with Jed. Perhaps his pub was in Erith. She'd traced the blue line of the Thames as it twisted towards the estuary and the open seas, recognizing seaside towns such as Margate and Whitstable. The trains ran from London as well and Freda knew that she could get to the capital city from her home in the Midlands. She would go to Erith, look for Lenny and stay there until she knew he was safe. The librarian had told her the names of some shops and factories, and Freda thought it would be easy to find work and lodgings once she arrived. After all, jobs were ten a penny where she came from, and it shouldn't be any different in a town so near to London, especially with it being close to Christmas too.

Perhaps once the warmer weather came along and she had a few shillings to her name, she could catch a train to the seaside or even go on a charabanc trip. That would be exciting.

The train jolted to a halt at Woolwich Dockyard, letting out a stream of early morning workers. Freda scrubbed the yellow, smoke-covered window with the cuff of her coat and peered through the clear hole. Perhaps, if she was lucky, she'd see Lenny. He had to be somewhere in the area. He may have found work here, as it was on the train line from Erith. She knew he'd find work and lodgings to try and keep his head above water. Then again, perhaps Woolwich was too far from Erith. The porter at Charing Cross Station had told her how many stops there were to Erith. No point in looking for Lenny just yet, then.

Freda yawned. It had been a long time since she left home and caught the milk train to London. She wondered what Erith was like. Too bad if it was a rotten place: she'd burnt her bridges and had to see things through now. Until she found Lenny, that was, and made sure he was safe. Her stepfather would never have her back in the house once he knew she'd pinched that five bob out of his pocket when he'd come home drunk again. No, she'd get a belt round the ear for that, at the very least.

As long as she was brave and stuck to her plan, she'd soon find Lenny, sort him out and things would be fine. She frowned as she looked at his words on the crumpled page.

Sorry, Freda, I couldn't stick it a minute longer. I

took me chance and legged it along with another bloke while we was on gardening duty. I just wanted you to know I was doing all right. Once the coppers get Tommy Whiffen, I'll be a free man. Take care of yourself.

Free man? She snorted to herself. He's no more than a kid with silly ideas, and it was his silly ideas that got him in with the wrong crowd to begin with and now look at him. Would she always have to go through life sorting out her little brother's problems? She'd have to stop worrying about Lenny until she had a bed to sleep in and had found herself a job. The few bob in her pocket wouldn't last long.

Her eyelids started to feel heavy as she sank down into her seat, resting her head on the edge of the window. The steam train chugged on towards Erith and her new life. Flakes of snow started to fall. She could see a dusting of white as it settled on the high banks of the railway line. Oh good, it might be a white Christmas, she thought, as her eyes closed.

'The next station's Erith, sweetheart. Do you want some help getting your suitcase down from the rack?'

Freda stretched her arms and yawned. The older woman sitting opposite her had been a big help when Freda had climbed aboard the train, not sure if she was heading in the right direction. 'Thank you, I think I can reach it, but mind your head.' She tugged at the case and it slid to the seat below with a thud.

A porter took her case as she climbed down from the carriage.

'Thank you. Where can I find the High Street?'

'Straight out the door, miss, and walk up the pathway over there. You'll see the start of the shops across the road.'

'Will there be somewhere I can buy a local paper?'

'At the top of the path. There's a newsagent's shop and a bit of a cafe as well. They do a good sausage sandwich if you're peckish.'

Freda thanked the porter and headed towards the town. She could do with a bite to eat but had to be careful with her money until she'd found herself a job and had her first pay packet.

Tall, elegant Victorian buildings appeared as she reached the top of the pathway. Shops of all kinds stood side by side with banks and other important-looking offices, their names etched into the glass windows of impressive-looking facades. Rows of houses faced onto the railway line with ornate tiled footpaths, their steps leading up to large front doors with polished brass door knockers. Even through the swirling snow and smoke from a passing steam train Freda could see it was a mite posher than where she'd come from. As long as that didn't mean lodgings were expensive. She crossed her fingers that there was a poorer area of the town that would suit her pocket. It was nice to look at, but the likes of her couldn't afford posh houses with brass door knockers. She hoped she'd made the right decision in coming to Erith.

In the end, she did go to the cafe. She'd managed to pick up a copy of the *Erith Observer* and needed somewhere to study the rooms to let as well as the job columns. The place was almost deserted, which suited Freda, as she felt scruffy and untidy for such a fine-looking town. However, looking around at the shabby cafe, with its nicotine-stained walls and scuffed tables, perhaps she would be more welcome than she imagined. The woman who'd served her was slowly wiping tables to pass the time.

'I've not seen you in here before. New to Eariff, are yer?'

Freda smiled to herself. So that's how the locals pronounced 'Erith'. It did sound strange.

'I've just arrived by train. I've never been here before. It looks like a nice place to live.'

'There's bits of good and bits of bad. You just has to know where to look,' the woman said, wiping her hands down her grubby apron. 'What can I get you, love? A bit of breakfast?'

Freda checked the coins in her purse and then peered at a few words chalked on a board behind the counter. 'I'll just have a mug of tea, please.'

The woman looked at the skinny girl in front of her. 'How's about a bit of bread and scrape? Tasty and filling – and on the house. Though it's on the stale side. I was about to make some bread pudding with it. I can spare a slice.'

Freda wrinkled her nose. '"Scrape"?'

'Yeah, dripping. You don't know what that is? I've just roasted a lump of beef, it's the gravy and fat out of the tin.'

Freda smiled. She knew well the rich juices and fat from the roasting pan that her mum saved in an enamel bowl. They had it on toast with a liberal sprinkling of salt each Monday for their tea. Her tummy rumbled loudly. 'Oh yes, I know.

We call it "bread and dripping" where I come from. Thank you very much.'

'Well, you sit yourself down and I'll bring it on over to you.'

Freda took off her coat. It wasn't that warm in the cafe, but she knew she'd never feel the benefit of the extra clothing when she went out into the fast-falling snow if she kept it on while she had her meal.

When the woman came over with the hot tea and a plate of bread and scrape, she peered at the page of the newspaper that Freda was carefully studying. 'Are you looking for somewhere to stay, love?' she asked, putting the food on the table.

Freda, confused by all the unfamiliar street names, nodded her head. Her mouth watered as she looked at the food. 'Yes, but I can't afford a lot of money.'

'Who can, love? But I knows just the place. Not far from here. There's a lady who lets rooms in Queens Road. Cheap enough.'

Freda scribbled down the address as the woman gave it to her. 'Is it clean?'

'Couldn't say, love, but beggars can't be choosers. You need a bed and she's got one. Can't say much more than that. Oh, and if you're looking for work, Woolies are taking on shop girls for the holidays. Get yerself round there this afternoon. I heard some posh-looking tart talking about it when she was in here. Look sharp, though, 'cos I reckon there'll be loads of girls after jobs there.'

Freda beamed at the woman. 'Thank you. Is Woolworths the best place to work in Erith?'

22

'Nah, you'll be wanting Hedley Mitchell for the best shop jobs.' She looked Freda up and down. 'But they're fussy who they take on.'

Freda grinned to herself as she tucked into her breakfast. That'd certainly put her in her place.

2

Sarah stood nervously fiddling with the gold chain at her throat. She was inside Woolworths, but what should she do next? Up ahead was a double door, while to the side was a smaller one. Which, she thought, led into the shop? Seconds later the outside door banged open again as two young women appeared in the long corridor. The taller of the two appeared to have stepped straight from a cinema screen. Sarah admired her stylish outfit. Why ever was she here? She had a perfect coiffure with not a hair out of place, and her eyebrows were pencilled so evenly. Sarah just stared. A fox-fur collar topped an elegant coat that must have cost a fortune. Sarah automatically felt gauche and young in her best Sunday coat. A waft of perfume invaded the space between them. Sarah inhaled deeply.

'Is that Chanel?' she asked. She recognized her mum's favourite scent but was surprised to find someone entering the staff door of Woolworths wearing such an expensive perfume, and in the daytime too. An exotic perfume like that was only worn by people with money, and even then very sparingly. She knew this well because her mum would often tell anyone who commented on her fragrance.

The woman nodded. 'Lovely, isn't it? My old man picks it up fer me. He works on the docks. I'll get you a bottle if you want?' She gave Sarah a broad wink. 'Keep it under yer hat.'

Sarah was surprised to hear the broad local accent come from someone she assumed had just stepped off a ship from America.

'Is this where we go see about a job?'

Sarah nodded. 'It's just up the corridor. Some other girls went through there just now. I would think that's where we have to go.' She couldn't quite believe that this stylish woman wanted to work for Woolworths.

'What about you, ducks? Are you here fer a job as well?' the woman asked the girl who had entered the building behind her as she tidied her fox fur and patted its head.

The younger girl nodded shyly. She looked that frightened she might just turn round and flee. 'Yes, if they'll have me,' she whispered.

'Well, all this chatter won't knit the baby a bonnet – let's go get ourselves a job,' the older woman declared, marching ahead of them.

Sarah gave the younger girl a smile. 'My name's Sarah. Do you come from around here?'

The girl shook her head so violently she had to grasp her brown knitted beret as it slid to one side of her head, allowing the mousy-brown hair to escape from underneath. Sarah noticed that her hair was none too clean, and her clothes were on the shabby side. 'No, I've just moved here. On my own,' she added quickly. 'I've done my best to get ready for this interview, but my lodgings don't have any hot water. My name's Freda,' she added.

Sarah wanted to hug the girl. She looked so afraid and far too thin. 'You look lovely, Freda. I do like your hat. Did you knit it yourself?'

Freda nodded. 'I like to knit.'

'Well, perhaps they'll put you on the knitting-wool counter. Wouldn't that be something?'

Freda beamed. 'I never thought of that. I just want a job. I didn't think about what they'd give us to do.'

A shrill whistle came from the other end of the long corridor. 'Oi, you two. Are you coming or not?'

Sarah linked her arm through Freda's and the girls giggled together as they headed towards the staff door. 'It's going to be a laugh a minute working with her.'

'She's ever so smart. Just like a movie star,' Freda said in awe. 'I've never seen anyone dress so posh before.'

'I doubt she is, though, especially not here in Erith and her wanting to work in Woolworths. It'll be fun finding out, won't it?'

'Here comes the new intake. Chop, chop, girls, or "Bossy" Billington will have your guts for garters.' A short, ginger-haired lad in a brown warehouse coat that almost met the floor smirked as he lifted a large broom and swept around the legs of the young women waiting to be interviewed. This caused Sarah to step smartly to one side before she had her freshly polished shoes covered in dust. She tutted in disapproval.

25

Another lad in a matching coat punched him on the shoulder. 'Leave it out, Ginger. You'll frighten the poor girls away before they've signed on the dotted line.' He turned to face Sarah and smiled at her. 'Are you looking for Miss Billington's office?'

Sarah nodded. She had to admit Ginger's taunts were not helping settle the butterflies in her stomach. She felt extremely nervous. 'Yes, I am.' She looked along the row at the other six girls. 'I think we all are.'

'I'll show you or you'll never find your way. Ginger, you're in charge of the broom until I get back.' The tall, fair-haired lad seemed to have an air of authority about him, as Ginger immediately took the proffered broom and set about sweeping the dusty floor with gusto.

Sarah felt relieved to have someone show her the way. The Erith branch of F. W. Woolworth, or Woolies, as it was affectionately known, was a complete warren. 'Thank you. Everything's so strange at the moment. Erith is very different to where I used to live.'

'And where might that have been?' the friendly lad asked as he led the young women towards the office.

Sarah looked sideways at him. He stood a head taller than her and had a twinkle in his blue eyes. His mop of unruly blond hair looked as though it would never behave. He seemed nice enough. 'Devon. I moved here to live with my nan. My parents originally came from around here, and my nan's lived here all her life.'

'That's near enough to make you a local, then,'

he said, indicating that they'd reached their destination, and held out his hand. 'I'm Alan, by the way. Alan Gilbert, trainee manager. Welcome to Woolworths.'

Sarah took his hand and was immediately, shaken by the warmth and strength that resonated from such a simple welcome. He held her hand for just a second too long. My goodness, she thought, I must be nervous if a simple handshake can affect me like this. 'Pleased to meet you. I'm Sarah Caselton,' she stuttered, looking up into his eyes.

'So, Sarah, do you have family working here?'

She shook her head. 'No, not now. My mum and my aunt both worked at the Dartford branch when they were my age. I only found that out when I told Nan I had an interview. I don't know very much about the company. It seems like a nice place to work, though,' she added as an afterthought. Sarah was keen to make a good impression, and with Alan being a trainee manager, she didn't wish to start off on the wrong foot with someone who might one day become her boss. 'I've just been told about when everything used to cost sixpence. Did you know that?'

Alan laughed. 'I thought everyone knew that! We still sell a lot of stuff for sixpence,' he added with a grin.

Alan knocked on the door of the office, opening it as he did so, and announced, 'The new intake are here, Miss Billington.' Smiling at Sarah, he squeezed her arm. 'Good luck, Sixpenny. I'll see you later,' he whispered so only she could hear him before heading back towards the warehouse.

Sarah blushed. She was quite taken with Alan

and could still feel the pressure of his hand on her arm, but pushed all thought of the young man from her mind as along with the other six girls she was called into the personnel office.

It was a tight fit. Sarah found herself wedged between a large metal safe and a filing cabinet alongside Freda. She hoped that Miss Billington would take her on. Glancing along the row of hopeful women, she wondered how many of them had enough experience to fill the vacancies. Sarah knew her own experience was minimal. Helping out in the village post office and general shop didn't seem enough. She felt very much out of her depth.

Miss Billington glanced at a list of names in front of her. 'Welcome, ladies. First I'd like you to complete an application form and sit a short arithmetic test. Miss Freda Smith?'

Freda held up her hand and took the proffered form and pencil, whispering a thank you as her eyes widened at the number of questions in front of her.

'Mrs Maisie Taylor?'

The fashionably dressed woman nodded and held out her gloved hand for the paperwork.

Sarah glanced at Freda and they both grinned. She had a normal name. A cough from the personnel lady had them looking down within seconds. It was just like being back at school, Sarah thought.

'That's me, ducks. You can drop the "Mrs" and call me Maisie; I ain't one for long names. And Mrs Taylor's me mother-in-law.' She laughed at her own joke.

Sarah chewed on the inside of her cheek so that she didn't laugh out loud at Maisie's joke too. She seemed to be a barrel of laughs and wouldn't take much notice of anyone in authority.

Miss Billington peered over the top of her spectacles, silencing any further remarks Maisie may have had. 'Here, you will be known as Mrs Taylor. I expect a certain respect among my staff, and I don't allow smoking in my office,' Miss Billington added as Maisie took a packet of Camel cigarettes from her handbag.

'OK, ducks.'

'My name is Miss Billington. Please remember that.'

'OK, ducks – er, Miss Billington,' the affable Maisie replied.

The personnel officer stared hard at Maisie. Sarah wondered if this meant that Maisie wouldn't be an employee at Woolworths. With seven applicants, surely there wouldn't be enough jobs?

Sarah was given her forms along with the other girls.

'I'll take you all through to the staff canteen while I leave you to complete your applications. I have to attend to an urgent staffing matter.' She looked at her wristwatch. 'I'll be back in half an hour. We can discuss your duties then.'

'So we all have jobs?' Freda asked hopefully.

Miss Billington turned to look at the young girl standing before her. She was aware that many of the applicants in front of her had responsibilities and needed to take home a wage packet. However, she required staff who would work hard for the company and not need watching every five minutes. 'There are three vacancies. Whoever is taken on will have to work a one-month trial. It does depend on how you complete the arithmetic test. We have just three weeks until Christmas, our busiest time of the year. We're short-staffed. I require three extra workers on the shop floor by tomorrow morning. I hope I will find suitable candidates among you.' She glanced at Maisie and sighed.

The three girls found a table away from the others and pulled off their coats. The room was warm. The windows were steamed up from the kitchen area, which was behind a counter, and the smell of baking made Sarah's stomach rumble. She had been too nervous to eat the sandwich Nan had made for her lunch.

The girls scrutinized the paperwork in front of them.

Maisie chewed the end of her pencil. 'At least I know how to spell my name.' She was thinking that she'd blown any chance of obtaining one of the three available vacancies. She'd always been one who 'dressed to impress', but perhaps this time she'd gone a little over the top. It was obvious that Miss Billington didn't approve of her outfit, or the way she spoke. She glanced at the two younger women sitting with her. The one called Freda looked as though she was down on her luck. The sleeves of her shabby coat were a little too short and worn threadbare at the cuffs. She reminded her very much of her little sister, Tessa, after... Maisie shuddered. No use in dragging up sad memories. She had a new husband and a new life now. No point in looking backwards. However, she'd make it her job to look out for the kid. That wouldn't hurt anyone.

She peered closer at the form in front of her. 'Blimey, I didn't realize that we'd 'ave to be so blooming clever just to work in a shop.'

Sarah giggled to herself. 'Woolworths expect their staff to be able to count and do basic arithmetic, as we have to add up and give the correct change. It said so in the advertisement in the newspaper.'

'I didn't see no newspaper,' Freda chirped up. 'Someone told me about the interviews. I've helped out on market stalls since I was knee-high to a grasshopper and can add up anything in my head and give the right change. I just don't know what to put on the paper here.'

'It's the same for me, ducks. I'm a dab 'and with adding up darts scores and serving behind a bar, as well as charging the right price for a round of drinks, but all this paperwork near on does me 'ead in.'

Sarah thought for a moment. 'Look, why don't I call out the questions and you both tell me the answers? Then I can show you how to write them down correctly.'

Freda beamed. 'Would you really do that for us? I'd be ever so grateful.'

'Me too,' Maisie added. 'Cheers, love. I owe you one.'

The girls spent the next ten minutes adding up pounds, shillings and pence, and working out change from ten-bob and one-pound notes.

Sarah was pleased to see that her idea worked well, and before they'd reached the last sum, both Maisie and Freda were writing down their own answers on the sheets of paper.

They were still poring over the application form when Freda let out a big sigh that made Sarah look up from checking she'd completed the form correctly.

'What's up? You sound as though you've got the cares of the world on your shoulders.'

'I have a problem with this bit that asks for references. You see, I don't have any.' Freda rubbed her eyes with the back of her hand as tears started to form. 'I really need this job. I don't know what to do,' she sniffed.

Sarah squeezed the young girl's arm. She was skin and bones under her thin cardigan. 'I'm sure we can think of something. Where did you work before you came to Erith?'

Freda shuddered. The last thing she wanted to do was tell these nice girls about her life. It was best she kept her secret. She needed a job to pay for her lodgings even if it wasn't for too long; besides, she liked this town, with its grand-looking High Street full of shops and the streets of Victorian houses. While getting on the train at London, she'd spotted a poster advertising trips to the seaside. Freda had never seen the sea, so if she was still here come the summer, she'd make sure she treated herself to a day out.

'I'd rather not say. I lived in the Midlands and wanted to come here for a fresh start. If I put my parents' address on the form, my stepfather will more than likely come and drag me back home.

Even if I put that I sometimes helped out in the market, it might get back to them, as the stall-holders see them most days.'

'Why did you come to Erith? Do you have family here?' Sarah enquired. Surely no one came to Erith out of choice? It wasn't as if it was anyplace special. She loved Erith, as it was where Nan grew up and her roots were here, but would a stranger love it as much?

'No, I'm quite alone. I decided it was as good a place as any.' Freda twisted the pencil between her fingers, knowing she'd have to get used to such questions if she was to make a life for herself in Erith. She'd never let on that she was here for a reason.

Maisie raised her eyebrows. She could tell the kid was not telling the truth. Her gut reaction was usually right. This girl was running from something or other. 'Look, ducks, it's not fer me to say, but I doubt whether old fussy knickers will follow up our references. Didn't she say she's run of her feet? Chances are that by the time she gets round to checking up on us, we'll have worked a month's trial. If she doesn't like us, we'll get the boot. If she's happy with our work, then she won't bother following up whatever we write here. Blimey, my references are just a couple of pubs up the East End of London. That'll impress her no end. Just make up a couple of addresses. You can always say you made a mistake if she asks.'

Freda looked shocked. 'A pub? I thought you were posh, what with those lovely clothes and all.'

Maisie snorted with laughter. 'What, me, posh? Gawd love you – I'm just 'andy with a needle and thread, that's all. I admit I like to look good, but posh? Dearie me.' She wiped her eyes as she continued to laugh.

Sarah looked at Maisie in amazement 'Why aren't you working as a dressmaker? There are plenty of factories taking girls on, from what I've heard.' She liked both the girls, but from the little they'd said, their lives were certainly different from her own. Sarah thought she was brave moving to Erith from her comfortable home in Devon and using Nan as the excuse, when in truth she just couldn't live with her mum's high expectations for a day longer. Thank goodness her dad had understood.

Maisie shook her head. 'That's not fer me. I tried it a couple of times, but it's too much like working in a sweatshop and being bossed around all the time. I like to make what I fancy. Then if it goes wrong, I only 'ave meself to blame.'

She stuck her pencil behind her ear and leant back in her chair. 'Now, I could make you two some outfits if you want me to? I brought me Singer with me when we moved in with the in-laws. I'd be only too glad to escape from the old bat and do some sewing. She fair does me head in with all her gossiping. That's why I wanna job. Get a few bob under our belts so me and the old man can rent our own place before the nippers come along.'

Freda's eyes opened wide and she blushed. 'You're expecting?'

'Gawd love you. No, not yet, but the way me and the husband are practising, it won't be long.'

Sarah didn't know where to put her eyes. She

didn't wish to insult Maisie by pointing out that she'd never heard people talk like that before. She was so embarrassed. 'A baby would be lovely,' was all she could think to reply.

Maisie looked pointedly at the two girls. 'So, what do you think?'

Sarah gasped. Did Maisie want her to comment on her plans to start a family? Her mother had never spoken about such things. Sarah didn't know what to say or where to look.

Maisie looked hurt. 'Well, either you both want some new clothes or not. It don't bother me none.'

Sarah felt a wave of relief wash over her. 'Oh, clothes. Yes, it would be lovely. How about you, Freda?'

'I'd love to say yes, but once I've paid my rent, I won't have much money left to spend on myself. Thank you for the offer, but I'd better say no.' Freda looked wistfully at Maisie's smart coat, which had been slung casually over the back of her chair.

'I don't take no for an answer, my girl. It'll hardly cost a penny to get you some new clobber on yer back. See this coat?' Both girls nodded as Maisie took hold of the smart tweed coat and waved it at them. 'Well, I made it from a man's overcoat I picked up at a jumble sale. Do you think I've got money to waste buying expensive cloth like this? I unpicked all the seams and copied a style I'd seen on some actress on Pathé News at the flicks.'

Sarah ran her fingers over the fabric and sighed. 'But we've only known each other for five minutes.'

Maisie snorted. 'Love, we're gonna be spending a lot of time in each other's company if we get these jobs, so we might as well get along. My way of doing it is to make clothes and be a shoulder to cry on when it's needed. What do you say?'

Sarah nodded enthusiastically. She liked Maisie's down-to-earth attitude. The thought of having ready-made friends to work with sounded wonderful.

Freda looked pleased as well. 'I'd like to be your friend too. Both of you. I've not really had any proper friends before. My stepfather didn't like it.'

Sarah wondered again why Freda had left home. She had worked out from the application form that she was only seventeen. She felt there must be a reason, and it probably wasn't a good one. 'Friends it is, then, but we'd better finish answering these questions or we won't even be offered a job.'

The girls bent back over the papers in front of them, deep in thought as they checked that every question had been answered, oblivious to what was going on around them in the busy canteen.

'Hello, ladies. How did your interviews go?'

Sarah looked up to see Alan close to her chair. 'We haven't finished yet. We still have to finish the arithmetic test. I don't suppose a trainee manager has to do such things?' she added cheekily.

'That and much more,' Alan said seriously. 'We have to learn every aspect of Woolworths if we want to advance to management level.'

'That's what you want?' Sarah asked, looking at his earnest face. Alan might like a laugh and a joke, but he also seemed to be serious about his work. Her dad would approve of him.

'We've all got our dreams, Sixpenny,' he said, looking into her eyes as if his plans included her. 'Can I get you girls a cuppa while I'm here?' Alan offered, bringing Sarah back to earth with a bump. She'd only met Alan less than an hour ago and already he had her dreaming.

By the time Miss Billington returned to the canteen, the girls had completed the long list of questions. Sarah chewed her lip nervously, wondering if she had given enough correct answers to gain full-time employment She had her savings, and her dad had handed her an envelope with five pounds inside, so she wouldn't be a burden to her nan, but even so she wanted to work and pay her way. Beside her, Freda had gone rather pale and was staring at the floor. Maisie had pulled a gold-coloured compact from her handbag and was busy powdering her nose.

'That all looks in order. I'll take these back to my office and check them through, then call you when I'm ready.' Miss Billington looked at her watch. 'We're coming up for staff tea breaks, so have a cup of tea while you wait. I'll follow up your references whenever I have the time. Goodness knows when that will be,' the older woman muttered half to herself as she stood up. She brushed down her tweed skirt with one hand, checked the buttons of the matching jacket were securely fastened and headed off to her office. Although only in her early forties, Miss Billington exuded an air of authority that the staff at Woolies would never dare question.

'Follow me, ladies. I'll show you the shop floor and point out where you'll be working.'

Sarah and Freda grinned at each other. They'd been called into the office last. Sarah had thought that they'd failed the interview, but no, they were the successful candidates. Maisie had been called in first and they hadn't seen her since.

Miss Billington looked at the excited girls. 'You will report here for duty tomorrow morning at eight o'clock. You'll be supplied with your uniforms and a list of your duties and staff rules. Keep the uniform clean and look presentable at all times or it will go onto your report. Now, follow me.'

Sarah glanced around her as she walked quickly, trying to keep up with the personnel officer. Rumours of war and general unrest in the country had not stopped shoppers trying to pick up a bargain to brighten their Christmas and to fill their children's stockings for Father Christmas to deliver. Polished wood counters were heaped high with products. Sarah spotted gleaming white china piled high on one counter, while on another glass-fronted boxes of loose biscuits tempted buyers. Customers were pointing to their favourite biscuits, and sales staff were busy weighing them on sets of large scales before placing them into brown paper bags, twisting the top of each bag securely. Sarah would have liked to stop and watch, but Miss Billington beckoned her to keep up before she was lost in the bustling crowd. They stopped by a long counter that stood in the centre of the shop under a canopy of brightly coloured paper chains. Sarah held her breath in anticipation. She would love to work on the seasonal counter, full of Christmas decorations and cheerful wrapping paper, but she thought that only the experienced staff would be placed there. She crossed her fingers behind her back and looked at Miss Billington in anticipation.

The woman looked at each of the girls in turn. 'I require two full-time employees to work here. It's hard work and I expect my staff to knuckle down and serve customers as soon as possible. We don't want queues and disgruntled shoppers going elsewhere. Sarah and Freda, you will join this section. There are six staff members working here.' She beckoned to a tall woman standing nearby, who was placing brightly coloured nativity figures into a brown paper bag. 'Daphne will show you the ropes and help you familiarize yourself with the stock. Report here after collecting your uniforms tomorrow morning.'

Sarah and Freda stopped to introduce themselves to Daphne as Miss Billington disappeared into the crowds of shoppers. Daphne welcomed the two girls and explained she had only been working in Woolies for two months. She showed them a small diamond ring on the third finger of her left hand and told them she only expected to be working there until the spring, when she was to marry. Both girls sighed as the older woman explained to a puzzled Freda that women never worked once married, as they would have a home and hopefully a family to care for. Sarah was already looking forward to the lead-up to Christmas, and their new colleague seemed very nice. By the big grin on Freda's face she knew her new friend was thinking the same.

Heading back to Miss Billington's office to collect their coats, their heads buzzing with all the rules that Daphne had shared with them, Sarah and Freda were both wondering if Maisie had been taken on.

'I reckon she'll be on the counter selling cosmetics. Or perhaps pretty scarves and jewellery,' sighed Freda. 'It would suit her down to the ground.'

Sarah wasn't so sure. 'I do believe that our Maisie hasn't made a good impression on Miss Billington. She may have passed the arithmetic test, but she's not your usual sales assistant. I wouldn't be surprised if she's been placed somewhere that doesn't fit with her glamorous appearance, or, perhaps she doesn't even have a job.'

Freda clapped her hand to her mouth. 'Oh, don't say that. She's a right laugh. I was looking forward to working with her. I even thought that in time she might sew me a new coat.'

'It's a shame we didn't think to swap addresses. I thought I saw that tall girl with the spectacles walking through the shop. It looks as though she might be the third person to be taken on.'

'You're right there, Sixpenny. Miss Billington has got the girl with the specs selling spuds on the veg counter. I was just humping sacks of carrots down there and spotted the pair of them deep in conversation by a pile of cabbages.'

Sarah turned to see Alan behind them. She blushed and stammered as she answered the handsome young man. 'Poor Maisie. I thought she'd be sure to be offered a job. I do hope we get to see her again. I've only known her a couple of hours and really liked her.'

Alan leant on the sack barrow he'd been pushing and wiped his brow with a handkerchief. 'Don't you worry about her – she's been holding court up in the canteen talking to some of the staff. Her kind always land on their feet.'

Sarah frowned. 'What do you mean, her kind? You shouldn't judge a book by its cover.' She didn't like his tone. Maisie seemed a decent sort.

Alan laughed. 'I didn't mean I didn't like her. She's the kind who can weather any storm. You shouldn't worry. We'll see her again, I'm sure. How about you, Sixpenny? Where will I see you working every day?'

Sarah was suddenly tongue-tied. She couldn't think of a word to say and just stood there blushing. Alan must think her a fool for not replying to a simple question. She felt such an idiot, as one minute she was snapping at him, and the next, when he showed interest in her, she was silent.

'We're both on the Christmas counter,' Freda piped up.

'I'll see you there, if I don't see you before, Sixpenny.' He winked at Sarah and headed off whistling.

'I think he likes you,' Freda giggled as they continued on their way upstairs.

'He's rather forward,' Sarah replied, although she was thrilled that he'd singled her out.

In the staffroom, they found Maisie applying lipstick and checking her appearance in a small mirror on the wall.

Sarah gave her a hug. 'I'm sorry to hear you've not been taken on.'

'Don't bother me none. I've heard they might be taking on at the Odeon. At least I'll get to see the flicks free of charge. If not, there's a job at the grocer's alongside the mother-in-law. Mind you, it would 'ave been fun here. Much more my cup of tea selling stuff over the counter, and I'd rather not be 'aving to wash me 'ands every few minutes or working in the dark.'

Snapping the lipstick shut and dropping it into her handbag, Maisie linked arms with Sarah and Freda. 'Anyone fancy a cuppa? We can still meet up after work if you two want to?'

3

Sarah shivered as she headed home through the darkening December afternoon. An icy blast of snow blew into her face as she tried to see her way ahead. Thank goodness she only had a couple of roads to cross and then she would be home. She thought of Freda and hoped that the young girl was home and warm in her lodgings.

Hugging her woolly scarf tighter around her neck to ward off the cold, Sarah was glad of her matching forest-green mittens, which were doing a very good job of keeping her fingers warm. The hand-knitted set had been a gift from Nan for her twentieth birthday in September. It may have been freezing cold, but inside she felt excited that she would soon be home and able to tell Nan the exciting news about her job.

A bitter wind whipped off the nearby River Thames as she headed along the deserted High Street towards home. The carol singers had long gone, as had most of the shoppers. In this weather, the best place to be was in front of a roaring coal fire. Nan had said it would be a hard winter, and she wasn't usually wrong. At least she didn't have far to walk to work and she would be able to get there – even if she had to dig through snowdrifts.

Sarah's stomach rumbled as she breathed in the delicious aroma of fish and chips from a nearby chippy. She'd be more than ready for Nan's warming mutton stew and dumplings by the time she got back. Teacakes in Mitchell's tea room, with Freda and Maisie, seemed an age ago now. They'd wanted to celebrate their new jobs and the possibility of Maisie finding work in the town. They'd talked non-stop as if they'd known each other for years, but with the weather getting worse by the minute, they'd decided to get themselves off home. Plans were made to treat themselves to a night at the pictures once they had their first pay packet in their hands. Even Freda, who had to watch every penny, was looking forward to their night out.

Sarah smiled as she thought about their conversation; she was excited about their new-formed friendship. Maisie had been adamant that she would make Freda a new coat once they'd visited a jumble sale to purchase some old clothing that could be unpicked and made into new garments, and Freda was keen to buy some unwanted jumpers to unravel so she could knit a cardigan. She'd explained how once the yarn was unravelled, it would be steamed over a kettle to take out any kinks and then it would be as good as new. Sarah wished she could knit and sew. Most girls her age were a dab hand with a needle, but her mother had preferred to buy clothes and turned her nose up at home-made garments. Well, now she'd ask Nan to show her how to knit so she too could be useful with her hands like her new friends.

Sarah didn't know why her mother was like she was. After all, she was an Erith girl born and bred, and from what she'd overheard her nan saying to her aunt Pat, she was just like the rest of them until her father had gained promotion and moved the family to Devon. This had been when Sarah was much younger. She only knew her mum as a smart lady who was always impeccably turned out and had someone 'come in' to do the housework. She didn't understand her mum wanting to move up in the world. It was Dad who was the breadwinner, and he was the salt of the earth and not at all snobby. She had many happy memories of Dad playing with her in the garden and taking her on trips to the seaside in Devon when she was a young child. She could confide in her dad more than she ever could her mum. He'd even driven her up to Erith so she didn't have to lug a heavy suitcase on the train. He was spending a few days with Nan so he could do some business at Vickers, in nearby Crayford. She wasn't sure what Dad's job was in engineering, but as news of war grew day by day, he became busier and busier.

Street lights flickered in the gloom of the late afternoon, blurred by the driving snow, as she carefully crossed the busy street to her nan's house, 13 Alexandra Road. She loved the long row of bay-fronted Victorian terraces and had always enjoyed visiting her nan. She was so happy to be living here. Pulling a string through the letter box, she let herself in with the key dangling at the other end. Nan was inside chatting to Mrs Munro from up the road. From the raised voices, it sounded like another of their heated discussions about whether or not there'd be a war. Was there ever a time when people didn't talk about war?

She stepped into the steamy kitchen. 'I'm home,' she announced.

Ruby Caselton got to her feet and hurried round the scrubbed kitchen table to envelop her grand-daughter in a bear hug. A short, plump woman with grey hair pulled back into a severe bun, she always had a smile for any child in her house and a toffee in her pocket for those she met in the street. Ruby was well liked among her neighbours.

'Now, sit yourself down and tell me all about your afternoon. I take it they hired you?'

'Yes! I had to sit a test along with some other girls. There were seven of us. I wasn't sure I'd get picked. Three of us got jobs. I start tomorrow.' The news tumbled from Sarah as she sat down, cheeks flushed from the cold outside.

Ruby placed a cup of tea in front of Sarah and sat to listen. 'There, didn't I tell you they'd take you on? I'm right proud of you, love.'

Vera Munro raised her eyebrows in disdain and

sniffed from where she sat in Ruby's armchair by the coal fire. 'If she was my granddaughter, I'd be prouder still if she was working in an office rather than a shop. My Sadie works in London. *In an office*. It's more fitting for a girl than shop work.'

Ruby stood up, her face going bright red. 'More fitting? Why, Sarah here has found herself a right good job that she's looking forward to doing and you turn your nose up at it?'

Sarah closed her eyes. Oh no, here we go again. Nan and Mrs Munro could have a right ding-dong of an argument one minute and be the best of friends the next. Sarah just didn't want to be the subject of their latest row. Tears pricked her eyes. 'Please don't worry about me. I like my new job.'

Vera bristled, ignoring Sarah's plea. 'Of course she's done well. It's just that she could do so much better, if she only tried. My Sadie's doing very well for herself and will make some man a good wife one day.'

'Well, we ain't snobs in this house, Vera Munro, and no amount of good jobs can make a good marriage. Our dinner's about ready to dish up, so I suggest you go home and get your own food on the table. Your Sadie's gonna be right famished when she gets home from her fancy job in London.'

Sarah sighed as Vera flounced from the room. She heard the front door slam shut as she wiped her eyes on the edge of the tea towel that Nan passed to her. 'I like the idea of working at Woolworths. Do you think I should be training to do something else like Mum suggested?'

Ruby went to stir the stew bubbling on the

stove. She looked thoughtful. 'There'll always be a place here for you, my love, and you take any job you want to. Life's about being happy. As long as you've a few pennies in your purse and food on the table, life isn't so bad. The Caseltons aren't ones for putting on airs and graces, and rubbing shoulders with the toffs. Even if your mum thinks we should be.'

Sarah started to cut slices from the crusty loaf that was sitting on the breadboard ready to accompany their meal. 'Thanks, Nan. I think I'm going to enjoy working at Woolworths. I've already made friends with a couple of girls who had their interviews at the same time as me. One of them comes from the Midlands.'

Ruby turned from placing large dumplings into the top of the bubbling gravy. 'Why did she come all the way down south to Erith? Has she got family here?'

Sarah frowned. 'She said she hasn't. She's a funny little thing. Very shy and doesn't look as though she's got two halfpennies to rub together. She's living in lodgings round here somewhere.'

'Well, you just bring her home for her dinner anytime you want to. There's always food in the cupboard. We'll take care of the girl. What about the other one? Is she local?'

'She's been living in the East End, but her husband's local. She didn't get a job at Woolies, as so many people applied. They've just moved in with her mother-in-law. Her husband works on the docks. You might know them. The name's Taylor.'

Ruby thought for a moment. 'The only Taylor I

know is that nosy old cow Doreen Taylor. She lives down the bottom end of Manor Road. I think she's got a grown-up son. Blimey, girl, your mate'll have her hands full if that's her family. Tell both your friends they're welcome here anytime. This is your home now and I want you to be happy.'

Sarah put the loaf of bread down and wrapped her arms around her nan.

'Here, what's all this in aid of? You'll make me spill the stew if you go all silly on me.'

Sarah grinned. Nan pretended to be hard, but Sarah could see she had tears glistening in her eyes.

Sarah was telling Ruby about Maisie's sewing skills when they heard the front door open.

'That'll be your dad. Go tell him his supper won't be long. He must be tired. He was out of here at the crack of dawn. Has he said anything about his job, love?'

Sarah wiped her hands on a towel hanging on a hook by the sink and shook her head. 'No. I just know that he was called to come up here as he was wanted for important work. Even Mum doesn't know what it's all about. Do you think this has got anything to do with all the talk about a war?'

Ruby looked worried. 'I don't like people talking about war. I told Vera as much just now. There's plenty of time to talk when it happens. God help us if it does. The last one was bad enough. We lost too many friends and family. We don't want that happening again. I'm sure your dad'll tell us in his own good time. Now hurry up and tell him about his grub or he'll fall asleep in

48

the armchair like he did last night.'

'Make us a cup of tea, Sarah, love.'

Sarah looked at the worried expression on her dad's face as he pulled off his overcoat and headed for the quiet of the front room. It was only used for high days and holidays, and housed a piano in one corner even though her grand-parents had never played. Ruby hadn't had the heart to throw it out when they moved into the house. The street was known as 'Piano Street' due to the many inhabitants, mostly shop owners, who kept a piano on view in the large bay window that looked out over the road. 'Whatever's the matter, Dad? Have you had bad news?'

'No, not bad news for me, love, but your mum won't be so happy. It looks as though my job will mean me travelling up and down from Devon for some time to come. Chances are, there'll be a war before too long and I'm needed where I can do the best job. I'm sure your mum will understand.'

'Does that mean you'll be moving back here for good?'

'I can't see that happening at the moment, love. I don't think she'd like it. Too set in her ways down in Devon. I'm needed at the factory in Plymouth, but meetings at Vickers mean I can see my favourite daughter more often.'

Sarah hugged her dad and giggled. 'I'd take that as a compliment if it wasn't for me being an only child.'

After telling her dad that his dinner was ready, Sarah headed to the kitchen to make the much-needed cuppa. She wasn't so sure that her mum would see things the way her dad had said. She wasn't sure at all. However, it meant she would enjoy her job at Woolworths more knowing she'd at least see one of her parents more often. It wasn't likely that she'd be able to get down to Devon much with only one and a half days off each week. At least there'd be time to spend with new friends, and she might even get to see more of Alan. She hugged herself as the thought sent a shiver of excitement through her body.

4

Freda gazed with awe at the buff-coloured envelope. 'Our first pay packet. I can hardly believe it.'

'You'll believe it all right when it's empty and you 'ave to wait a week for another one,' Maisie said as she tore open her own envelope and poured the contents into her purse.

'And I still can't believe that you ended up working here,' Sarah exclaimed, 'and only three days after we started. Who'd have thought that tall girl with the spectacles would have left so soon? Do you think it was because she didn't like serving on the vegetable counter?'

'I heard it was because she spent too much time chatting to the lads rather than serving the customers and someone complained.' Freda frowned. 'There's a name for girls like her.'

'Whatever the reason, I'm bloody glad I'm here.

You could 'ave knocked me down with a feather when the letter came from Bossy Billington. I was round here like a flash, I was that surprised.'

Sarah nodded. She too was surprised. She'd heard Maisie before she'd seen her as she'd bellowed across the shop, 'Oi, what the 'ell do you think you're up to, my lad?' Sarah had turned to view Maisie in her Woolworths uniform pulling a young boy by his ear towards the front doors. 'Now don't you come back in 'ere till you've learnt some manners.' It seemed Maisie had caught the lad rolling his wooden train across the rear end of a portly woman in a tweed coat as she bent over the haberdashery counter. Maisie had caught the lad just as the woman had shrieked in surprise.

Maisie snapped the clasp of her purse shut. 'Once I've given the mother-in-law her whack and put some away for a rainy day, I'll still 'ave a few bob left. Thank goodness.'

Freda nodded. 'I have to pay my landlady for my room, and at least I can pay extra for more hot water so I can have a proper bath.'

'I think she's got a bloody cheek charging you for so many extras. Whoever heard of a landlady wanting more money for 'ot water and a slice of toast? If I was you, I'd tell her to go take a jump and find another lodging house.'

Sarah had been as shocked as Maisie when she heard of the landlady's demands on her young tenant. 'I agree with Maisie. I'm sure you could find somewhere more suitable. Nan said she'd listen out for decent lodgings for you.'

Freda tucked her pay packet away safely in the pocket of her overall. 'It'll do me for now. Once I

51

know I have a permanent job, I can plan for the future. I'll think about it more in the new year. We'd best get back to our counters or we won't have a pay packet to collect next week. See you later, Sarah. Don't be late.'

Sarah watched her friends disappear back to work. She'd started her afternoon tea break later than they had. She was surprised how much Freda had blossomed in just one short week. The young girl now had colour in her cheeks and was so much happier than the day they'd first met. She finished her tea and stood to take it back to the counter in the staff canteen.

'Whoa – watch it, Sixpenny. You nearly knocked me over.'

Sarah turned to see Alan Gilbert staggering in an exaggerated way. She grinned at his antics. 'Don't be so daft. I didn't even touch you.'

Alan straightened up and grinned back as he placed his mug of tea and a sticky bun on the table that Sarah had just vacated. 'No harm done. How's your first week been? I've only seen you at a distance and not been able to stop and talk. I don't know about you, but I'll be glad when Christmas is over.'

'I love Christmas. This year particularly, as there's been so much doom and gloom about. At least it's taking people's minds of things. The snow's helping with that as well.'

'You can say that again. Mr Benfield's had me outside clearing the pavements every half-hour so our customers don't slip over and can still get inside to spend their money.'

Sarah didn't mention that she'd seen Alan outside and watched him as he worked. In fact, a few times she'd been so busy watching him that customers had to call her for assistance. Thank goodness Miss Billington hadn't spotted her being slack. Alan seemed to have a word and a smile for every person who walked by. He was certainly a charming young man.

'Now, Alan, don't you go bothering this young lady; we don't want her in trouble for getting back to her counter late,' an unfamiliar woman's voice said. Just then, a shrill bell echoed through the building. 'There you go – that's the bell for the end of this break.'

Alan pulled a face at Sarah. 'I can never escape this woman.'

The older woman cuffed his ear playfully before saying to Sarah, 'I'm Alan's mum, Maureen. He won't tell you, so I'd better do it myself.'

Sarah could see a likeness between Maureen and Alan. Although Maureen's hair was as dark as night, they shared the same sparkling eyes and warm smile.

Maureen added thoughtfully, 'You're Ruby Caselton's granddaughter, aren't you?'

Sarah nodded. 'Yes, I live with Nan. I moved up from Devon.'

'Then George must be your dad. I went to school with him. I even knew your mum from our days working at the Dartford Woolworths. That was a long time ago. We both worked together at one time. Give them my regards. Well, I must get back to the kitchen – there's lots needs doing there.'

Sarah grimaced to herself as she bade goodbye

to Alan's mum. She'd pass on the greetings to her mum when she next wrote, but she had a feeling Irene Caselton wouldn't appreciate them. That part of her life seemed to have been wiped from her memory.

'So we're almost family, Sixpenny?'

Sarah frowned. 'What do you mean?'

'My mum went to school with your dad and worked with your mum. That must mean something.'

Sarah blushed and turned away quickly. She didn't wish Alan to see that she was so flustered by his words. Was he just joshing with her? She hoped not, as she liked talking to him. 'I have to get back to work,' she whispered, before dashing from the canteen.

'Eat up, girls. There's plenty more where that came from,' Ruby said as she placed plates piled high with steak-and-kidney pudding in front of Freda and Maisie.

'My goodness, Mrs C., there's enough here to feed an army,' Maisie declared. 'If I eat all this, I'll fall asleep during the film.'

'It's delicious,' Freda said in between mouthfuls.

'I've made you up a bowl to take home with you, love. We've too much here and it'll only go to waste. Sarah told me you don't have much in the way of a kitchen where you live.'

Sarah threw Ruby a grateful glance. She seemed to know just how to help people out without making a fuss about it. 'You'll be doing us a favour, Freda. Nan'll be giving it to me for breakfast at this rate.'

'Blame your mum, Sarah. If she hadn't called your dad back to Devon for the weekend to some posh dance, I wouldn't have so much left over. Trust him to forget to say anything.'

Sarah giggled. 'You always make loads of food, Nan.'

Ruby put a steaming-hot apple pie and a jug of custard in the centre of the table. 'I like to make people happy.'

Maisie dipped her finger into the jug and licked it appreciatively. 'You've sure made me happy, Mrs C.'

Ruby slapped Maisie's hand playfully. 'Eat your dinner or you'll miss the start of the film. What are you going to see?'

'It's a Jessie Matthews musical at the Odeon, Nan.'

'Now, she is good. I could watch her all day. Such a beautiful actress, and she's British. None of your American movie stars for me.'

Freda glanced at Sarah, who knew only too well that she was remembering when they both thought that Maisie had been a movie star when they first met her. Only two weeks later they knew better. 'I've not seen her before, Mrs Caselton. Is she a singer?'

Ruby put down her washing-up cloth and bowed to the girls before bursting into song – *'Over my shoulder goes one care. Over my shoulder goes two cares...'* – ending the rendition by throwing her leg high, but not quite as high as the popular songstress.

Freda couldn't believe her eyes and started to

cough as she swallowed her food.

'Cough up, love – it might be a gold watch,' Maisie said as she thumped her on the back. 'That was some performance, Mrs C. Why don't you come with us to see the film? A night at the pictures will do you good.'

Ruby straightened her crossover pinny and fanned herself with a tea towel. 'Be off with you, Maisie. You don't want an old woman coming along with you. Besides, I have the washing-up to take care of.'

'Get yourself ready, Mrs C., and we'll do the washing-up. It won't take long. We can leave the pots to soak until we get back.'

'In that case, I'll do just that.' Ruby turned at the kitchen door and smiled at Sarah and her friends. 'It's changed my life having you here, Sarah, and that's no lie.'

'She's all right, your nan,' Maisie said as she took a slice of the apple pie. 'Did you give her Maureen Gilbert's message?'

'Yes, I did. She knows Maureen. I think it was my parents that the message was really for. Nan's lovely. She's more like a mum to me, to be honest. I'm pleased I'm living here now. I was worried at first, but with Dad travelling back and forth from Devon, it's like I'm still living at home.' She didn't add that it was less stressful with a couple of hundred miles between Erith and her mum.

'I'm so glad to hear that. When you told us that your mum thought your dad's job would mean them moving to London, I was so worried you'd be moving with them.'

'I thought the same as you, Freda, love. So are

they still going to London, Sarah?' Maisie asked as she passed plates to Freda to be stacked into the sink.

'No, Dad's just travelling between Devon and Vickers. Mum is really angry, as she'd taken into her head that they'd be living in London and visiting the theatres and everything, and going home to Devon at the weekends. Nan said I can live with her whatever happens. That's why Dad's gone back to Devon for the weekend for a dinner dance. He thought it'd cheer Mum up a bit.'

'I can't see why she wants to live out in the sticks like that. Erith has more than enough for me to enjoy, and we can get to London if we want to.'

Sarah sighed. She didn't know how to explain to her friends that her mum looked down her nose at everyone who lived in Erith, and that included her in-laws and friends from her past. 'Mum's involved in lots of clubs and things where she lives. It's close to Plymouth, so we aren't particularly isolated.'

'Well, I'm pleased that you decided to move to Erith. We make a good team, don't we?' Maisie declared.

Freda nodded enthusiastically. 'I agree!'

Sarah smiled. 'Me too. I couldn't think of nicer friends to have... We'd best hurry or by the time we get to the Odeon, it'll be the interval and the usherettes will be selling ice cream. I for one haven't got room for another mouthful. Not even a bag of chips on the way home.'

5

'If only those ruddy bells would stop ringing. I swear I 'ear them in me sleep.' Maisie stretched her arms above her head and yawned.

'Watch it or you'll be in trouble. There are still customers in the shop,' Sarah hissed. 'We've only got another ten minutes to go. At least pretend to be doing something.'

Maisie lazily flicked a feather duster over a pile of delicate tree baubles. She'd been moved to the seasonal counter to help out in the days leading up to Christmas Eve. 'Why does there 'ave to be so many bells ringing all over the shop?'

Sarah sighed. She too was tired. The girls had been working non-stop and were grateful for their short tea breaks. 'So that we know what the time is and the customers know when the shop is closing. If there wasn't a bell ringing, how would you know you could go for a cup of tea or pack up and go home?'

'You've got a point there, love. I'd hate to be stuck in here overnight with old Benfield.'

Sarah giggled. It was well known that the manager, Mr Benfield, was the last to leave and the first to arrive each morning. They did wonder if he ever went home, as he seemed to be a firm fixture in the shop.

'Here, which one of these calendars should I buy me mother-in-law for Christmas?'

Sarah looked between the two that Maisie was holding up. There were so many scenes to choose from. Everyone in Erith, as well as the surrounding villages, would have a calendar from Woolworths in their stocking. Each large piece of card showed a pretty picture that would grace the walls of many a home for all of 1939. 'I like the cottage scene, but perhaps your mother-in-law would prefer the seaside picture.'

Maisie shrugged, her perfectly painted lips pouting despondently. 'She'll moan whatever one I buy. I'll get her what I like. After all, I'll probably 'ave to look at it for all of next year.'

'No chance of you finding your own place, then?' Sarah asked as she pulled a dust cover from under the counter as yet another bell rang to indicate that all customers had left and the staff could start to put the shop to bed for the night.

'Nah – and now Joe's talking about joining up. He reckons it's better to jump in now before all this conscription lark starts. He says it'd be safer for me to stay with the old girl. Safe from what? I'll go insane stuck in the house alone with that old bat.' Maisie ran her fingers over a calendar that depicted a thatched cottage. 'Now, if I had a place like this to live in, I'd be in heaven. I fancy 'aving a few chickens and some kiddies running around in the garden.' She sighed wistfully.

'I'll buy the thatched-cottage calendar for my mum,' Sarah said. 'My parents have a lovely house, but she's always wanted to live in a cottage with a thatched roof.'

'How's she doing, ducks? Yer nan said she wasn't so happy with you being up here and yer dad travelling back and forth so much.'

'She's not so good, Maisie. Nan told me that when Mum and Dad moved away from Erith, it changed Mum's world. I was only a toddler at the time so can't remember any of it. Mum liked joining the clubs and meeting new people. Most of them owned businesses and were well-do-to. Nan said it turned her head a bit and gave her airs and graces. It seems that my aunt Pat wouldn't speak to her when we came back to Erith to visit and Mum looked down on everyone.'

'Sounds as though she's a bit above everyone else, don't it?'

Sarah nodded. She hated talking about Mum like this, but Maisie was a friend now.

'At least your dad's all right. It'll be nice to see him when we get to your nan's place. It was good of her to let us get ready for the Christmas party at her house. She's a right laugh.'

Sarah grinned. 'Yes, she is. She's always happy when the house is full of people.'

'Here, look sharp – Bossy Billington's coming along to empty the tills. If we aren't quick, she'll have us doing more work and we'll never get away on time. Where's Freda?'

'She went to the warehouse with a pile of empty boxes. She said she'd meet us in the cloakroom. She's so excited about tonight.'

Maisie threw the last of the covers over the counter and, grabbing Sarah's arm, steered her away from the counter so they could escape. 'Bless her. I don't think she 'ad much of a life before she came here. I wish she'd open up a bit and tell us, but even I can't get anything out of her. Do you know, she was even thrilled when Miss Billington told us we'd have proper made-to-measure uniforms in the new year? Mind you, it'll be better than wearing these second-hand rags.'

'Well, it's a sign that we have permanent jobs to look forward to. Maureen said the bosses wouldn't be bothered with our uniforms if they weren't planning to keep us on.'

'You're pretty chummy with her, aren't you?'

'She's nice. She likes to chat about my family and the old days when she serves me in the canteen.'

'Whether we get to stay on or not, I for one am glad to be getting a new uniform. I look like a sack of spuds in this old thing.'

Sarah grinned at Maisie as she followed her upstairs to the staffroom. Whatever Maisie wore she looked a million dollars. Considering she'd taken her overall apart and remade it to fit her slim shape, she had nothing to complain about. She looked a hundred times better than all the other staff members lumped together. Sarah was looking forward to seeing everyone's faces when they saw what Maisie was going to be wearing at the staff Christmas party that evening.

'You look like a princess, love.' George Caselton put down his evening newspaper and stood up as Sarah walked into the front room dressed in her new party frock – courtesy of Maisie's dressmaking skills. Sarah twirled round for her father, the pale green chiffon swirling around her ankles. With a simple fitted bodice and short puffed sleeves, the dress emphasized Sarah's slim figure.

She'd washed her hair that evening, and she'd clipped back the soft waves that bounced around her shoulders.

Sarah kissed him on the cheek. 'Thank you, Dad. Isn't Maisie clever?'

'She certainly is. It's a rare talent to be able to create something so beautiful. Speaking of which, where are your friends?'

'They're just finishing getting ready. Freda needed another stitch in her hem, so Maisie is doing it now.' Sarah sat on the arm of his chair and breathed in the aroma as George puffed on his pipe. This was what she identified with her dad: the distinctive tobacco smell, and the way she could speak to him at any time about anything that troubled her.

'Dad, I'm worried about Mum. Is she all right on her own in Devon? With you travelling so much, she's on her own. I thought perhaps she could come and stay here sometimes?'

George grimaced. 'I don't think she'd like that, love.'

'Why didn't Mum like living in Erith? I know you both came from here, and we've always visited Nan, but Mum has changed so much, from what I've been told, and I'm worried.'

George patted her knee. 'Don't you worry about your mum, Sarah – she's just fine. I'll try to bring her up at Christmas. I can hear your mates coming downstairs now. They sound excited. I wish I was coming along to this party myself!'

'Why don't you, Dad? You'd be more than welcome.'

'I don't think so, love. Not this time. I'm about

all in. It's been a hard day. I'll finish the crossword and be making tracks for my bed before too long.'

Sarah bent and kissed his forehead, wondering why was it she could always speak so openly to her dad and not her mum.

'Now, look at the pair of you. Aren't you both a sight for sore eyes?'

Freda grinned at George and curtsied in response. Sarah had never seen her look so pretty. She scrubbed up well, as her nan would say. In a deep red velvet dress, with the sweetheart neckline edged in lace, she looked a million miles away from the frightened young girl Sarah had met when they started work at Woolworths. It certainly showed what friendship could do if Freda could blossom within weeks of starting her new life. Sarah wondered again what it was that her friend was running away from. It seemed that Freda had secrets that she was not yet ready to share.

Maisie's dress of oyster satin was equally beautiful; it skimmed her hips and fell into soft folds that floated as she moved across the front room. Her blonde hair was pulled back into a severe pleat at her neck, which showed off the tiny pearl studs clipped to each ear. A multitude of small curls topped the pleat, giving the overall appearance of a sophisticated, assured woman.

'You've done a grand job, Maisie,' George said. 'You've a rare talent there.'

Maisie went red. Sarah had never seen her blush before. 'Thank you, Mr Caselton.'

'My, my, don't you all look a picture?' said Ruby. She turned to Vera Munro, who had followed her through the front door. 'Look at these girls all done up for their Christmas party. As pretty as a picture, all three of them.'

Vera sneered. 'Such a shame to spoil all that get-up on a Woolworths party. Don't you agree, George? I reckon your Irene wouldn't be so keen to see her only child dressed up for a shop do.'

'I'll have none of that in my house, Vera. The girls look lovely, and if some don't like it, they can just pick up their coat and go elsewhere.'

Vera snorted. 'It's only my opinion. However, some might consider toning down their appearance. No husband this evening, Maisie?'

Sarah was horrified. Her friend was standing, hands on hips, glaring at Vera. 'I'm so sorry, Maisie. I'm sure Mrs Munro didn't mean what she said.'

'That's OK, love. You ain't responsible for what other people say. My husband is working a late shift, Mrs Munro. At least he doesn't have to go to the pub most nights to escape his nagging wife.'

Vera stood with her mouth opening and closing, resembling a goldfish. 'Well, I never.'

Ruby took Vera's arm. 'One too many sherries, eh, Vera? I think we'd best get ourselves off to the bingo before anyone else gets upset. See you all later – and you girls have a good time.'

Ruby could be heard berating her mate even after the front door had closed behind them.

George folded his newspaper. 'Now, you girls have a lovely time and, er ... be careful what you drink, eh?'

Sarah hugged her dad. 'Are you sure you don't want to come with us?'

'Please do, Mr Caselton. I need someone to

teach me to do the waltz,' Freda begged.

George took his daughter by the shoulders and turned her towards the door. 'Now off you go and enjoy yourselves. Freda, there will be no end of young men waiting to lead you round the floor. You don't need lessons. Now, be off with you before I change my mind.'

Outside, the girls linked arms. Huddling under their winter coats, they stepped carefully through the pathway the neighbours had swept through the snow-covered pavements. The night was clear and stars twinkled down on the excited trio as they walked the short distance to the Prince of Wales public house, where the party was to be held.

'I never thought I'd see Vera so squiffy,' Sarah said. 'I know Nan went along to the vicar's wife's get-together this afternoon and Vera went with her, but even so...'

'That's probably why she took so badly after just the one glass of sherry,' Freda added helpfully. 'Drink can do some funny things to people. I know it did with my stepfather.'

'I've got a feeling it was more than the one that loosened her tongue,' Maisie said as they crossed the road.

'All the same, she was blooming rude considering her own home life ain't so clever.'

'How did you know about her husband?' Freda asked.

'If anything's worth knowing, my mother-in-law knows it. Why do you think I do so much dressmaking? With my sewing machine whirring away, it blocks out her chatter.'

Sarah chuckled at Maisie's comment, although

she was surprised at what went on behind people's front doors. 'Here we are. Thank goodness it wasn't far. I'm frozen to the bone,' Sarah said as they approached the pub, where music could be heard from the function hall behind the main bar.

'Do we have to go in through the bar?' Freda asked nervously.

'No, there's a door at the side. It says on the tickets to use that entrance.' Sarah opened the door to the hall and the girls stepped inside, banging their feet on the floor to remove the icy snow from their smart shoes. A wall of noisy chatter and a band playing a quickstep welcomed them, along with the overpowering fug of cigarette smoke.

Sarah had only just taken off her coat when Maureen Gilbert caught up with her. 'There you are, love; I was beginning to wonder where you were. Your dad and nan not with you? Staff can buy tickets for close family.'

'No, Dad's had a busy day. He doesn't know from one day to the next if he's working up here or back in Devon. Nan's been out with her friends today, so I think she wants a quiet night once she's been to bingo.'

Not that it would be quiet, with Vera the state she was in, Sarah thought to herself with a grin.

'Well, you get your coat off and enjoy yourself. My Alan's around somewhere. He's been looking for you,' Maureen said with a knowing smile as she turned to take tickets from a group of staff entering the hall.

Sarah joined Maisie and Freda after leaving her coat and checking her hair in the cloakroom. They'd found seats along with some of the other shop girls, who were exclaiming over their lovely party dresses.

Sarah was turning round, showing off her own dress, when someone touched her arm. 'Would you care to dance?'

Sarah spun round to see Alan holding out his hand. Ignoring the giggles from younger colleagues, she slipped her hand into his and followed him onto the crowded dance floor. Alan pulled her close. The lights dimmed and the band started to play the well-known ballad 'Isn't It Romantic?'

Sarah closed her eyes as Alan held her tight. Couples shuffled around them, but Sarah was oblivious to everything except Alan. He was a competent dancer and appeared so much more mature than the jovial lad she knew from work, who was always up for a laugh with the other staff She felt safe in his arms. It felt right. She could feel his hand on the lower part of her back; her skin was tingling under his touch as he held her close. Sarah ached to run her fingers through the golden hair at the nape of his neck, but instead she concentrated on keeping time to the music while breathing in his masculine smell. She could stay in his arms forever.

As the song ended, the dancers clapped politely. Alan held on to her hand, rubbing her palm with his thumb. It sent shivers of delight through her body. She could hardly bear it. Alan started to speak to her as the band burst into 'The Hokey-Cokey'. They both grinned. The spell was broken. Alan led her back to her seat.

Alan didn't dance with her for the rest of the evening, although Sarah dearly hoped that he would. She couldn't forget the way he held her close and could still smell the fresh, clean tang of his shaving soap and feel the strength of his firm shoulders under her hand as they danced. It was as if time had stood still and no one else was in the room until the music ceased.

She'd still had fun, jumping up to join the girls as they danced to 'The Lambeth Walk', and she had also taken a spin round the floor with the shop manager, Mr Benfield, to do the Gay Gordons. They'd even won a prize in a spot waltz, much to the amusement of the revellers. The band suddenly stopped playing and declared there would be a prize for the first couple to reach the stage with a ladder. Mr Benfield looked perplexed, but Sarah grabbed his hand and ran to the front of the hall, just beating Maisie, who'd been dancing with Alan's colleague, young Ginger. She raised the hem of her skirt and showed a small ladder in her stockings, to cheers from the other dancers. She'd been thrilled to win three pairs of new stockings and decided, straight away, to share them with her two friends. Mr Benfield was more than pleased with a pouch of tobacco.

Throughout the evening, Sarah watched Alan. He seemed to be busy all the time dancing with the older staff members and helping behind the free bar. He'd even been called upon to help Maureen when a table heavily laden with sandwiches and cakes had been uncovered. The management had certainly done the staff proud with the spread and there wasn't an unhappy face to be seen.

Sarah checked the dainty watch round her wrist. It was almost eleven. Not a chance for another dance with Alan. Soon she'd be queuing to get her coat and then facing the cold night air to walk the short distance home with Freda, who was staying with her for the night. She thought she may as well go for her coat now to beat the rush. Taking a few steps from the table, where she was seated with her friends, being careful not to step on the toes of those seated nearby, Sarah was brought to a sudden stop by a person in front of her. Looking up, she saw it was Alan standing before her.

'You wouldn't deny me a last dance, would you?'

Lost for words, Sarah allowed Alan to lead her to the dance floor and to hold her close again. Around them, the party revellers were joining in with Maureen, who had jumped onto the small stage to sing along with the band.

'*Goodnight, sweetheart, till we meet the morrow...*'

'I've been waiting to do this all evening,' Alan said softly to her.

Sarah felt herself tremble as his lips brushed her ear. 'You have been busy. I didn't expect...'

'*...Goodnight, sweetheart. Sleep will banish sorrow...*'

Dancers jostled close to the couple. She slid her hand to Alan's collar. Running her fingers through his hair, she leant her head against his chest, feeling the roughness of his suit jacket. Time seemed to stand still once more.

'*...Tears and parting may make us forlorn, but with the dawn, a new day is born...*'

'It's not that I didn't want to,' he murmured. 'We're together now.'

Sarah closed her eyes as they moved slowly together, feeling Alan's touch on her lower back, the other hand holding hers, as if he never wanted to let go. She hoped he didn't. The light dimmed and a glitter ball above their heads turned an already unforgettable night into a magical one.

As everyone around them joined in with Maureen, Sarah realized the song was coming to an end.

'...*Goodnight, sweetheart, goodnight.*'

Alan held Sarah close until the last possible moment. 'Can I walk you home?'

She gazed up into his eyes. 'Yes, please.'

6

Sarah wriggled deep under the warm blankets and peered over the top of the eiderdown. From her cosy bed she could see fresh snow heaped on the window ledge through the gap in the flower-sprigged curtains. Her bedroom had an icy chill, and the stone bottle at her feet was now cold. Perhaps Nan was right. She should have worn a woolly hat to bed too. At least she didn't have to worry about walking to work on the icy pavements until the next morning. There would be a busy few days in the lead-up to Christmas, but at least she'd get to see Alan.

Sarah hugged herself with glee at the thought of Alan, the Christmas party and the way he held her close during the last waltz. He'd walked her home too. It wasn't as romantic as she'd imagined, because Freda was staying the night, so Alan had escorted them both the short distance to Alexandra Road, offering an arm to both girls.

Sarah could hear her nan in the kitchen below as she prepared breakfast. Sunday meant egg and bacon with fried bread. By the sound of pots and pans rattling in the room below, she'd soon have to brave the nippy room and get herself dressed. As she contemplated leaving her warm nest, there was a tap on the door and Freda crept in holding two cups of steaming tea.

'Here you go. Ruby said breakfast will soon be ready and you'd best shake yourself or there'll be no fried bread left. Mrs Munro popped in to borrow a cup of sugar and invited herself to breakfast as well. I don't think she's eaten for a week. Brr ... it's a bit on the cold side in here. There's ice on the window. Budge up a bit.'

Sarah moved over so her friend could slide under the warm eiderdown. 'Thanks. I'll drink this and get myself dressed. I take it there was another fall of snow in the night?'

Freda's eyes lit up. 'I'll say. It's lovely out there. *"Deep and crisp and even"*, as the carol goes. The kids up the road are going to build a snowman later. Do you want to help?'

Sarah looked sideways at Freda. She was no more than a child herself. 'Are you sure? You'll freeze to death out there.'

Freda grinned. 'It'll be fun. Come on. Do say you'll join in.'

Sarah relented. 'OK, but only for a while. I have some presents to wrap and there won't be much chance once we are back at work tomorrow. Two evenings working late and then it's Christmas.

We're going to be rushed off our feet.'

'I'm looking forward to it. I love to see everyone buying their Christmas presents and decorations and being able to help them make decisions.' Freda plumped up the pillow behind her and snuggled down. 'It's such a happy time of the year. I wish it would go on forever,' she added wistfully.

Sarah placed her cup and saucer on the bedside table. 'Can't you get home to see your family for a few days?'

Freda shook her head, looking fearful. 'No. I'd rather stay in Erith. Your nan has just invited me for Christmas Day. She said I can stay over like I did last night.' She looked at Sarah. 'You don't mind, do you? Please say if you do. What with you going out with Alan and all.'

'Of course I don't mind. Anyway, I'm not going out with Alan. He just walked us home last night.'

Freda giggled. 'I think it was more than that. I peeped through the letter box after I left you both on the doorstep and he was kissing you.'

Sarah thumped her on the arm. Freda was just like a naughty younger sister. 'You minx. He did kiss me, but only to say goodnight. It was nothing special.'

'Nothing special. You were almost floating on air when you came in. Your nan had to ask you twice to get the sugar out of the cupboard and then you passed her the gravy browning.'

Sarah felt herself blush and started to rise from her bed to hide her embarrassment. It was true. She had felt as though she'd flown to heaven after Alan's kiss. If she closed her eyes, she could feel his arms around her and his lips as they brushed against hers. She wanted to stay there on the cold doorstep, with snow swirling around them, for all eternity, but all too soon the moment was over. He'd stroked her cheek with one finger and simply said, 'See you at work, Sixpenny,' before striding out into the night.

She didn't wish to tell Freda how she felt about Alan. Well, not just yet. She wanted to savour her feelings and wait and see what happened next. Perhaps it was that special Christmas magic and the wonderful music at the party. The days ahead would show whether Alan really liked her or if he was swept up in the moment.

'That's enough of this silly talk. I'd best get dressed or Mrs Munro will have eaten all the bacon as well.'

Freda didn't like this part of Erith. It was a world away from where Sarah lived in Alexandra Road and the streets in the busy town, with their many shops and people going about their business. It had taken a little while to find out where the Ship public house was in Erith, as Freda didn't want her new friends to know why she was looking for the pub. She would then have to explain about Lenny, and for now she wanted to keep the reason she'd travelled south a secret. It was the local newspaper that gave her a clue as to the where-abouts of the pub, as there had been a report of a violent fight and a man being stabbed. The pub was in West Street, down by the side of the river.

Freda stepped over the threshold of the pub and headed towards the bar. The air hung heavy with the smell of cigarettes and beer. She wrinkled her nose; it reminded her of the pubs back home. Trying not to look around, as she didn't wish to draw attention to herself, Freda wondered what to do next. She was aware that women who frequented some public houses by the docks did so for a reason. She did not wish to be mistaken for one of those women.

Noticing an elderly woman behind the bar, she waved discreetly for her attention. 'Excuse me. I wonder if you can help...'

The women sucked on a cigarette and looked Freda up and down. 'Depends what you want.'

'I'm looking-for a man named Jed Jones. I believe he may be the landlord's son.'

'He might be. What do you want him for?'

'My brother, Lenny, was in... He was with Jed for a while. I need to get in touch with my brother.'

The woman didn't say a word but stared for some time before reaching for a scrap of paper from under the counter. 'If I see 'im, I'll say you was 'ere. Write yer address down and I'll see if I can pass it on. I'm not promising, mind.'

Freda quickly scribbled down the address of her lodgings and handed the piece of paper back to the woman, who tucked it into her pocket. 'Thank you,' Freda whispered, almost too scared to speak.

The woman nodded and turned away. Freda fled from the pub and hurried back to the safety of Woolworths and her new friends.

The lead-up to Christmas was busy in the shop. Sarah didn't get a chance to speak much to Maisie and Freda, let alone Alan. She'd thought that after the Christmas party they'd have been closer in some way, but it didn't appear to be the case. While working hard, serving queues of shoppers, wrapping purchases and advising on the best products to give as gifts, Sarah kept an eye out for Alan. When she did spot him, he was struggling under boxes of goods or pushing heavy trolleys through the store so that counters were fully stocked. Occasionally he accompanied Mr Benfield or one of the senior assistants as they removed cash from the tills. It was while he was assisting with the collection of cash that he finally spoke to Sarah.

'I've been hoping to catch you.'

After days of wondering whether Alan's kiss had been a spur-of-the-moment thing, and questioning her feelings towards him, Sarah wasn't sure what he was about to say and bowed her head so as not to look him in the eye. If he apologized for kissing her, she would cry. She knew she would.

'Hey, there's no need to look as though I'm about to bite you,' Alan said, taking hold of her hand beneath the highly polished mahogany counter they were standing behind.

'I thought... Well...'

'Go on. You can tell me,' he urged, a worried frown on his face.

Sarah gulped. This was silly. If Alan was leading her on, then she shouldn't let him hold her hand like he was at this moment. She pulled away, but he was holding too tightly.

'Is there something wrong, Sarah?'

'After not seeing you to speak to, I thought you didn't like me anymore.' There, she'd said it. If he laughed at her words, she'd know the truth. It would break her heart, but at least she'd know.

Alan did laugh. 'You silly thing. Like you? Sixpenny, I "like you" to distraction. Every time I'm on the shop floor I can't concentrate on anything, as I'm too busy trying to catch a glimpse of you. I almost ran someone down with the sack barrow when I spotted you yesterday.'

It was Sarah's turn to laugh.

'Look, it's hell working here at this time of the year. When I finish work, I'm exhausted and fall into my bed. You must feel the same?'

Sarah nodded. Alan was right.

'Let's get Christmas out the way and then see how things go, eh? Don't forget we work late tomorrow for the old soldiers to come shopping. Some of them were too old to serve in the last war, would you believe? But the stories they tell! It's always a good evening. More fun than work, and we will get to have a sing-song and some food in the staffroom. Have you volunteered to help?'

'We didn't have much choice. Miss Billington gave us all one of her stares when she came round with her clipboard asking for volunteers. Not that I don't want to help,' Sarah added quickly, in case he thought she was a bad sport.

She'd looked forward to helping out at the annual event. It was always held the night before Christmas Eve, and from what the other girls had said, was such fun that it carried them through the very busy last shopping day before Christmas. There would be a gift for every guest and food laid out in the staff canteen. She was told that there'd even be a piano brought in for the evening, as well as a barrel of beer so they could entertain the old soldiers and raise a glass of cheer in the spirit of the season. First, though, staff would each accompany one of the elderly guests as they made their small purchases in the shop. Sarah and Maisie were to be paired together to assist a man in a wheelchair. Sarah was looking forward to the evening. It would make a nice change.

'Mr Gilbert, may we have your attention, please? Miss Caselton, you have customers waiting.'

Sarah and Alan both jumped. Caught up in the moment, both had forgotten their duties until a senior colleague had called their names.

Alan squeezed her hand before letting it drop to her side. 'I'll see you later.'

Sarah nodded and turned with a smile to the queue that had formed on the other side of the counter. Surely her worries about Alan were unfounded? Her heart skipped a beat as she imagined him once more holding her hand and standing close.

'May I help you, madam?'

The rest of the shift rushed by. Sarah, her head in the clouds as she thought of Alan, couldn't even come down to earth when the grumpiest shoppers tried their utmost to upset her. She hurried home in order to be able to wash her hair and make sure she had ladder-free stockings for the next day. Although all staff had to wear their uniforms during the evening, she wanted to look clean and presentable, even after a full day on the shop floor.

7

The day of the party for the old soldiers dawned bright, although there was still snow on the ground. She'd heard that the men would be collected by staff to ensure they would be at Woolworths as the doors closed to the other shoppers at half past five. They would be able to browse the shelves with help from staff before enjoying their tea party.

During her midday break Sarah was summoned to Miss Billington's office. She looked around her as she stepped into the room. Rows of box files covered the shelves, each labelled with neat handwriting. Paperwork was stacked tidily in wire trays on the desk, and next to them a row of pencils, each sharpened to a point, were lined up ready to be used. Miss Billington certainly ran a tight ship.

'Take a seat, Sarah. I don't wish to take up too much of your lunch hour. I just wanted a quick word with you to ask if you were happy working for F. W. Woolworth.'

Sarah frowned. Had their colleague reported her and Alan because of the few minutes they had held hands while on duty the previous day? 'I'm very happy here, Miss Billington. I hope I haven't given cause for complaint?' She chewed her lip nervously as Miss Billington looked at a sheet of paper on the desk in front of her. To be denied a permanent job now would be awful. Not being able to work alongside Maisie and Freda, and not having the chance to see Alan each day, would break her heart. She knew that Alan still hadn't asked her out, but to miss the thrill of seeing him around the shop, the anticipation of a few snatched words, the touch of his hand, a smile or a cheeky wink was simply unbearable. Perhaps if she begged, Miss Billington would change her mind. But what could she say?

Miss Billington cleared her throat. 'I know I said that you were on probation until January, but I've reason to change my mind.'

Sarah closed her eyes and clenched her fists in anticipation of being sent away without a job and without seeing Alan again.

'Sarah, I'm more than happy with your work, to the point that I feel you have the makings, in time, of a supervisor. You are already aware that I'm arranging uniforms for the probationers in January, but I wanted to have a quiet word about your future with Woolworths.'

Sarah gasped. From expecting to be given her cards to being told that management were happy with her work had taken her breath away. She was determined to show she was worthy of Miss Billington's trust in her. 'Thank you. I promise I'll do my best to make you proud of me.'

Miss Billington smiled and checked her watch. 'I'm sure you will, Sarah. I have faith in you. Now, finish your lunch and get back to your counter before we have queues running the length of the shop. I don't need to tell you that this is the busiest time of the year and we in the Erith branch of F. W. Woolworth pride ourselves on our service to our customers.'

'I will, Miss Billington. Thank you, oh thank you.' Sarah rushed from the room and was halfway to the shop floor before she remembered she had left her handbag in the staffroom, along with her half-eaten lunch. Turning quickly, while chiding herself for her stupidity, she bumped into Maisie.

'Whoa, watch where you're going!' Maisie said, grabbing Sarah's shoulders to slow her down.

'Gosh, I'm sorry. I don't know whether I'm coming or going.'

'You look all of a fluster, love. Not been in the store cupboard sharing kisses with that Alan, have you?'

Sarah blushed. Maisie certainly had a way of saying things. 'Goodness, no. I was called in to see Miss Billington and forgot where I was going when I came out of her office, that's all.'

Maisie nudged her with her elbow. 'I'm only kidding you. Mind you, I bet you wouldn't say no if he asked you. I saw the way you were dancing together at the party. He couldn't keep his eyes off you.'

'I do like him.'

'And it's obvious he likes you.' Maisie linked her arm through her chum's. 'Now, where are we heading?'

'I'm going to the staffroom to finish my sandwich and then I'm back on the shop floor.'

'I'll come with you. I've got time for a quick cuppa.'

The girls headed for the staffroom and found Freda already sitting at the table that Sarah had vacated earlier. She held up Sarah's handbag. 'I thought you'd be back. You forgot this. I've got you a fresh cup of tea as well. Yours was stone cold. Want one, Maisie?'

'I'll get me own. You start cross-examining this one here. There must be a reason she looks like the cat what got the cream.'

Sarah giggled. 'I am quite excited.'

'Go on, do tell,' Freda begged. 'Is it to do with Alan?'

'Not you as well. I've had Maisie making all sorts of suggestions. He hasn't even asked me out.'

'He will,' Freda said with certainty. 'His mum reckons he will as well.'

Sarah glanced over to where Maureen Gilbert was serving Maisie her tea. 'I didn't realize I was the subject of everyone's conversations.'

Freda looked hurt. 'Sorry. I didn't mean any harm by it. I like Alan. Your nan does too.'

'I'm sure you didn't mean any harm. I like Alan too.'

The girls giggled as Maisie joined them, balancing her cup and saucer in one hand and a plate with slices of tart in the other.

'What's that?' Freda asked, peering closely at the pastry-based confection with its creamy-brown filling.

'Gypsy tart. It's a Kentish cake. You'll love it,' Sarah said, passing Freda a slice.

Freda bit into the sweet filling, wiping the crumbs from her lips. 'It's delicious,' she declared. 'We have nothing like this where I come from.'

'There'll be plenty more of it. It's Maureen's

speciality, along with bread pudding, from what I've been told,' Maisie said, sitting down at the table and pulling out her cigarettes. 'So come on, spit it out. I know you've got news of some sort.'

'It's nothing, really. Miss Billington wanted to tell me that I have the makings of a supervisor, that's all. Nothing definite.'

'Nothing definite? That's blooming marvellous. Well done, kid!' Maisie cheered, and had to be shushed by the other two, as heads turned their way in the crowded staffroom.

Freda squeezed Sarah's arm. 'I'm made up for you. You'll be in charge of the both of us in no time at all. Perhaps we should celebrate?'

Sarah shook her head. 'No. It's not as if I have a proper job offer. It might be years before I get the position. Besides, we have enough celebrating to do, with Christmas only a couple of days away and entertaining the old folk this evening. Are you sure you and your husband can't come to us for Christmas, Maisie? Nan said the invite still stands.'

'No, sorry. We've got to spend some time with the old bat. Thanks all the same. To be honest, I'd rather be sharing your Christmas than what we have planned, but needs must where the family's concerned. Thank your nan for me, will you? We'll share a glass or two to see in the new year, though.'

'Of course I will. You've not changed your mind and want to go see your family, Freda?'

Freda shook her head and shuddered. 'No. I'd much rather be at yours. That's if it's still OK?'

'Of course it's all right,' she reassured Freda. But Sarah wondered why a young girl wouldn't want to be at home with her family over Christmas. Freda had a secret and Sarah wasn't so sure it was a pleasant one.

That evening Sarah immediately fell in love with Alfie, the elderly ex-soldier she was escorting around Woolworths. The men exclaimed with delight at the Christmas tree that stood just inside the entrance to the shop. Almost touching the ceiling, it set the scene for the delights of the store as visitors stepped over the threshold. Sarah had to admit her own counter, stocked high with boxes of greetings cards, calendars for 1939 and a large assortment of wrapping paper, looked suitably festive, with its canopy of paper chains and Chinese lanterns. Maisie pushed Alfie's wheelchair, while Sarah picked out books, packets of toffees and tins of sweets as possible gifts for his grandchildren. She asked about them and tried hard to find presents that would suit the characters he described. Although a warm rug was tucked around his legs, Sarah could see he wore what must have been his best suit and a row of medals across his chest. She recognized one as the same as her granddad had proudly owned. As a young child, she'd sat on her granddad's knee and been allowed to look at his medals, displayed in a velvet-lined box. She knew that one had been earned for service long before the Great War.

'So tell me, my dear, why are you helping an old man when you should be out with your friends enjoying yourself? Are you courting?'

Maisie laughed. 'You're not slow in coming forward, Alfie.'

Alfie waved his walking stick at Maisie from his wheelchair. 'None of your lip either, young woman. I'm asking because she's a pretty young thing who shouldn't be hanging around with old goats like me. It's Christmas – she should be with her young man. Now answer my question, young miss.'

Sarah looked up from where she was wrapping a small bottle of eau de cologne. Alfie was a lovely man. He reminded her of Granddad Eddie – straight-talking, as many of his generation were. 'I don't have a boyfriend, Alfie, and even if I did, I still wouldn't miss this evening for a hundred pounds. I've loved helping you with your shopping.'

Alfie looked up at Maisie. 'Is she having me on? No young man?'

Maisie grinned at Sarah. 'Not at the moment, Alfie, but I reckon there's one who has set his cap for our Sarah.'

The old man guffawed with laughter and Maisie joined in.

Sarah tried hard not to join in with their mirth. But try as she might, she had to laugh.

'Now, is there anything else you need? We will have to get upstairs to the canteen before too long or there won't be any food left.'

'Don't you go worrying about me, my dear. I may not be able to walk that far, but with one of you young ladies on my arm and my faithful walking stick, stairs hold no fear for me.'

Sarah smiled to herself. What a lovely man he was. It was a pleasure to help him. This evening was so much fun.

Alfie took her hand as she bent to place his purchases in his bag. 'Hark up, my love. You get yourself out and have some fun. If there's a lad that sets your heart a-fluttering, then get him up that aisle and a ring on your finger as soon as you can. I don't hold with all this talk of "peace in our time". Mark my words, there's gonna be another war and you youngsters are going to lose loved ones and miss growing up among family and friends just like the last generation did. I was lucky – my sons returned in one piece, just as I did when I served my country.' He tapped his legs with his stick. 'Even if me pins never worked proper afterwards, at least I came back. A lot didn't. Grasp your happiness while you can, my love. While you can.'

Alfie fell silent for a moment as a faraway look came into his eyes. 'Now, enough of my ramblings. Let's go have that food, shall we?'

Sarah stood watching as Maisie pushed Alfie away. A sudden chill made her shiver as if something had walked over her grave.

The party was in full swing when the girls pushed Alfie through the doors of the staff canteen. The shop manager, Mr Benfield, was dressed as Father Christmas, complete with a pillow stuffed inside his costume to enhance his already portly figure.

Plates piled high with ham, pickles and crusty bread were being tucked into, while a large Christmas cake, in the centre of the table, was waiting to be sliced. Maureen, assisted by Freda, was busy pouring out cups of strong tea. The barrel of beer would be put to use soon afterwards when the entertainment started.

Sarah could see Alan in the kitchen with a tea towel tied round his waist as he set to work on the already mountainous pile of washing-up. The ex-servicemen may be elderly but they could still put away an enormous amount of food, Sarah thought to herself. She was just thinking of going to help him when she spotted Miss Billington waving to her from where the piano had been positioned.

'Sarah, would you be a dear and turn the pages as I play? It's been a while and I'm all fingers and thumbs. Thankfully Maureen Gilbert will take over when she's finished serving tea.'

Sarah squeezed onto the long piano stool beside her boss. 'Of course I will, Miss Billington.'

'There's no need to be so formal, Sarah. You may call me Betty as we aren't at work.'

'Thank you, M– Betty. That's a pretty name.'

Betty Billington smiled. 'Thank you. It's Elizabeth really, after my grandmother, who died long before the last war. But you know how names are shortened by family. I have vague recollections of her, but time does strange things with our memories. Shall we start with "By a Waterfall"? I'm rather partial to a Busby Berkeley tune.'

It was the first time that Sarah had thought of her boss as a person who had likes and dislikes. Betty Billington was probably not more than forty years of age, but with her hair pulled back in a severe bun and her tweed suits, she looked much older.

'That's my favourite song as well.' Sarah beamed and reached for the sheet of music, ready to turn the page when her boss indicated. Members of the party started to hum and tap their toes to the music. As the tables were cleared and cigars passed round, Mr Benfield made his appearance, sack over his shoulder and many 'ho, ho, ho's as he got into the part. He was the perfect Santa.

Betty stopped playing so that Father Christmas could take centre stage, to much cheering and ribbing from his staff. He handed out a small parcel to every guest, who each tore it open with gusto, voicing their appreciation.

Sarah watched with glee as the men showed their gratitude, shaking the hands of staff sitting nearby. 'Is this the same every year?' she asked Betty.

'There's always a party, but this year we've made it more special, as who knows what will be happening by next Christmas. These men know more than any what our country will face. It's only right we show them some respect. Apart from the cigarettes and tobacco we've wrapped for each man, there's also a small hamper of Christmas foods that will be delivered when we take our guests home. For some, this will be the only Christmas celebration they'll have and here at F. W. Woolworth we feel that we should be saying thank you to these brave men.'

Sarah found she couldn't speak properly as her throat had tightened and tears had started to form. She was seeing another side to her boss, and the job she was beginning to enjoy, this evening. 'I think it's wonderful that we are able to treat these men to such a lovely party,' she said eventually. 'My nan has told me that she lost many friends and family in the last war. It must be awful for the older folk, as they know it could happen again. I couldn't bear to think I'd lose family and loved ones to war.' Her gaze drifted to where Alan was chatting to a group of old soldiers. She had known him for such a short time. It would be unbearable never to see Alan again under such circumstances. 'How do women cope when they lose the love of their life?' she murmured.

'We carry on, Sarah. That's all we can do, but we never forget.'

Sarah could see that Betty's hands were shaking. 'I'll get us a cup of tea. Would you like a slice of cake to go with it?'

'Thank you. You're a good girl, Sarah. I hope you aren't faced with the sadness that my generation have had to bear.'

Sarah slipped into the kitchen, where she found Freda and Maisie cutting cake and laying it out on a tray to hand round to the guests.

Maisie licked the icing sugar from her fingers. 'You're getting a bit cosy with old Bossy Billington, aren't you?'

Sarah shrugged her shoulders. 'She's not so bad. She was getting a bit upset talking about the last war. I said I'd get her a cuppa to cheer her up. I think she must have lost someone close and it's shaken her up seeing the old soldiers here tonight. It's rather sad to think about, isn't it?'

'I suppose lots of women lose their loved ones during a war,' Freda said as she continued to cut the cake, unaware of Maisie and Sarah, who had stopped work and were looking at each other in fear.

'This could happen to us if Hitler has his way,' Maisie whispered.

'Please, God, no,' was all Sarah could say.

8

'...*down at the Old Bull and Bush, la, la, la, la, la...*'

'This is fun,' Freda exclaimed as she stopped singing and sat down beside Sarah. 'I've never heard so many old-time songs being sung before. The old soldiers seem to be enjoying themselves.'

The barrel of beer had gone down well and many of the men were waving their pint pots as they joined in with the songs. Some had stood by the piano and sung a ditty. Alfie had performed an extremely long version of 'The Man Who Broke the Bank at Monte Carlo', quickly followed by a rousing rendition of 'Take Me Back to Dear Old Blighty'.

Maureen clapped her hands for everyone's attention. 'We've come to the part of the evening where the Woolies staff are going to entertain you. First we have Mrs Maisie Taylor, with her rendition of "Hello, Hello, Who's Your Lady Friend?" A round of applause for Maisie, please.'

Freda and Sarah clapped until their hands ached as Maisie performed her song, with much swishing of her feather boa and winks to the older men. They then giggled uncontrollably as Mr Benfield, red-faced in his Father Christmas outfit, marched about the room booming out, slightly off-key, 'On the Road to Mandalay'.

Sarah cheered loudly when Maureen curtsied at the end of her version of "When Father Papered the Parlour". 'I must say everyone is being a great sport. I never thought the staff would all be singing a song.'

Freda nudged her as Alan walked to the centre of the room, a large fake moustache stuck to his face.

'Ladies and gentlemen, for your delectation I would like to dedicate this next song to all the beautiful women here today. And I will require the services of a certain young lady.'

Alan stepped forward and took Sarah's hand, leading her back to the centre of the room. Kneeling down, he invited her to sit on his knee. Maureen, at the piano, played a grand opening and he burst into song. *'If you were the only girl in the world...'*

Sarah knew she should have been embarrassed. She wasn't one for being the centre of attention. But here, sitting on Alan's knee, his arms around her, she really did feel as though they were the only boy and girl in the world.

All too soon the song came to an end and they both stood up. Sarah curtsied to the audience before Alan took her back to her seat, kissing her hand as he saluted her. Again the old soldiers cheered.

Maisie leant over and whispered loudly into Sarah's ear, the feather boa she still wore tickling Sarah's cheek, "'Ere, I told you there was nothing to worry about. That Alan has fallen for you hook, line and sinker.'

'I'll say he has,' Freda said, pretending to fan her face. 'That was so romantic. I could swoon just thinking about it.'

'It was romantic, wasn't it? But best not get carried away... Let's go help the men on with their coats. It looks as though the evening is over,' she laughed. However, deep in her heart, Sarah held on to the thrill of being close to Alan as he showed his love for her. This had to be real. It just had to.

Sarah found Alfie's coat and helped him into it, making sure his scarf was wrapped securely round his neck. Snow was still falling outside and the air was freezing.

Alfie tugged at her arm for her to lean close. 'Now, take note of what I said earlier. Marry your young man before he goes off to war.'

'Alfie, he's not my young man. He's just a friend.' Sarah couldn't explain that they hadn't even been out together.

'Don't you go saying things like that, 'cos I know better. The two of you are made for each other – any fool can see that. I'm just saying don't wait too long, that's all, or you'll regret it.'

She kissed his cheek, wished him a happy Christmas and promised to visit him in the new year, before heading to the kitchen to help with the last of the washing-up. As she ran hot water and scattered soap flakes into a bowl, the kitchen door opened behind her. She was delighted to see Alan standing there.

'Oh, Alan. I thought you were taking the old folk home?'

Alan looked a little sheepish, with no hint of the bravado he'd had during his performance. 'I am. I just wanted to give you this. You'll have probably gone home by the time I get back.' He held out a small, square box wrapped in green paper and tied with a red bow. 'Don't open it until Christmas Day. I won't be in Erith over the holiday, as I'm taking Mum to see Dad's family. It's a long-standing invitation,' he added by way of an apology.

Sarah took the box. 'Thank you. You didn't have to. I've not got anything for you.'

He held up his hand to silence her apology. 'There's no need. I hoped that you wouldn't think too badly of me for not asking you out yet. I want to. I really do. Perhaps in January when we aren't working all hours?'

Sarah smiled. 'I'd really like that.'

Alan stepped towards her. Sarah held her breath. Was he going to kiss her?

At that moment the door flew open and Freda and Maisie burst in.

'Oops! Sorry. Did we interrupt something?' Maisie asked. 'My hubby's here. He said he'd walk us all home.'

'No, I was just going,' Alan said. 'Have a lovely Christmas, girls. Don't work too hard tomorrow.'

Sarah slipped the small box into her pocket, hoping that the Christmas holidays would soon pass so she could be alone once more with Alan and truly be his girlfriend.

Christmas Day passed in a flurry of visitors. Ruby always kept an open house for family and friends, and this year was no exception. Young Freda had stayed over after going straight to number thirteen after work on Christmas Eve. Both girls, tired after working until ten o'clock, had gratefully tucked into the sandwiches Ruby had ready for them and enjoyed the cocoa they all shared before retiring for the night.

Sarah had hoped to see her parents over the short Christmas period, but it wasn't to be. She'd rung her mother from the phone box at the end of the road during her lunch hour on Christmas Eve, hoping that by speaking to her mum she'd convince her either to come up by car or catch a train to Kent. But Irene Caselton had flatly refused to travel in such bad weather. Besides, there was a party at the golf club on Boxing Day and she couldn't be seen to miss it. Sarah felt sad not to be seeing either of her parents, but her dad had assured her he'd be heading back to Erith for work early in January and had a pile of parcels with her name attached. She may have been twenty years old, but the thought of opening a parcel still gave her a thrill. She just couldn't wait to open the gift from Alan. As she drifted off to sleep, she slipped her hand underneath her pillow to where she had placed the small box. A sigh of happiness passed her lips as she fell into a deep sleep.

'Cor blimey, my feet are killing me,' Ruby declared as she lowered herself onto the overstuffed sofa in the front room.

'I'm not surprised, Nan. You've been on the go since early morning. How about I pour you a glass of stout, or would you prefer a port and lemon?'

'Sarah, love, a glass of stout would go down a dream, along with a slice of Christmas cake. If we have any left? Those kids of Pat's are like gannets. I've never seen so much grub cleared away in one sitting. I reckon the lot of 'em have got worms.'

Sarah giggled. Nan always said what she thought. It was true. Her aunt Pat's kids could pack away a fair amount of food. 'I've hidden some in the pantry, along with the ham and the chicken left over from our Christmas dinner. So don't worry – we won't starve just yet.'

'I don't think I'll be able to eat another bite for a week,' Freda exclaimed as she tidied cushions and straightened the antimacassars on the armchairs. 'You're a great cook, Mrs Caselton. The roast chicken and plum pudding were the best I've ever tasted. I loved playing party games with the kiddies as well. How many grandchildren do you have?'

'Seven. Sarah here and Pat's six. Anyways, I think it's six. They never stand still long enough for me to count them.'

Freda nodded her head. 'I think I counted six, unless one is hiding somewhere.' She started to look behind the settee and under the table, which set Ruby laughing until her sides ached.

'Freda, you're a right tonic.' She patted the empty seat next to her. 'Come sit down here and tell me about your family. I assume a young thing like you still has parents alive?'

Sarah held her breath. Both she and Maisie had given up asking questions of Freda, as she would duck and dive around whenever asked.

Freda sat next to Ruby and wrung her hands together as she spoke. 'I do have a family. A large one, as it happens, but if you don't mind, I prefer not to talk about them. It's best I don't. It may seem ungrateful after the way you've been so good to me, all of you' – she smiled at Sarah – 'but for now I want to enjoy my present life and not think about the past. If that's all right?'

Ruby patted the young girl's knee. 'That's all right by me, but do remember that you can turn to us anytime, night or day, if you need some help or just want to talk. Now, what about that slice of cake?'

Freda jumped to her feet. 'Thanks, Ruby. I'm lucky to have met you. You too, Sarah. I'll get that cake, shall I? Then I must go back to my lodgings. I don't like to be away too long in case my landlady thinks I've run away and lets the room. I'll only be a tick with that cake.'

Ruby frowned as Freda left the room. 'She wouldn't kick the kid out, would she, Sarah?'

'I dunno, Nan. It doesn't seem that nice a place to live, from what she's said. I tell you what, I'll accompany her home; then I can tell you what it's like. It's not far. Just down Queens Road.'

'There's a good girl. I'll pack up some bits and pieces for her to take for her dinner for Boxing Day tomorrow. I wish she'd stay here. At least until tomorrow. The kid's stubborn. I've a mind to offer her the spare room. We could have a bed put in the front room for when your dad stays.'

Sarah hugged Ruby. 'You're a diamond, Nan. I'll try and convince her to come live with us.'

'You know, Sarah, this is the first chance we've had to talk today, what with all the visitors. I thought Mrs Munro was going to stay until the sherry bottle was empty. That woman can put it away. I've been meaning to ask you about the pretty brooch you're wearing. I've not seen it before. Was it a gift from your mum and dad?'

Sarah ran her fingers over the small spray of flowers picked out in coloured glass that she'd pinned to her navy velvet dress. The stones sparkled in the light of the coal fire. She'd been delighted when she opened the small box and found the brooch nestling among a bed of cotton wool. 'No, it's a gift from a friend.' She blushed as her nan raised an eyebrow.

'Friends don't usually make you blush like that. Was it from young Alan? Is he keen on you?'

Sarah nodded. 'Yes, Alan gave it to me. Nan, he wants to take me out once Christmas is over. Do you think it's OK?'

Ruby thought for a moment. 'You're twenty, and he's a good lad. I can't see any problem with that. But think on what your mother will say, and don't do anything to upset her, will you?'

'Aw, Nan, do you think I would?'

'No, I don't, love, but you seem smitten with him, and love can make us do some silly things sometimes. Just take things slow. There's no rush. You're both only kids.'

Sarah nodded as her nan spoke, but then she recalled Alfie's words and wondered. Did her generation have the luxury of time to fall in love?

'You really don't have to help me, Sarah. I can get home on my own.' Freda had looked worried when Sarah suggested helping her carry her small suitcase and the box of food that Ruby had thrust into her arms as she prepared to leave.

96

Slices of chicken and ham with cold cooked potatoes and cabbage, which she just needed to fry up to make delicious bubble and squeak, as well as a couple of mince pies and a large slice of Ruby's home-made Christmas cake.

'I don't mind. It's nice to have a walk after eating so much today. Besides, you can't carry this lot yourself. Here, give me the box to carry.'

Freda passed the box over and they walked in companionable silence. The snow had not long stopped falling and seemed to glisten in the light from the street lamps. The world had a perfect silence about it as the two friends created fresh footprints in the virgin snow.

Sarah looked up the ten steps to the shabby front door of a Victorian terraced house. At one time the street would have seen the wealthier inhabitants of Erith living under its roofs, but now many of the houses were home to multiple inhabitants or were lodging houses to the poorer population. As Freda pushed open the door, Sarah was hit by the smell of boiled cabbage, mixed with something she couldn't quite distinguish. She tried not to wrinkle her nose in distaste in case her young friend noticed.

Freda went to the bottom of the wide staircase. 'It's a bit of a climb, I'm afraid. I'm on the top floor.'

They'd not gone halfway up the first flight of stairs when a voice boomed from behind them. A woman wearing a wraparound apron that had seen better days, with her hair in curlers, stood with her arms folded across her ample bosom glaring up at them. 'Miss Smith, I'll ask you not to take one more step up those stairs.'

Freda frowned. 'Good evening, Mrs Carter. Is there a problem?'

Sarah held her breath, which was easy to do considering the cabbage smell had been joined by the acrid aroma of burnt onions wafting from an open door. Mrs Carter must live in the basement of the building, as she could see steps leading downwards. Was this the money-grabbing landlady whom Freda had mentioned, who charged her tenants for every small convenience that many took for granted? Perhaps Freda had not kept up with her rent. From the stern look on the woman's face, this was something serious.

'Yes, you could call it that. I understand you've not been staying in your room...'

'I told you I was spending last night at my friend's house in Alexandra Road, just in case you were worried by my absence.'

Sarah doubted that the landlady was worried about any of her tenants.

The woman huffed. 'That's as maybe, but I don't expect to have to chase away male callers on your behalf.' She pulled the collar of her blouse closer to her neck. 'He was an unsavoury sort and I feared for my life.'

'I'm sorry, Mrs Carter. I don't know what you mean.' Freda placed her suitcase on the step in front and leant across the banister to face her landlady head on.

Mrs Carter was in full flow. 'I was ready to call the police. I asked him if he wanted to rent a room, but he said he was just looking for you.'

Sarah wondered if Mrs Carter would have been

more welcoming to the stranger if he'd held out cash for a room. But who was looking for Freda?

'He gave me such a scare. Strange, brooding sort. Scruffy; with a scar on his cheek. A bad lot, I'd say.'

Freda went to take a step down the stairs but was blocked by Sarah standing behind her still holding the box of food. 'A scar, you say? Where is he now?'

Mrs Carter looked down her nose. 'So you do know him? I'm surprised you associate with the likes of him. I sent him packing, of course. Told him I'd get my old man to call the coppers. That worried him. He soon took off after that.'

Freda put her hand to her mouth, looking worried. 'Did he say anything at all?'

'I closed the door on him. I don't want his sort over my threshold, and I'll ask you to do the same. I don't hold with the likes of him, so I don't want you under my roof either.'

Sarah felt it was time to speak up. This may have something to do with Freda not wanting to speak about her past life, but right now her friend needed support.

'Miss Smith has a new place to live, Mrs Carter. In fact, we only returned to collect her belongings.'

'Sarah?' Freda looked bemused.

'Come along, Freda – let's go get your things.' She handed the box to Mrs Carter. 'Here is a gift for you. I hope it will be accepted in the spirit of the season.' She wrinkled her nose. 'Not untimely, as it seems you may have burnt your supper.'

'Well, I never,' was all Mrs Carter could say as

the two girls climbed the stairs together.

Ruby gazed at the clear night sky through her kitchen window as she dried the last of the cups and saucers. It had been a good party considering they hadn't planned to celebrate seeing in 1939. This time last year she'd not long buried her Eddie and wasn't up to thinking much about the future. Now, with Sarah having made number thirteen her home, life was moving on, and that's as it should be. She sighed thoughtfully as she turned the cups upside down on their matching saucers before placing them carefully on a shelf in the kitchen cabinet. The evening had been fun. She'd expected to feel sad thinking back to times gone by, but no, the young women had included her in their happiness, and yes, it was catching.

Maisie had arrived with her husband. Ruby had seen him from afar as he'd grown up in Erith but had to admit he was nothing like his foul-mouthed mother. He liked a glass of beer, though, and had undoubtedly knocked back a few before he stepped over the threshold of number thirteen. Saying that, he was a quiet lad and only showed a spark when someone mentioned the chances of a war, at which point Ruby had got to her feet from her armchair and announced she was making herself a cup of tea and did anyone else want one. Even with their gas masks safely stored in the cupboard under the stairs, she didn't want to think of what lay ahead. Let those politicians sort it out. That was their job. Hers was to make a home for her family.

With young Freda now living under her roof,

Ruby didn't worry about the girl so much. She was welcome to stay as long as she wanted, although the girl kept saying she wouldn't stay long and would continue to look for new digs. She was too young to be alone. Ruby made a mental note to give her a talking-to. It was a rum do when Sarah came home with Freda on Christmas night. The kid hadn't wanted to talk much and was adamant the strange man was not something she wished to discuss. She'd tucked herself up in bed with a hot-water bottle but Ruby could hear Freda crying gently before she'd even closed the door.

The world was going mad, but she'd ignore all of that and just concentrate on those who ventured under her roof. Time for everything else later.

9

'Sit yourself down, Alan. She won't be long. Would you like a cup of tea?'

'Not for me, thanks, Mrs Caselton.'

Ruby wiped her hands on her pinny and sat down opposite Alan. Her cheery face for once had no trace of a smile. 'Now, lad, I'll ask you this before Sarah gets herself downstairs. I don't want her thinking I'm fussing over nothing.'

Alan loosened the thick woollen scarf round his neck. He suddenly felt a little too warm. It was unusual to see Sarah's nan so serious. The only sound in the room was that of coals settling in the grate and the ticking of the clock as he waited for

Ruby to speak. He'd expected Sarah's dad to ask about his intentions towards Sarah, not her nan.

'Now, you might think me worrying when there's no need, but it's that contraption of yours out on the pavement. Is it safe?'

Alan relaxed. Early on a chilly March morning was not the time to have a conversation about his feelings towards Sarah. Anything else, he was more than happy to discuss. As his mother was always saying, there was a time and place for everything.

'That's no contraption, Mrs Caselton; that's Bessie, the love of my life.'

'Whatever you call it, lad, it looks none too safe to me, and there you are about to put my grand-daughter on it and drive off God knows where.'

'It's as safe as houses. There's no safer motor-bike in the whole world,' Alan said proudly. 'I've tuned it to perfection and every part is tickety-boo.'

'Well, you just make sure that you bring her back here in one piece. All I'll say is you won't get me on one of those contraptions. I'll keep my feet firmly on the ground, thank you very much.'

'There's no need to worry. I'd not do anything to harm a hair on Sarah's head. She's too precious to me to put her in danger.'

Ruby's stern face softened. She'd watched the young couple as they'd gradually got to know each other since Christmas. Alan's mum, Maureen, had grown up with Sarah's dad, George. The whole family were a hardworking, decent lot. 'I know that, lad. It's obvious to anyone who looks at the pair of you that you have something special. It makes my heart proud to know Sarah's met a boy who'll take care of her.'

Alan felt his face start to go red. Sarah's nan was a good sort. Even so, he was embarrassed to talk about his feelings to someone when he'd not yet discussed them with Sarah. He cleared his throat. 'Mum and Dad did their courting on Bessie. I remember Dad always polishing and tinkering with her when I was a small kid.'

'He was a good man, your dad, and taken far too soon. You're a lot like him.'

Alan grinned. 'Do you think so? He died when I was ten and sometimes my memory isn't that clear about him. I'm lucky so many people knew him.'

Ruby patted his knee before rising to her feet. 'There's many that do, Alan, so rest assured you'll never be short of a person around here who can tell you about your dad. Now, let me go shake that granddaughter of mine or it'll be teatime before you even leave the house.'

Ruby left Alan sitting by the coal fire and went to the foot of the steep staircase in the narrow hallway and bellowed up to a closed door, 'Sarah, get yourself down here or I'm putting my coat on and going off with this boyfriend of yours for a jaunt. Freda, come down here as well before the teapot goes cold.'

She glanced back over her shoulder to where Alan was looking thoughtfully into the fire, nervously clutching a pair of leather gauntlets. He seemed to have something on his mind. Ruby liked the boy. Sarah could do much worse than settle down with Alan, but not just yet. She'd only known him a short while and it was best that youngsters enjoyed themselves and had some fun before they thought about settling down with babies and the like. Yes, time for such things in the future, and hopefully not for a few years. Ruby preferred to think of her great-grandchildren not coming along just yet.

'So where are you off to today?' Freda asked as she peered at her face in Sarah's dressing-table mirror, dabbing a touch of scarlet lipstick to her lips before pulling a face and scrubbing it off with her handkerchief. 'It can't be dancing with all that clobber you're wearing.'

Sarah pulled a second jumper over her head before leaning towards the mirror. 'Budge up and pass me the lipstick. Alan's taking me for a ride on his motorbike. I'm not sure I'm wearing the right clothes, but at least I'll be warm.' She pouted as she added a dab of red to her lips, pulling a couple of curls from the confines of a red beret that sat jauntily on her head. 'That'll have to do.'

Freda gave her a sideways look. 'You look good in anything. I looked like I'd been dragged through a hedge backwards after five minutes on Alan's bike, and he'd only given me a ride round the block. So where are you going?'

'I'm not sure, but he's been going on about taking me somewhere special for ages. Now the snow has cleared, he said it was time. It's the wrong time of the year to go to the coast, although I've hinted like hell. Dad has always told me about the trips he made to Margate and on the paddle steamer to Southend when he was a kid. I'd love to go when the weather's a bit warmer.'

Freda nodded. 'Me too. Living in the Midlands, I've never been to the seaside. Let's go when we have a day off in the summer, shall we?'

'It's a deal. We can take Nan with us for a treat. She's been an absolute brick putting up with the pair of us.'

'I wanted to talk to you about that.' Freda suddenly seemed glum. 'I'm going to look for new digs as soon as possible. Ruby's been great taking me in since Christmas, but I don't want to put on her too much. It's best I move out and find somewhere else. Maisie said she'd ask around and find something for me.'

Sarah sat on the edge of her bed looking downcast. 'There's no need. You're not putting anyone out. Dad still has somewhere to sleep when he comes up to Erith to stay, and Nan says you're good company. No one wants you to move out. Please don't. It's like having a sister to live with.'

Freda almost gave in and agreed, but she knew that she couldn't risk bringing trouble to Ruby's doorstep. However much she had settled into day-to-day life in this riverside town, she had to remember she was here for a reason: she had to find her brother. Moving out was the best thing. 'I won't be that far away. After all, I've still got to get to work. Ay up, that's your nan calling. You'd best get yourself downstairs or Alan won't wait much longer and you won't get to ride on his motorbike at all.'

'I'm not sure I want to go now. I wasn't much looking forward to it, and now you've sprung your news on me, I'd rather stay home.'

Freda grinned and nudged her in the ribs. 'Don't be daft. Just hang on to Alan for dear life, – you'll be OK. I'm sure you'll enjoy that.'

Sarah nudged her back. 'Less of that, please!' However, secretly she couldn't think of anything better than being close to Alan. Unless it was being held in his arms while he kissed her. Of late his kisses had been more passionate, more demanding. Sarah knew he held back, but there were times she wondered what would happen next. She increasingly wanted to find out but knew that they would be letting down their families if anything came of their closeness. She sighed. Oh, to be married and be able to stay with Alan as his wife. She felt her cheeks redden at her thoughts and stood up to leave the room in case Freda noticed.

'What do you plan to do on your day off?'

Freda shrugged. 'I might go and visit Maisie, see if she wants to go to the pictures. Her Joe's working a long shift, so she's stuck at home with her mother-in-law.'

'Well, have a good time and tell Maisie I'll see her at work tomorrow. I want to find out how she likes working in the china department.' The three girls had been kept on at Woolworths after Christmas and the previous week had been given permanent duties in different parts of the store. Freda was kept busy on the household goods counter, while Sarah had been transferred to a counter selling books and stationery.

Freda agreed that she would and kept quiet that the real reason she was visiting Maisie was to go to see a room that was advertised on a card in the newsagent's window. Maisie would be able to check things out and wouldn't let Freda be brow-beaten into paying too much. She'd miss her cosy room in Ruby's house, but she had to stick to the plans that she'd made back in December when she'd moved to Erith.

'Are you warm enough?'

Sarah nodded as she sipped the hot cocoa that Alan handed to her. She didn't like to say that her cheeks were numb with cold and she didn't think she'd ever be able to speak again. So much for the romantic notions she had of holding on to Alan as they drove through the Kent countryside. She felt as though every bone in her body ached from bumping over the stony roads, and her head buzzed from the roar of the bike engine. They'd stopped at a small roadside cafe and Alan had left Sarah sitting beside a rather sad coal fire while he fetched their drinks.

'We're nearly there, but I thought you'd like a bite to eat before we reach our destination.' He looked around the cafe, which was empty apart from a young woman, cigarette hanging from the side of her mouth, frying eggs behind the counter. 'It's nice here, isn't it?'

Sarah didn't know what to say. It certainly wasn't what she'd been expecting when Alan said he was taking her out for the day. She knew he was excited at showing her something of his life, but she still didn't like this cafe. She decided not to answer just in case she said the wrong thing.

'The place is usually buzzing with bike riders and cyclists, but I suppose it's still a bit too cold for many of them to come out. I'm sure you'll meet some of them another time,' he grinned.

Sarah groaned inwardly. There would be another time? 'That will be nice,' she said, just to be polite.

The woman put a plate in front of them and Alan bit into his fried-egg sandwich with relish. 'Tuck in. These are the best around. People ride miles for one of Milly's egg sarnies.'

She nibbled the sandwich, feeling the greasy fried egg moving around her mouth. It was hard to swallow. She held her breath and forced it down. 'I'm not very hungry, Alan. Nan made us a big breakfast this morning.' She slid the plate across the cracked oilcloth table cover. 'Here, you eat it. It's a shame to waste good food.'

Alan took the plate and squirted brown sauce in between the slices of bread. 'We'll just have this and be on our way. We should be there by midday.'

It can't be the coast, then, Sarah thought to herself, although she couldn't face the time it would take to reach the Kent coastline on the bike. 'Where are we going?'

Alan grinned. 'All in good time. The only hints I'll give you is that I've spent many a weekend there, and it was Dad who got me interested.'

Sarah didn't know much about Alan's dad apart from the fact that he had died fifteen years ago, when Alan was only ten years of age, from injuries sustained during the Great War. Ruby had mentioned that Burt Gilbert had never been a well man, but had provided for Maureen and his son by repairing motorbikes and bicycles from a small workshop behind their house in Crayford Road, where Maureen and Alan still lived. The house almost backed onto Ruby's house in Alexandra Road, with just the small railway sidings in between their back gardens that led from Erith docks. When sleep eluded her, Sarah often looked out across the darkened railway line to Alan's house and thought of him sleeping in his room.

'Right, let's get moving or we'll never be there in time.'

'In time for what?' Sarah asked as she pulled on her coat and checked the clips securing her beret were in place.

Alan winked. 'You'll soon see.'

'Are you sure we're allowed to go in here?' Sarah looked at the sign for the Royal Air Force, Gravesend, that stood proudly outside the entrance to the airfield. 'There seems to be a lot of people in uniforms.' She hung on to Alan's arm as he pushed the motorbike towards a barrier across the narrow road, where an officer was checking names on a clipboard. She dared not let go, as not only was she frightened of entering such an official area, but she was also trying hard to keep the one mouthful of egg sandwich in her stomach. The bumpy ride and the greasy food had not made her first motorbike journey an enjoyable one.

'It'll be OK. They know me here,' Alan said confidently as he waved to the airman with the clipboard.

'Hello, Alan. We've not seen you for a while. Go straight through. You'll find Syd out near the airfield.' He nodded to Sarah. 'I'll just make a note of your name, miss. Security has tightened up of late,' he added as Alan looked at him with a frown.

109

'You can park your bike around the back of the hangar.'

'Things have definitely tightened up,' Alan said as he steered the bike towards a large, shed-like building.

Sarah could see a couple of aeroplanes inside, with others on the expanse of grass outside. Under normal circumstances she would have been interested in the scene unfolding in front of her, but the airman's words about security and seeing so many men in RAF uniforms had her worried. 'Why are we here, Alan?'

Alan set the bike up against the metal side of the hangar and beckoned Sarah to follow him. He took her hand and squeezed it. 'My dad was a flyer in the war, and his mate Syd, who you are about to meet, is my godfather. He's worked here on and off for years and is now a flying instructor. He tinkers with the planes as well. Even though the RAF have taken over the airfield, Syd was kept on. I come here when I can and help him. He taught me to fly.'

Sarah gasped. 'You can fly those things?' She pointed to where a plane was making a bumpy landing on the grass. She could imagine the fragile plane breaking easily into small pieces and those aboard perishing. Sarah held her breath as a wave of sickness washed over her. Why ever would Alan wish to risk his life in such a contraption?

'And I can pull one apart and put it back together again,' Alan said proudly, not aware that Sarah was unimpressed. 'In fact, that's why we're here. I wanted to show you more of my world and how it affects my future.' He squeezed her

110

hand. 'I hope it will be our future.'

Sarah's breath was taken away by Alan's words about their future together. She hoped that meant marriage, but at the same time she couldn't help but worry as to how he could fit a good job working at Woolworths alongside flying aeroplanes and also have a family to care for. It didn't make sense. 'It's all such a shock. I had no idea...' was all she could think to say. She was saved from further comment by shouts from inside the hangar.

'Alan, over here, mate.'

Sarah looked around to see where the voice came from. Alan pointed to a small aircraft. 'It's Syd, over by the Tiger Moth. Come on, let's go see him. I really want you to meet him.'

Sarah had no idea what a Tiger Moth was, but followed Alan as he ran over to a small aircraft and shook an elderly man warmly by the hand. She held back as the man clamped Alan in his arms and then held him at arm's length, laughing. 'You're looking more like that father of yours every day. How's your mother doing? I've not seen her for a while.'

'She's fine, Syd, she's fine. Mum sends her best wishes and said you should go over for dinner sometime.' He turned to where Sarah was standing nervously watching the older man beam at Alan as if he hadn't seen him in years. 'Syd, this is Sarah. I want the two of you to meet, as you both mean so much to me.'

Syd wiped his greasy hands down his overalls before grasping Sarah's small hand and pumping it up and down enthusiastically. 'I've heard a lot about you. You're prettier than this lad lets on.'

111

Sarah smiled back at the man. His enthusiasm was contagious. 'I had no idea I was being talked about,' she laughed. 'In fact, I had no idea you or the airfield existed.'

It was Syd's turn to laugh. 'I've seen many a young woman flee from her beau when she realized she had to take second place to one of these beauties.' He slapped his hand on the side of the aircraft.

Sarah frowned. 'Second place? I don't understand.'

'When a lad gets to grips with a Tiger Moth, he'd rather be in the air than have his feet on the ground, even with the most beautiful girl. Alan's one of our best flyers. Comes from hanging around here since he was a child. He grew up around the planes. He's a natural. In fact, Alan, you can take this one up for a test run. She should fly as sweet as a bird.'

Alan laughed. 'Do you want to come up with me, Sarah?'

Sarah felt her head spin at his words. 'Do I what?'

'Fly with me. There are two seats,' he added quickly. 'You won't have to sit on the wing.'

Both men laughed at his joke.

Sarah's head spun again. This time she really did feel sick and dashed from the hangar as her stomach and its contents parted company. She was just wiping her face with her handkerchief when Alan and Syd caught up with her. Alan looked concerned. Syd stood back a little, expecting there to be words between the couple.

'Are you all right, Sarah? You look awfully pale.'

Alan put an arm around her waist to support her.

'Sorry, Alan,' she whispered. 'It was all a bit much, and when you ask me to go up ... up there...' Feelings of dizziness overcame her once more. She was grateful for his arm around her.

'You don't have to, Sarah. I got caught up in the excitement. I forget that some people have no interest in aeroplanes.' He looked crestfallen.

Sarah took a gulp of air. She didn't wish to disappoint Alan. She wanted to be interested in his hobbies. After all, if they married, she would have to put up with him disappearing for the day to visit the airfield. A man needed a hobby. Wasn't that why her mum tried to encourage her dad to take up golf?

'I'll be fine, Alan. I'm feeling better already. Look, why don't you go and fly the aeroplane? I'll wait until you return.' She looked around for somewhere she could sit and wait.

Syd stepped forward. 'I'll take good care of her, Alan. Go find yourself some overalls and get this baby up in the air. Why don't I take you to the mess and find you a cup of tea?' he said, turning to Sarah.

'That would be nice, thank you.'

Alan kissed her cheek. 'Are you sure?'

She pushed him away playfully. 'Go play with your aeroplane. I'll be fine.'

Alan didn't need a second bidding as he ran towards a row of lockers and began to pull out overalls and a flying helmet.

'Come on, love – I think we've lost him for now.' Syd led Sarah towards a single-storey building on the corner of the airfield, where she could hear

113

loud voices behind the steamed-up windows. 'It can be a bit rowdy in here at times, but the lads have good hearts, and you'll get a decent cuppa and perhaps a bite to eat.'

Sarah looked forward to the warm drink but thought it better to avoid food for now.

Freda gazed up at the house in front of her as she stopped at the gate. 'It's certainly different to the last place I rented in this road.'

'It couldn't be much worse, from what Sarah told me,' Maisie said as she peered down to the single cellar window. 'You could eat yer dinner off that doorstep.'

'The windows are sparkling clean, and look at the shiny brass door knocker. Whoever owns this place keeps it spick and span.'

Maisie frowned. 'Mind you, the woman could be a tyrant. Probably makes you take yer shoes off at the front door and say prayers before you can eat yer grub. Do yer want to leg it now?'

Freda liked the outside of the house. It looked clean and respectable. She felt bad at leaving Ruby's home after the Caseltons had taken her in, but she knew they needed the room for when George came to stay. It wasn't fair that George slept on the put-you-up in the front room. 'No, I like this house, and whatever the landlady is like, I'll handle it. After all, I'm at work most of the time or out with you and Sarah, so it's not as if I'm going to be stuck here all day, is it?'

Maisie shrugged and knocked on the door. 'Well, it's your funeral. Me and Sarah can always come and rescue you if she has you knitting doilies or blacking the hearth and such like.'

'Don't be daft,' Freda giggled as they heard footsteps approaching the door.

The door was opened by a rosy-cheeked woman who was drying her hands on a tea towel. She beamed at both of the girls. 'Hello, my loves. What can I do for you? Collecting for the church jumble, are you? I've got a bag of bits put by.'

The woman turned to pick up a string bag stuffed to bursting with clothes as Maisie tried not to laugh out loud.

'No,' Freda blurted out. 'I'm here about the room. That's if it's not already gone? I spotted your advert in the newsagent's window. You are Mrs White, aren't you?'

'Well, bless my soul. Here's me giving you a bundle of old clothes and you wanting a room. Dearie me.' She laughed before wiping her eyes on the tea towel. 'Get yourselves in, ladies, and let's show you the room. I've not long taken a fruit cake out of the oven, so perhaps we can have a slice with a cup of tea while I gets to know you. You looking for a room as well, are you, love?' she asked as she waved Maisie into the front room.

'I think me 'usband and mother-in-law would 'ave something to say if I did, Mrs White,' Maisie laughed. 'Mind you, if yer cakes are any good, I'll give them a week's notice and move in with you. The mother-in-law can only burn things.'

'Bless my soul,' Mrs White exclaimed to Freda. 'Your friend's a right laugh, isn't she? Now, park yourselves down there – move my knitting, that's it – and make yourselves comfy. I'll go put that kettle on.'

Maisie looked around her as she made room for them to sit on the chintz-covered armchairs. The room was very cosy, with a rag rug in front of a glowing fire and a long sideboard covered in china figurines. 'Blimey, you've landed on yer feet here. It's knitting heaven.'

Freda could only nod. Her chums were always joshing her about the amount of knitting she did, but going by the hanks of wool and the piles of patterns on a side table, Mrs White must be running a wool shop from her front room. 'It's wonderful,' Freda sighed, before adding, 'Pinch me – I must be dreaming.'

Over tea and slices of warm fruit cake, Mrs White told them all about her home. Freda was amazed to hear that indeed Mrs White and her daughter had run a wool shop in the town, but had closed the business when the daughter had married and moved to Wales.

'It was time I thought about retiring, but I still do a bit of selling, and I have my weekly knitting-circle ladies to keep me company. Now, let's show you the rooms. You must be dying to see them.'

'Rooms?' Freda looked dismayed: she could only afford a small bedsit. 'The advert said one room. What if I can't afford it and we've spent all the afternoon eating her fruit cake?' Freda whispered to Maisie as they followed Mrs White down the basement steps.

'Now, it's not much to speak of, but it is clean and warm. My husband used the basement as his work room when he was alive. He was a watch-maker,' she added proudly. 'Tell me what you think.'

Freda stepped into a small room with white-washed walls, an armchair and a small table with two chairs set against them. A small coal fire with a bright scatter rug were opposite.

'This room looks out to the main road. There's a bit of a window box, which makes up for the room being at basement level. You do get a fair amount of sun in the afternoon, though. Now, if you step through that door, you can see the bedroom.'

Freda found she couldn't speak. The bedroom was slightly smaller than the living room, but there was space for a single bed, as well as a chest of drawers and hanging space. Again, the walls were whitewashed, and the one window looked out onto a small, low-level yard with steps up to a garden area.

'This room does tend to be a bit gloomy in the wintertime,' Mrs White said, 'but then, it's only meant for sleeping in, so why worry?'

'I think it's lovely, but I'm not sure I can afford the two rooms. I've only got a job at Woolworths, and I'm not on full pay until I'm twenty-one.'

Mrs White named a figure and both the girls gulped with shock. 'Surely that's not right, Mrs White. You must want more money than that for the two rooms?' Freda couldn't believe what she'd heard.

'I'm happy with that, and after all, you'll have to share my bathroom, although I'm more than pleased to cook an evening meal with the price. There's a key to the door, so you can come and go as you please, and if you want to join in with my knitting circle, you're more than welcome. I can see you're a knitter: I've been admiring your cardigan. We'll get on like a house on fire. Now, let's go have another slice of cake, shall we?'

Sarah sighed and looked at the clock in the mess. Alan had been gone over two hours. She wasn't sure how long it took to fly an aeroplane, but surely he'd be back soon.

Syd slid another cup of tea across the table. 'He shouldn't be too long now, love. It must be boring for you having to wait.'

Sarah didn't wish to offend Syd, although she had the desire to yawn and stretch her arms. It had been interesting to hear about Alan's family and how Syd had known them since the war. It seemed that Syd looked upon Alan as the son he'd never had, as he'd lost his own wife in child-birth when Alan was a toddler.

'Does it take long to fly the plane? I mean, where does he fly to, and when does he know to came back?'

Syd laughed, making Sarah feel silly for asking such things. 'Once you get up in the clouds, love, you lose all sense of time. Alan's a natural flyer. Lads like him will be in demand before too long.'

Sarah didn't understand. 'I'm sorry, in demand for what?'

'Fighting the enemy. Once the war starts, and it's only a matter of time, all the lads who are trained to fly will be up in the clouds protecting England against the Huns.'

'But flying's just fun for Alan. He has a job. A good job. Surely he wouldn't give all that up and risk his life?'

It was Syd's turn to look confused. 'I'm sorry,

love. I thought you knew.'

'Knew what?'

Syd looked uncomfortable and started to concentrate on the cup in front of him, turning it round in his hands, trying not to make eye contact with Sarah. 'It's best you talk to Alan, love. I think I've said too much. If I'd realized he'd not told you, I'd have kept my big mouth shut.'

Sarah felt an anger she'd never felt before stir inside her. How dare Alan keep such a secret from her? She thought he loved her, but obviously not if he was making changes to his life that did not include her. It was bad enough waiting these few hours for him to return, let alone a life of not knowing if he would crash and die, and then she'd never see him again. No, she wouldn't put up with it. Alan had to change his plans or she would walk away from him forever. She looked around her at the men in the room. The only women were the ones serving behind the counter. It was a male reserve and she didn't feel part of it. No doubt that was why Alan hadn't told her how he felt or included her in his future plans.

Syd looked sad. It wasn't his fault, she thought. In a way, she should be thankful that he'd let slip that Alan planned to spend his life in the air and not on the ground with her.

'I have a bit of a headache. I think I'll go outside for some fresh air.'

Syd reached for his jacket.

'No, stay in the warm, Syd. I'll be fine.'

'If you're sure, love? I have to be back at work soon. I've got planes to patch up and get in the air.' Syd could see the look of horror on Sarah's face and knew he'd said too much again. He reached out and patted her hand. 'He'll be OK. Alan knows what he's doing.'

Sarah pulled her hand away and just made it outside before tears cascaded down her cheeks. She sobbed until she thought her heart would break. As her tears subsided, she made a decision. It was too soon to speak to Alan. She needed time to think. She could only do that at home and on her own. She ran back to where the airman with the clipboard was still standing by the barrier.

'I'm sorry to bother you, but I need to get home as soon as possible. Where would the nearest railway station be?'

The airman scratched his head. 'That'll be Gravesend, but it's a fair walk. Isn't Alan going back with you?'

'No, no, he's still flying. I need to go now. If you point me in the right direction, I can walk.'

'I can do better than that.' He whistled to where a man was offloading crates of vegetables from a lorry. 'Jack, can you give this young lady a lift to the station?'

Jack nodded.

'He'll look after you OK. He's here most days and lives locally. Are you sure you don't want to wait for Alan? I think that's his plane landing now.'

'No, I'll go with Jack. In fact, can you tell Alan I couldn't wait and I'll see him at work?' Sarah hurried over to the lorry, where Jack was preparing to leave. She wanted to be away from this place and Alan as quickly as possible.

10

Ruby got up from her armchair. Whoever was knocking on her front door this late at night would have the paint off the wood if they didn't stop soon.

It had been a rum day. Young Freda had been a bag of nerves when she arrived home. Even Maisie didn't stop long, refusing a meal and saying she had to get herself off home. Freda played with the sliced meat and boiled potatoes, pushing them around her plate until Ruby had asked what was ailing her. You could have knocked her down with a feather when Freda blurted out that she was moving out. The girl was almost in tears. Ruby gave her a hug and told her she was free to do whatever she wanted. She reassured her that there was always a place for her in the Caselton home, and if she didn't come round for her dinner at least twice each week, Ruby would go find her.

Freda had calmed down after that and told Ruby all about Mrs White and the basement rooms. Ruby remembered the White family and knew that Freda would be in safe hands. She still had a nagging fear that Freda was hiding something, but all the time she was friends with Sarah and Maisie, she knew there were people looking out for the girl.

They were washing up when Sarah came into the kitchen.

'Did you have a lovely day?' Ruby asked. 'Is Alan not with you?' She thought Sarah looked tired, and her eyes were puffy. No doubt that motorbike had something to do with it.

'No. I think I'll have an early night. I've a bit of a headache.'

'Wait for me and I'll come up and tell you about my new digs,' Freda said, completely forgetting that Sarah knew nothing of her looking for a new home.

Sarah blinked. 'You're moving out?'

'Yes, at the weekend, but it's not far away.' Freda was full of excitement and oblivious to the look on her friend's face.

Sarah started to cry and ran from the room. Freda went to follow.

'Leave her, Freda. I don't think it's you she's upset about.'

'Oh no, I hope she hasn't broken up with Alan. They are such a perfect couple. Just like Jeanette MacDonald and Nelson Eddy in *Rose Marie*,' Freda sighed.

'Oh, you and your movie stars,' Ruby laughed.

As Ruby pulled back the bolt on the front door, she thought there was never a dull moment at number thirteen these days. 'Why, Alan, whatever brings you out so late?'

Alan stood on the doorstep looking worried. 'Is Sarah home?'

'Course she is, lad, and safely tucked up in her bed.' Ruby peered at his face. 'Didn't you bring her home?'

Alan looked sheepish. 'No, I couldn't find her

at the airfield after I landed the plane I'd been flying. It was ages before someone told me she'd made her own way home. Then I got a puncture and had to push my bike the last couple of miles. All the while I've been worried about Sarah, so I've come to see if she is OK.'

Ruby wouldn't tell him that Sarah had taken to her bed in floods of tears. Whatever they'd fallen out about would soon be mended, and they didn't want an old woman poking her nose into their business. Sarah would talk to her soon enough if she wanted a shoulder to cry on.

'Can I see Sarah, Mrs Caselton? I really need to speak to her.'

'Lad, it's gone nine o'clock. Leave it until the morning when you see her at work. You look fair done in. Best you both sleep on whatever has happened.'

Alan turned away. 'I suppose you're right. Sorry to be bothering you so late in the evening.'

'It's no bother, lad. No bother at all.'

As Ruby slid the bolt back in place, then turned off the hall light, she hoped that all was well between her granddaughter and Alan. They were well suited, and Ruby thought again that Sarah could do a lot worse than settle down with Alan.

Sarah gazed at Mr Benfield. She was aware that all eyes were on her but had no recollection of what he had said. She'd been miles away, thinking of Alan and what had happened at the airfield two days previously. She could hear some of the Woolies girls tittering at her confusion.

'Stirrup pump, you dozy cow,' Maisie hissed,

causing female staff nearby to giggle again. 'He asked you to pass the bloody stirrup pump to me.'

Sarah pulled herself together and handed the contraption to Maisie, who held it at arm's length as if it was about to bite her. She knew she should stop avoiding Alan and tell him why she'd run away. The shock when she realized that he intended to join the Royal Air Force and fly planes still made her sick every time she thought of it. She didn't want a future in which she feared that every knock on the door would tell her he had crashed. She couldn't think of him so high in the sky when he could be safely on the ground working at Woolworths and by her side. If the threat of war, which seemed to get more real every day if the newspapers were to be believed, became reality, then the thought he could be killed in action was unbearable. No, she would tell him that if he joined the RAF, they were through. If he loved her, he wouldn't do such a thing and then their lives would be back to normal. Pleased that she'd made a decision, Sarah turned her mind to what was happening in front of her.

'Ladies, please, pay attention. We only have half an hour before we have to open our doors to customers. Head office want us to make use of the late opening time to be aware of how to put out a fire, if one should start during working hours.'

'And the only way that's going to 'appen is if someone doesn't put out their dog ends properly in the sand bucket,' Maisie muttered. She was enjoying the break from selling cups and saucers to the customers and unpacking the patterned dinner plates that nestled among straw in the large packing cases. Each had to be polished and displayed on the mahogany counters. Maisie liked to see her counter presented to perfection and would mutter angrily when customers wanted something from the bottom of her carefully arranged crockery.

Mr Benfield clapped his hands. 'Now, ladies ... and gents,' he added as he spotted Alan and a couple of the warehouse men standing at the back of the crowd of shop staff, 'for this exercise, we will not add water to the bucket but will carry out the full procedure with the aid of Mrs Taylor, Miss Smith and Miss Caselton. Ladies, if you will proceed, please, but don't forget the first warning.'

Freda stepped forward swinging a large bell in both hands. 'Fire, fire,' she shouted. 'Fire, fire.' Passing the bell to a colleague nearby, she next pretended to pour water from a row of jugs into the metal fire bucket, all the time fighting hard to keep a straight face. She stepped back and bowed as her colleagues gave her a round of applause.

It was then Maisie's turn. 'Stand back, folks.' She rolled up the sleeves of her overall and placed the stirrup pump into the bucket. 'Ready, Miss Caselton?' she enquired primly.

Sarah lifted the hosepipe attached to the pump and aimed it at a pile of kindling Mr Benfield had placed on the polished wooden floor. It was supposed to denote a roaring fire. 'Ready when you are, Mrs Taylor.'

Maisie, much to the mirth of her colleagues, pumped the contraption up and down as if her life depended on it. She stopped to mop her brow as Freda stepped forward to add more water to the bucket. 'Bleedin' 'ell, this is too much like 'ard work. How long are we supposed to keep this lark up, Mr Benfield?'

Mr Benfield tried not to smile. 'Until the fire is out, Mrs Taylor, or until the fire department arrive. I must say you've done an admirable job. Step down, ladies, and we will move on to the rear of the store. Follow me, staff.' He waved his arm and the Woolies staff obediently followed. Sarah, Maisie and Freda stayed behind to tidy the area.

'Do you think we'll really have to put fires out?' Freda asked.

'Seems a bit far-fetched to me,' Maisie said, rolling down her sleeves and fastening the cuffs. 'Probably just the big shots at head office worrying over all the talk of war and thinking that their precious shops will burn to the ground.'

Sarah was thoughtful. 'I'm not so sure. Everything seems to be heading that way, and I'm beginning to believe it.'

Freda nodded her head. 'That Mr Hitler seems a bad sort. There was something in the paper the other day about him invading some country or other and making nasty speeches.'

'What country? The mother-in-law won't have the wireless on indoors, so I've not heard any news lately. We'll 'ave to rely on you to keep us up to date, Freda!' Maisie said as she checked her face in a mirror on a nearby counter. 'What else did the news report say?'

'I don't know. It was the wrapping on my chips and I didn't have the rest of the page.'

Maisie hooted with laughter. 'You'll just have to eat more chips. Speaking of which, I could go for

126

a bag of chips for me dinner. What do you say, Sarah?'

Sarah shrugged. 'I'm not really that hungry, and I'm sure Nan will've cooked dinner, so I'd best say no. Why not join us, Maisie? Joe too if he's not working.'

'Ta. I'll take you up on the offer. Joe's on a night shift. Gawd knows how I'll ever get pregnant with the both of us working opposite shifts.'

Sarah blushed. As much as she loved her friend, her language could be ripe at times. 'Look out – here comes Mr Benfield. We'd better get to work.'

At that moment the bells rang and Sarah turned to see Alan opening the shop doors to let in the customers who'd been waiting patiently on the doorstep.

'Miss Caselton, you may as well take your tea break. We must be more organized if these fire drills are to be a regular occurrence.' Mr Benfield walked away checking his watch and muttering to himself, not listening as Sarah replied that she could wait until the later tea break. The last thing she wanted to do was bump into Alan right now. Even though she'd made up her mind about their future, if there was to be a future, she wasn't ready to talk about it on her break. She looked around. He seemed to have vanished, so perhaps she could slip upstairs to the staff canteen if she was quick.

Sarah had just reached the top of the stairs and was heading towards the canteen when Alan stepped forward from a side room. 'Alan, you made me jump!'

Alan looked as though he hadn't slept in a

week. His skin was grey, and there were shadows under his eyes. 'Sarah, I need to speak to you.'

Sarah pulled away as he reached out to hold her hand. 'Not now, Alan. Work is not the place to talk about something so serious.'

'Where is the right place, and why have you been avoiding me? It's been two days since you left me at the airfield. I'm at a loss to know what has happened. Even your nan couldn't tell me.'

'Nan? When did you speak to her?' Sarah hadn't told Ruby about what happened on Sunday, although she'd seen Ruby looking at her a few times in a questioning way.

'I went to your house Sunday evening to see if you were home safe and sound.'

Sarah couldn't understand what Alan was telling her 'But the message I left – didn't you get it?'

He shrugged. 'Not straight away. I didn't think to ask if you'd left a message. I looked everywhere for you. Syd said he thought he'd overstepped the mark telling you about my flying plans. He did, but that's beside the point.'

'But why didn't you tell me, Alan? You're a trainee manager with Woolworths. I thought that meant you wanted to stay with the company and one day be a manager with your own store?'

'I do. I am. I mean, well, when the war comes, I can't stay here. I have a duty. I meant to tell you, but you ran away, and then the bike had a puncture. Oh, it's such a mess.' Alan ran his hands through his hair. 'I'm begging you to let me explain. Please, Sarah?'

Sarah pushed Alan away from her as he stepped forward to take her in his arms. A sob escaped her lips as she ran blindly down the passage. She turned a corner and bumped into Miss Billington coming out of her office. 'Oh my. Sarah, whatever is the problem? Come in, child.'

She put her arm around the now sobbing Sarah and led her into the office, making her sit down before patting her shoulder to comfort her. She locked the door and sat watching until Sarah's tears subsided. 'Whatever is the problem, Sarah? Have you been upset by a customer?'

'N-no, it's Alan. He wants to join the RAF and fight if there's a war. I can't let him do that. I just can't.' She dissolved into tears again.

Betty Billington slid her own cup of tea across the desk. 'Sip this. It will make you feel better.'

Sarah fumbled in her overall pocket for a handkerchief.

'Here, have this one.' Betty took a crisp, white lady's handkerchief from her drawer. 'It's clean. I keep a stock of them in case of emergencies.'

Sarah gave a weak smile and wiped her eyes. 'Thank you. I'm sorry to be so much trouble.' She went to get up. 'I'll get back to my counter.'

Betty Billington held up her hand to stop her. 'No, Sarah. Sit down. I want to know why you are so upset. You say it is Alan?'

Sarah nodded. 'Yes, he took me to Gravesend airfield on Sunday and I discovered he intends to join the RAF and ... and I just can't bear the thought of him leaving here and being in danger.' She started to cry again. 'I've decided we should stop seeing each other. I couldn't bear to lose him. I just need to tell him...'

Betty sat thoughtfully watching Sarah as she

129

sniffed into the tear-dampened handkerchief, before reaching for her handbag. She pulled out a small, worn envelope, taking from it a photograph of a young man in uniform, along with a faded yellow letter. She slid them across the desk. 'I've never shown anyone these before.'

Sarah picked up the photograph and saw the pain in Betty's eyes. 'You knew this young man?'

'He was my fiancé. We'd been courting for a year when he went away to war. He wanted us to marry before he left, but I said it was too soon. We should wait. I was only seventeen. I wanted a proper wedding with a lace gown and a bottom drawer. I'd dreamt about it all my life. With friends that I'd seen marry, I wanted the same.'

'You never married?' Sarah asked as she picked up the letter and looked at the few lines of writing.

Betty looked sad. 'As you can see, we almost made it. I missed him so much that I wrote and told him I'd changed my mind and that when he returned home on leave, I'd marry him. But it was too late. They found the letter after he was killed. So many young men died that day at Ypres. A politician is quoted as saying at the start of the war that the lamps went out all over Europe. For me, they were never to be lit again.'

Sarah gasped at the horror of what Miss Billington had told her and reread the few words.

17 August 1917

My dearest Betty,
Your words cheered me no end, my darling. When this bloody battle is over, I'll get leave and we will become man and wife. Buy the ring and I'll place it

130

on your finger the moment I disembark…
Fondly,
Charlie

Sarah could only read those few lines, as the ink had faded, but Charlie's name could still be seen clearly at the bottom of the page. She looked at Betty. 'He never came home?'

Betty took back the photograph and letter, and placed them into the envelope. Holding them close to her heart, she looked Sarah straight in the eyes. 'What I'm trying to advise you is to grab your happiness while you can. No one knows what's round the next corner. You love Alan, so accept him for what he is. Don't question him. Don't try to change him. Just enjoy what time you do have, whether it be a year or fifty years.'

Sarah could see the glint of a tear in Betty's eye.

Betty held up her right hand. 'We never walked up the aisle, but I wear the ring my Charlie would have placed on my finger. I may not carry his name, but in my heart I'm Mrs Charlie Mann. It wouldn't have been right to wear the ring on my left hand, so I keep it safe here until we meet again. I'm as much a widow as the women who were fortunate enough to marry their beaus. I honour Charlie's memory by not taking a husband.'

Sarah knew then that she couldn't let what happened with Betty and her Charlie happen to her and Alan. Whatever the future brought, she'd be with him. 'Thank you for sharing such a private part of your life.'

Betty smiled. 'Most of the staff think I'm a

grumpy old spinster.' She held up her hand as Sarah went to protest. 'No doubt that's how I appear, and it suits me to have people think of me that way. But my life is not that bad. I'm no different to thousands of other women my age. I have my memories.'

For want of something to do, Sarah lifted the cup to her lips. By this time the tea had cooled.

Betty stood, slipping the envelope into her pocket. 'I'll go fetch us both a fresh cup of tea.'

'I really should go back to my counter.'

Betty waved at her to stay where she was. 'Time for that later. Another ten minutes won't hurt. Pull yourself together. You'll be making big changes to your life before too long, so best you start with a cup of tea inside you.'

Sarah smiled. 'You sound like my nan. She always says the same.'

'Then she's a sensible woman,' Betty said as she left the room.

Sarah wiped her eyes. She must stop this crying. What must her boss think of her? She noticed a small mirror on the wall and went to check her face. Her eyes were red from crying, and her nose was beginning to match. If she were Maisie, she'd have a powder compact and lipstick in her pocket to make some repairs. But she wasn't. She'd go to the washroom shortly and splash her face with cold water before heading for the shop floor to join her colleagues – they must all be wondering where she'd got to. Once Miss Billington had brought her the cup of tea, that was. She was a decent sort, and next time Sarah heard one of the girls joking about her boss, she'd make sure to hush them up.

She heard a noise in the hallway. Miss Billington must be trying to open the door. No mean feat with two cups and saucers in her hands. She opened the door, pinning a smile to her face at the same time so that her boss could see that she was getting over her tears. Alan stood there looking anxious.

'Alan?'

'I was worried about you, Sarah. You were so distressed. Miss Billington saw me and said I was to come and speak to you.'

Sarah smiled to herself. Was her boss pushing her and Alan together? 'I was just a little upset, Alan. Miss Billington allowed me to sit in her office for a while. Don't stand there in the passage. Come in.'

Alan looked uncomfortable. Miss Billington's office was not somewhere he frequented often. Staff meetings and requests for days off came to mind. 'Look, Sarah, about Sunday. I'm sorry I didn't get to tell you about the flying and everything. I just didn't think straight.'

Sarah watched Alan. He looked so upset. She felt her love for him surge in her heart. 'I'm sorry too, Alan. I shouldn't have run off like that. You must have been so worried. It's just that it got too much for me.'

Alan took her by the hand. 'Will you ever forgive me?'

'Oh, Alan, I should be the one asking for forgiveness. I'm such an idiot. If you have a dangerous hobby, I shouldn't complain. After all, you did it long before you knew me.'

'Sarah, it's much more than that. I've been trying to tell you that if there's a war, and it's more than likely going to happen, then I will sign up. Can you see that it's something I've got to do?'

'But, Alan, there'll be plenty of people to fly planes and join the RAF. You have a good job here. Why change things?'

Alan led Sarah to a chair and knelt in front of her as she sat down. He took both of her hands in his. 'Do you think I really want to fight the enemy and possibly kill other chaps who are no older than me and also have sweethearts waiting for them at home? I'd rather stay here and see you every day and go to the pictures and have a laugh at work. But would you want your boyfriend to be a coward?'

Sarah snatched her hands away. 'No one could ever call you a coward, Alan. You're a decent person. I wouldn't be seen with a coward.'

Alan sighed. 'That's why I need to sign up. Hopefully these politicians will sort something out and we won't go to war, but if we do, I need to do my bit. Don't think I'm not afraid, Sarah. I'm as worried as you are. I want to live to see my children grow up and to watch my grandchildren ... our grandchildren live in a happy world free of bullies like that Hitler.'

Sarah stroked his cheek tenderly. 'Oh, Alan, I want that as well, but I just can't bear to lose you.'

'Could you bear it if I was branded a coward? Because that's what will happen if I don't play my part. Years ago the families of cowards were given white feathers. Do you want that to happen to our families?'

'No, of course I don't,' Sarah sighed. She knew then she had to give in. This was one battle she wouldn't win. She loved Alan for his principles and determination, even if it did mean she may lose him. She held back that fear. Perhaps it would never happen. 'Alan, go with my blessing, but promise me you'll never do anything to endanger your life, and as soon as you can, you must come back to me.'

'I'll do my best, my love. The RAF may not even want me. I've only just completed the application form. The chaps at Gravesend will put a good word in for me, but chances are they won't want a shop boy from Erith flying their planes. They usually have a load of toffs do those jobs. I may not be good enough.'

Sarah was indignant. 'Now, none of that talk, Alan Gilbert. I'm sure you are the best at flying planes that there is. They'd be lucky to have you. You go tell them I said so.' She then went quiet for a moment, before adding, 'But like I said, you stay safe and come home to me as soon as you can.'

Alan pulled Sarah into his arms. 'I promise you I will, my love. Nothing will keep us apart for a moment longer than necessary.' Alan silenced Sarah's next words as his lips claimed hers.

The door opened quietly and Betty Billington entered the room with a tray holding two cups of tea and a plate of biscuits. She smiled. It was good to see that Sarah had made things up with Alan. There were bound to be dangerous times ahead. With all her heart she hoped this couple would make it through and she'd be there to see them celebrate a happy future together.

She cleared her throat. 'Drink this up, the pair of you, and then get back on the shop floor. Mr Benfield will be wondering where all his staff have disappeared to. I'll take my tea in the staff-room. There may at least be a chance I get to drink it.'

'Where the 'eck have you been?' Maisie peered at Sarah. 'You may be smiling, but yer eyes are puffy. Something's happened. You've been really strange the last couple of days. What's up?'

'Sshh! I'm sure Sarah will tell us when we have a break,' Freda said as she pushed Maisie back behind her counter. 'We'll be for it if we're caught off duty.' She could tell from Sarah's happy face that whatever had been troubling her friend had been resolved. She'd abided by Ruby's request not to speak to Sarah when she'd come home in tears at the weekend, and now she too wanted to know. However, the shop floor of Woolworths was not the right place. Not when there were so many customers about and they were already behind with their duties due to the regular Tuesday morning fire practice.

'Well, roll on dinner time, 'cos me tummy's rumbling and I won't do an ounce of work until I know what's going on,' Maisie muttered as she picked up a feather duster and half-heartedly flicked it across a row of brown earthenware teapots.

Sarah returned to her counter and turned her attention to the customers who were waiting patiently to be served. She'd not long been working on the stationery counter and was enjoying being in charge of keeping the stock tidy and

136

helping customers with their numerous enquiries. She could see Maisie across the aisle making pretty displays with cups and saucers, and knew that Freda was only yards away working hard on her counter.

'What the 'eck is that?' Maisie asked, rubbing her head as a bell started to ring long and loud from the other end of the store. 'I was under the counter fetching some bags and banged me blooming 'ead with fright.'

'It's the fire bell,' Sarah said as she counted change into a customer's hand and thanked her.

'I can't smell smoke. Why would anyone be ringing it now?'

Freda dashed up and took Sarah by the hand. 'You've got to come now. It's Alan.'

Both the girls followed Freda to the centre of the store, where Alan was standing on a chair, ringing the fire bell as if his life depended on it.

'Gawd, whatever is he up to?' Maisie puffed as she pushed Sarah past customers who had stopped to stare. A few ladies had rushed to the front doors alarmed at the prospect of a fire. Mr Benfield was holding the door open and trying to explain that to his knowledge there was nothing untoward happening in his store. He was not having much luck.

Sarah wriggled past the last of the shoppers and headed to where Alan had stepped from the chair onto a counter piled high with saucepans. 'Alan,' she hissed as she tugged at the hem of his brown warehouse coat. There was no point in shouting, as he wouldn't have heard her above the din of the bell. 'Alan, whatever are you doing?'

Alan stopped swinging the bell as he saw Sarah. He jumped to the floor, leaving the handbell behind. Sarah's ears were still ringing. 'Sarah, my love, sit down.' He pushed her towards the chair he'd used to climb onto the counter, first wiping the seat clean with his sleeve.

'For heaven's sake, Alan, what are you doing?' Sarah felt her cheeks burning as dozens of customers stood in a semicircle watching with puzzled looks on their faces. Colleagues had left their counters to see what the fuss was about. Sarah could just see Alan's mother, Maureen, on the edge of the crowd. She must have come down from the staff canteen to see what was causing the noise. Sarah couldn't understand why she had a smile on her face. Surely Mr Benfield would sack Alan for causing such a disturbance?

'Look, Alan, I think we ought to get back to work, don't you?'

'Stay right there, Sarah.'

To Sarah's utmost embarrassment, Alan went down on one knee in front of her. All around her she could hear people sighing. Sarah just wanted to dig a big hole and hide in it. Whatever would Mr Benfield say about this?

Reaching into his pocket, he pulled out a small, square box. Taking a ring from the box, he held it out to her. 'Miss Sarah Caselton, will you do me the honour of taking my hand in marriage? I may not have much to offer you, but I swear to love you my whole life through and never give you cause to question me.'

'I'd be worried already if a man surprised me in Woolies like that,' someone shouted from the back of the crowd.

'Ignore them – say yes,' Maisie urged from nearby.

'Yes, yes, yes!' Freda exclaimed.

Sarah closed her eyes. Was this really happening? It had been a strange day and she hadn't slept properly since the weekend. Perhaps it was a dream? She opened her eyes. Alan was still there, waiting for an answer. It wasn't a dream after all.

'Oh, Alan, of course I'll marry you.'

As the crowd cheered, Alan took Sarah in his arms and swung her round before kissing her tenderly. A cough from Mr Benfield made the happy couple step apart.

'Sorry, Mr Benfield. I don't know what came over me. I knew that if I didn't propose to Sarah there and then, I'd lose the confidence to ask her.'

'Don't you be so sure, Alan. Her friends would have encouraged you,' Maisie called out to much laughter from the customers.

Mr Benfield stepped to the front of the cheering crowd. 'Well, well. I'm not sure quite what the protocol is when a man proposes to his young lady in an F. W. Woolworth store. However, being a forward-thinking company, I'm sure I can speak for the owners when I wish our employees the very best for the future. Also, as our saucepan counter played such a big part in this auspicious occasion, I shall make sure that the happy couple are presented with a full set with the compliments of their employers.'

'Blimey,' Maisie called out. 'It's a shame Woolies doesn't have a diamond counter!'

11

'Happy, darling?'

Sarah snuggled up to Alan as he put his arm around her. Even though it was only mid-afternoon, the sun was hiding behind a few grey clouds and there was a chill in the air as they left Woolworths and headed towards Alexandra Road. 'I couldn't be happier if I tried. I want to pinch myself to check I'm not dreaming.'

'If you're dreaming, then so am I. I must say it was pretty good of old Benfield to let us off work this afternoon, don't you think?'

'He's a sweetheart. How many other bosses would put up with what happened in the store today, then give us both the rest of the afternoon off?'

'Don't forget the set of saucepans.'

Sarah giggled. 'I'll never forget the saucepans. It's been an unusual day.'

'I should hope so. How often does a man propose to his girl?'

'I didn't mean that, silly. I was thinking about Miss Billington. It's her we have to thank for bringing us together. Did you know that she was almost married but her intended was killed in the war? She told me that she would never marry another man and would always respect his memory. That is true love... Would you?'

'Would I what? Marry Bossy Billington?'

'No, marry someone else if anything happened to me.'

'But we're not married yet, you silly thing. Speaking of which, when do you want to get married?'

Sarah stopped and turned to Alan. 'Do you know what I'd really like?'

'Another kiss?' Alan said, pulling her into his arms.

Sarah pushed him away but held on to his hand. 'Not here in the street. People will talk. I meant when I'd like to get married.'

'Tomorrow wouldn't be soon enough for me,' Alan said as he steered her across the busy road towards number thirteen.

'Me neither,' Sarah sighed as they reached the gate, 'but we have to be practical. Weddings need to be planned. What I'd really love is to be married on my twenty-first birthday.'

Alan frowned. 'I don't believe I've ever asked you when your birthday is. I hope it's soon.'

'It's 3 September and she will be twenty-one, so until then you'd best not make any plans until you've spoken to her father, young man.'

Sarah was startled and turned to see Ruby on her knees scrubbing the doorstep. 'I didn't see you down there, Nan. Do you want a hand?'

Ruby rose to her feet, holding on to the wide concrete ledge of the bay window for support. 'I'm all done. I think the pair of you have someone else you should be speaking to. Don't you?'

'Nan?'

'Your dad's indoors. Don't forget there are ways of doing things, Alan. I gather from what I overheard that the two of you are making plans. I'm pleased for you both, but you should have spoken to Sarah's dad first. You'd best do it now before he hears it from someone else in the street. They've only got to look at the pair of you to guess what's happening. Now, you get yourself in there and ask for Sarah's hand, and when I've shaken this doormat out, I'll go fetch the sherry.'

Alan turned pale but headed for the front door. Sarah went to follow.

'You stay here, my girl. That talk is for men only. You can help me wipe down the window ledge. I curse those pigeons. Why men want to keep them in the backyard I'll never know. It just makes more work for us women.'

George puffed on his pipe thoughtfully. 'You've placed me in a bit of a quandary, Alan.'

Alan ran his finger round his collar. He felt as though he was being choked, and the room felt extremely warm for March. 'I'm sorry, sir. I love Sarah and I wouldn't do a thing to harm her.'

'I'm sure you wouldn't, son, but we have another problem.'

'Sir?'

George tapped his pipe into the ashtray on the arm of his chair. 'Sarah's mother is the problem.'

Alan frowned. 'I don't understand.'

'It may be customary for the man to ask his girlfriend's father for her hand in marriage, but in reality it is the mother who has the final say. Mrs Caselton, as you know, is in Devon. She would be most hurt to know that such an important decision in her only child's life was being discussed

without her.' George knew his life would be unbearable if Irene was not in control of the situation.

Alan breathed a sigh of relief. At least George
had not sent him packing with a flea in his ear.
He'd heard talk of Sarah's mother always wanting
the best for her family. Would she want him, a
shop boy from Erith, as a son-in-law?

George cleared his throat. 'I think it's time to
call Sarah and her nan in. They've been polishing
that window for the past ten minutes. If it's not
clean by now, it'll never be,' he smiled as he
beckoned to Ruby through the heavy net curtain.

Ruby stuck her head round the front parlour
door. 'Do I fetch the sherry?'

'In a minute, Mum. Come in and sit yourself
down. You too, Sarah.'

Sarah walked in behind Ruby. She glanced from
Alan to her dad, but wasn't sure whether to laugh
or cry. What had been said to make Dad look so
serious? She sat on the edge of the sofa next to
Alan. He took her hand and gave it a squeeze.
Ruby took one of the hard upright chairs and
fiddled with the polishing cloth she still held in
her hand. She had a feeling she knew what
George was about to say.

George looked at Alan and how tenderly he
held Sarah's hand. He knew that this man would
care for his daughter long after he and his wife
weren't around.

Ruby nodded, encouraging George to speak.
'Come on, son, spit it out.'

'I'm pleased, very pleased that Alan feels he
wants to marry our Sarah.'

'Oh, Dad, don't make it sound like you never thought I'd have a husband,' Sarah exclaimed.

Alan shushed Sarah. 'Let your dad speak, love.'

'As I was saying, I'm pleased that Alan wants to marry Sarah. I'm grateful that he came to ask for her hand in marriage. There's nothing wrong in doing things the right way. However, we have to consider your mother, Sarah.' He held up his hand for silence as Sarah tried to interrupt him. 'Sarah, one day you will be a mother. How would you feel if your own daughter became engaged to be married and you were hundreds of miles away and couldn't contribute to the discussion? So, I've made a decision.'

Sarah chewed her lip and waited for George to have his say. Please don't let him say no.

'I've decided that we should keep your engagement a secret until you have visited your mother and made your request to us both. Do you think you can manage that? I'd hate your mother to feel left out.'

'That seems fair to me,' Ruby nodded. 'You don't want to leave your mum out of things, do you? Why not go down on Sunday, see your mum for a few hours and get back here in the evening? We can have a little party here next week and tell your friends at the same time.'

Sarah and Alan looked at each other. 'That does sound like a good idea, Mrs Caselton, but there's one problem,' Alan said.

Sarah continued. 'It's just that when Alan proposed to me, a few people overheard. So it's not quite our little secret.'

'I'm sure a few people won't make any difference to your mum knowing. After all, you do have friends in Erith,' George said.

Ruby frowned as she looked at Alan and Sarah's serious faces. 'How many people, exactly?'

Sarah looked down in embarrassment. 'All the staff in Woolies and the customers. Alan stood on the saucepan counter and did it.'

George and Ruby burst out laughing.

'Oh my, I've never heard anything like it,' Ruby gasped as she wiped her eyes on the cloth she'd been using to clean the window ledge, leaving a large black smudge on her cheek.

'Oh, Nan, you look as though someone's given you a right old shiner.'

Ruby stood to look at her face in the large mirror placed over the fireplace. The more she rubbed her eye, the blacker it became. 'I'll go wash my face and get the sherry. I'm sure everything'll come out in the wash. You two aren't to worry. We'll sort it out.'

'Irene, Irene, where are you? Come and see who I've brought home with me.' George hung his coat on the carved wooden coat stand, placing his suitcase neatly against the wall. He ushered a nervous Sarah and Alan through to the lounge.

Sarah felt as though she was visiting a stranger's house. It didn't feel like the home she had left only months ago. 'Give me your coat, Alan. You'll not feel the benefit when you go out otherwise.' She clapped her hand to her mouth. 'Goodness, I'm turning into my nan. I've never said anything like that before. It just shows how nervous I am.'

Alan brushed her cheek with his finger. 'You're

probably tired as well. Leaving home when it was still dark has made it a long day.'

'It's only just midday and I'm ready for my bed. I don't know how you can make this journey every other week, Dad.'

George had already made himself comfortable in his armchair and was pulling out his pipe. 'The difference is, love, that I've never arrived and departed on the same day. It's such a shame you couldn't get time off to stay for a few days. It's a fair train journey down to Devon from home.'

It's not just me who thinks of Erith as home, then, and Dad's been living here since I was a kid, Sarah thought.

'Hello, darling. What a lovely surprise.' Irene Caselton kissed Sarah lightly on the cheek, taking care not to smudge her perfectly made-up face. Sarah hugged her mum back, although Irene stood still, not returning the embrace. She spotted Alan and frowned slightly. 'Who do we have here?'

Alan stood up and shook hands with his future mother-in-law. 'Good afternoon, Mrs Caselton.'

Before he could speak further, George took control of the conversation. 'Sit yourself down for a few minutes, Rene. We have some news for you.'

Irene almost flinched as George used the shortened version of her name, but did as she was told, a questioning look on her face. 'I wish I'd known you were visiting, as I have an afternoon committee meeting I just can't miss. Can this keep until later?'

'No, dear, it can't. Sarah has to get back to Erith, as does Alan.'

'Why the rushed visit? It's the first I've seen of you since you left to live with your grandmother.' She suddenly put a hand to her mouth in shock. 'My goodness, you're not...?'

Sarah opened her mouth to reply. How dare she think she was expecting a child? Did her mum not even trust her own daughter?

Again, George took control. 'Don't jump to conclusions, Rene. Young Alan here has been courting our Sarah for a while now. With the future so uncertain, they are determined to marry, but they want to do it properly. They've come to ask us both to give them our blessing. It made sense, what with their work commitments, to travel down with me. They intend to catch the five-o'clock train back.'

The frown on Irene's brow deepened. 'Sarah's far too young.' She waved her hand in Alan's direction. 'We know nothing about this young man.'

Sarah wanted to speak out and protect the man she loved. Her mum was reacting just as she had feared.

George tapped his pipe carefully into the ashtray. 'Now, now, Rene. Let's keep calm, shall we? Sarah will be celebrating her twenty-first birthday in September; she'll be able to make up her own mind about her life. Aren't you pleased that both she and Alan want our approval?'

Irene looked between the young couple and her husband. 'This is just too much to take in.' She checked the dainty watch on her wrist and sighed. 'I suppose I have an hour before I rush off. So, Alan, how did you meet my daughter?'

147

Alan visibly relaxed. 'We work together at Woolworths.'

'You know Alan's family, Mum. You used to work with his mother, Maureen. Dad went to school with her, so he isn't exactly a stranger, is he?'

Irene's face dropped. 'You work at Woolworths?'

'I'm a trainee manager, Mrs Caselton. My mother works in the staff canteen. She sends her best wishes and hopes to catch up with you at the wedding.'

Irene rose to her feet. 'I'll put the kettle on.'

As Irene headed to the kitchen, Sarah gave a small smile. 'Not as painful as we thought, Dad?' she whispered.

George winked at his daughter. 'Don't you be so sure, young lady. Now, go help your mum with the tea while I ask Alan about his prospects. I believe that's what happens next?'

Sarah giggled. Perhaps things would go smoothly with Mum.

In the kitchen, Irene placed biscuits onto a plate and fetched napkins from a cupboard. 'Really, Sarah. I think you could have been a little more considerate. I don't understand the rush. What will your future be like married to a shop worker? How can he provide you with a proper home? You can't live with Ruby forever or, God forbid, his mother.'

'Mum, Alan is well thought of at Woolworths. One day he will have his own store to run.' She thought it best not to mention Miss Billington's suggestion that one day Sarah could be a supervisor. After all, once she was married and child-

148

ren came along, she wouldn't be working. She would be a wife and mother.

'You're throwing your life away, Sarah. Goodness knows why you won't come home and settle down into life here. With my contacts, you could meet the right people and make a good marriage.'

'Mum, please.' Sarah took Irene's hand so that she could look her in the eye. 'I love Alan. For me, it is the perfect match. I'm a lucky girl to have found someone who will care for me, just like you are lucky to have Dad. Whatever happens in the future, I'll know that I married the right man.'

Irene pulled her hand away and picked up the tea tray. 'I don't know what you mean about the future, I'm sure.'

'Mum, there will be a war. I want to marry Alan before he goes away to fight for our country. God knows I don't want him to go, and I know he'd rather be here with me, but we'll have no choice in the matter.'

'So you'll just be another soldier's wife. You could wait.'

'You're wrong, Mum. I'll be a pilot's wife and proud of my husband.'

Irene put the tea tray down on the table so quickly that the teaspoons rattled on their saucers and tea slopped through the spout of the teapot. 'A pilot's wife? How?'

Sarah smiled. She knew that her mum would be much more interested once she knew Alan would have a responsible role to play if there was a war. She didn't give a hoot what Alan did, but if it helped with her mum's approval of the marriage, she would say he was to be prime minister.

Irene hugged her daughter. 'I'll cancel my meeting. The ladies will understand once they know that my daughter is to marry an officer in the RAF. We need to make plans. Book the golf club, agree on the wedding breakfast and make a trip to London to pick a wedding gown.'

12

'Happy, darling?' Alan said, echoing their earlier conversation.

Sarah snuggled closer to Alan as the train sped towards London. It would be the early hours of the next morning before they reached Erith, but the trip had been worth it. 'Yes, I'm happier than I've ever been. Once we'd convinced Mum that the wedding would be in Erith and Maisie was to make my dress, I was able to breathe a sigh of relief.'

'It was harder convincing her that I wasn't an officer. I thought she was going to salute me at one point. I may not even make the final cut with my application to be a pilot. I'd love to fly Spitfires, but even a job with the ground crew means I'll be doing my bit. If there is a war,' he added quickly as he saw a look of concern spread across her face.

'Let's hope there isn't and we can live our life in Erith with no worries. Now, I'm going to try and sleep for a while and dream of orange blossom and wedding cake.'

Alan lit a cigarette and stared out into the darkening sky, one arm around the woman he loved, as she slept nestled close to his shoulder. He wished he could have the same positive dreams as Sarah; however, he knew that war was inevitable. Come what may, he would play his part to defend his country and protect his loved ones.

'For heaven's sake, stop yer wriggling. I've never seen anyone not be able to stand on two feet before. You got ants in yer pants or something? Whatever's wrong with you?' Maisie muttered as she held a dressmaking pin between her teeth.

'I can't help it. I need to go to the lavvie. I've been standing on this chair for an hour now. Haven't you finished the hem yet?' Freda replied as she wriggled from foot to foot.

Maisie sighed and stood up. 'Time for a rest. My knees have gone to sleep. Your bridesmaid frock has been more trouble than Sarah's wedding dress and all the dresses put together. I've had to let it out once, and if you aren't careful, it's likely to split a seam on the day. Now, let's get you out of this so you can go sort yerself out. I think I'm done for now.'

Freda allowed Maisie to undo the hooks at the back of the dress and hang it on the front-room door. 'It's lovely. Sarah's wedding is going to be so posh.'

Maisie beamed; she wasn't one to blow her own trumpet, but she was proud of the work she had done on the bridal-party outfits. She particularly liked Ruby's two-piece suit. It fitted to perfection, and the deep burgundy colour suited the older woman to a T. She hadn't minded in the least having to let out Freda's gown. The girl had blossomed with the help of all the good food since living at her new lodgings and also having Ruby look out for her too. She was nothing like the frightened kid Maisie had met that first day at Woolies. Now she was a young woman with rosy cheeks and a confidence that had not been there eight months ago. Occasionally Maisie would see a shadow pass over Freda's face and the younger woman would go quiet for a short while. Then it passed and she was as bubbly as before, the moment forgotten. Maisie would get to the bottom of what was troubling Freda if it was the last thing she did. That kid was like a sister to her, and a young sister was what Maisie missed most.

She shook herself and stabbed a few stray pins into her pincushion. 'Stick the kettle on, Freda,' she called out as she heard her come through the back door. 'I could do with a cup of Rosie. Ruby and Sarah will be home soon. I bet they'll be parched. Sarah was hell bent on buying Ruby a new hat. I just hope they found one that Ruby likes.'

Freda returned to the room and helped Maisie cover the dress with an old sheet. 'I love the colour. I'm so pleased Sarah asked us both to be her bridesmaids. I've never been one before.'

'Oh, you get used to it after a few times,' Maisie said loftily.

'What? How many times? I bet you looked lovely in all them dresses.'

Maisie punched Freda's arm playfully. 'I'm kidding you. I've done it three times, but this'll

152

be the first time I've worn a long frock and walked up the aisle in a church. The other times 'ave been a bit of a quick dash to the registry office and a pint down the pub.'

Freda's face dropped. 'Oh, I know what you mean. I've been to a wedding like that as well.' Then she grinned. 'This wedding will be the best there's ever been. Sarah will float down the aisle and we'll be right behind her.' Freda sighed. 'It's going to be a lovely wedding, as well as being Sarah's twenty-first birthday.' She ran her fingers over the bridesmaid dress, which was now hanging on the door leading to Ruby's kitchen. 'What's the fabric named again?'

'Taffeta, and the bodice and underskirt are silk. I was lucky to get the colours to match. I thought for a while we'd 'ave to go with the pale blue, and it wasn't 'alf as nice as this.'

'It's such a lovely colour. The pale green suits all of us, and the little headdresses are just beautiful. I could wear mine all the time.' Freda couldn't contain her excitement.

'You'd look right silly with that on yer 'ead at work, you daft brush!'

Freda giggled. 'I suppose I would. It is lovely, though. I could dream about weddings all day long.'

'Well, you'd best buck up your ideas and get that tea brewed. When Ruby and Sarah get back, we've got another important job to get on with, and get that dress upstairs to Sarah's room before Alan sees it. I know it's unlucky to see the wedding dress, but I'm not letting him see ours either until the big day.'

'I'll do it right now. I'm ready for this afternoon. I've borrowed a pair of wellington boots from Alan's mum, Maureen, so I don't spoil my shoes. I'm looking forward to digging the hole and planting Ruby's Anderson shelter, aren't you?'

'It's not a blooming rose bush. Besides, I can think of better ways to spend my afternoon,' Maisie sniffed as she checked the polish on her fingernails.

'Isn't your Joe at home?'

'Yes, but he's distempering the outhouse for the mother-in-law and I don't want to get roped into 'elping him. She'll give me no peace, telling me where I've missed a bit and how to do it better. I'd end up shoving her 'ead down the khazi.'

'Looks to me like digging a hole for Ruby is the best option, then. Do you fancy a bite to eat? Ruby said there was some corned beef on a plate in the pantry if we wanted it.' She looked at the clock standing on the dresser. 'In fact, I'll make some sandwiches for everyone so we can get stuck straight in with the shelter.'

Maisie reached for her cigarettes. 'Don't get so blooming excited. It's not gonna be a barrel of laughs if this war does start, and you won't catch me 'iding down some hole in the ground.'

Freda looked at Maisie with a puzzled expression. She could see her friend's hands shake as she lit her cigarette. Perhaps it was all bravado and Maisie was truly frightened about what lay ahead. 'I tell you what. I'll make us some bubble and squeak to go with that corned beef. It'll put hairs on our chest for when we start digging that hole.'

'Now you're talking. I'll give you an 'and.'

The cabbage and potato were sizzling nicely in Ruby's large frying pan as the girls heard the front door open.

'Do you want tea? I bet you're dying for a cuppa after all that shopping.'

'You can say that again,' Ruby said as she poked her head round the scullery door. 'Something smells good.'

'We thought you'd like something filling in your stomach before we got stuck into all that 'ard work this afternoon,' Maisie explained as she added another dollop of dripping to the frying pan. 'Do you think there's enough to go round if we have this with the corned beef?'

Ruby peered into the pan. 'Best fry a few eggs as well. Alan'll be here in a few minutes. He's just dropped his mum home, and then he's parking Mr Benfield's car back at Woolies.'

'I must say it was good of Mr B. to loan the car. He's been a darling over all this wedding,' Maisie said as she took a bowl of eggs from the pantry. 'Is it right that him and Mrs B. don't have any children?'

Ruby pulled off her scarf and started to wash her hands at the stone sink. 'From what Maureen told us, they've never been blessed and that's why he takes such an interest in his young staff. He's a good sort. In fact, you girls have got some nice bosses at Woolworths. I do like that Miss Billington too.'

'I'll say,' added Sarah, taking the bar of carbolic from her nan to wash her own hands. 'We'd have never got up to Petticoat Lane and back so quickly without the loan of Mr Benfield's car. It's a shame Maureen's got a headache. She's not so good travelling in a car. She's gone to lie down for a while and might join us later for tea.'

'Have you invited Miss Billington to the wedding, Sarah?' Freda asked as she cracked eggs into a pan, watching them sizzle in the hot dripping.

Sarah nodded. 'Yes, she's been a good sport all round. Did you know that she managed to find us all matching gloves for the wedding? Actually, I wanted to ask you something.' She looked worried as she faced Maisie by the cooker. 'It seems such a cheek when you've gone to all the trouble of making so many dresses for the wedding, but do you think you could make another bridesmaid dress?'

'I think we've got enough fabric. If not, I'm sure we can pick up a bit more. Why? Who were you thinking of asking? Not that it's my business,' Maisie said as she shook the pan to stop the bubble and squeak from sticking.

'Well, I think it is your business. You've both been so good helping me and Alan with everything. It's just that Betty was such a dear when she found me in tears over Alan. She made me realize I should grab my chance for happiness while I could. So you see, I'd like to ask her to be one of my attendants but wanted to ask you both, as she is our boss and you might not think it's the right thing to do.' She looked from Freda to Maisie. 'Well?'

Freda grinned. 'I think it's a lovely idea. What about you, Maisie?'

Maisie nodded. 'I don't see a problem. We've got two months to go, so I've plenty of time to make her dress. That's if I've not got to keep taking out your dress, young madam,' she said, and flicked Freda with the tea towel as she caught her pinching a piece of fried potato from the pan. 'Let's get this lot on the table, shall we? Alan should be here anytime and we don't want him 'earing about frocks and things, as it'll spoil the surprise. Mind you, it'll feel a bit strange measuring up me own boss for a dress,' she laughed. 'You can help me with that, Sarah.'

Sarah hugged Maisie. 'What would I do without you? Both of you. You're the best friends a girl could have. I'll ask Betty tomorrow; then we can get cracking. She said she wants to see me in the office about something, so I can kill two birds with one stone.'

'I'm fair whacked,' Ruby said, flopping down into the armchair. 'Who'd have thought we'd have to dig such a lot of earth just for that shelter? I wondered where we were going to put it all. It's a good job Alan knew what he was doing.'

'He's helped a couple of Maureen's neighbours, so he's got the hang of it now. He said that next weekend he'd build a wall in front of the door to stop draughts, and knock up a seat and that for inside,' Sarah said, handing her nan a glass of water.

'He's a good lad. I hope he's had time to build Maureen's shelter?'

'She's not having one. They've got a bit of a cellar under the house, so Alan's cleared it out. It looks quite cosy.'

'Has he heard anything about the RAF yet?'

'No. It can't be much longer. I just hope we don't have to change the wedding date if he's called up. It would be such a shame.'

Ruby patted her hand. 'Don't you go worrying yourself. We'll face things as they happen, and your wedding day will be a day to remember. I promise you. Now, what shall we plant in all that earth Alan packed on top of the shelter? I don't think flowers would be fitting somehow.'

'How about some potatoes and cabbages?' Maisie asked as she joined them. 'Though we'd need to grow a lot going by the amount of bubble and squeak we put away earlier.'

'I'll have to put me thinking cap on. The old man was the one for the garden and I never took much notice of how he grew things. My goodness, he'd be upset to see what we planted today and there's no mistake.'

Sarah put her arm around her nan. 'He'd understand, Nan. In fact, he'd already have put his name down for this fire-watch training and all. I think perhaps we should start digging over the rest of the garden and see what else we can grow, don't you? We can have a look at what Gramps had in the shed, and what we don't know about we can ask. After all, we sell seeds and such like in Woolies, so we might as well make the most of what we have at our fingertips. It'll be fun.'

'That's a good idea, Sarah, and you're right, love. He'd have been organizing everyone. He'd be right upset to see the state of his garden at the moment. I'll make it my job to put it all straight. Besides, if we have a nice summer, it'll be good to be outside and doing something to keep our minds off things that might not 'appen.'

'It's gonna 'appen, Mrs C., so you might as well plan ahead to be on the safe side. Me mother-in-law has already started stockpiling tins of food.'

'Well, that's enough of this miserable talk. Here comes Alan and we haven't even thought about some grub to feed everyone.'

'Don't you worry none about me, Mrs Caselton. I'll pop round the corner and help my mum. She said she'd make some sandwiches and such and bring it round for five. She knew we'd all be too busy to think of Sunday tea,' said Alan, wiping perspiration from his face with the back of his hand. He'd left his muddy wellingtons at the rear door and was wearing the overalls he usually wore when working at the airfield.

'That's really good of her. I've got a sponge cake in a tin in the pantry. We can have that as well.'

Alan went into the scullery to wash the mud from his arms. They could hear him whistling from where they sat.

'You've got a good one there, Sarah, and no mistake. His mum's all right as well, but then, they are a local family. No airs and graces there.' She looked pointedly at Sarah, who knew that Nan was thinking of Irene.

Alan returned, rolling down his sleeves. 'I'll shoot round to Mum's just in case she's set off on her own and is struggling.'

Sarah leapt to her feet. 'I'll come with you.' She thought it better to escape before her nan got into full flow about her high-and-mighty daughter-in-law. Apart from one trip over to Erith, Irene hadn't taken much notice of the wedding. She had tried

159

to convince Sarah that a wedding gown from a store in London would be more fitting than a home-made dress, but had had to agree that Maisie was indeed a skilled dressmaker and was doing a good job. She left an envelope for Sarah that generously covered the cost of all the wedding outfits, although she'd declined Maisie's offer to make an ensemble for the mother of the bride.

13

'Sit down, Sarah. I'll be with you in a minute.' Sarah took a seat opposite Miss Billington and waited as she finished adding a row of figures, then shut the leather-bound ledger. 'No need to look so glum. I have good news. F. W. Woolworth usually supports the local cottage hospital at their summer fete. This year they've decided to have a carnival queen, and we've been requested to nominate one of our assistants to take on the role along with an entourage. Mr Benfield and I have had a discussion and we can't think of anyone more fitting than you, Sarah. Would you like to be the Erith Carnival Queen of 1939?'

Sarah didn't know what to say. She'd expected to discuss work and had been wondering how to invite Betty to be her bridesmaid; then she had this thrown at her. 'I really don't know what to say. What would I have to do? What would I wear? When is it to be held?'

Betty laughed. 'I think you have a lot to say,

160

don't you? It's next month, in August, and will be held in the grounds of the cottage hospital. There will be a parade through the town. I'm told that there will be a band, and a lorry will be decorated so that you and your maids of honour can travel in style. I've already spoken to head office and they are going to supply velvet capes and a crown for the carnival queen to wear. It's hoped that the hospital will keep the regalia to use in years to come. They may even ask you to present the crown to next year's queen. I think it will be splendid. The fete at the hospital is bound to attract a big crowd and take our minds off what may be ahead in the months to come. Would you like to represent us, Sarah? I know it's rather short notice, but it will be such a happy occasion.'

Sarah took a deep breath. If she didn't ask Betty now, the moment would be missed. 'I'll do it on one condition.'

Betty's eyes grew large as she peered at Sarah. 'Condition? I don't understand. Whatever do you mean, Sarah?'

Sarah gulped. Perhaps she had made a mistake wanting her boss to take part in her wedding, but it was too late to back down now. 'I'd really like you to be one of my bridesmaids. If it wasn't for you, I'd never be marrying Alan. You made me see sense, and you also put up with me crying all over the place. Most bosses would have given me my marching orders, but you understood. It would mean a lot to me if you were there on my wedding day. Please say yes.'

Betty Billington looked astounded. Sarah could see she was trying hard to say the right words.

'Oh my. In all the years I've supervised staff for Woolworths I've never been asked that question before.'

Sarah looked crestfallen and rose to her feet to leave the room. 'I'm sorry. It was stupid of me even to think you'd be interested. Please, just forget I was here.'

Betty reached out and grabbed Sarah's hand. 'Don't be a ninny. I would love to be in attendance at your wedding. It's the greatest honour anyone has ever bestowed on me. I don't have a large family, so I've never been a bridesmaid. Most of my friends are either in the same boat as me or married quickly while their husbands-to-be were on leave. Losing Charlie, like so many women my age, I knew I'd never be part of a wedding party.'

'So you'll do it?' Sarah asked, somewhat amazed that Betty was so thrilled.

Betty reached for her handkerchief and dabbed at her eyes. 'Look at me acting so silly. Thank you, Sarah. I'm honoured you asked me, and yes, I'd love to share your wedding day. Now, would you like me to purchase my own gown? I appreciate that these occasions can be expensive.'

Sarah shook her head. 'No, Maisie is making our outfits. I have the fabric. If you would like to come to tea on Sunday, Maisie could measure you up and I can show you the plans for the wedding.'

'I can't think of anything I'd rather do. I'll bring along the details of the carnival queen and we can have a splendid afternoon chatting about dresses and special occasions.'

Sarah chewed her lip, still unsure about her role

as queen. 'Is there no one else you think could do the job? How about Maisie? She's so glamorous she would be perfect to sit on the lorry and wave to the crowds.'

Betty shook her head. 'No. The carnival queen has to be an unmarried woman.'

'Freda, then?'

'Freda is too young. I had her in mind as an escort. In fact, Maisie would be ideal as the second escort to the queen. We can sort out the details on Sunday.' She clapped her hands together in delight. 'How exciting this is all going to be. I can't wait. Can you?'

Sarah smiled. She was looking forward to her wedding and was counting the days to her twenty-first birthday, when she would become Mrs Alan Gilbert. As for her duties as carnival queen, she just hoped that she didn't fall off the lorry or trip over her cape. At least she'd have Freda and Maisie with her to pick her up off the floor if things went pear-shaped.

'Blimey, I didn't expect to 'ave to be on me good behaviour today. It's worse than being at Sunday school, isn't it?'

'Ssh. They'll hear you, Maisie. They're only in the next room.' Freda poked her friend in the arm. 'I don't think that Sarah expected her mum to turn up unannounced like that. It must have been the mention of Miss Billington in her letter that had her mum rushing up from Devon like that.'

'I wonder why. Perhaps she's not keen on all the bridesmaids being Woolies girls?'

'Well, let's get this tea tray in the front room

163

and we may just hear something. Poor Alan looks right uncomfortable in his best suit sitting between his boss and his future mother-in-law. It's a shame Ruby is off at her whist drive. She'd have loved to witness what was going on this afternoon.'

Maisie nudged the door to the front room with her bottom and carried the tea tray into the stuffy room. Freda followed with a cake stand containing a large chocolate cake, one of Ruby's, which she'd quickly made when she heard that Betty Billington was coming to tea. It didn't hurt for her daughter-in-law to see that she could also put on a spread fit for a queen. She'd left strict instructions for the girls to use her best tea plates and had even polished the silver cake knife that had been a wedding gift from her husband's employers. It only came out on high days and holidays.

'Help yourself, ducks,' Maisie said as she held a plate piled high with salmon sandwiches in front of Irene Caselton's face.

Irene wrinkled her nose at Maisie's words and took just one small sandwich from the pile. 'Thank you.' She smiled politely before turning to Betty. 'So, Miss Billington, I understand you work with my daughter?'

Sarah cringed. She knew she shouldn't have mentioned in her letter that she'd invited Betty to be a bridesmaid. Her mother's response had been a postcard showing her intent to travel up to Erith to 'sort out a wedding that was turning into a circus full of shop girls'. Now Irene was interrogating her boss. 'Miss Billington is in charge of all the staff at our branch, Mum.' She looked up to

164

see Alan wink reassuringly at her. She tried not to grin.

Maisie sat on the side of Sarah's armchair and bit into a sandwich. 'If it wasn't for Miss Billington, none of us would have a job.'

Irene raised her pencilled eyebrows. 'You're in management?'

Betty smiled her thanks as Freda placed two sandwiches onto a plate and passed them to her. 'Yes, Mrs Caselto–'

'Please, do call me Irene.'

'Yes, Irene. I started out on the shop floor, just like your daughter, and gradually worked my way up. First as a supervisor, then as staff manager.'

'You never married?'

'Please, Mum. I'm sure Betty doesn't want to be questioned like this. I invited her to be my third bridesmaid, and once we've had tea, Maisie is going to measure her for her gown, and then we are going to talk about the carnival queen's duties.'

'It's all right, Sarah. Your mother should know about me. After all, I'm going to be present at one of the most memorable days of her life, when her only daughter gets married. Irene, I lost my intended in the war, so instead of having a husband and family, I devoted myself to my career.'

Irene showed no sympathy as she sipped tea from Ruby's best china cup. 'Very commendable. I wish my own daughter would think more of her future than just being a wife and mother. But then, she is going to be the wife of an RAF pilot, so I shall console myself with that instead.'

Sarah closed her eyes. Would this tea party ever end?

Maisie jumped to her feet and grabbed Sarah's hand. 'Come on, ladies. Let's go measure up Betty in yer bedroom. We can have a slice of Ruby's cake afterwards. Alan, why don't you show Mrs Caselton the Anderson shelter? She might like to see the rhubarb we planted as well.'

'You are a very talented seamstress, Maisie.' Betty ran her hands over the full skirt of the dress that Freda was holding. 'Are you sure it's no trouble for you to make another gown, especially as we now have the carnival to prepare for as well?'

Maisie waved her hand in the air to dismiss the question. 'It'll only take me a day or two to run up. Now that the queen's attendants are going to wear their own party dresses underneath the cloaks, there's not much to prepare for the carnival – just Her Majesty's frock to alter. I really hope it doesn't rain, as water is a bugger on satin.'

Betty flinched at Maisie's turn of phrase and smiled at Sarah. 'It was fortunate that the carnival committee had a gown that had been donated.'

'And that the girl who wore it before was larger than Sarah,' Freda added quickly. 'It only needs taking in at the waist and the hem shortening slightly.'

Sarah looked sad. 'I just wish it wasn't white. I wanted my first full-length white dress to be my bridal gown, not a second-hand carnival-queen outfit. Not that I'm not grateful for being given the honour to be queen,' she added quickly, in case Betty thought she was being fussy. After being shown photographs and being told the history of how money was raised for the local cottage hospital, along with the part that the Erith branch of Woolworths played in events, she understood how memorable a day it was for the residents of Erith.

'Hmm, I have an idea.' Maisie pulled some green taffeta round Sarah's waist. 'How about if I make an overskirt of taffeta and add a matching collar to the dress? Once you're wearing the cloak, there won't be much white left to see.'

Sarah frowned. 'But that's my bridesmaid material and everyone will see it before my wedding day.'

'Don't be a ninny. This is the material for Betty's dress. I can pop up to Woolwich Market and get a remnant for your frock. Give me some ideas for colours and I'll see what I can do.'

Betty grinned. 'You are certainly resourceful, Maisie. I'll make sure you are reimbursed for any money you spend and insist that you are given an afternoon off to complete the preparations.'

Maisie was just finishing the measurements for her boss's bridesmaid dress when there was a tentative knock at the bedroom door.

Sarah jumped to her feet from where she was sitting on her bed with Freda. She quickly covered her wedding gown in case it was Alan. She felt bad that he'd been left to entertain her mum for so long. 'Yes. Who is it?'

'It's Mummy, darling. Can I come in?'

'Is Alan with you?' Sarah called back.

They all heard Irene sigh from outside. 'Certainly not, and I do hope that you don't make a habit of allowing young men upstairs.'

167

'Come in, Mum. Of course I don't.'

'No need to worry about yer daughter, Mrs Caselton. She's as pure as a lily is Sarah. No man will step over the threshold of her bedroom till she's got a ring on her finger,' Maisie called.

The girls all giggled as Irene entered the room and looked around at the fabric and other sewing implements scattered about the small bedroom. 'This all looks very cosy. I hope Miss Billington doesn't feel uncomfortable being measured for a home-made dress in your nan's little house, Sarah?'

Alan had no doubt answered many questions about Betty Billington while keeping Irene company downstairs. She had adopted a deferential air, almost doffing her cap in front of the other woman, who was presently standing on a stool in her petticoat while Maisie pinned fabric round her waist.

'Goodness, no,' Betty exclaimed. 'I grew up in a house just like this one in Deptford, and my own house is a two-up, two-down in Belvedere. It's very good of Sarah's grandmother to invite me to her home. In fact, Sarah, you must remind me that I have a small gift for Mrs Caselton Senior in my bag. I don't wish to forget and take it home with me again. It's just a selection of seeds for her garden. I know how much she is enjoying her new hobby, as she told me about it when she visited the store.'

Irene nodded her head graciously and observed Betty as she stepped from the stool and put on her grey woollen dress. 'Are there many women in management at F. W. Woolworth, Miss Billington?'

168

'More by the day, Mrs Caselton. I've already informed Sarah that she too could be in a supervisory position one day.'

'Not if she's a married woman, and no doubt with child before too long.'

Betty picked up her handbag. 'Times are changing, Mrs Caselton, and women will be required to do their bit if the menfolk go off to war.'

'So Sarah could be in management just like you even though she is destined to be a housewife?'

'That's correct,' Betty agreed. 'Now, shall we go and taste that delicious-looking cake that is waiting for us downstairs?'

As Freda and Maisie followed Sarah down the steep stairs, Freda whispered, 'Miss Billington is very nice, isn't she?'

Sarah nodded. Betty seemed to have summed up her mother straight away, and in her eyes that wasn't such a bad thing at all. She was sure, that Betty would be a good friend, and that was marvellous considering her position at work.

Sarah was happy that so much was happening at Woolworths to distract her, as her wedding was beginning to play on her mind. Mr Benfield not only had the staff practising fire drills, but had also arranged for gas-mask training so that customers and staff could join in too. She hated the smell of the rubbery mask but knew that it may well save her life. It was the children who upset her most, as many feared the scary masks, and to see a small baby placed inside such an ugly contraption had brought her to tears more than once. Even Maisie, who could be guaranteed to liven up any occasion, was growing tired of fire drills, although she'd taken up a new hobby making pretty covers for the gas-mask cases. Mr Benfield had pointed out that it wasn't prudent to fill the small box with lipstick and compact, but Maisie had just laughed. She assured her boss that if there was the slightest chance of her being required to use the mask, she would be the first to pull it out of the carrying box and pull it over her perfectly styled hair.

Alan hadn't heard a thing from the RAF, but Sarah knew it wasn't worth getting her hopes up that he would not be accepted for training, as she knew he'd be bitterly disappointed. Whatever she thought of her future husband joining the forces, she had to keep it to herself. It was just a matter of time before he received the official letter. She only hoped that it wasn't before the wedding.

Another problem that kept her awake at night was Irene. Her mother wanted the wedding break-fast to be catered at a hotel, or even a nearby golf club. Each time a letter arrived from Devon, her mother had included more suggestions for posh hotels and fancy food. Sarah considered taking her nan's advice and using her mother's favourite fancy pink notepaper as tapers for the coal fire that Ruby had ready to be lit if the nights should turn cold. As it was, she tried to placate her mother by explaining that everything was in hand. Ruby had told her not to worry so much and that the day of her wedding and her twenty-first birthday would be one she would always remember. Every bride had worries before the big day and Sarah was no different.

It was with a heavy heart that Sarah pulled on her hat and coat, and picked up her handbag to head for work. Tomorrow was the carnival, and try as she might, she could not find the enthusiasm required to be Erith's carnival queen. Pulling the front door closed behind her, she was surprised to see Alan standing at the gate.

'Thank goodness I didn't miss you,' he said, kissing her cheek and putting his arm through hers. 'I have a surprise for you.'

Sarah's heart skipped a beat. 'You've heard from the RAF?'

'No, darling girl. It's a special treat. I've arranged it with Betty. You're taking the day off from work and we are going on a little trip.'

'But where and why?'

'Why? Because I love you to distraction and want you to myself for the day. You are constantly fussing over dresses with your friends and being drilled on your royal duties as carnival queen. I can see you look tired with so much on your mind. It's time we stopped thinking about weddings and me joining the RAF and everything, and just acted like two young people in love with each other. Where? Just you wait and see.'

Sarah felt the weight she'd been carrying on her shoulders almost vanish. She was the luckiest girl in the world to be engaged to such a caring, thoughtful man. 'Oh, Alan, a day to ourselves would be lovely. Wherever you are taking me, I'm sure I'll love it.'

'Well, come on, my love, our transport awaits.'

Although puzzled, Sarah happily walked the short distance to town before heading down the

High Street towards a small jetty by the River Thames, where passengers were boarding *The Kentish Queen* paddle steamer. A wooden board announced, 'Day trips to Margate.'

'Oh my goodness, this is so exciting. I've wanted to go on a trip on the Thames for ages. Freda will be so jealous when I tell her what I've been up to.'

'Don't you worry about Freda. She knows about your surprise, and I've promised that once the wedding is over, we can all have a day out together. Now, mind your step – I don't want to have to dive in and fish you out of the water.'

Sarah hung on to Alan's hand as she climbed aboard. The steamer bobbed slowly up and down as gentle waves lapped against its sides. A smiling young woman took the tickets Alan held out and welcomed them aboard. She pointed out where they could sit and admire the view.

'Do you think that she works on the boat?'

Alan nodded. 'The Sayers family have run the paddle steamer for generations. Gracie works with her dad, Ted. They're a local family just like us.'

'I do believe I've seen her shopping in Woolies,' Sarah said as she looked out over the Thames towards Essex.

Seagulls flew overhead, dipping and diving and calling out to each other. The river was a hive of activity, as around her, ships that had travelled from exotic locations around the world unloaded their goods at the many warehouses and jetties. She felt the warm morning sun on her face and visibly relaxed from the worries that had kept her awake for so many nights.

'This is lovely. I feel better already. Will it take

long to reach Margate?'

'I'm not sure, but let's just enjoy the journey and some time to ourselves. There never seem to be enough hours in the day for us to spend time together.'

Sarah snuggled up against Alan. 'You're too generous with your time. How many people have you helped erect Anderson shelters? You must be an expert at the job. Then you're busy decorating Maureen's house. There can't be an odd job left to do.' Sarah was proud of Alan, but there were times when she thought he gave too freely of his time.

'About half a dozen or so, but our neighbours are elderly and can't manage on their own. Everyone's doing their bit to make sure folk will be safe when the war starts.'

'*If* the war starts.'

'OK, if.' Alan squeezed Sarah closer to him. 'You know it's going to happen, though, don't you?'

Sarah sighed. 'Yes, there's more chance now of war than I ever thought there would be, but I want things to stay the same and for everyone to be safe and happy, so if you don't mind, I'll continue to say "if" rather than "when".'

Alan took Sarah by the shoulders and looked her in the eyes. She looked sad and he wished he could make everything right in her world, but it was beyond his capabilities. 'My love, you must face up to things. Now is not the time to close your eyes to world events. Those Nazis are a pretty bloodthirsty lot and we need to sort them out before they turn our country into another part of their empire. There will be a war and there's no way we can avoid it.'

Sarah tried to pull away from Alan's grip, but he was strong and kept hold of her. Why was he spoiling their day with talk of war? She didn't want to think about it. 'But, Alan…'

Alan placed a finger under her chin, turning her head so she looked into his eyes. He didn't like to see Sarah upset, but she had to face up to the future. 'Look, love, I'm going to be away for long periods of time, and when I am, I want you to be brave. Promise me you'll take care of my mum as well as your nan, and keep an eye on young Freda too? That will keep you busy and stop you worrying so much. Once this is all over, we can plan for the future. Our own home and perhaps even a family. Promise me?'

Sarah blinked to stop a tear from falling. 'I promise, but I'll be counting the hours until you're home and safe. You're just not to do anything dangerous, do you hear me?'

Alan laughed and pulled her into his arms, holding her close. 'I hear you, my love. I'm not exactly keen to be shot at by the Hun, you know.' He silenced any further protest by claiming her lips. Sarah melted into him, content to stay that way for as long as possible, until the sound of tutting from nearby made them part.

'Well, really. I know a date has been set for the wedding, but there's no need for such goings-on in public.'

They both turned to see Vera, from up the road, sitting nearby with her daughter.

'Good morning, Mrs Munro. Isn't it a lovely day?' Alan called, before grabbing Sarah's hand and pulling her to her feet. 'Let's go find those refreshments, shall we?'

Sarah giggled. She'd enjoy her day with Alan. Nan had told her how she treasured all her memories of Granddad and how important they were to her now he was no longer with them. She'd do her best to create some of her own memories today to hold close and cherish. Whatever happened in the future, she would remember Alan's love of life, his smiles and his laughter. Today would be an entry in her album of memories. Hopefully there would be many more to come and she could look back on them in her old age and relive their day together.

'So, did you go on the waltzer? What about candyfloss? Did it taste nice?'

'For Gawd's sake, Freda, stop nattering and wave yer bloody hand like the Queen does and smile at the punters. Anyone would never think you'd been to a funfair or the seaside.' Maisie beamed around her and winked at the butcher's boy, who was pedalling fast to keep up with them.

Freda gripped the side of the lorry as it moved slowly down Pier Road towards Woolworths and waved enthusiastically at the crowds that lined the pavements. Youngsters ran alongside the lorry calling out to Queen Sarah as she sat on her throne on the low-backed vehicle. 'I've never been to the seaside, so of course I want to know all about it.'

'What, never? Why's that?' Maisie asked, grabbing Sarah's shoulder to balance herself as the lorry bumped over a hole in the road.

''Cos I come from the Midlands and it's in the

middle of the country, that's why,' Freda hissed back indignantly.

'Blimey, I never thought of it like that,' Maisie said, nudging Queen Sarah, who was trying not to listen to her friends and to remember all that Betty Billington had told her about the rest of her duties.

'What do you think "midland" means, you dunce? We lived miles from the sea, and not having much money, we didn't get to have days out and such. I spotted the poster for Margate and Dreamland at Charing Cross Station and thought that it was somewhere I'd go to one day. Fat lot of chance of that, what with working all hours.'

'All right, keep your hair on,' Maisie hissed back. 'It's only the seaside.'

'It might be "only the seaside" to you, but it would be heaven to me. I'll most likely never get to paddle in the sea or eat cockles and all.' Freda looked sad.

'Well, pin that smile back on yer face or you'll be for it if Mr Benfield catches you looking miserable. I'll see what I can do to get you to the seaside.'

'Really? You'd do that for me?' Freda jumped up and down, waving to the crowd frantically as the lorry pulled to a halt in front of Woolies. 'I can't believe it. When? When can we go?'

Sarah looked around for Mr Benfield. Surely he would see that Freda's mind wasn't on her duties. 'Look out, you two. Mr Benfield is on his way over. Freda, we'll sort out your trip later. Let's finish the job in hand, shall we?'

Freda calmed down as they alighted from the

lorry, assisted by their beaming manager. They stood on the pavement watching as the Dagenham Girl Pipers marched by, resplendent in their brightly coloured kilts and playing well-known marching tunes on the bagpipes. Following behind were local groups of Brownies and Scouts, as well as the nurses that could be spared from Erith Cottage Hospital, where the fete was in progress. The plan was to return to the hospital and attend the fete once Queen Sarah had toured the store and greeted the staff and customers. Mr Benfield, accompanied by the mayor, led Sarah and her entourage into the shop, to much cheering from the staff. Sarah blushed with embarrassment. If she'd known that there was going to be so much fuss, she would have declined the invitation to be the carnival queen. Inside the shop, she sat on a specially made throne, while the mayor made a speech thanking F. W. Woolworth, which was followed by Mr Benfield and staff demonstrating their skills with firefighting material and gas masks.

Betty sidled up to Sarah as she was watching Alan skilfully putting out a pretend fire, much to the mirth of the Brownies, who were enjoying a bag of sweets each courtesy of Woolies. 'You do look pretty, Sarah. You all do,' she added, turning to Maisie and Freda. 'I can't thank you enough for volunteering to help.'

Maisie gave the girls a wink behind their boss's back. All three knew that if there had been any volunteering involved, they'd have been hiding at the back of the queue. 'I'm sure I speak for all of us when I say we wouldn't have missed this for all the tea in China, ducks ... er, Betty ... I mean, Miss Billington.'

Betty patted Maisie's hand. 'Betty will be fine for today, and please, you must think of me as a friend, as we will all be bridesmaids together very soon.'

'Only three weeks to go now,' Freda added. 'It will be Sarah's twenty-first birthday as well, so it's twice as special.'

Betty nodded. 'Yes, the third of September will indeed be a day for rejoicing. I haven't looked forward to something so much since I don't know when. Now, let's get you girls a cool drink before you climb aboard your chariot and head back to the cottage hospital and the fete.'

Maisie rubbed her backside and grimaced. 'Chariot? I could have sworn it was Clarke's coal lorry we were riding on, and it was none too comfortable either. I'm sure my seat was a bag of nutty slack.'

14

'Now, now, love, you've got to stop this crying. Your Alan is not going to be too pleased to see his bride walking up the aisle with puffy eyes and a red nose, now is he? Just unlock the door and let me in, there's a love. You still have birthday presents to open downstairs and a few more cards to read. People have been so generous. I've got a nice cup of tea for you with a dash of brandy in it to perk you up. There's a couple of slices of toast as well, as you missed your breakfast with all this hoo-ha going on.'

Ruby heard muttering from behind the bedroom door and then the key turning in the lock. A worried Freda opened the door and whispered, 'It's gonna take a lot to convince Sarah to get married today. I hope you can talk her into it. She's refusing to put on her wedding dress.'

Ruby entered the crowded bedroom and placed the tea and toast on top of a chest of drawers, moving a photograph of Sarah and Alan in the process. The image showed the young couple standing close together. Their eyes were full of love as they gazed at each other, caught by a photographer in Dreamland. Was it only weeks ago that her granddaughter had returned from her day trip to Margate so full of plans for the future?

She sat beside Sarah on the bed and took her hand. 'Now, love, there's no reason for you not to go ahead with the wedding. The whole day is planned, and who is to say that this radio announcement is going to tell us war has started with Germany? I reckon it's all a load of rubbish.'

Maisie reached for her cigarettes and offered them to Sarah.

'Not in here, Maisie. The smoke will make my dress smell.'

'It's not going to matter if you ain't wearing it,' Maisie pointed out as she put a cigarette between her own lips and reached for her lighter.

'Perhaps go downstairs and smoke that, eh, Maisie?' Betty said. 'You could let Sarah's mother know how Sarah is feeling.'

Maisie sniffed but did as she was asked. She wasn't keen on going to chat with Irene Caselton, but Betty was still her boss, even if she was sitting in Sarah's bedroom covered from neck to toe in her dressing gown and admiring her recently polished nails.

She looked at the dainty watch on her wrist. 'OK, but don't forget the prime minister is on the wireless before too long and we don't want to miss that.' She saw Sarah's startled look and added quickly, 'Not that we know what it is he is going to tell us. He might just be telling the country that it's Sarah and Alan's wedding day.'

Sarah's face broke into a sad smile. She knew her friend was trying to cheer her up, but it would take a lot to make her happy today, and even more for her to step into her wedding gown. Why of all days did this have to happen today? She'd woken early in such good spirits, only to hear that the prime minister, Neville Chamberlain, was going to broadcast to the nation at a quarter past eleven. Everything had gone downhill after that, with Vera dashing round full of excitement to tell them all that war was going to be declared this very day and that no doubt no one would want to go to a wedding. Nan had sent their neighbour packing with a flea in her ear, but by then Sarah had fled to her bedroom, followed by her bridesmaids, where no amount of coaxing would convince her that the wedding should go ahead. How could she celebrate the happiest day of her life when the country was possibly going to war? It didn't seem right somehow, and it seemed wrong for her to be happy when so many people would be waving off loved ones as they joined the forces and left home – possibly for good.

'Someone ought to let the guests know that the wedding has been cancelled.' She looked at her nan, who was still holding her hand. 'Can you let Alan know, please, Nan?'

Ruby nodded and got to her feet, beckoning Freda to follow her.

'Well, this is a right to-do,' Ruby exclaimed as she joined her son and daughter-in-law in the front room. 'I'm at my wits' end trying to think how we can convince Sarah to go ahead with the wedding. I feel for the girl, I really do, and on her twenty-first birthday as well.'

'Thank goodness we didn't book the golf club for the wedding breakfast. I wouldn't have been able to face my friends after all this. At least there's been no money wasted.'

Ruby puffed up her chest ready to give Irene what for, but George beat her to it.

'Now, Irene, I've kept my mouth shut these past few weeks, but I think this time it needs saying. You've just insulted not only my mother with your words but also young Freda here. Everyone's worked hard to put on a wedding fit for a queen, and whether it's at a bloody golf club or Buckingham Palace it doesn't matter. What concerns me is that our daughter is upstairs right now crying her eyes out and wants to cancel what should be the happiest day of her life. Now stop being such a snob and put your thinking cap on so we can decide what to do.' He ignored his wife's gasps and his mother's snort of laughter and looked at the clock. 'There's still three-quarters of an hour before the broadcast. Let's listen to what Neville Chamberlain has to say and then we can move forward. The wedding's not until three o'clock and I'm of the opinion that we have time to make Sarah change her mind.'

Ruby nodded. 'I'm with you there. I'll put the kettle on. We might need a cuppa while we listen. George, you ought to warm up the wireless so it's ready in time.'

Freda, who had been standing quietly listening to Sarah's family, wondered what her own family would be doing at this time. It was Sunday and normally they'd all be heading for the pub. As for her brother, she only hoped that he was safe somewhere. It was nine months since she'd received his letter with the postmark 'Erith' that had brought her to this town. 'Can I suggest something?'

George nodded to the young girl. He'd come to like Freda, and whenever he was working in Erith would treat her like a second daughter, taking her and Sarah to the pictures and joining in with their lively conversations at the dinner table. 'Go ahead, love.'

'I think that the only person who can talk Sarah round is Alan. I want to go and tell him what's happening.'

'What a silly idea. Everyone knows that the groom shouldn't see the bride before the wedding.' Irene Caselton frowned at Freda.

'Well, there ain't going to be a wedding if someone don't do something. I reckon Freda's idea is spot on. I'll come with you to get him. He can talk to Sarah from the other side of the door if that makes you feel any better,' Maisie snarled at Irene.

'Come on, let's get our coats and go find the groom.'

George tapped on the bedroom door before entering. Sarah was sitting on the bed staring into space. Fresh tears were scattered on her cheeks. Betty had been tidying up the room and had hung the wedding gown on the side of the large mahogany wardrobe. George recognized the wardrobe as it had been in his bedroom when he was a lad. Apart from the furniture from his boyhood, it was now a very feminine room. His daughter had made her mark on the little space, which overlooked the back garden, where a row of similar-sized plots now had Anderson shelters in pride of place, with cabbages and potato plants replacing rows of gladioli and chrysanthemum.

He stopped to look at the layers of white silk that had been so carefully stitched together by Maisie. 'Your friend has a remarkable talent. I would have been so proud to walk you down the aisle, my dear, but it's your decision not to marry. You're twenty-one today and that makes you an adult. An adult who can make her own decisions. Don't worry too much about all the people who worked hard to make your wedding day special. I'm sure they will understand,' he said nonchalantly, before checking his watch. 'Ten minutes to go before Mr Chamberlain's broadcast. I'd better go check the wireless set. Your nan does like to twiddle with the knobs, and today isn't the day to miss such an important announcement.' George kissed Sarah's cheek, placed his pipe in his mouth and left the bedroom.

Sarah closed her eyes as a great weariness overcame her. She could hear her dad's footsteps as he went downstairs and her mum's shrill tones as she called him into the front room. She ran her hands through her hair and gazed at Betty, who had sat quietly on a stool in front of the dressing table observing what had gone on in Sarah's bedroom.

'Oh, Betty, it's such a mess, and now Dad is disappointed in me. Whatever should I do?'

Betty knelt on the floor in front of Sarah and took both of her hands in her own. 'Sarah, do you mind if I give you some advice?'

Sarah nodded. 'Yes, please. I do value your opinion.'

'I'm led to understand that on the day a girl marries, she will be worrying over many things. The months that lead up to the big day can be exciting, but the day itself marks many changes in her life. She is leaving home as a daughter, and granddaughter, and will be planning a new life with her husband in a new home. You also have your twenty-first birthday today, another excitement, and to top it all we've had the build-up to this bloody war.'

Sarah raised her eyebrows. She had never heard her boss swear before.

'Of course, I've never experienced being married, but I know that after I wrote to Charlie to say I was wrong not to have married him before he left for France and that I'd marry him upon his return, I did experience that stir of excitement as I planned our wedding. Of course, it wasn't to be.' Betty stopped talking, lost in thoughts of what might have been. 'I just wish that I'd not been such a fool and had married him before he went off to war.'

The room fell into silence, with only the ticking of the clock taking the two women towards the time when the prime minister would spell the fate of the country, perhaps even the world.

Sarah looked towards the beautiful gown. She only needed to take it down from the hanger to make her first step towards her new life. The delicate froth of veil was draped across the bottom of the bed. A headdress of silk orange blossom was waiting to be placed upon her head. She stood up and folded her dressing gown around her. 'I do believe I've been rather silly. I'm so sorry, Betty.'

Betty smiled. 'I'd never use that word, Sarah. You've had a lot to think about. I'm sure Alan will come back and you will live happily ever after, as the fairy stories tell. However, I don't want you to live the life I've led. Yes, I've been happy, but in a different way to what I planned. I don't want you to miss out on being Mrs Alan Gilbert and having the chance of a normal life, for however long.'

Sarah hugged Betty. 'Yes, you're right. I hope no one listened to me and started putting the wheels in motion to stop the wedding, as that would be just too awful.'

'I'm sure they haven't, Sarah. You have to remember how much everyone loves you and Alan. Why, look at the wonderful party that the staff threw for you yesterday at work. I've never witnessed anything like it, and I've worked at the Erith branch for many a year.'

'It was lovely, wasn't it? It was a complete surprise when we walked into the staffroom at the end of the day to see the bunting and so many presents. And to have invited Nan as well was so nice of everyone.'

'I'll remember it forever. In fact, the staff magazine is going to feature it in the next edition, which is such a bonus for the branch. Now, why don't we go downstairs and join your family? We will just be in time to listen to the broadcast on the wireless. I don't know about you, but I could do with a hot cup of tea.' She peered to where Ruby had left Sarah's tea and toast on the chest of drawers. 'I think this is past saving.'

'Yes, and I must open my birthday presents. I keep forgetting I have the key of the door today.'

The two women had just reached the bottom of the staircase when the front door burst open and Alan rushed in, followed by Freda and Maisie.

Sarah was shocked to see her intended standing out of breath and red-faced in the hallway. 'Alan?'

'Bloody 'eck, you mustn't see the bride before the wedding. It's unlucky,' Maisie shrieked, grabbing Alan by the jacket and trying to pull him back out of the open door.

'I think it's just the dress he mustn't see,' Freda advised.

'No, it's the bride and the dress,' Betty added helpfully. 'However, it's too late now, so let's leave the pair of them alone while they talk.' She ushered the two girls towards the front-room door. 'I'll call you before the prime minister makes his speech. I'm sure you won't wish to miss that.'

Alan led Sarah to the bottom of the stairs and

they sat down together. 'What's all of this about, my love? I was just having a shave when Maisie and Freda burst in to tell me you'd changed your mind about marrying me. Look, I've nicked myself.'

Sarah ran her finger over the small cut on his jawline. 'Oh, Alan. I'm so sorry. I've been an utter fool. Everything just got on top of me, and then this news about Neville Chamberlain making an announcement on the wireless was the final straw. No one is going to want to go to a wedding on a day like this, are they? Surely they won't want to celebrate our happiness on such an awful day?'

Alan put his arm around Sarah. 'I was thinking about this while I was shaving. Mum's house is full to brimming with family and friends popping in to say good luck. Not one of them said we should cancel the wedding. We've given everyone cause to put on their finery and have a happy few hours sharing our joy. Why let Hitler spoil our plans?'

'You're right. Come on, let's go join the family. I don't intend on anything else spoiling our day.' Sarah rose to her feet.

'But just before we do, come here, Mrs Gilbert.' Alan pulled Sarah into his arms.

'Aren't you being a little presumptuous, Mr Gilbert?'

'What's a couple of hours between a husband and wife?'

'When you put it like that...'

'What on earth is happening here?' Irene Caselton stepped into the hallway and pulled Sarah away from Alan just as their lips met. 'Don't you know it's unlucky to see the bride before the wedding, let alone be so familiar?'

'I think it's just the dress he mustn't see,' Freda said again from behind Irene's back, where she was trying to see what was happening.

'No, it's the dress and the bride – Betty told us just now,' Maisie called out.

'Whatever the superstition, it's too late now,' Ruby added. 'Get yourself both in here and sit down. The wireless has warmed up and we want to know what's going to happen.' She ushered her family into the crowded front room as the solemn announcer introduced the prime minister.

'*This morning the British ambassador in Berlin handed the German government a final note stating that unless we heard from them by eleven a.m. that they were prepared at once to withdraw their troops from Poland, a state of war would exist between us.*

'*I have to tell you now that no such undertaking has been received, and that consequently this country is at war with Germany...*'

'Oh my God!' Ruby exclaimed, reaching for her son's hand.

'Ssh, Mum. He's still speaking.' George patted his mother's hand, even though he felt just as shaken.

The family continued listening, leaning towards the wireless so as not to miss one word of the life-changing speech.

'*...The government have made plans under which it will be possible to carry on the work of the nation in the days of stress and strain that may be ahead. But these plans need your help.*

'*You may be taking part in the fighting services or as a volunteer in one of the branches of civil defence.*

188

If so, you will report for duty in accordance with the instructions you have received. You may be engaged in work essential to the prosecution of war for the maintenance of the life of the people – in factories, in transport, in public utility concerns or in the supply of other necessaries of life. If so, it is of vital importance that you should carry on with your jobs.

'Now may God bless you all. May He defend the right. It is the evil things that we shall be fighting against – brute force, bad faith, injustice, oppression and persecution – and against them I am certain that the right will prevail.'

'Well, there it is. The country is at war. What do we do next?' Irene looked around the room at the shocked faces.

'First we put the kettle on; then we have a wedding to get to,' Ruby announced. 'Why don't you open your birthday presents, love? There'll not be much time later. We can worry about the war tomorrow.'

Sarah nodded and reached for a small package that Maisie held out. 'It's a joint present from me and Freda. We chipped in together.'

Sarah carefully peeled back the layers of tissue to reveal a flat, square box. Inside, she found a powder compact, the lid inlaid with mother-of-pearl. 'Oh, thank you. I'll treasure it forever.' She hugged both of her friends closely.

George returned with a tray of cups and saucers. Freda followed with another containing a large brown teapot and a plate of sandwiches. 'Before we do anything else, we should drink this and eat something. It's going to be a busy afternoon and no doubt we won't eat until we tuck into the lovely spread that Mum and the girls have prepared for the wedding breakfast.'

There was a frantic knocking on the front door. Irene turned to look through the bay window. 'It's that irritating woman from up the road. What is her name?'

'It's "Vera from up the road",' the girls all chanted together, and burst into a fit of giggles.

'Well, there's a fine thing,' Vera exclaimed as she entered the room. 'The world is at war and you are all sitting here giggling. Why, Sarah, I thought you of all people would have been distraught not to be getting married.'

Alan, who had stood up as Vera entered, faced up to her. 'Mrs Munro, there is to be a wedding today. In fact, once I've drunk my tea, I'm going to jump on my bike, ride over to Crayford and check that everything is ready for us at St Paulinus Church.'

'You shouldn't be here – it's unlucky to see the bride before the wedding,' Vera spluttered as she heard Alan's words.

George smiled politely at Vera. 'I'm glad he is, Mrs Munro. It's been a strange day, but now we know what's what, we can get stuck in and win this war. Once we've enjoyed Sarah and Alan's wedding, that is. Would you like a fish-paste sandwich?' He held out a tea plate, but just then a low moaning noise could be heard. The sound continued to gain speed as it grew higher and louder.

'Oh my God. It's an air raid. Quick, everyone – into the shelter. George, where did I put my insurance policies?'

'Don't worry, Mum. They're all in the little case

by the door, along with your gas mask. I'll pop this tea into a flask.' George started to marshal his family into action. 'You never know how long we might be in the shelter. Irene, dear, close your mouth and move yourself. There's a love.'

Tea and sandwiches were put down as Sarah, her family and her bridesmaids headed towards the back door.

Just then Vera put her arm across the door, stopping the frightened wedding party from heading towards the Anderson shelter. 'There are too many of us. The shelter will only hold six at a squeeze.' She pushed to the front of the queue. 'The last three will have to stay here.'

Ruby frowned at her neighbour. 'Well, for a start, you, Vera Munro, have your own shelter, so I suggest you scuttle up the road and join your daughter.'

'But I might be blown up in the street,' Vera moaned, going rather pale at the thought.

'Not if you run fast. I'm sure the Germans aren't looking for you. More likely it's the docks.'

Sarah felt Maisie grip her arm. Joe, Maisie's husband, was working a Sunday shift on the docks. Was he safe? 'It may be a false alarm, or perhaps they are testing the sirens,' Sarah suggested.

'Best to be safe anyway. Come along, everyone, let's get to the shelter,' Irene insisted, pushing Vera out of the way and taking Betty's arm. 'Miss Billington, I'll show you the way.'

It was Alan who took control. 'I'll just see Mrs Munro up the street and I'll return. Sarah and I can sit it out in the cupboard under the stairs, the rest of you, please hurry and get to the shelter as

191

soon as you can.'

'I don't think that you should be alone in such a confined place,' Irene objected. 'It's not proper.'

George took his wife by the arm. 'For goodness' sake, Irene, they will be married in a few hours, as long as we or the church aren't blown to kingdom come. Now come along.'

Sarah pulled a couple of overcoats from the hooks on the wall in the cupboard and laid them on the bare boards under the stairs. One had been the old coat that her granddad had worn when gardening. She held it to her face and inhaled. She could still smell her granddad and she ached to have him with her once more. 'Oh, Gramps, what would you make of all this?' she sighed.

'I'm back. Shove over.' Alan sat next to Sarah and pulled her close to his side.

'That was quick. Did you see Vera home?'

'By the time I got out of the front door, she was running up the road. I watched her go into her front door, then came back in. Are you comfy?'

'Mm, I could stay like this forever.'

'I hope not – we have a wedding to go to, and don't forget a certain twenty-first birthday as well.'

'I keep forgetting my birthday, what with everything going on today.'

'That reminds me – I have a present for you. I was going to give it to you at the church when we signed the register, but now is as good a time as any. The light's not very good in here, but you can just about see by the cracks around the door frame.' He fumbled in the pocket of his jacket and produced a small jewellery box. 'Here you are. I hope you like it.'

Sarah took the box and opened it slowly, savouring the anticipation of wondering what her husband-to-be had bought for her. Inside the box, nestled in a layer of cotton wool, was a small key on a chain. 'Oh, Alan, it's the key to the door.'

'No, my love, it's the key to my heart.'

'I'll wear it forever, I promise. Please help me put it on.'

Alan fastened the fine chain round her neck, took the empty box from her hand and tucked it into his pocket, alongside an envelope he had placed there this morning.

Sarah reached for Alan, sliding her arms around his neck. 'Thank you, my darling,' she whispered as she sought his lips in the darkness of their shelter.

Alan responded eagerly. He would wait until tomorrow to tell his wife-to-be about the contents of the envelope.

15

'The vicar should know better than to be ringing those church bells, Ruby.'

Ruby sighed and stretched her legs. As lovely as they were, her new shoes were a bugger to wear for very long. She'd crept away from where the wedding guests were standing in the sunshine, while George took photographs of the bride and groom with his box Brownie camera. She'd found a bench close to Eddie's grave and was deep in thought, thinking how proud her late husband would be of his eldest granddaughter today.

Sarah had looked beautiful as she walked down the aisle on her husband's arm and out into the late-afternoon sunshine. This afternoon there had only been tears of happiness. Her silk gown, lovingly made by Maisie, would not have looked out of place in a Paris fashion house. Ruby marvelled at the fine pleating on the bodice and the many tiny silk-covered buttons at the cuffs of the long sleeves and again to fasten the back of the dress. The bridesmaids' pale green dresses were in a similar style, although nothing could outshine Sarah on her special day. A slight breeze caught the long veil, causing it to fly out behind Sarah. Bride and groom laughed as her attendants hurried to catch the cloud of white before it caught on a rose bush. Ruby smiled. She wouldn't need a photograph to remind her of this day.

St Paulinus held many memories for the Caselton family, both happy and sad. She gazed up at the old church, set on the highest point in Crayford. Sarah had wanted to share her wedding day with her family and this was the right place to do just that.

She patted her husband's headstone. 'Eddie, I hope you are looking down on us all today. We miss you, my love,' she murmured.

'Did you hear what I said, Ruby?'

Ruby looked up as Vera came storming up the path, shattering the peace. 'Yes, Vera, I heard you the first time. I was just having a few minutes with my Eddie.'

Vera nodded towards the grave and stopped

speaking for a few moments. 'That vicar shouldn't be ringing the bells. I've just told the verger, but he wasn't interested. He muttered something about cassocks and walked away. I told him in the last shout church bells were only to be used if we had an invasion. He's not that young that he can't remember.'

'Well, I'm sure that even Hitler won't be marching up the High Street yet, so a few bells to celebrate Sarah and Alan's big day shouldn't make much of a difference. Surely you wouldn't begrudge the kids the sound of church bells ringing on their wedding day?'

Vera sniffed. 'Far be it from me to spoil their day, I'm sure. I'll get walking back to Erith or there'll be no ham left, and I'm not partial to fish paste.'

'Now, Vera, don't be a daft so-and-so. There will be a seat for you with our Pat. They brought the horse and cart from the farm. It looks a fair treat all dressed up with ribbons and the like.'

Vera wrinkled her nose. 'I don't want me best coat smelling of horses.'

'When did you get so fussy? Your old man took you everywhere on his cart when he had his milk round. You never complained of horses back then.'

Vera smiled. 'They were good days, weren't they? My Don and your Eddie down the boozer on a Sunday and rolling home for their dinner with bags of winkles and cockles for our tea. I'm feeling fair famished just thinking about it. How much longer do you think the photographs are going to take?'

'We're going to be a bit longer, what with

George playing with his camera. He bought it special for the wedding. Irene hasn't stopped telling everyone how much it cost and how it's got all the latest knobs and bits on it. As long as I have a nice picture to put in a frame for the sideboard, I don't care how much his camera cost.'

Vera nudged Ruby. 'Here, do you think George would take a picture of me? I'd like one of me in all me finery.'

'I'm sure he'll take one of you – that's if he doesn't run out of film. He's pointed the box at everything in sight. I even caught him taking a photograph of the vicar and the verger having a fag. That'll go down a bomb with the Mothers' Union. Now, help me to my feet and let's join the fun.'

'Happy, Mrs Gilbert?'

Sarah squeezed next to Alan as he sat on a bench in Ruby's back garden. They'd done the right thing by having the reception at her nan's house. Family and friends were packed into every room, as well as sprawling out into the back garden and the road out front. Trestle tables had been borrowed from the Methodist hall and groaned under the weight of food that the family had prepared in the days leading up to the wedding. Nearby, a group of young children ran in and out of the Anderson shelter, shrieking with laughter and without a care in the world. 'I've never felt so happy. Our wedding has been wonderful.'

'Despite Hitler not playing cricket today and you wanting to cancel the wedding this morning?'

Sarah giggled. 'You know what I mean. Even war being declared didn't spoil our happy day. Whatever happens in the months to come, we will have made some wonderful memories.'

Taking a sip of brown ale from his pint glass, she wrinkled her nose. 'How can you drink that stuff? It's awful.'

'Then stick to your port and lemon or whatever it was you were sharing with Freda.' Alan placed his glass on the ground and pulled Sarah into his arms. 'That's better. Did I tell you how beautiful you looked as you walked down the aisle?'

Sarah leant her head to one side, considering his question. 'I do believe you did, at least ten times, but you can say it again if you wish.'

'Then I'll tell you again. Now give me a kiss, Mrs Gilbert.'

'With pleasure, dear husband.' Sarah closed her eyes and surrendered to Alan's kisses.

He held her tightly as if he'd never let her go.

She squealed. 'You're squeezing all the air out of my body. How can I kiss you when I can't breathe?'

Alan reached for his glass and took a deep gulp, a look of fear on his face. 'Sorry, love, I just didn't want to let you go.'

Sarah shuddered as if something or someone had walked over her grave. 'Alan?'

'Here, you two, are you coming indoors?' Freda said as she popped her head round the corner. 'Maureen's going to play the piano. We can have a sing-song. What are you doing out here, anyway? It's getting a bit chilly.'

'I thought so as well,' Sarah answered, remembering how she felt as Alan held her far too tight. 'I only came out to find Alan. It was so noisy in the scullery. Maisie and Joe were having a bit of a ding-dong. The poor bloke's only been here a few minutes and she's laying into him like no one's business even before he's had a beer.'

Freda grinned. 'He's only gone and joined the army. Maisie's livid, as it means she'll be living on her own with Joe's mum, and the pair of them never see eye to eye.'

'Oh, poor Maisie.' However funny it was for Sarah to think of her friend being left alone under the same roof as her dreadful mother-in-law, she knew just how Maisie must be feeling. Although Alan hadn't yet heard from the RAF, she knew that one day he would go away and she would be distraught too. At least she had Ruby and her friends nearby, and her dad would visit often. At the moment George was living more in Erith than Devon, with him being in demand at the vast Vickers factory in nearby Crayford. 'Perhaps we ought to go in and rescue Joe?' Sarah rose to her feet to follow Freda back into the kitchen. 'Are you coming, Alan?'

Alan picked up his glass. 'I'll finish my beer first, love.'

Sarah gave Alan a backward glance as she followed her chum into the kitchen. Her husband seemed quiet. Already he was looking into space and a million miles away from Ruby's back garden.

Alan lit a cigarette, his fingers touching the letter in his jacket pocket as he reached for his lighter. It had been a wedding gift from his new wife and was engraved with their initials. He knew the words of the letter off by heart. How could he tell Sarah that he would soon have to travel north to start his training with the RAF? He'd had the letter for two weeks now and there hadn't been the right time to sit her down and explain. How could he spoil what was supposed to be the happiest day of their lives? He snorted to himself. Happy? The country goes to war and he is supposed to be happy?

'There you are, Alan. I thought by now you'd be at the piano joining in the sing-song.' George sat next to his son-in-law, and took a cigarette as Alan held out the packet. 'Not changed your mind about marrying my daughter, have you, lad?' he asked with a smile on his face. George liked Alan and in the few short months since he'd got to know him, he'd grown to consider Alan part of his family and the son he never had.

'Not for one moment, George.'

'Then why the glum face?'

Alan knew he had to tell George his secret. 'I've kept something from Sarah and now I don't have the nerve to tell her.'

'Not been hiding a wife and six kids away, have you?' George laughed.

'Nothing as simple as that, I'm afraid.'

George looked serious. 'I think you'd better tell me all about it'

Alan reached into his pocket for the letter and handed it to his father-in-law. 'You'd best read this.'

George turned the brown envelope over in his hand. He could see that it came from the Royal

Air Force due to the mark stamped on the back. He pulled out the single sheet of paper and read the words before replacing it inside the envelope and handing it back to Alan. 'And you say you've not told Sarah?'

Alan nodded.

'Well, Alan, you're about to learn the first rule of marriage. Never keep a secret from the wife. She'll know a mile off if something is wrong. Believe me, my Irene can spot a secret almost before there is one. They can make you suffer for weeks if they think you're up to something. Now, it's none of my business, but I take it you've planned a honeymoon?'

'Yes, I was going to surprise Sarah. We were to go touring on my motorbike for the next week and stop over at pubs along the way. I thought she'd like it. We will only be back at Woolworths a few days before I have to report for duty.'

George thought for a moment. How could he tell this young man that his daughter was not as keen on riding on two wheels as her new husband was? Ruby had told George how quiet she was after her trip with Alan earlier on in the year. 'Leave it with me, lad. I'll pop down the phone box and make a call. You go enjoy the party, and whatever you do, don't say one word to my daughter until I give you the nod.'

'OK. Cheers, George.'

'You'll learn, Alan. Get a few years of marriage under your belt and you'll know how to keep out of trouble.'

'Don't forget to save the top tier for the christening!' Vera called out as Sarah and Alan cut the wedding cake together.

'That's jumping the gun. Or at least I hope it is,' Irene sniffed, giving Alan a glare. 'Plenty of time for children later on, when this war is over.'

'Mum, please,' Sarah hissed, feeling embarrassed to be discussing her married life in front of the many people who had crowded into number thirteen to share the couple's happy day.

Ruby spotted Sarah's discomfort. 'Let's cut the cake up and have a slice with a cup of tea, shall we?'

'I'd rather have a sherry with mine, if it's all the same to you,' Vera said, holding out an empty glass.

'I'll help you, Mother,' Irene said, getting to her feet. 'There's a knack to cutting a wedding cake and pouring sherry,' she added, taking the glass from Vera.

'I'd like to say a few words,' George announced.

'Whatever for, George?' Irene asked as she brandished Ruby's best bread knife ready to cut up the cake. 'You made your speech this afternoon. There's no need to hog the limelight. It's Sarah's day, not yours.'

George ran his fingers round his starched collar trying to ignore Irene and the knife. 'I'd just like to give Sarah and Alan a wedding present.'

Irene frowned. 'We gave them a canteen of cutlery, George.'

'This is a little extra.' He cleared his throat. 'With everything that's gone on today, we can all agree that perhaps the outbreak of war is not the best time to start married life, but I know we all

201

wish Sarah and Alan the very best.' He held out an envelope to Sarah. 'Here's a little something for you to start off your life together. It's to help build on those memories you are always talking about, Sarah.'

Sarah took the envelope from George. She spotted Betty nodding wisely from where she was sitting by the piano with Alan's mum, Maureen. Sarah had taken Betty's advice and had told her dad about making memories. Inside was a key and a slip of paper with an address. She passed it to Alan, who looked equally puzzled.

'Come on, lad, tell us what it is,' Ruby called out as she placed slices of rich fruit cake covered in marzipan and sparkling white icing onto her best meat plate. 'This cake will be ready to hand out soon and we all want to know what the gift is.'

George helped himself to a chunk of white icing with a silver leaf attached and licked his fingers. 'It's the key to my car so Alan can borrow it to drive Sarah to their honeymoon.'

'Honeymoon?' Sarah asked, looking puzzled. 'Alan, I thought we'd decided to take a few day trips rather than go away?'

'Now you can enjoy yourself for a few days instead of being under your nan's feet,' George added.

'Don't bother me none who's under my feet. I like a full house. Besides, you and Rene will still be here,' Ruby butted in.

'No, you're wrong, Mother. We are driving back to Devon tomorrow, as I have a luncheon appointment with the ladies' golf team on Tuesday ... George?'

'Sorry, love. We can go back by train. Alan and Sarah need the car more than we do at the moment.' He leant close to his wife. 'I'll explain later.'

'I hope so, George. Here, have some cake.'

Sarah peered at the slip of paper. 'What does it say, Alan?'

Alan looked at George with a puzzled expression on his face.

'It's an address in Whitstable for a boarding house. I stayed there once when I had to travel to the other side of Kent for work. The landlady is expecting you there in the morning, and you are booked in for the week. It's all paid for, so enjoy yourselves and try and stop worrying about everything, Sarah. What will be will be,' George said.

Sarah flung her arms around George. 'Thank you so much, Dad. It's the perfect present.'

'The warm sun is marvellous. You wouldn't think it was September, would you? I feel quite sleepy.' Sarah stretched out on the rug that Alan had laid on the beach. They'd found a sandy patch between the pebbles and, after sharing a picnic, were enjoying the sun on their faces while looking out to sea. Among the few fishing boats out in the estuary were gunmetal-grey ships heading with determination out to sea. Just looking at them gave Sarah the shivers. She'd close her mind to everything except the beautiful weather, the honeymoon and her devoted husband. Alan was an attentive lover. Any fears she'd had about their first time together had been swept away as they explored each other's bodies and he gently showed her just how much he adored her. Sarah spent the night in Alan's arms, her head against his chest, listening to his steady heartbeat as he slept, unable to believe how much she was loved and how wonderful their life together would be…

'Wake up, sleepyhead. Are you going to snooze all afternoon?'

Sarah awoke to find Alan leaning over her. 'Goodness, did I sleep for long? You should have woken me.'

'I didn't like to. You looked so peaceful and without a care in the world. I want to memorize every detail of your beautiful face, even the scattering of freckles that you hate so much.'

Sarah rubbed her face. 'It's the sun. It always happens.' She stopped rubbing her face and froze. 'Why do you need to memorize…? Oh, Alan, no! The RAF can't have you yet.' She sat up quickly and reached for her husband. 'When?'

Alan took her hands and kissed both palms before looking into her eyes, where he could see unshed tears. 'Be strong, Sarah. We knew it was going to happen soon. I've had the letter since before our wedding. I didn't want to spoil our day. God knows Hitler did his damnedest, but we managed to have a great day despite the outbreak of war, and I swear to you nothing will spoil our life together. I may be away for a while, but you'll be here in my heart and I'll be thinking of you all the time.'

Sarah smiled; she had to be brave for Alan. He mustn't see that her heart was breaking. 'Perhaps you shouldn't think of me too much while you're flying your plane. We don't want you having an accident, now do we?'

'Oh, my love, I'll hate being away from you, but I promise it will pass quickly; then we can plan for our future. I'll be manager of a branch of Woolworths and you can be mother to our brood of children and make our own mothers proud grandmothers.'

Sarah smiled and bit her lip to remind herself not to cry. 'I'm not sure that my mother will like the title. She's sure to say it makes her feel too old.'

'Whatever name she uses, she is sure to love any child of yours. George will be chuffed to bits. I can see him taking our lad fishing and teaching him to ride a bike.' He helped Sarah to her feet and reached for the rug. 'I told George about my call-up letter on the day of our wedding.'

'Is that why he sprang this honeymoon surprise on us?'

'Yes. He thought you would like it more than what I had planned, and he wanted us to have some time to ourselves before I left.'

'My goodness. Whatever did you plan?'

Alan's face lit up. 'A tour on Bessie, and we would stay overnight in different pubs and inns.'

Sarah tried not to laugh. Bless Dad for stepping in she thought, as she linked arms with Alan. 'I'm sure it would have been lovely, Alan, but Dad's surprise means we can spend more time together, rather than me sitting behind you as we travel around the countryside.'

There, she thought, my first white lie to my husband, but it was for the best. She'd not tell him just yet that she preferred to walk on her own two feet than sit on Bessie and be shaken to pieces. For the short time she had him to herself, she didn't wish to disappoint Alan in any way.

'When do you have to leave, Alan? Please don't say we have to cut our honeymoon short.'

'No, we have a few days at home before I set off for Scotland and my training period. I'm hoping that if I pass all my exams, I'll be posted at an airfield in the south of England so I can come home as much as possible. It'll give us something to look forward to.'

'Alan, please, there's no need to try to cheer me up. Wherever you are posted, we will find a way to be together as much as possible. I won't lie. It will be strange not to see you every day. I don't think we've missed seeing each other ever since the day I started work at Woolworths.'

'Dear old Woolies. Make sure you write to me as much as possible and tell me everything that happens at work. Keep an eye on young Ginger so he doesn't get the sack for slacking.'

'I will, I promise.'

'There's something else I need to ask you,' Alan added as he helped Sarah over the pebbles, away from the beach and pretty harbour, and towards a narrow passageway between fishermen's cottages that led towards the High Street. 'Do you think we could move into Mum's house? She's all alone apart from her friends at Woolies, and once I'm in the RAF, I don't like to think of her alone when the air raids start. I've decorated the whole house for her, and the cellar's as safe as Ruby's Anderson shelter if things get bad.'

Sarah liked her mother-in-law a lot, but to

move from Nan's would be a big wrench. Then again, it was only a street away, and Nan had more people close to hand, as well as Dad visiting most weeks for his work. She didn't like to think that Alan would be miles from home worrying about his mother.

'Of course I will. I'm sorry I never thought of it myself. Why don't we buy some of those funny postcards and let her know to expect us? We can move in properly before you leave for training.'

Alan kissed her cheek. 'You are an absolute darling. I can go away knowing that everyone is happy and taken care of. Why don't I treat us to afternoon tea and we can write the cards and get them in the post this afternoon? There's a tea room just over the road. We may even get toasted teacakes if we're lucky.'

'Here you are, loves. A pot of tea for two, toasted teacake for one and a slice of Victoria sandwich for the other. I'd leave the pot to brew for a few minutes if you like it stronger, and I'll bring you out a jug of water to top it up.'

'Thank you. It looks lovely,' said Sarah, gazing at the enormous slice of cake sandwiched with strawberry jam. 'It looks delicious. I'm not sure I can eat it all.'

'I'm sure you'll do your best, and what you can't eat I bet your young man can finish off.'

'Husband,' Alan said as he bit into his teacake. 'We're on our honeymoon.'

'Well, bless my soul. With all the awful news we've had lately, you nigh on made my day. When was the wedding?'

Sarah blushed. 'Sunday just gone.'

The waitress sat down. 'That's a day to remember and no mistake. So where do you hail from?'

'Erith,' they both said at the same time.

'I know it well. I come from Woolwich. Moved down here and took on the cafe after my husband's brother retired. It's a good life, but I miss the area I grew up in. I go back as often as I can to visit the family and go shopping. You can't beat the shops up that way, but then you'd know that, as Erith has a fair few.'

'We do have some good shops, as well as the river. In fact, we both work at Woolworths. That's where we met,' Sarah said proudly.

'You don't say? I worked at the Woolwich branch myself for a while before I married. If we ever moved back home, I'd be on their doorstep like a shot asking for a job.' The lady, who had told them she was called Mavis, looked wistful.

'Surely it's safer down here than nearer to London?' Sarah asked.

'I dunno, love. Look up the estuary. See those large things that look like flying elephants? They're barrage balloons. Supposed to stop enemy planes getting to London. My old fella says if they can't get up to the Smoke, then they're more likely to bomb us. Well, that did it for me. We had the grandchildren evacuated last week, the pair of 'em packed off who knows where – somewhere in Wales is all we know – and now my daughter, Sandra, won't leave her bed she's that upset. I told her she's bound to hear where they are living before too long and they're probably having a whale of a time.'

'She must be upset. I know I would be too,' Sarah sympathized. She'd seen a crocodile of young children heading for Erith Station only last week wearing labels tied to their coats and carrying small bags for their clothes and a gas mask over their shoulders. The children seemed excited, but she recalled well the drawn faces of the parents and that some of the mothers were reduced to tears.

The woman wiped her eyes with her pinafore and stood to her feet. 'I'll get you that hot water. Enjoy your tea.'

'It seems wrong somehow.'

'What, writing a few postcards?' Alan asked.

'No, us being so happy and all. This is a seaside town – why would little children be in danger here?'

'I'm no expert,' Alan said, wiping melted butter from his chin, 'but I'd think the whole Kent coast would be tempting to the enemy. Think of all the boats heading in and out of London, let alone the fishing boats. Hit this area and it could affect our navy as well as supplies of fish and all that.' He didn't add that they could also be invaded from the Channel if the Germans reached the coast-line of France.

Sarah shook her head. 'So would the RAF protect the seaside towns as well as the cities?'

'I dare say they would, but until I've done my training, I won't know what's expected of me.' Alan saw Sarah's face drop. He reached across the table and squeezed her hand. 'I did promise you that I wouldn't do anything dangerous, so stop looking so sad and pour me a cup of tea. I've got a feeling that if we don't polish off every crumb, we're going to be in trouble with our new friend.'

Sarah grinned and poured milk into their cups before picking up the teapot. All the same she felt the now familiar shiver run through her as if someone was walking over her grave.

Later that night, as they snuggled up in the large double bed, Alan whispered into Sarah's ear, 'I've had an idea.'

Sarah giggled as his breath tickled her neck. 'What would that be?'

'Let's make ourselves a promise that we will come here next year to celebrate our first anniversary, shall we? We can sunbathe on the beach and go to Mavis's tea room for one of her roast dinners she told us about.'

Sarah shoved Alan playfully. 'Alan Gilbert, I think you're more interested in coming back to Whitstable for a roast dinner than to celebrate our marriage.'

Alan laughed and pulled his wife close. 'I think we both know that isn't true.' As his lips met hers in the room, which was lit only by moonlight, he fervently hoped that a year from now the war would be over and they would both be safe.

16

'This is for me? It's so pretty. Thank you.' Freda admired the dainty bracelet made of shells that Sarah had just given her and put it on her wrist.

'It's just a little something from Whitstable to say thank you for looking out for Nan while I was away.'

'It was more like her looking after us. I swear I've doubled in size with all the food she's stuffed into us,' Maisie added as she admired her brooch, made from similar shells to Freda's bracelet. 'We took her to the Odeon to see *Goodbye, Mr Chips.*'

'It was lovely. I did cry at the end,' Freda sighed.

'I thought they were closing the cinemas for the duration?' Sarah said.

'The Odeon was only closed a few days, and when it opened, we thought we'd better nip round there quick before the government changed its mind and closed the cinemas for good.'

'That would be unbearable,' Freda said indignantly. 'I couldn't go without my weekly visit to the pictures. How does Alan feel now he only has a couple of days left at work before he joins the RAF?'

'He hasn't said much. As for me, I'm dreading the day he leaves Erith.'

'Chin up. He'll be home on leave before you know it. Fancy another cup of tea?' Maisie said, getting to her feet. 'We've got time before the end of our tea break. We came up late.'

Sarah checked the clock on the wall. 'I'd best not. I have to see Betty in five minutes.'

'Miss Billington,' Maisie called over her shoulder as she headed to the counter. 'No familiarity, please. We are at work now.'

Freda and Sarah laughed together as Sarah leant close to her friend. 'It's good to be back to normal after the wedding and everything. Tell me, how is Maisie coping now that her Joe's off in the army?'

'You know what Maisie's like – always the life and soul of the party, but it's a game she's playing. For all their arguing, Joe and Maisie are devoted to each other and she's missing him so much, but me and your nan have kept her busy. Maisie might think she's been looking after Ruby, but the truth is, it's been the other way round. Ruby kept asking her to help out in the garden, and then she hinted she'd never seen *Goodbye, Mr Chips* when she'd been to Dartford to see it with Vera from up the road only a couple of days before. We had a good time, though.'

Sarah checked the clock on the wall of the staff canteen again. 'Look, I have to dash, but I've had a thought. It means talking to Nan, and it also affects you, as you may want to move back into number thirteen. You know there's always a place for you there. I just wondered if we could talk Maisie into moving into my old bedroom. She'd be happier living with Nan than with her mother-in-law. Now that me and Alan are living with Maureen until we get our own place, there's plenty of room at Nan's. What do you think?'

Freda nodded her head. 'It sounds like a good idea to me. I'm not planning to move out of my digs just yet. Perhaps we could talk about it more on Sunday? There'll be time while we're in Margate. That's if you don't mind? It'll be your last day with Alan before he heads off for his training camp.'

'I think Alan will be able to spare me for a few minutes. He'll probably have his own views on it as well. I'm looking forward to the trip. I heard it may be the last time the paddle steamer does pleasure trips, as it's going to be used for more important work while this war is going on. Such a pity, as it is fun to travel on the Thames down to the seaside.'

Freda grinned. 'I can't wait. I've wanted to go to the seaside ever since I saw the poster on the platform at Charing Cross Station when I travelled down here. It'll be such fun. Even if we are at war,' Freda added quickly.

'Thank you for coming to see me, Sarah. There are a few things I need to go over with you.'

Sarah sat in front of her boss in the small office. Paperwork was heaped upon the desk and Betty looked harassed. The last time she'd seen her was as family and friends waved her and Alan off on their honeymoon. They'd spent their first night in the Wheatley Arms Hotel in the town before setting off for Whitstable after breakfast. Thanks to her dad, it had been a wonderful honeymoon that she would never forget. Betty had still been wearing her bridesmaid dress as she waved from the pavement, her pretty headdress slightly askew after hours of singing. It seemed strange now to see her in a formal suit sitting across from her desk. Sarah wondered if she should call her Betty or Miss Billington.

'Sarah, I'm so relieved to see you back at work. As you can see, I'm snowed under here. Half the male staff have either joined up or given us notice of when they leave our employ. Some of the female staff have left to work at the Vickers factory as well. I understand the pay is very good.' Betty didn't look happy as she checked a list in front of her. 'It does leave us with rather a staffing problem.'

'If it's any help, I don't plan to give up my job. Alan leaves for his RAF training on Monday and I'd like to work as many hours as possible so I don't have time to think about what is happening to him.'

Betty smiled. She knew that Sarah would be worried about her husband while he was away but would still work hard when called to do so. Sarah Caselton, or Sarah Gilbert, as she was now, would not shirk her duties. 'I'm pleased to know we shan't lose you just yet. In fact, I have a change of job for you. That's if you are interested?'

Sarah frowned. She liked working on the stationery counter. She wouldn't be so keen to be moved to some of the other areas of Woolies. Especially not the vegetable counter, or indeed haberdashery and knitting wool. Nan and Freda had both patiently taught her how to fashion items out of wool, but it was still a struggle, and she was still surprised when a sock or balaclava appeared after hours of sweating over those knitting needles. To be faced with wool and needles every day at work would only remind her that she just didn't have the skill required to be a proficient knitter.

'I'll help if you think I'm suitable, but I'm not sure I'd be much good on some of the counters.'

Betty could see that Sarah was concerned. 'There's no need to look so worried, Sarah. I'm thinking more of a promotion than moving you to another counter.'

'Promotion? I know we had a conversation about me one day possibly making supervisor, but I didn't think it would be so quick.'

'We live in changing times. With our menfolk off to war, it leaves us women to keep things on an even keel ready for their return.'

Sarah nodded. She could see the sense in her boss's words. 'What would my duties include?'

'To begin with, you will assume the job title of supervisor, and there will be a pay rise alongside your increase for reaching twenty-one years of age, but I'd like you to work with me rather than on the shop floor.' She waved her hands above the pile of ledgers and papers on her desk. 'Not only do I have extra duties working alongside Mr Benfield, but there's all this paperwork. New staff require training, and then there are the duties of fire watch and making sure all our staff know what to do if there's an air raid.' She ran her hands through her hair and sighed. 'I'm drowning under all this work.'

'Well, you have me to help you now. Where shall we start?'

Betty checked her wristwatch. 'I have to be in a meeting with Mr Benfield in half an hour. We have visitors coming down from head office. There are three young ladies starting this morning and I have to finish a report. Would you take the new staff? They need to collect their uniforms and have the beginner's talk. I usually do that in here, as you know. Perhaps if you took the girls to the staffroom, there should be time before the next tea break to go through the ropes and give them a tour of the shop floor.' She rummaged on her desk and pulled out a file and a clipboard. 'Here are their details and the sections where I'd like them to work. Use your judgement as to where you feel each girl should be placed. Their uniforms are on the top of the cupboard by the door.'

Sarah took the paperwork and tucked the overalls under her arm. Before she left the office, she turned to Betty, who was already busy writing in a ledger. 'Betty, thank you for trusting me with this job. I promise I'll do my best to make you proud of me.'

Betty smiled. 'I know you'll make a good supervisor, Sarah. That's why I offered you the job. I think we will make a good team.'

'I think so too,' Sarah grinned as she headed outside to where three young girls were waiting to start their new jobs.

'Follow me,' she beckoned, leading them towards the staffroom, where the delicious aroma of lamb stew was coming from the kitchen area. She waved to Maureen, who was busy mixing flour and beef suet to make dumplings. 'Take your coats off and find yourselves a seat, ladies. Would you like a cup of tea?'

The three girls accepted shyly, not making eye contact with the self-assured woman they saw in

216

front of them.

'Bless 'em, they look terrified,' Maureen said as she poured strong tea into the four cups on the counter. 'A new intake, I suppose?'

Sarah, who was piling slices of seed cake onto a plate, licked her fingers and nodded. 'Yes, I'm about to show them the ropes before they start down on the shop floor. It's part of my new job,' she added quietly, not sure how her mother-in-law would view Sarah's promotion. She needn't have worried.

Maureen wiped her floury hands on her apron, rushed round to the other side of the counter and hugged Sarah until she was fit to burst. 'I'm that proud of you, my love. Alan will be too. I take it he doesn't know yet?'

'No. Miss Billington has only just told me about it. It's not a management job or anything. It's just that she needs help while we are short-staffed.'

'Don't you put yourself down, my girl. It's as good as being management. You're in the office. Look at Alan. He might be a trainee manager, but he's never out of that warehouse coat, and nine times out of ten he's got a broom in his hand.'

'He's got prospects, though,' Sarah added quickly in defence of her hard-working husband, 'and Woolworths have told him that his job will be here for him when he returns after the war.' She chewed her lip thoughtfully. 'I wonder how long that'll be.'

'Well, it can't be soon enough for me. If I could get my hands on that Mr Hitler, I'd wring his bloody neck for making all this trouble. Whatever does his mother think of him, causing all this war

217

nonsense? If he was mine, I'd box his ears for him.'

Sarah smiled. Maureen sounded just like Nan when she got talking about the war. They might only be a week in, but it was all anyone spoke about. She knew her mother-in-law was worried, even though she put on a brave face.

'Alan will do his best, Maureen, and I'm sure he will be back to visit us both as soon as he can. He won't be away training forever; and with a bit of luck he will be based down our end of the country.'

'But he won't be at home in the mornings to bring in the coal and eat the breakfast I put on the table, will he?'

Sarah could see Maureen was getting upset. 'No, he won't, and we will both miss him, but I'm living with you now and we must both show him we can cope on our own until he comes home. We don't want him worrying about us, now do we? Mind you, he'll moan something rotten if you don't have that stew cooked when he comes up here for his dinner break later on. Him and everyone else at Woolies.'

'Oh my,' Maureen said, straightening her apron and rushing back round the counter. 'I'd best get on. Now, can you tell that Miss Billington that if there are any spare staff to be had, I'd like some help here? More people seem to be eating at work at the moment and I'm fair pushed at times to get all my jobs done.'

'I'll make sure to mention it – don't you worry.' Sarah picked up the tray of tea and cake, and took it to the table, where she spent the next half-hour running through the duties required of the

218

three young newcomers before heading towards the narrow staircase to show them to the counters where they'd be working.

Arriving at the door to the shop, she bumped into Alan as he struggled through with a couple of boxes in his arms. He placed them on the ground before kissing his new bride soundly, much to her embarrassment. Sarah was proud that her new husband had insisted on returning to work for the few days between their honeymoon and heading off to join the RAF. At least she got to see him while he was at work too.

'Alan, please,' she scolded as she wriggled away from him. 'I'm working.' She indicated the three young girls, who had burst into giggles. 'It's not that funny,' she insisted, trying hard not to grin and to act as she thought a supervisor should. 'This is my husband, Mr Gilbert. He is a trainee manager and is about to join the RAF to fly Spitfires.'

This silenced the three young girls, who looked at Alan in awe.

'Now, let's get you three working or it'll be time to stop for your dinner break.' She ushered the girls through the door as Alan caught her arm and frowned.

'What's all this about?'

'Miss Billington has promoted me to supervisor and I'm helping her by getting the new staff working, as she has a meeting with people from head office.'

He quickly stole another kiss before Sarah could escape through the door. She would love to have lingered in his arms but was aware of her charges waiting and the possibility of being seen by other staff members, let alone the customers. 'Well done, my love. I'm really proud of you. We will have to celebrate before I leave for Scotland.'

'Don't be daft – it's not important. Besides, we're off to Margate the day after tomorrow, and you will be leaving early the morning after.'

'Then we will have to celebrate when we are alone,' he said, running a finger across her lips.

Sarah shivered with delight. She would miss Alan when he left Erith. However would she cope?

'You look like a mother hen with yer little chicks,' Maisie called out as Sarah passed by her counter. 'Where are you going with the youngsters?'

Sarah stopped and ushered the girls to where Maisie was unpacking teapots from a hamper and wiping each one with a cloth before adding it to an impressive display on the high mahogany counter. 'These are the latest intake of new staff. Two are working with Freda on haberdashery, and the other is on household goods.'

'Two more on haberdashery? Whatever is the world coming to?'

'They're short-staffed. Freda was thrilled to be transferred to that counter. She's wanted to work there ever since she joined Woolies. Two girls have gone off to work in a factory. I just hope Freda doesn't get any silly ideas about joining them.'

'Too late for that. She's got some bee in her bonnet about doing her bit for the war effort and reckons working at Burndept's factory will mean she's doing something more than working in a shop,' Maisie said as she blew hard on a teapot lid,

220

sending dust and bits of straw towards the three girls, who stood staring at Maisie, looking as glamorous as ever even though she was hard at work.

'Oh dear, that's all we need. I'll have a word with her. I don't like to think of her down at the factory. They employ hundreds of staff and it's hard graft. I'm not sure Freda's up to it.'

'She can take care of herself. It's not as if she'll be working miles away. The factory is only down the road, and her digs are close by. Then again, perhaps she'll move in with Ruby now she's on her own?'

Now that Maisie had mentioned the living arrangements at number thirteen, Sarah couldn't miss the opportunity to ask if she would move in with Ruby herself. 'No, I think she's happy where she is, and if she does go to work at Burndept's, it'll be even closer than Alexandra Road.' Sarah fiddled with a box of silver teaspoons, which Maisie had displayed close to the teapots. 'Actually, Maisie, I wonder if you'd do me a favour.' She looked to where the new girls were waiting patiently nearby.

'Well, spit it out. We ain't got all day.'

'I wondered if you fancied moving in with Nan. I'm worried about her now she's on her own. I know Dad will be popping in when he's up this way, but with the chance of bombing and all, she shouldn't be on her own, should she?'

'Gawd love you. That's the best thing I've been asked in a long while. I'd go home and pack right now if I didn't have these bleeding teapots to sort out. I swear if the old bat reminds me one more time that her son has done me a favour by marrying me, I'll swing for 'er.'

Sarah was relieved that her friend accepted the invitation so quickly. She knew that behind Maisie's bravado there was a very sad woman who was missing the man she loved. She looked at the large clock on the wall of the store. If she didn't get a move on and get the new girls to their sections, she would be stripped of her supervisor status before she'd even done a whole day's work. 'Look, I need to get cracking. Do you mind if I tell Nan a little white lie?'

Maisie grinned. 'As far as I'm concerned, you can tell her a whopping great big lie as long as I can move into number thirteen and escape the mother-in-law as soon as possible. She does nothing but harp on about how her Joe could have done so much better than me. She thinks I've got nowhere to go.'

'Well, she's wrong, isn't she? Look, I just want Nan to think that you are moving in because of Joe being away and the situation with his mum. I need to know she won't be alone if anything should happen.'

'It's hardly a lie, is it, ducks.'

Sarah felt a tug of guilt. Was she really tricking her friend into moving in with Nan? Really, it was all for the good. 'As long as you don't let on to Nan. You know how independent she is.'

Maisie tapped the side of her nose. 'A nod's as good as a wink, ducks. Now, you go sort yer young brood out, while I finish stacking the crocks. I'm supposed to get this job finished before dinner break and it's a bit touch and go as it is without standing here chatting to you.'

She gave Sarah a broad wink before turning to the task of displaying her teapots.

Sarah ushered the girls through the queuing customers, content that she'd done her best to keep her mate cheerful and her nan with a companion during the dark days ahead.

'What time are you off, Alan?' George asked as he handed his son-in-law a pint of bitter.

Alan took a gulp of the dark brown liquid and wiped his mouth. 'Early tomorrow morning. They've given me a train pass, so at least Sarah won't be worried about me riding Bessie all the way to Scotland.'

George patted Alan's shoulder. 'It's for the best Women don't take to motorbikes like we do. They fuss about their hair and their clothes. I always fancied one myself. I told Irene we could have a motorbike with a sidecar and she nigh on went through the roof. She was hell to live with for weeks until I bought the car. Don't tell her I said so, but I'm glad now we got the car. It's handier for when I have to drive up from Devon. I'm not as young as you, Alan. I like to keep dry and warm these days.'

Alan nodded. He could see George's point. No doubt when he was older and had a couple of nippers, he'd feel the same. He looked at his watch. 'I suppose we'd better go find the women-folk. Is Irene in Dreamland with the others?'

'There's no rush, lad. We've got time for another pint. Irene went for a walk. She's not one for funfairs. She said she'd meet us all for tea later before heading back to *The Kentish Queen* and home. Ted Sayers was telling me there won't be many more leisure trips on the steamer. He's talking about carrying cargo up and down the Thames instead.'

'I can't see many people wanting to take pleasure trips. There's no knowing how safe it's gonna be on the river.'

The two men gazed out over the Margate seafront deep in thought. The mild September weather had drawn families out for a day on the beach. Children were digging in the sand making castles, while their parents sat on deckchairs and enjoyed the warmth of the autumn sun. If it weren't for a number of visitors in uniform and most people carrying gas masks, it could have been any sunny day at the popular Kent seaside resort. Behind the pub where George and Alan were enjoying a pint could be heard the screams of excitement from people tasting the delights of Dreamland.

'Do you think they'll all be here this time next year enjoying the sunshine?' Alan asked.

George finished the last of the beer. 'There's no point in asking things like that, lad. Who knows? As long as Dreamland is open and people are allowed onto the beach, there'll be those who will come and enjoy themselves like they always have. This war could run on for a few months or years, but people won't let it get them down. Fancy another?'

'Just half, thanks, George. Then I'll go see what the girls are up to. Young Freda's that excited. You'd think she'd never been to the seaside before.'

'There you are!'

The two men turned to find Sarah approaching them.

'I've come to see if my husband wants a trip through the water caves with me. Mum'll have your guts for garters if she finds you the worse for wear, Dad.'

'I've only had the one, love,' George was quick to point out.

Sarah kissed her dad's cheek before linking her arm through Alan's. 'Why not go find Nan? She said she fancied a plate of winkles. You know you like them, Dad.'

George licked his lips. 'I might just do that while your mum's not about. She's not as partial to seafood as we are.' He rubbed his hands together and headed into Dreamland ahead of Alan and Sarah.

'Bless him. Dad likes the simple things in life. Not like Mum.' Sarah giggled. 'It's such a shame they don't share the same interests anymore,' she added thoughtfully. 'You don't think we'll ever get like them, do you?'

'What, me sneaking off for a plate of winkles with your nan, you mean?' Alan asked, tucking her hand into the pocket of his jacket.

'No, well, yes, I suppose that is what I mean. Let's enjoy everything together, Alan. Let's never have secrets from each other or drift apart. We have to be together forever, just like we said in our wedding vows.'

'Forever's a long time, Sarah.'

'But we vowed we would, and in church too.'

'I'm sure we will share as much as we can and

be as close as any married couple can be, but we also have a war to get through, and who knows how long our own forever is going to last?'

Sarah stopped and faced her husband, pulling her hand away from his. 'No. I won't listen to you talking like this. I refuse to think we will be parted for long. This war won't last forever and then we'll be together until we grow old and grey. Promise me, Alan?'

Alan could see the fear in his wife's blue eyes. This wasn't how he wanted to spend his last day as a civilian. He needed Sarah to be brave and happy. He couldn't bear to leave knowing she was sad. 'Darling wife, I promise we will live to be a hundred years old and be overrun with grand-children and great-grandchildren. We'll be a proper Darby and Joan. How does that suit you?'

'That'll do for now. But I'll hold you to your promise, Alan. Look, here are the water caves. Let's join the queue before the others find us.'

Sarah cosied up to Alan as the round tub-type boat headed into the darkened caves. It was chilly, and the sound of water dripping down the man-made walls caused her to shiver and hug Alan even closer. She could hear the whispers of other day-trippers in front and behind them, but here, in the darkness, for all intents and purposes they were alone. 'Say goodbye to me now, Alan.'

'Darling, I'm not leaving until tomorrow morning.'

'But this might be the last time we are really alone. Even at Maureen's house we won't really be alone, as she will be in the next bedroom.'

Alan understood what Sarah meant and for the

next few minutes they whispered their goodbyes and planned what they'd do when they next met. Sarah promised not to cry as she waved him off at the station, and Alan promised to wave to his wife until the train left Erith Station, heading towards London and then Scotland on his own personal adventure. They both fervently hoped that by Christmas Alan would be able to join her in Erith, a fully trained Spitfire pilot.

'That was so much fun. When can we go again?' Freda was still excited from her day in Margate.

'Blimey, ducks, we ain't even home yet. You've just stopped feeling sick from too much candy-floss and chips. It's a bloody good job you didn't have those jellied eels as well or you'd be hanging over the side of this boat all the way home to Erith,' Maisie laughed.

'Honest, I'm all right, Maisie. I wouldn't mind a cup of tea, though, if there's one going?'

'You stay here and get some fresh air and I'll bring up the tea. You don't want to be below deck, as it's a bit on the stuffy side down there. It's not the best place to be if you are still feeling a bit rough, and you do look it to me, whatever you say.' Maisie gave Freda a quick hug and disappeared down the steps to where the refreshments were on sale.

Despite her happiness, Freda *was* still feeling a little green around the gills, but she didn't want to be a bother to her friends. The mention of jellied eels hadn't helped. All the same, it had been a grand day and she swore to visit the seaside again soon, regardless of Hitler and the war.

She gazed out across the darkening sky towards the riverbank on the Essex side of the Thames. If only she knew where her brother, Lenny, was. It had been over nine months since she arrived in Erith, and apart from the letter postmarked 'Erith' and sent while she was still at home, and that dodgy-looking chap arriving at her old digs, she was no closer to knowing where he was. However, she did know he was not in prison, or whatever it was they called the place where he'd been locked up, otherwise that bloke wouldn't have come looking for her to get to Lenny.

Shifting her view of the river to look towards London, past the many ships that were on the skyline, she could see barrage balloons high in the sky like giant elephants, waiting to stop any enemy plane that dared get near the capital. She sighed. Was she wrong in coming to Erith? Should she instead be looking for her brother elsewhere? And was it safe for Lenny now that war had been declared? How would a young lad cope alone at a time like this? She knew the one place he wouldn't be, and that was at home. No, neither of them was likely to return to the Midlands if they could help it. She would have loved to have moved back into Ruby's house at Alexandra Road, but she didn't want to bring any trouble to number thirteen if the dodgy bloke came calling again. It was best she stay put for now. Besides, she liked her digs, and if she did decide to work at Burndept's, it was closer to the factory. She may hear something about Lenny if she worked among hundreds of people rather than at Woolworths. She'd give it some more thought once she felt a bit brighter.

'Why the glum face, Freda? Are you still feeling sick?' Ruby stood beside her and sniffed the air. 'It can be a bit ripe on the river sometimes, but today ain't so bad. Although, if you aren't so used to the pong, it can turn your stomach.'

Freda shook herself. She didn't want the Caseltons to think she had a problem. They were like a second family to her now. In fact, a first family, as she could barely recall her own dad anymore. 'I'm fine, thank you, Mrs C., just a bit tired what with all the excitement.'

Unbeknown to Freda, Ruby had been watching the young girl as she'd stood deep in thought. There was something on the kid's mind and she'd be sure to get to the bottom of it or her name wasn't Ruby Caselton.

17

'It's not quite the same, is it? But it'll have to do.' Betty Billington stepped back from the front-window display of the Erith branch of Woolworths, carefully avoiding passing pedestrians, and placed her hands on her hips. 'What do you think, Sarah?'

Sarah tipped her head to one side and looked intently at the main window, as well as the two smaller windows either side of the double doors that led into the store. 'It's not the same as last year, but it's still festive. Not that our customers can see much with all this anti-blast tape stuck over the windows.'

Sarah thought it was a shame that the usually highly polished curved windows, set in dark mahogany frames, blocked out so much of what was on display for the Christmas shoppers. The months leading up to Christmas 1939 had been full of anticipation for the residents of Erith. So far no bombs had dropped, but everyone wondered whether today would be the day that Hitler's armies tried to invade or a bomb would drop on their home. There was also thought at all times of loved ones who were serving in the forces. Were they overseas or still at home? No one knew for sure, but in each home wives and mothers prayed for their menfolk's safe return. Daughters, too, were joining the services or volunteering in other ways. The country was prepared, but when would it all really begin?

Gas masks were still diligently carried everywhere, and in each branch of Woolworths staff had been trained in what to do if their store should be damaged in an attack or if there was a fire. One of Sarah's duties as supervisor was to make sure that all staff knew their place and the part they needed to play if there should be an attack. They already participated in fire-watch duties, although the time was usually spent knitting or playing cards.

'I do wish we could light the window display more, but the government have been so strict about us illuminating the street and alerting the enemy if they should fly over.'

Maisie, who had been sweeping the pavement in front of the store, another one of her duties since young Ginger had been called up, looked towards the sky. 'It makes you wonder why Hitler would want his planes to fly all this way just to drop a bomb on Erith Woolies, doesn't it? A bit of light in front of our shop shouldn't do any harm.'

'It's not just Woolworths, though, Maisie. Think of all the shops in the High Street and Pier Road. If they all had their lights blazing away, then the enemy pilots would be able to see from their maps that this is Erith and nearby are the docks, as well as factories that are doing important war work. Put them out of action and we could have Hitler marching through our towns in no time,' Betty explained.

'Blimey. It makes you think, don't it?' Maisie gasped as the women all looked skywards.

'At least we are no different to all the other shops in town,' Betty added, 'with the Ministry of Home Security allowing us to use only lighting that doesn't reflect into the street.'

Sarah pointed across the road to the Hedley Mitchell store. 'We're in the same boat as Mitchell's, and if I do say so myself, Woolworths has a better window display.'

'I don't even know why you're worrying about a bit of light. It all has to be turned off at dusk so no one can look into the windows anyway,' Maisie declared. 'Now, I'm really cold, so if we've finished out here, can we go in and get warmed up before we all freeze to death?'

'I just want to check that the display of men's gifts looks all right. Do you think we should add anything else?' Betty peered through the gaps in the anti-blast tape. 'What do you think? Will women be interested enough to buy items to send to their loved ones? You both have husbands in the forces. Would you buy presents from Woolworths?'

Sarah glanced at Maisie. They had both laboured for many weeks under the watchful eye of Freda as they knitted warm pullovers for Alan and Joe. More than once Freda had stepped in and helped when Sarah had dropped a row of stitches or Maisie had forgotten which part of the pattern she should have been following and threw her work out of the back door in annoyance. 'I'm wrapping a few little gifts to put under the tree for whenever Alan comes home. He told me he might be back at Christmas for a few days before he is assigned to a squadron. It all depends on what's happening, though. You've made a good selection, Betty. I'll most certainly make some purchases from Woolworths.'

Maisie had gone quiet. Sarah could see her chin starting to wobble. There'd been no news from Joe in months, apart from a postcard with a few brief words. 'I'm sure you'll hear from Joe soon. In no time he'll be back and you will forget he's been away,' Sarah told her chum.

Maisie tried to smile. 'I hope so, but from all the gossip I'm hearing, he'll be in France some-where by now, and look at how many were killed over there in the last war.' She swept the pile of dust and leaves she'd removed from the entrance of the store into the gutter and stretched her back. 'It must be time for a tea break, and I'm chilled to the bone standing out here.'

Sarah went to follow Maisie back inside, but Betty took hold of her arm. 'I sense problems with Maisie and her husband. Am I right?'

'Not a problem between them, but Maisie is missing him so much and her mother-in-law blames Maisie for her son joining up.'

Betty frowned. 'That is ludicrous. Joe would have been conscripted by now even if he hadn't decided to join the army when he did. Is there anything we can do to help?'

'I don't think so, Betty. She brightened up when she moved into number thirteen, but with Christmas approaching and all the magazines she reads telling women to soldier on alone and suggesting ideas for presents for the men at the front, she just seems to be so sad.'

'Oh dear, and there's me asking her about the window displays. Trust me to put my foot right in it. There must be something we can do to cheer her up. How about a trip up to London to see a pantomime? Perhaps we could go as a group and ask Maisie to organize it? That would take her mind off things, wouldn't it?'

'I'm sure it would, Betty. It's a splendid idea. I reckon Maureen and Nan would love to join us. A proper family group.'

Betty smiled at her assistant. 'You have no idea how it warms my heart to be thought of as part of your family, Sarah.'

Sarah linked arms with her boss. 'I'm the one who should be thankful. You've been so good to me and Alan since I joined Woolworths. Goodness, I've cried on your shoulder so many times it's a wonder you haven't turned rusty.'

'I'm sure that one day it'll be my turn to cry on your shoulder and it's good to know you'll be

233

there. Now, let's catch up with Maisie and thaw out with that cup of tea she mentioned. We need to be bright and chirpy for the old soldiers' party this evening.'

'...*down at the Old Bull and Bush, la, la, la, la, la...*'

Maureen grabbed Sarah by the arm as her daughter-in-law entered the staffroom. The sing-song had already started and Maureen, true to form, was leading the old soldiers in the first number. They swayed together side by side, singing loudly until the song finished with a rousing cheer. 'Where have you been, love?'

Sarah yawned. It had been a long day. 'The man I was allocated couldn't make his mind up between a pair of socks or a calendar for his son. Twice we got as far as the door and he changed his mind. I wouldn't have worried, but I'd already wrapped the gifts. After the third time, I raced him up the stairs as quick as possible before he changed his mind again.'

'Rather you than me,' Maureen chuckled. 'I might moan about the long hours in the kitchen to prepare for the party, but I'd rather do that than shop for a grumpy old man.'

'He wasn't too grumpy, but not as much fun as shopping for Alfie last year.' Sarah looked around the crowded room as staff members and guests tucked into sandwiches and cake. Mr Benfield was filling glasses with beer from a barrel balanced on the edge of the counter where Maureen usually dispensed her tasty meals. Every one of them had a smile on their face. 'I can almost imagine he is here with us.'

Sarah still thought fondly of the old man who told her to follow her heart. Was it only a year ago that she'd met Alan and fallen in love? It felt like a lifetime. So much had happened. So many new friends, and hopefully so much to look forward to in the future. A cold chill crept through her body and she shivered.

'What's up, love? Chilly? Have a drop of this – it'll warm you up.' Maureen held out a glass containing a nip of whisky.

'No, I'm fine. It's just something walking over my grave.'

Maureen looked at her daughter-in-law. The girl's face had turned ghostly white. 'Don't you mean *someone* walked over your grave?'

Tears formed in Sarah's eyes. 'I do hope not.'

'Sit yourself down, love. Your breakfast is ready.' Ruby placed a plate of eggs, bacon and fried bread in front of her granddaughter.

'Crikey, Nan. There's enough to feed an army on this plate.' She picked up her knife and fork, unsure of what to eat first.

'You've got a busy day ahead of yourself. The world and his wife'll be wanting to shop in Woolies today. I've even got to pop in there myself to pick up a few last-minute bits and bobs. Thank goodness Christmas Eve is a Sunday. It makes the Christmas holiday a bit longer this year for you girls.'

'I can get them for you, Nan. Write me a list and I'll do it in my break.'

'Oh no, you'll be run off your feet. Besides, it'll be good to stretch my legs and walk into town. I won't be leaving the house again this side of Boxing Day with so many to cook for.'

'You know we'll all help you, Nan. It was good of you to let me stay over Christmas. I know it's a squeeze with Maisie living here now and Mum and Dad due this afternoon.'

'Now, don't you say another word, my girl. It'll be a cold day in hell when I can't have my own granddaughter under my roof at Christmas time. I'm not having you sleeping alone at Maureen's while she's away. Now, tuck in and eat up all that bacon. There'll not be any to be found once it's rationed in January. Have some more butter on your bread before that's scarce as well.'

Sarah smiled to herself. It was lovely to be back at number thirteen with Nan. Even though Maureen made her feel at home, it wasn't the same without Alan there. Tonight Freda would be staying over, so the three girls would be sleeping top to tail in the two single beds and drawing straws for who would have a bed to themselves. Freda had suggested a rota and couldn't understand why her two friends had laughed so much. Since Freda had started helping out with the Girl Guides pack up at the mission hall, she was forever trying to organize them all. Fortunately, Freda had stopped mentioning working at Burndept's factory and Sarah hoped she was happy to stay at Woolworths.

Sarah wondered what Alan was doing. He was nearing the end of his training and she'd hoped that he'd be able to come home for Christmas. She hadn't spoken to him since he left for Scotland. Apart from postcards and a couple of letters signed by her devoted husband, she may well have been a single girl again. Perhaps he was now with his new squadron. At least with this phoney war continuing, she knew he was safe.

'Did I tell you that Vera thought she saw some German soldiers last week?'

Sarah placed her knife and fork down on her plate. 'Wherever did she see them?'

'Woolwich. She'd gone up to the market and there was a couple of them getting off the London train.'

'Oh, Nan. I know I shouldn't laugh, but did she honestly think the Germans would invade by train?'

'You know what Vera's like. Once she gets a bee in her bonnet, she won't let it alone.'

'What happened?'

Ruby sat down and buttered her toast before continuing with the story. 'She decided to follow them to see where they were heading. You know there are barracks in Woolwich?'

'Yes, I know, Nan.'

'Well, she followed them to the gates and was amazed to see the sentries let them enter, so she went up to the sentries as bold as brass and asked what they were playing at. She gave them a right tongue-lashing.'

Sarah held her breath, waiting to hear what happened next.

Ruby stopped to wipe her eyes as tears of laughter ran down her cheeks. 'It turns out they was Canadian soldiers. The silly woman had walked all that way and the lads were on our side. I swear it was hard to keep a straight face when she told me. She was quite indignant that the sentry guards had laughed at her.'

Sarah joined in with her nan's laughter. 'Bless her, we shouldn't really laugh. With a few more like Vera, we could win this war.'

'What's all this giggling about?' Maisie staggered into the kitchen, her dressing gown wrapped haphazardly around her and curlers still in her hair. She stopped to kiss Sarah's cheek. 'Nice to 'ave you back home with us, mate. Blimey, I've never seen so much bacon in me life. Are we breeding pigs now, Ruby?'

'Nan was telling me about Vera and the Germans.'

Maisie pinched a piece of bacon from Sarah's plate. 'Yer nan told me the other day. I thought she was 'aving me on! This bacon's a bit of all right.'

'I'll throw some in the pan for you, Maisie. D'you want some eggs too?'

'A sarnie'll do me with a bit of brown sauce, ta, Mrs C.'

'Here, take mine. I'm full up. Nan's going overboard in case we never see another slice once rationing starts.'

'You don't wanna worry about that. My Joe'll always be able to lay his hands on some. You know he has contacts on the docks...' Maisie went quiet, realizing that Joe wasn't working on the docks anymore; he was somewhere in France.

'He'll be home soon, love, and then we can have bacon every day,' Ruby said.

Sarah hugged her friend. 'Yes, Nan's right. Perhaps even some more of that perfume you like.'

Maisie smiled. 'You're right. I'm going to try hard not to be miserable today. After all, it's nearly Christmas and it's our last day at work. I'd best get myself dressed. Freda said she would be here before work to drop off her suitcase and leave her bits and pieces for Christmas.'

'Have you girls got time for another cuppa before you get to work? It's icy cold out there, so it'll keep you warm on the walk to Woolies,' Ruby said as she headed for the stove, trying not to smile. 'I heard that part of the Thames has frozen over further upriver, and it's chilly enough for it to happen on our stretch. I've never known it so cold.'

'Go on, then,' Maisie said. 'I might even be able to squeeze in that last rasher of bacon Sarah left on her plate. I'll be back in a flash.'

Ruby cut the sandwich in half and left it on the table ready for Maisie, then placed the large frying pan into the stone sink to soak, pouring on hot water from the kettle. 'I've been thinking, Sarah – we need to keep an eye on Maisie over Christmas. She's missing her Joe more than is healthy for her. She puts on a brave face, but every so often it cracks and I can see a very unhappy young woman. What with Maisie and young Freda not having much in the way of close families to speak of, I'm thinking we are very fortunate.'

Sarah hugged her nan. 'You're right there. Thank you for caring for my friends.'

'Well, they look out for me as well. I've not slept alone under my roof since you moved to Maureen's house. Don't think I don't know when you've engineered something, my girl.'

'Nan! I don't know what you mean.' Sarah tried to sound indignant. Had Nan found her out?

'Let's just say I enjoy the company of young people. Now, get yourself ready for work or that nice Miss Billington will be giving you what for.'

'Phew, I'm fair whacked out.' Maisie leant dramatically against Freda's counter. 'How much longer until we can go home?'

'It's only half past two and you've just come back from a late dinner hour. You'd better watch it or you'll be in trouble if the supervisor catches you away from your counter.'

'It's only Sarah on duty.'

'Only? You know she has eyes in the back of her head. It wouldn't be fair if she had to tell you off for not doing your job. Think how it would make her feel.'

Maisie shrugged her shoulders. 'What I meant was, she's upstairs working with Betty, so she can't be down here as well, can she? You've turned into a right goody-goody since you started helping out with the Girl Guides.'

Freda finished counting a customer's change into her hand before turning back to Maisie with a hurt look on her face. 'That's not a nice thing to say, is it? What I do with the Guides has nothing to do with my job here. I'm only helping out as their regular leader has been evacuated with her class to Cornwall. It's left Brown Owl shorthanded, and as I lodge with her mother, I felt as though I should offer to help out a bit.' Freda didn't add that she thoroughly enjoyed herself at their meetings and doing all the war work they were involved with. Working at Woolies, she had begun to feel as though she wasn't playing her part in the war effort, even though nothing much had happened yet. Like everyone else, she was starting to get fed up with this 'phoney war', as they called it, and wanted it all to end. From the bits she'd heard on the wireless and on Pathé News at the pictures, all their soldiers were safe, but some ships had been sunk. She couldn't help wondering what had happened to the seamen on the ships and hoped they were all safe.

'Don't listen to me. I'm just not looking forward to Christmas much without Joe at home. It might be a bit different by next year. I reckon this lot'll all be over and we'll be back to normal.'

'What, you moaning about work and skiving, you mean?' Freda added with a laugh. 'Get back to your crockery before the queue that's forming starts to complain.'

'Blooming 'eck,' Maisie declared. 'I 'ope they don't all want to buy tea sets or I'll never serve them all.'

'I'll send over one of the new girls to help you. There's not a lot of call for haberdashery so close to Christmas. I'm sure if our supervisor was here, she'd say the same.'

'Cheers, Freda. I'll see you when we get our coats at closing time.'

Sarah linked arms with her two friends as they headed through the dark night towards Alexandra Road. 'Sorry I wasn't on the shop floor much today. I did miss it.'

'I bet you did, sitting up there in your warm office,' Maisie chided her.

'Honest I did. It wasn't much fun sorting out

241

piles of paper and filing away staff records. Poor Betty has got herself in a right mess since Mr Benfield's assistant left to be a land girl.'

'Why has she left a cosy job to grow spuds?' Maisie couldn't believe what she was hearing.

'Some people think they should do more for the war effort, Maisie,' Sarah pointed out. 'The woman is single and didn't have a family to worry about, so decided to join the land army.'

'I know how she feels,' Freda said quietly. 'I think I should be doing more as well.'

'Don't think I'm being rude, Freda, but I really don't think you're strong enough to be a land girl,' Maisie replied.

'I don't want to be a land girl. I wouldn't know a turnip from a marrow, let alone be able to milk a cow. No, I'm still thinking of going to work at Burndept's factory. At least I'd feel as though I was doing my bit.'

'Doing your bit? But, Freda, you don't have to think that way. You're needed at Woolworths, especially now that so many of the men have joined up,' Sarah was quick to point out.

'Thank you for saying that, Sarah, but I thought you ought to know that I'm thinking about it.'

'Burndept's do pay more than Woolies,' Maisie said, 'but it's dirty work.'

'Freda, if it's the money that's the problem, you know you can move back into Nan's house. She keeps telling you that you're more than welcome. She won't charge as much rent as you pay to your landlady.'

Freda smiled to herself. As much as she'd love to move back to number thirteen, she preferred to be independent, at least until she knew that Lenny was safe and she wasn't likely to be visited by the unsavoury man who turned up at her digs last Christmas. She'd heard no more about him, so perhaps he wouldn't return now. Was it really a year since she'd been kicked out of her old lodgings and Sarah had rescued her? She was no closer to finding her brother, even though the letter she received that had sent her rushing to Erith had been clearly stamped with an Erith postmark. She'd thought working in a public place like Woolworths would mean that she may spot her brother. On the other hand, would the men who were undoubtedly after Lenny do her harm unless they found him first?

Maisie nudged Freda. 'A penny for them?'

'Sorry – I was miles away. Perhaps you are right and I should stay at Woolworths. I promise that if I change my mind, I'll let you both know first.'

Sarah patted her hand. 'I'm so pleased. Oops, mind how you go – the pavement is rather slippery. Thank goodness we are almost home.'

The girls turned into Alexandra Road, thankful to be almost out of the cold weather.

'It looks as though there's someone waiting on the doorstep,' Maisie pointed out.

'I hope Nan hasn't forgotten her key. It's too cold to be waiting outside.'

'Surely Mrs C. would have popped to Woolies and borrowed a key from us?' Freda asked.

'It's most likely Vera come to tell us she's spotted some more German soldiers,' Maisie laughed.

'Oh my goodness. It can't be!' Sarah pulled away from her two friends and ran towards number thirteen. 'Alan! It's Alan!' In the darkened street, she could just see the outline of the man she loved.

She reached the gate as Alan turned and saw his wife and swept her up in his arms. They were locked in an embrace, only parting as a polite cough from Freda and Maisie brought them back to earth.

'Good to see you, Alan,' Maisie said as she held out her door key. 'Let's get ourselves inside before we freeze to death.'

'How long have you been waiting on the doorstep? I thought Nan would have been home,' Sarah asked her husband as she ushered him into the front room, closing the curtains before switching on the light. Freda and Maisie had discreetly gone through to the kitchen, leaving the young couple alone.

'Not long. I went to Mum's house first, but it was locked up and empty. I thought I'd find someone here, but all I've seen is a dog. I didn't know your nan had one. He seems friendly enough, even though he finished off my sandwiches.'

Sarah frowned. 'Nan doesn't have a dog. Perhaps it's that stray that's been hanging around. You know what Nan's like with waifs and strays. I reckon she's been slipping it some food, even though Dad has chased it off a few times.'

'That sounds like your nan all right. Is Mum still at work?'

'Maureen's gone away for Christmas to visit your aunt Joan in Ipswich. I did mention it in my last letter. It'll probably be waiting for you when you get back to Scotland.' Sarah started to remove her coat, wishing she was wearing something prettier than her maroon Woolworths overall and comfortable old shoes. 'Shall I light the fire?'

'No, don't bother. We may as well go into the living room with the others.'

Sarah felt a stab of disappointment. She thought Alan would have preferred some time alone with her, as they hadn't seen each other since September. Perhaps he was tired. 'Did it take long to travel down from Scotland?'

Alan looked away as he removed his overcoat. 'I'm no longer in Scotland.'

'But ... but why didn't you tell me? Where are you based now?'

'I'm not really supposed to say, Sarah.'

Sarah felt impatient. 'For heaven's sake, Alan. I'm not likely to tell the enemy.' She thought of Vera and her 'Germans' and felt a nervous giggle escape from her throat.

Alan looked annoyed. 'It's no laughing matter, Sarah. It's all right for you women, staying home and not having to train to fight the enemy. You can go on as if life is just the same, but for us men, it's different. Damn you. Men are going to die and all you can do is stand there and laugh.'

'Alan?' Sarah didn't recognize this man standing in front of her. Had he changed so much in three months? His face was thinner, and there was a guarded look in his eyes.

Alan ran his hands through his short hair. 'For your information, and please don't share this with your friends, I'm based in Kent.' He raised his hand to silence Sarah as she was about to say how pleased she was that he would be close to home. 'Don't say a word. From the little I know,

245

it's likely that this part of the country will take a pounding, and it will be our air force that will stop an invasion.'

Sarah frowned as she looked at her husband. He had never spoken to her this way before. 'Alan, all I want is – for you to be safe. Please let's not argue.'

Alan sighed. 'I'm sorry, my love. It's been a long day and I expected to find Mum home as well as you. Come here.' He held out his arms and Sarah stepped gratefully into them. This was more like the Alan she knew and loved. She traced the lines on his face before pulling his lips down to hers. His face was more lined than she remembered, and his eyes didn't shine quite as much, but once their lips met, none of that mattered anymore.

'Cooee! I'm home!' Sarah pulled away from Alan as Ruby let herself into the house, closely followed by Vera. 'My goodness, is that you, Alan? Come here and give me a hug. It's so good to see you, lad. You look a sight for sore eyes in that uniform.'

Alan hugged Ruby and shook Vera's hand.

'Now, have those girls offered you any food yet? ... I thought not. You come along with me and we'll sort that out right now.'

Alan followed Ruby without a backward glance to his wife.

For the next hour Sarah sat quietly and watched as Alan chatted to the women about his life in the RAF and told them things he had not mentioned in his letters to her. I may as well not be here, she thought, as she went to the scullery to wash up.

She didn't hear Maisie come up behind her

until she whispered in her ear, 'Don't look so glum. I reckon your husband's a little bit shy after being away for so long. Come with me.'

Sarah wasn't sure that Maisie was correct in her assumptions but followed her upstairs to the room the girls were sharing over Christmas.

Opening her wardrobe, Maisie pulled out a parcel. 'I suppose you'll be going back to Maureen's tonight?'

'Oh, I hadn't given that a thought. I suppose we will, as there's no room here, is there. Not with Mum and Dad arriving tomorrow evening.'

Maisie laughed at her friend's innocence. 'Here, this is your Christmas present. I think it'll be a good idea if you open it now.'

Sarah took the parcel. 'But it's not Christmas yet. I'd rather wait until Christmas Day.'

'No, open it now. You'll thank me later.'

Sarah untied the ribbon and pulled back the wrapping paper. Beneath a layer of tissue was a confection of fine lawn and lace. Lifting the garment, she found herself looking at the most beautiful nightdress she'd ever seen. 'It's adorable. Did you make this?'

Maisie nodded. 'I thought that it would come in useful once that husband of yours returned home.'

'Won't you be needing this yourself, Maisie?'

'Don't you worry about me, my love. My fingers haven't been idle. My Joe will see me in something equally as alluring.'

'Alluring?' Sarah felt her cheeks turn pink. 'My goodness,' she spluttered. Now she did feel shy.

Maisie delved back into the wardrobe and

247

pulled out her second-best dress, of green velvet, and held it up to Sarah. 'Hmm, that'll do. Now, get yourself ready and take that husband of yours back to Maureen's. You have the place to yourself. We don't want to see you until Christmas Day.'

'But that's—'

'Yes, it's the day after tomorrow. Don't worry about the potatoes and the sprouts. Freda and me'll help Ruby. You just get to know your husband again before he vanishes up into those blue skies for months on end.'

Sarah hugged Maisie. 'You are the best friend a girl has ever had.'

'Don't go saying that in front of Freda or she'll never forgive you. Not that I can see Freda running up a nightdress like this and giving it as a Christmas present.' She checked her watch. 'It's late, so you get dressed and I'll go tell Alan to wait for you at the front door. Oh, and there's some of my perfume in the top drawer. Help yourself.'

'Cheers, Maisie. I don't know what to say.'

Maisie paused at the door. 'Just name the first baby after me.'

Sarah cuddled up to Alan and watched as the night sky turned to dawn through a crack in the curtains. They'd not bothered about the blackout, as there had been no time to turn on a light. Maisie's gift had worked its magic, but Sarah felt as though the man she was lying next to was not the person she had married. It was Alan who had held her close. It was Alan who had covered her body in kisses, but where was the Alan who would whisper tender words to her and cuddle

248

her close until they fell into a deep sleep? She could see his uniform jacket draped across the seat by the dressing table. It was alien to her, as was the way he now held himself, upright and proud. No doubt this was the RAF's doing, but she felt there was more. They needed to talk, and it had to be before he returned to his duties.

She slipped out of bed, careful not to wake him. Her hand fell upon the nightdress that Maisie had sewn with such care for her friend, but instead she reached for her normal attire. Pulling the dressing gown tight, she slipped her feet carefully into her slippers and crept from the room. A good breakfast would put matters right. Maureen may be away, but she always kept the larder well stocked. Perhaps they could go for a walk afterwards. That would be nice, she thought, as she put the kettle on the stove and lit the gas beneath. Humming happily to herself, she cracked eggs into a pan and sliced bread ready to fry to a crispy brown just as she knew Alan liked it.

'That smells good.'

'Oh, Alan, I was just about to bring it to you.'

Alan stretched his arms above his head and yawned. He was wearing just the bottom part of his pyjamas. Sarah's heart skipped a beat as she saw strong, well-defined muscles that hadn't been there three months ago flex across his broad chest. She resisted the urge to trace them with her fingers, instead pouring milk into his cup. They needed to talk. She had to keep her head clear.

'Sit yourself down, Alan, before it gets cold.'

Alan tucked into his breakfast. Sarah watched

him as he ate hungrily.

'You don't know how much I've missed decent grub these last months. I've thought about nothing else all the way home on the train.'

Sarah felt her heart sink. 'Haven't you missed me at all?'

Alan's eyes never left his plate as he mopped up the last of his egg with a piece of bread. 'Goes without saying, don't it?' he muttered.

'I don't think it does, Alan. I've missed you like hell. I was missing you before you'd reached the end of the street. Now you're back, I'll tell you again. I miss you, Alan Gilbert, and if I had it my way, you'd never leave me again. As it is, bloody Hitler is stopping us being together and I'm not happy about it. Now, tell me all about your life these past months and the people you've met.'

Alan sighed. 'You know I'm not supposed to talk about things, Sarah.'

'I don't mean the war. I want to know if you've made friends. What are the people like you are living with?'

'They're just chaps. Nothing to write home about.'

'But I'm interested, Alan. I want to be able to imagine what your life is like when you are off duty. Are these chaps like us? Do they have wives and children? Did they work at Woolworths or in factories?'

Alan laughed. It wasn't his usual carefree laugh but harsh and cynical. 'For Christ's sake, Sarah, of course they aren't like us. I'm the odd one out, if you must know. I wasn't born with a silver spoon in my mouth like many of my fellow pilots.

I never went to the kind of school one boasts about that opens doors for the rest of one's life. No, Sarah, they aren't like us ... me.'

Something inside Sarah died at that moment. Looking back, she could pinpoint the time, the room and even the remains of breakfast on the table at the moment she realized her husband had changed.

She reached across the table to take Alan's hand, but he pulled away. 'Alan, it's what's inside us that matters. You wouldn't be a pilot if the RAF didn't think you were good enough.'

Alan rose to his feet. 'You don't understand. It's not just about flying planes. I'm going for a walk.'

'If you wait until I've washed up and tidied around a bit, we could go together. It would be lovely to walk down by the river and get some fresh air.'

'I'd rather be alone,' he said, walking from the room.

Sarah collected the empty plates and headed to the scullery. She'd clear up and then make herself presentable. Perhaps when Alan came back, he would be in a better frame of mind and they could make a fresh start with the day.

Sarah put her knitting to one side. It was starting to get dark outside, even though it was only mid-afternoon. She needed to check the blackout curtains were secure before turning on the light. Her fingers felt numb from knitting for so long, but it helped stop her from pacing the floor worrying about where Alan had gone and why he had not returned. Freda had popped round earlier with a basket of food from Ruby, so at least she didn't have to think about what to prepare for their evening meal. Slices of roast beef with vegetables would see them through until they went to number thirteen on Christmas Day. Freda had not questioned Sarah about Alan once she explained that he'd gone for a walk. Thank goodness Maisie had not accompanied her, as she would have seen through Sarah's bright smile and Alan going out alone.

Knowing that she would be away over Christmas and that Sarah would be staying at Ruby's, Maureen had not bothered putting up her few decorations or bringing in the tree from the garden, where it had been planted the previous year. The greetings cards on the mantelpiece did not make the room look at all festive and Sarah switched off the wireless with a sigh. The carol service that had been playing had done nothing to lighten her mood.

She'd just picked up her knitting when she heard a key turning in the lock of the front door.

'Alan, is that you?'

There was no response. Surely it wasn't Maureen come home early from her visit to her family. Sarah prayed it wasn't, as she was bound to notice the difference in her son and Sarah could not face the questions. She picked up the poker from the hearth and crept into the darkened hall. The door had swung open. Sarah jumped as she spotted Alan sitting on the floor.

'Alan, whatever are you doing down there?' She pushed the door closed, retrieving his key, which had been left in the lock. Flicking on the hall light, she tried not to laugh at the state of her husband.

'Sorry, love,' he slurred, finding it hard to form his words. 'I bumped into young Ginger and we stopped off at the New Light for a pint. He's home for a few days before he's shipped out. Look, I won the raffle.' He held up a rather bedraggled-looking chicken. 'It needs plucking.'

Sarah helped him to his feet and he staggered to the over-stuffed horsehair sofa, sitting on Sarah's knitting, which she'd left when she went to investigate the intruder. 'I'll make you some food and then I think you should lie down for a while,' she said, retrieving her knitting and checking that Alan hadn't knocked any stitches from the needles. 'I'll take this as well,' she added, prising the chicken from her husband's arms. He lay in an untidy heap, his head dropping onto his chest as he started to doze off. She had no idea what to do with the bird, or if it would remain fresh for when her mother-in-law returned home. She'd leave it in the pantry and ask Nan for advice.

Returning to the front room ten minutes later with sandwiches made from the beef that Freda had dropped off earlier in the day, Sarah found Alan snoring loudly on the sofa. She pulled off his shoes and jacket, retrieved his cap from the floor and made him more comfortable. Despite the way she had to roll him over to get his arms out of the jacket sleeves, he didn't wake. It was pointless making a proper meal, as it was unlikely Alan would wake for a few hours and it would be wasted. It was better he slept off his excess of ale. She frowned. She'd never known him drink this much before.

Sarah topped up the coal fire and picked up her knitting. Christmas Eve would be quiet for once, but at least Alan was home and safe.

18

'Happy Christmas, darling. Where is that handsome husband of yours?'

Sarah hugged her mum and pulled off her coat, checking her hair in the mirror above the fireplace. 'He's chatting with Dad in the garden.'

'I just hope they are seeing off that mangy dog that's been hanging around. I read in the newspaper the government are putting down all dogs so they aren't a burden on the country while we're at war. Someone should do something about that animal before we all catch something or he attacks us in our sleep. Now, shall I pour Alan a sherry, or do you think he would prefer a glass of beer?'

'Mum, I don't think the dog is a danger. He's quite sweet really.'

Irene frowned. She didn't look convinced. 'I'll have a word with your father about it. Now, how about that sherry?'

'Perhaps wait and ask him when he comes in?' Sarah doubted Alan could face alcohol today. After trying unsuccessfully to wake him the night before, she'd covered him in a blanket and spent the night alone in their large double bed. It had taken some urging the next morning to have Alan pull himself together enough to wash and shave, let alone eat the breakfast Sarah placed in front of him. He'd picked at the poached eggs and toast before turning rather green and heading to bed for another hour. By the time he materialized, Sarah was ready to walk the short distance to number thirteen and start the Christmas festivities.

Alan had gone back into his shell and was as uncommunicative as he had been the previous day. Sarah had hoped that by letting his hair down at the pub, he would return to his old self, but no, Alan was a stranger once more.

'Hello, my love. Give us a kiss for Christmas.' George swept his daughter up in a big hug and swung her round.

'Good grief, George. Have you been on the rum again? Put the girl down and hand out the presents.'

'Whatever you say, dear.' George winked at his daughter and reached under the tree, pulling out two parcels. 'The large one is yours, Sarah, and this is yours, Alan.'

Sarah passed two packages to her parents. 'These are from the two of us. I made them myself.'

'How quaint,' Irene said as she pulled out a pale pink shawl. 'Fancy you making this. You've turned into a proper little housewife. I'm sure I will find a use for it.'

George was pulling on the woolly scarf and gloves he'd found in his parcel. 'Perfect, my love. Just what I need for these cold days.'

Sarah grinned. 'I'm so pleased you like your presents. Freda had to help me with the fingers on your gloves, Dad, as I went wrong and you only had three fingers on the left one.'

George kissed his daughter. 'I'm sure I'd have loved them with six fingers. You are a clever girl.'

'I'll never be a perfect knitter, but I wanted to give it a go. The government says we mustn't overspend, so I thought by making presents I'd be doing my bit.'

'That is very commendable, my dear. Now, open your presents from us. I'm afraid they are not home-made, but I've put a lot of thought into them. I wish I had time to be the perfect housewife and make things, but my life is just too busy.'

Sarah flinched. Mum had long ago perfected the art of the put-down while giving a compliment, but it still hurt. She undid the string round the large box and the paper fell away. She didn't know what to say.

'They are the best of their kind, Sarah, and should last a lifetime. I always say invest in quality and it will last.'

Sarah gazed at the shiny set of saucepans and summoned all her strength to put a smile on her face. 'Saucepans. Thank you very much.' She did her best to look pleased, but did her mum not recall being told about Alan's romantic proposal and Mr Benfield's generous gift on behalf of Woolworths?

She fixed the smile on her face. It was Christmas; she would try not to get upset. 'Open your present, Alan.'

Alan picked at the knot on the small package until a small jewellery box was uncovered. He pulled back the lid to reveal a smart set of gold cufflinks. 'Thank you, Irene and George. I don't know what to say.'

Irene waved away his thanks and reached for her sherry. 'You have a new social standing, Alan – you need to be turned out correctly. Now, sit down here with me and tell me all about your fellow pilots. Do they come from good families?'

Sarah sighed. Was this how her future was going to be? She would be the housewife, while Alan was the key to her mother mixing with the upper classes? She couldn't quite believe that the RAF was full of the upper classes, whatever Alan and her mum seemed to think. Then again, if Alan was mixing with a different class of person, then that could be why he wasn't happy to be back in Erith or, more importantly, with her. 'I'm going to help Freda and Maisie with the vegetables.'

'I'll give you a hand, love. Unless your mother wants to. Irene?'

Irene Caselton gave her husband a horrified look. 'Not in this outfit, George.' She turned to continue to question Alan about social gatherings and mixing with the officers' families.

'It's just me and you, then, love,' chuckled George. In the hallway, he turned to stop Sarah entering the kitchen, where Freda was in control of the women, who were peeling sprouts and scrubbing carrots. 'I've got something else here for you, just in case you weren't over the moon with the saucepans. I mentioned you already had a set, but...' George shrugged his shoulders. 'Your mother means well, but she gets some funny ideas in her head sometimes.' He handed her a small brown envelope. 'Sorry. You know I'm no good at wrapping presents.'

Sarah opened the envelope and a pair of earrings slipped into her hand. 'Oh, they are beautiful.' She held up the dainty golden hearts so the light caught them, before hugging George. 'Thank you, Dad. I love them.'

'I know you women love saucepans, so these are just a little stocking-filler,' George laughed, 'and you make sure Alan shares those pots and pans – don't keep them to yourself.'

'Dad, you are funny. I love both my gifts.'

'You don't have to fool me, Sarah. Now, let's go sort out those sprouts or we won't be eating before the King makes his speech.'

'Oh my goodness. I don't know what to say.' Sarah looked at the pile of presents in front of her. She'd thought that once she was grown up and married, Christmas wouldn't be so exciting, but this year was different to the Christmases she'd spent at number thirteen as a child. Ruby, aided by Maisie, had put up the paper chains that had been stored in the loft. Freda had dug up the tree from the garden and decorated it, and Sarah had purchased some new Chinese lanterns from Woolies. With cards hung on string from the picture rail and a roaring fire in the hearth, it was Christmas as Sarah remembered from her childhood.

Aided by George, the girls had helped Ruby prepare the dinner before sitting down for ten minutes to exchange gifts, while George stepped outside to smoke his pipe. Irene had banned him from the house, as she didn't like the smell. Alan sat quietly nursing a large whisky that George had poured earlier. He was gazing into space and taking no part in the festivities. He may as well not be here, Sarah thought sadly. He is usually the life and soul of a party. Then she felt guilty for her thoughts. She would hand out the presents she had carefully chosen for her friends and try to remain cheerful.

Freda gasped as she opened her parcel and found a small jewellery box inside. 'I love it. Thank you so much, Sarah.'

'You have somewhere to put your pieces of jewellery now, Freda,' Sarah smiled.

'However did you manage to find this?' Maisie shrieked, jumping up to kiss Sarah. 'I've not been able to find my favourite face powder for over a year.'

'I spotted it in a chemist's window in Whitstable when we were on our honeymoon. I'm so happy you like it.'

Sarah ran her hand over the soft wool she found in her parcel from Freda.

'I know you're keen on knitting, now you've learnt how to do it, but I'll make up the cardigan if you like?' Freda said. 'You too, Maisie.'

'And Maisie said she'd help you run this up into a winter dress,' Ruby added, as Sarah shook out some deep red woollen fabric, which had been carefully wrapped. 'I picked it up at Woolwich Market. The colour caught my eye as soon as I spotted it on the stall.'

'It's lovely, Nan. Thank you so much.' Sarah jumped up from where she was kneeling by the coal fire to hug and kiss Ruby. 'Now open your present, Nan. It's a joint gift from me, Maisie and Freda.'

Ruby opened the small package to reveal a navy-blue silk scarf with a delicate white pattern round the edge. 'Why, it's beautiful. I do believe it is pure silk. Fancy that! Thank you so much, girls. I've never had anything so posh before. I can see this didn't come from Woolworths.'

'Nan, you have to shake out the scarf and see what it's hiding,' Sarah urged.

Ruby carefully removed the whole of the scarf from the wrapping and carefully shook it. Four pieces of paper fell into her lap. 'Oh my goodness, whatever can this be?' She peered closely at the wording on the tickets. '"*Cinderella* at the London Coliseum." Well, I'll be blowed. I've not seen a panto in many a year.'

'It's for the day after Boxing Day. It's half-day closing, so we can go up town and have afternoon tea at Lyons Corner House before going to the show, Nan. We've got tickets for Betty and Maureen as well, but they are wrapped in their Christmas boxes.'

'What generous girls you are thinking of an old woman and including her in your outing. I'm truly blessed.' Ruby wiped her eyes on the edge of her best pinny.

'Are you sure you wouldn't like to come with us, Mum? I'm sure I can get another ticket. You too, Alan?' Sarah felt as though she should include Irene in the group trip and was uncomfortable that Alan was home and she was abandoning him.

Irene Caselton waved away her daughter's words. 'I'm not one for comedy theatre. Besides, we will be heading back to Devon that morning.'

'And I'll be back on duty by then,' Alan added.

'So soon?'

Alan got to his feet and knocked back the whisky. 'Some of us have a war to fight, Sarah. I don't have time for gadding about.' He left the room.

Sarah went to follow her husband, but Ruby placed a hand on her shoulder. 'You stay there, love. He'll be all right. It's the drink talking. I need to check the spuds and call George in before he freezes to death out in the garden. The last time I looked, he was talking to Nelson.'

'Nelson?'

'The stray. I've named him Nelson and given him a new home for Christmas. He's good company, but don't tell your mum.'

Sarah smiled at her nan. Yet another mouth to feed. She was such a caring person. Sarah dared not speak about Alan or she knew tears would soon flow. It was Christmas and she didn't want to spoil the day for her family. She started to flatten the paper and roll up the string and ribbon. 'Waste not, want not. We may as well save this for another occasion.'

Freda joined in and soon the floor was clear of the mess. 'What did you give Sarah, Maisie?' she asked. 'I didn't see her opening anything.'

'Let's just say she had her Christmas early, shall we?' she said, giving Sarah a large wink and a nudge with her elbow. 'I just hope it worked its magic, eh, Sarah?'

Sarah blushed bright red. 'It was appreciated, thank you, Maisie.'

She looked around the room at her happy friends and family. Alan's empty glass was still

261

balanced on the wide arm of the armchair where he had left it. She just wished she had the husband she knew back with her once more. Perhaps now he'd spent time away from his home town and the people he'd grown up with, he wasn't happy with his lot. Maybe he'd met someone else. No, he wouldn't have, would he? Sarah didn't know anymore, but she tried to push the thought firmly from her mind. She just hoped that whatever had caused Alan to change wouldn't bring a wedge between them. After all, it had only been three months since they vowed to stay together until parted by death. Perhaps they shouldn't have married so soon. What was that saying? Marry in haste and repent at leisure? She shuddered. She'd had too many of these feelings lately.

The family and friends sat round the table, the remnants of their meal not yet cleared away, as they listened to King George address the Commonwealth on the wireless.

'...I believe from my heart that the cause which binds together my peoples and our gallant and faithful allies is the cause of Christian civilization. On no other basis can a true civilization be built. Let us remember this through the dark times ahead of us and when we are making the peace for which all men pray.

'A new year is at hand. We cannot tell what it will bring. If it brings peace, how thankful we shall all be. If it brings continued struggle, we shall remain undaunted.

'In the meantime, I feel that we may all find a message of encouragement in the lines which, in my closing words, I would like to say to you.

'I said to the man who stood at the gate of the year, "Give me a light that I may tread safely into the unknown." And he replied, "Go out into the darkness and put your hand into the hand of God. That shall be to you better than light and safer than a known way."

'May that Almighty hand guide and uphold us all.'

George raised his glass as the last bars of the national anthem faded on the wireless. 'After that rousing speech, I just want to say good luck to us all and may we face with fortitude whatever the year ahead throws our way.'

The family and friends raised their glasses as one.

'That was a grand spread, Mum,' George said, rubbing his stomach.

'I didn't do it on my own, George. The girls were a great help to me. Many hands make light work, as they say,' Ruby replied.

'They also say that too many cooks spoil the broth, Mrs C., so thank goodness I only 'elped with peeling the veg or we'd all have stomach ache tomorrow,' Maisie added with a grin. 'Now, shall we clear the table and then we can play some games?'

'You ladies stay where you are. The washing-up is man's work today. Come on, Alan, shift yourself. I'll wash and you dry.'

Alan managed to raise a smile as he headed to the scullery, his arms piled high with empty dinner plates.

'That was a lovely meal, Mrs Caselton,' Freda said. 'I've never tasted turkey before.'

'I'm glad you liked it, love. We usually have a

263

chicken, but with more of us here this year, I thought I'd have a big bird instead. It should see us through a few meals yet and then I'll make a stew.'

Maisie groaned. 'Please stop talking about food. I don't think I can eat for another week I'm so stuffed. Who fancies a walk?'

Sarah stretched her arms and yawned. 'That is such a good idea. I'm feeling quite sleepy. How about you, Nan and Mum?'

'Not for me, love. I'm going to have ten minutes on my own in the front room if you all don't mind. You go and enjoy yourselves,' Ruby said.

'I'll decline. I'd like to listen to a music programme on the wireless. You might remove your paper hats before you go out,' Irene added.

'Oh, I don't know. I think mine's quite fetching,' Maisie laughed as she patted the green crown that sat on her head at a jaunty angle. 'Come on, Freda, Sarah, let's go get our coats before it gets too dark to see a foot in front of us out there.'

'I'll be with you in a minute. I just want to see if Dad and Alan want to join us.' Sarah slipped out to where her dad was up to his elbows in pots and pans, and Alan was drying cutlery. 'You look quite fetching in Nan's pinny, Dad. Some of us are going for a walk. Do you want to join us?'

'Needs must, Sarah. Your mum will kill me if I mess up my Sunday best. I think it suits me, don't you?' George said, spinning round with the washing-up brush in his hand. 'I'll be a while finishing up here. You go with the girls, Alan.'

Alan shrugged. 'No, I'll help you, George. You

264

go out with your friends, Sarah.'

Sarah had been looking forward to holding her husband's arm as they took a brisk walk through the quiet streets. She wanted to spend as much time as possible with Alan before he disappeared from her life once more. 'Are you sure?'

Alan just nodded and turned back to the draining board and the pile of crockery.

Taking her coat and scarf from Maisie, Sarah headed to the front door. 'Ooh, there's a letter on the doormat. Someone must have delivered it. I wonder why they never knocked.' She picked up the small envelope and peered at the writing. 'It's for you, Freda. Looks as though it was delivered to your old lodgings. The landlady must have remembered you came to live here. Why, you haven't lived there since last Christmas.'

Freda took the envelope and slipped it into her coat pocket. Her stomach flipped as she recognized the handwriting. It belonged to her young brother, Lenny. She'd read it later when she was alone.

'Do you remember that awful landlady and how rude she was to you?' Sarah asked as she opened the door and the girls stepped out into the darkening afternoon.

'And how she charged you extra for a bit of hot water and a slice of toast? Gawd, it's a good job you're shot of her,' Maisie laughed. 'Thank goodness you found Mrs White and her lovely house, even if it does resemble a wool shop. Blooming 'eck, it's brass monkeys out here!'

The girls linked arms and carefully walked along the icy street. 'Where shall we go?' Sarah asked.

'How about up Pier Road past Woolies and then down to the riverbank?' Freda suggested.

'Blimey, can't you keep away from the place for one day?' Maisie joshed the young girl.

Freda smiled but thought that Woolworths had been her saviour this past year and she had much to thank God for now that she had a regular pay packet, good friends and a happy life. If only she knew where Lenny was and if he was safe.

Maisie, too, was thinking of life since joining Woolworths. She had no idea what Joe was doing right now. He'd been her rock these past few years. She knew if it wasn't for her mates and Woolies, she'd be back in that dark place she tried so hard to forget.

Sarah smiled. 'Woolies and the river it is, then. Best foot forward, girls, and mind the icy patches.' She would look at the window display that Betty had been so worried about and report back to her friend on how it looked to passers-by on the most magical day of the year. But was it as magical this year? Just one year ago she had fallen in love with Alan, the old Alan, not the silent, angry man who had returned. Was it her fault he was like this? A small shiver ran down her back. Again she felt as though something was amiss. Was it an omen?

Freda decided to make her excuses and head up to bed early. Sarah had left, hand in hand with Alan, to go back to Maureen's house in nearby Crayford Road. Ruby, her feet propped up on the settee, looked cosy and it wouldn't be long before she fell asleep, going by the way her eyelids were dropping. George was already snoring quietly in his armchair, his paper hat falling down over his eyes. Freda straightened his hat and picked up the book that had slipped to the floor. She was very fond of Sarah's dad. His caring ways reminded her so much of her own dad, although she had been a mere child when he passed away.

Maisie and Irene were in the living room, listening to *A Christmas Cabaret* on the wireless, so the coast was clear for Freda to head upstairs and open up her own Christmas surprise.

Quietly closing the bedroom door, she sat on the bed and looked at the envelope that had been burning a hole in her pocket since that afternoon. It had been posted a week ago, and the postmark was smudged. Perhaps this letter would disclose where Lenny was and what he was up to. She realized then how desperate she'd been to find her brother and prayed that within the envelope her questions would be answered. Most of all, she needed to know he was well. They weren't much of a family for writing letters, so this had to be important. She pulled the single page from the envelope and quickly read the words, her heart beating as she worried what Lenny had to say.

Dear Freda,
It's your brother, Lenny. I know I've not kept in touch, but it's been hard what with them still looking for me since I skipped out of prison. Freda, I'm not staying there when I ain't done nothing wrong, and especially when I know it was Tommy's gang that did the robbery and shot the night guard at the warehouse.

Freda shuddered. She could remember well the

day that the police barged into their house and took Lenny away. He professed his innocence, but it was only Freda who believed him. Their stepfather didn't want them in the house anyway, so he was glad to see her brother go to prison. It was one less mouth to feed and more money to spend in the boozer. Freda's mother had turned away when she asked her for help to free Lenny. Even to tell a small lie and say he was home the night of the robbery. Since their stepfather had placed his foot over their threshold, no one had dared question him, and that included Freda's mum. She sighed. Lenny was no lily-white, innocent kid, and getting in with the wrong crowd had not helped. That Tommy Whiffen was a bad lot, and once he had Lenny under his spell, throwing him a few quid to run errands and deliver knocked-off goods, he was as good as guilty.

Her silly brother had kept quiet and carried the can for what happened that night at the warehouse. He was in too deep once he was told that a man had been shot.

It's like this, Freda. Tommy knows you've moved south and he thinks you know where I'm hiding. You need to move from your digs and change your job to be on the safe side. I'd say go back home, but the old man would dob you in to Tommy for the price of a pint.

I'm all right. I'm lodging with a bloke who was inside when I first got banged up and offered me a bed if I ever needed one. I'm picking up a bit of work as well, so I'm keeping me head above water. It's best you don't know where I am in case Tommy finds you. Once Tommy gets caught and people know the truth, then we will be safe. Until then, Freda, keep yer eyes peeled and I'll not be far away.

Lenny

Freda folded the letter and hid it away in her handbag. She was glad that Lenny was safe, but by escaping from prison, he had made things so much worse. It was time to leave Woolworths and possibly change her lodgings so she would be safe. First, she would leave Woolworths. It was time to disappear among the hundreds of workers at Burndept's. If she remained safe, then Lenny was safe too.

19

Sarah stared into her cup of tea. It was almost four months since Christmas and her worst fears had been confirmed that very morning. In the staff canteen, Maureen was humming happily to herself as she served the Woolworths staff their mid-morning refreshments. At least someone was happy with the news, Sarah thought to herself.

'You poor girl, you look dreadful,' Betty declared, sitting beside Sarah in the canteen. 'I think you should go home and go to bed. I don't want one of my most devoted staff members working herself into the ground.' Betty looked at Sarah's white face. She looked so drawn. 'What did the doctor say?'

'I'll be fine when I've had this cup of tea, Betty.

Then I'll get working on the stock sheets you gave me yesterday afternoon. I should have finished them by now.'

'You'll do no such thing. I want you to go home and put yourself to bed. You look as white as a sheet.'

'Here you go, my love.' Maureen slid a plate of dry toast in front of her daughter-in-law. 'Get that inside you and you'll feel as right as nine pence in no time. I was the same when I was carrying my Alan. It won't be for long and then you'll be blooming.' She touched Sarah gently on the shoulder. 'Alan will be that excited when you tell him.' She returned to her duties, a broad smile on her face.

Betty's face was a picture. Sarah wanted to laugh, but it really wouldn't be the done thing to laugh at her boss in public, even if they were good friends. She nibbled on a piece of the toast instead.

'Oh my. You're...?'

Sarah nodded her head. 'Yes, I'm expecting a baby.'

Betty pulled herself together and grinned. She shouldn't automatically be thinking of her staff rotas when Sarah had such exciting news to share, but if truth be known, she had no idea how she would cope without her right-hand woman. 'That is splendid news. When can we expect to welcome Master or Miss Gilbert into the world?'

Sarah smiled weakly. 'Thank you, Betty. My doctor told me it would be around 18 September. It's rather a shock. I still can't take it all in.'

'I'm sure you can't. Why, you only visited the

doctor this morning.'

'It was good of you to let me come into work late.'

Betty dismissed Sarah's comment with a wave of her hand. 'Nonsense. You were that pale yesterday I thought it was the start of something serious. Never in a million years did I expect such wonderful news. Now, who have you told apart from Maureen?'

'No one else knows. Apart from you, that is.'

'Well, I think it would be a good idea to take the rest of the day off and let your nan and your parents know before your secret leaks out. Maureen has that broad a smile on her face that everyone she meets is going to guess before too long.'

'Betty, it's nice of you to be so generous, but I have work to do. I can write to Alan and my parents this evening. I'm going to Nan's for my dinner tonight, as Maureen is off to her WI meeting, so I can tell her then. I must complete those stock sheet calculations or we will have head office down on us like a ton of bricks.'

'That paperwork can wait. You must go home and rest.' Betty was insistent.

'Then let me take the work home with me, please? I'll be at Nan's house and she won't let me overdo things.'

Betty sighed. She admired Sarah's strength of character but knew she shouldn't really put upon the girl. Especially now she was expecting a child. She knew that they should be planning her leave from work, not piling more onto the poor girl. 'Well, if you're sure, but I won't have you carrying that paperwork, even though Ruby's house is only

271

a couple of streets away.' She gazed around the staffroom and spied Maisie entering and heading towards the counter. She beckoned. 'Maisie, can you spare me a moment, please?'

Maisie approached the table with a frown on her face. Betty Billington usually conducted her work in her office, not in the open staffroom. Then she saw Sarah and exclaimed at her pale face. 'Gawd, Sarah, you look a right sight, there's no mistake. What's wrong, ducks?' She pulled out a chair and sat next to her friend, taking her hand.

Sarah put her finger to her lips. She didn't want her friend to draw attention to her, and she didn't wish to have to tell Maisie such a private piece of information here in the staffroom. Maisie was a good friend and it was only proper that she gave her the news of the baby in the right way.

Betty could see that Sarah was disturbed at having her news announced within earshot of colleagues. 'Sarah is feeling a little peaky. I would like you to accompany her to Mrs Caselton's house and carry her bag. Take as much time as you require. Please do not rush back until you are sure Sarah is settled.' Betty raised her eyebrows, indicating that Maisie should do as she was told and not make a discussion out of the request.

Maisie linked her arm through Sarah's as they left Woolworths. 'So when is it due?'

'What?'

'The baby. I ain't daft, you know. I can spot the signs even though I've not had one of me own yet.'

'Oh, Maisie, I'm so sorry. I know how much you've longed for a home of your own as well as a child, and here I am newly married and a baby on the way. It seems so unfair, what with your Joe away goodness knows where and all.'

Maisie squeezed Sarah's arm. She would never tell her friend that she was green with envy: her friend's wellbeing came first. 'Your Alan's away as well, so we're both in the same boat as far as absent hubbies are concerned. So don't you worry about me. All I can say is that my lack of kiddies ain't for the want of trying. As soon as Joe's back, I'll be doing me damnedest to catch you up, I can tell you. For now, I want to share every minute of your pregnancy, and that includes the shopping. This little baby is going to have a doting Aunty Maisie who will spoil it to bits. Let's plan a trip to Hedley Mitchell when Freda is free so we can look at prams and cots.'

Sarah wasn't fooled for one minute. She recalled one of their first conversations, in which Maisie had declared her yearning for a child. Sometimes life just wasn't fair. 'I promise you will be fed up with baby talk by the time this child arrives. As for buying a pram, I do believe it's bad luck to have one in the house before the baby is born. But there's no reason why we can't go shopping and take a closer look, is there?'

'Now, can you get in touch with Alan to give him the good news?'

'I'm going to write to him today. There was no point in doing so before I was sure. It's not like he can come rushing home.'

'Nah. Men aren't that good at times like this anyway. Apart from some back-slapping and 'anding out of cigars after the birth, they can't do much.'

Sarah smiled to herself. Maisie did have a point, but she liked to believe her Alan would be a little more involved. She could imagine him proudly pushing the pram when they walked through the town, stopping to chat to friends and showing off his child. They would take a picnic and go up to the recreation ground or walk down to the river-front on, sunny days. They would be a proper family. However, he'd been so distant on his last leave this past Christmas that perhaps she didn't know the man she married as well as she thought. Only time would tell if he was pleased that the family they'd discussed on their honeymoon had started to become a reality. She crossed her fingers, silently praying that all would be well.

'Now, let's get you settled on the sofa. Put your feet up and I'll make you a nice cup of tea. It was good of Maisie to walk you round. Did you discuss your leaving dates with that nice Miss Billington?'

'Nan, I'm not four months gone yet. Please don't fuss. I feel fine, and I have some work to do. After an afternoon's rest I'll be well enough to go back to work tomorrow. A cup of tea would be lovely, though.'

Ruby stood, hands on hips, watching her grand-daughter. Sarah did look a little peaky, but she came from good stock, and as she was quick to point out to anyone who would listen, the Caselton women never had a problem carrying a child or rearing them. However, she wasn't sure that Sarah should go back to work so soon. 'You won't be fit for man or beast if you go rushing back to Woolworths too soon, my girl. That boss of yours is female, so she knows that at times like this a woman should be at home and not working. You've only got a few weeks until you pack up work for good, so no need to even be worrying about it.'

Sarah sighed. She felt such a fraud to be putting her feet up and taking it easy when there was a war on and women were doing men's jobs. Why, Freda was holding down a manual job and working long shifts at Burndept's. It had been a shock when she announced just after Christmas that she was leaving Woolies and doing her bit for the war effort by working in a factory. What puzzled Sarah, although she didn't like to mention it to her family and friends, was that Freda had asked to move back to number thirteen and was now sharing the large front bedroom with Maisie. Although the two girls protested loudly, Ruby insisted on moving into the smaller back bedroom, leaving the third room free for when George was staying over. The excuse for Freda leaving her comfortable lodgings had been that she didn't like to be coming and going at ungodly hours due to her shift work. Sarah hadn't liked to mention that Freda had her own entrance door to her rooms so wouldn't be bothering her landlady. Ruby had been thrilled to have Freda back in the nest, and it didn't seem right to question the young girl's sudden decision not only to move from a job she loved but also to leave lodgings that she had made into a comfortable home over the past year. No doubt Freda would explain what she was up to when she was ready.

Sarah took the welcome cup of tea from her nan.

'Ta, Nan.' She sipped the hot brew thoughtfully. 'Nan, I've been thinking. What with the war and all, do you think I'd be doing the right thing by working as long as I can before the baby comes along? We are so short-staffed at the moment. A lot of my work is in the office these days, so it's not as if I'm doing any heavy lifting or anything.'

Ruby sat on the edge of the sofa and rubbed Sarah's ankles as she thought about what to say. 'Hmm. It's usual for women not to work after six months, but as long as you feel all right, you might as well be sitting in the office as sitting at home, I suppose. See what Miss Billington has to say about it first, but perhaps don't mention it to your mother. We don't want her up here fussing over nothing. Which reminds me – don't forget to let her know about the baby or there'll be all hell let loose if she finds out after everyone else.'

'I'm going to write a letter as soon as I've finished adding up these stock sheets for Betty. I can post it along with Alan's letter when I walk back to Maureen's house later on. I do wish I still lived here with you, but it wouldn't be fair to leave Maureen all alone. She worries about being bombed when she's on her own.'

'I'd feel the same way if I was in her shoes. You know you are welcome anytime you want to stay over – and bring Maureen with you too. After all, she's family now. And if you want to put a few hours in at Woolies once the nipper comes along, you can leave him or her with me if you like.'

'Oh, Nan, that would be lovely. Thank you. I don't want to appear to be a bad mother leaving the baby when it's so young, but the money would be handy, as I can put a bit by for when we have our own home.'

'You just concentrate on getting the roses back in your cheeks and we can talk about all of this later. It'll be grand to have a baby to spoil. Your aunt Pat's brood are growing up far too quickly. Not that I see much of them these days, what with them being evacuated to Wales. Did I tell you that Pat is thinking of bringing them back? Seems young Eric is homesick and Pat is missing them something awful.'

Sarah placed her hand on her stomach and rubbed it protectively. 'I can understand how she feels, but will it be safe having them back? Wales is a long way away and they must be safer there. Can't Aunt Pat stay with them?'

'No, she's needed on the farm. Don't forget that they live in a tied cottage and if they aren't both working, the farmer could hand it over to someone else. By all accounts, he is already talking about getting some extra help now that they've had instructions to up production. I'll have a word with her and tell her it's best those kids stay where they are. I've got a feeling in me water that this war's about to kick off good and proper before too long and we don't want anything to 'appen to those youngsters.'

Sarah nodded. When her nan had one of her feelings, it was best to take notice. She wasn't often wrong.

'Betty, I'm just popping down to the shop floor to help Maisie with the staff training. Some of the new staff aren't taking the fire drill nearly as seriously as they should. I'm worried they won't know what to do if they are left alone on fire duty.'

Betty looked up from her ledger and peered absentmindedly over her spectacles. 'Would you like me to come with you, Sarah?'

'I can manage, Betty. I wouldn't like to take you away from your important numbers,' she laughed.

Betty stretched. 'I could do with a break. I'm almost seeing double peering at these columns of figures. Since Mr Benfield was moved to another store, all I seem to do is look at lists of numbers and write reports. I don't know how he managed it all, and he also used to be on the shop floor so much. The man was a marvel.'

'And so are you, Betty. There aren't many women who can say they hold the position of manager at Woolworths.'

'Temporary stand-in manager, Sarah. We are only holding the fort until the menfolk are back from fighting this awful war.'

Sarah nodded. Only the day before, she had spent her lunch hour with Maisie down by the riverfront eating their sandwiches and feeling the late-May sun on their faces. It had been good to get away from the store for a while. What had surprised them was the number of small craft sailing downriver towards the estuary. There were more than usual, and they were in some kind of formation. She felt a familiar shudder run down her spine, but then couldn't help but smile to herself as she thought of Ruby having a feeling in her water of things afoot too.

Betty and Sarah had just reached the shop floor when they were aware of someone hammering on the locked shop door. 'My goodness, whoever can that be? Surely they can read the sign that says we open late on Tuesdays for staff training and fire drill,' Betty muttered as she rushed towards the door before the glass pane was shattered.

She was still pulling the door open when she was almost knocked to the floor by an agitated woman rushing in. 'Where is she? Where is the murdering cow?'

Betty tried to catch up with the woman as she ploughed her way through the bemused staff who were lined up in front of Maisie as she demonstrated how to use a stirrup pump.

'There you are. I might have known I'd find you flaunting yourself in front of a crowd. You're no better than you ought to be!' The woman stopped in front of Maisie, a wild look in her eye. Steel-grey hair flew out behind her, escaping from a bun, and her coat hung from her shoulders. She wore threadbare indoor slippers on her feet.

Sarah had managed to reach Maisie, while Betty had opened the shop door. 'Maisie, is that your mother-in-law?'

Maisie stood dead still, the usual affable smile disappearing from her face as she noticed the piece of paper the woman waved in her hand.

Maisie reached out blindly and Sarah took her hand. 'Maisie?'

'You may well look surprised, you trollop, but you can wipe that innocent look off your face. You've got blood on your hands and there's no mistake.'

Betty tried to intercede but was pushed away by the agitated older woman.

'You're a murderer, Maisie Taylor, and there's no denying it! You pushed my lad into the army and now he's dead.' She rammed the telegram into Maisie's face.

Maisie looked stunned and stared from Sarah and back to her mother-in-law. 'My Joe...?'

'He's not your Joe any longer. He's dead, gone forever and it's *all your fault.* You sent him to his death. When I think how my lovely boy took you on after you killed your own sister and now he's paid for it with his life. I'll see you rot in hell if it's the last thing I do, I swear by all that's holy.' The woman screwed the telegram into a tight ball and stuffed it into her pocket. Pushing her way back through the startled staff, she stormed out of the store.

Betty caught Maisie in her arms as the shock turned to oblivion and she sank into a deep faint.

20

'How is the poor love?'

'She's still sleeping, thank goodness. The doctor gave her something earlier and she went out like a light. I've been that worried about her, Vera. The girl's like one of my own.' Ruby wiped her eyes on the corner of her apron. 'That was no way for her to hear that her husband is dead.'

Vera nodded. 'The girl's a bit on the brassy side, but she's always meant well.'

Ruby nodded. She could have taken Vera up on

her comment about Maisie, but now wasn't the time. In a strange way, she was being kind. 'Sarah and Freda are sitting with her at the moment so she's not alone when she wakes up. I was truly blessed to have my Eddie with me for so many years. I can only imagine what it must feel like to be young and have all your dreams and plans for the future dashed to nothing.'

Vera patted Ruby's hand. 'Don't go getting yourself upset, Ruby. You've got to be strong for the girls. From all accounts Maisie hasn't got any family to speak of, so she needs her friends right now. What I don't understand is what that old cow Doreen Taylor said about her murdering her own sister. We know that Maisie loved Joe and she didn't send him off to be killed. But her own sister?'

Ruby nodded. 'From what Sarah told me, the woman was demented and then stormed off out of Woolworths. Everyone was too worried about Maisie to bother much about what Doreen said at the time. Why, that Betty Billington was a marvel getting people to help Maisie and controlling the customers waiting outside the shop who all wanted to know what was going on.'

'Do you think Woolworths will want to get rid of Maisie after this? Accusations of murder can't be ignored, can they?'

'The girl is well thought of at Woolworths. Why, she's the life and soul of the place. For Maisie's sake I need to get to the bottom of what happened to Joe. The only way to do that is for me to go visit Doreen Taylor and find out what she was ranting about,' Ruby declared.

Vera was quiet for a moment. 'I don't envy you that. Do you want me to come with you for support in case she lays into you?'

Ruby reached for her coat and hat. 'That's good of you, Vera, but this is something I should do on my own. I'd be grateful if you could stay here and keep an ear out in case the girls need anything.'

'I'll put the kettle on and take a brew up to them.'

'You're a love. You might keep an eye on the time, as Freda needs to get to work in a couple of hours. She doesn't want to be late for her shift at Burndept's.'

'That's another puzzle if you ask me.'

'What's that, Vera?' Ruby asked as she picked up her bag.

'Freda. Why did she leave her job in Woolworths to go do shift work at Burndept's factory? It's a right mucky job apparently. In fact, what do you know about the girl apart from her moving down here from the Midlands?'

Ruby sucked in her breath and silently counted to ten. Vera had been a good neighbour stepping in to help when Maisie had been brought home from work in deep shock that morning. Truth be known, she was probably being nosy, but she was still a help to Ruby as she fussed around the girls and tried to keep Sarah calm. None of them wanted anything to happen to the baby.

'There's nothing mysterious about Freda, Vera. The girl wanted to do some war work and Burndept's were calling out for workers now they have shifts running round the clock. By all accounts it's essential war work, so she's more than doing her bit. I reckon that when this war is over, she will return to Woolies and be back working with her mates.' Ruby didn't add that she was also more than a little puzzled about Freda's sudden change of heart about moving back to number thirteen and leaving her shop job. No doubt she would get to the bottom of things in time. For now it was good to have Maisie and Freda living safely under her roof. She'd sort out Maisie's problems and worry about Freda when the time came.

'I'll be off now, Vera. Keep your fingers crossed Mrs Taylor will talk to me civilly and not be as verbal as she was to poor Maisie. Oh, and if you hear a scratching at the back door, it'll be Nelson. There are some scraps for him in the pantry.'

'Nelson?'

'My dog.' Ruby had put off mentioning she'd taken in the dog, as she knew what Vera's reaction would be. 'I've got to calling him Nelson because of the black patch on his eye. He's been sleeping in the Anderson shelter.'

Vera was horrified. 'He'll be full of fleas. You don't want a mangy dog hanging around, not with a baby in the house before too long.'

'He hasn't got fleas, Vera. Freda dragged the tin bath into the garden and gave him a good scrub. He's company for me for when the girls are at work and George ain't visiting. Right, I'll be off. See you later.'

Ruby marched down Manor Road trying hard to be brave. There was no knowing what state she'd find the Taylor woman in when she reached her door. Doreen was a proper docker's wife: she stood for no nonsense from anyone and seemed to have a nasty word to say about all and sundry. She'd even been known to black another woman's eye. Ruby would rather leave well alone and not speak to the woman, but what she did to Maisie in Woolworths was unforgiveable, and as Maisie had no family around to care for her, it was Ruby's duty to fill the gap. Besides, it was only fair that Maisie knew the circumstances surrounding her husband's demise, and Doreen Taylor was the only person in the know. Ruby was also eaten up with curiosity as to what Doreen Taylor was on about when she accused Maisie of murdering her sister. Not that she'd confess that to Vera.

The house was at the end of the long road just before it turned into the dirt track that led down to the riverbank and the Erith Marshes. Ruby breathed in the saltiness from the river and composed herself for the task ahead. If it wasn't for the barrage balloons bobbing in the sky along the river, no one would have known there was a war on. But Ruby, now standing on the doorstep, was only there because a soldier had died, and she knew only too well that the war had truly entered their lives. She prayed that Maisie would get over this and lead a normal life once more.

Ruby tapped on the door and it swung open slightly. Rather than a hallway like the houses in Alexandra Road, the door to this small two-up, two-down abode led straight into the living room.

'Mrs Taylor ... Doreen, are you there? I'm Ruby Caselton. Your daughter-in-law works with my granddaughter.' She listened for a sound that told her Doreen was home: 'Do you mind if I come in?' There was no sound to suggest there was anyone at home. Ruby stepped slowly into the dark interior. 'Oh my God...'

'Tea up, girls. I found a few biscuits to go with it. There's nothing better than a cup of tea to perk you up.' Vera pushed into the bedroom and placed a tray on the spare bed. 'Tuck in, everyone.'

Maisie propped herself up on one elbow and looked around her. 'I don't... What happened...?' A look of horror crossed her face as she slumped back into the pillows. 'Joe?'

'There, there, dearie. No need to upset yourself, and I'm sure what your mother-in-law said about your sister isn't true. Is it?' Vera leant in to look at Maisie's face before patting her hand.

'Thank you for the tea, Mrs Munro,' Sarah said, guiding Vera towards the bedroom door. 'We will bring the cups downstairs when we've finished with them.'

'Well, if you're sure, dearie. It's no trouble for me to stay...'

'You must have a lot to be getting on with,' Freda called out to the older woman. 'Please don't let us keep you.' She grinned at Maisie, who gave a weak smile back to her friend.

Sarah checked that Vera had gone downstairs before closing the bedroom door. 'I'm sure she means well, but she is so nosy at times. How are you feeling, Maisie? You gave us quite a shock when you fainted like that.'

'I just didn't expect to hear news of Joe while I was at work. I always thought a letter or telegram went to the next-of-kin at their home. I was his next-of-kin, and I know he put that on his papers 'cos he told me he did.' She reached for a sodden handkerchief and wiped her eyes. 'You both know I didn't want him to join up. That bloody woman has made it look as though I put on a Jerry uniform and shot me own husband.'

Sarah put her arms around her friend and held her close. 'I'm sure no one thinks badly of you, Maisie. Why, most of the staff were calling out to your mother-in-law as she left Woolies, and the comments weren't polite. So many people care for you, Maisie, whatever that horrid Doreen Taylor says.'

Maisie nodded. Always so perfectly coiffured, her face always powdered and her lips always painted red, it was a shock for her friends to see her in such a state, with no care for how she looked. 'She's never liked me. That's why I was so grateful to Ruby when she invited me to live here. I know I was doing you a favour, Sarah, what with you not wanting Ruby to be on her own, but if the truth be known, I didn't want to be living with the old witch once Joe was away.' At the mention of her husband's name, fresh tears threatened to fall, but Maisie forced them back. 'I didn't do what she said, you know.'

Freda perched on the bed next to Sarah. 'You don't have to explain yourself to us, Maisie. We don't give a fig what that horrid woman says.'

Maisie sat up straight and took the cup and saucer that Sarah held out to her. 'No, I want to tell you both about it. I'm not proud of what 'appened, but I don't want any secrets between us. I'd only ever told Joe and he must have men- tioned it to his mum. Look where that got me...

286

Not that I'll blame Joe for one moment. He was good to me and there's no mistake. He put me on the straight and narrow after what 'appened and I'll always be grateful to him for that, whatever anyone says.'

Freda chewed her lip. Perhaps she shouldn't have secrets from her friends either. But how could she explain about Lenny and what happened?

'Drink your tea and stop looking so sad, Freda. I'm gonna tell you what 'appened and then there won't be any more secrets. I was brought up in Bermondsey near Tower Bridge. That's South London,' she explained to Freda. 'There was me, Fred, who's two years older than me, and our Sheila, who was the baby of the family and five years younger. Mum and Dad worked at the Courage brewery not far away, so I was expected to look out for Sheila when Mum wasn't 'ome. I was fourteen and planning to get myself a job at the biscuit factory the summer it happened. It was a bloody 'ot day and we'd gone with a crowd of other kids to the Serpentine. Sheila wanted to paddle, and Fred's mates planned to play football.' Maisie's eyes took on a faraway look. A flash of pain shot across her pale face.

'You don't have to tell us now, Maisie. It can wait,' Sarah said, aware that talking about the loss of her young sister must be a painful experience.

'No, I need to get this of my chest once and for all. I never want to keep another secret as long as I live. Well, I had a new swimsuit, and even though I wasn't much off my fifteenth birthday, I fancied meself as a bit of a movie queen, like Jean

Harlow, and when a couple of lads hung around and started to chat to me, I forgot about Sheila and only had eyes for them. It was when someone screamed that a kid was unconscious in the water that I remembered our Sheila, but by then it was too late...' The sobs that Maisie had so valiantly held back while she told her story burst forth and it took both girls a while to calm her.

'Why not try to have a little sleep, Maisie?' Freda stroked her friend's hair back from her damp face.

Maisie brushed her hand away. 'No, no, I want to get this all of me chest now. The police said that Sheila had hit her 'ead, and with it being so crowded and her being such a little kid, no one had seen her in distress. I should have been watching her. It was my job and I let everyone down – especially our Sheila.'

'But, Maisie, it was an accident,' Sarah soothed her friend.

Maisie shook her head violently. 'No, my parents blamed me and they were right. Dad said I might as well have murdered her meself for all the care I took, and Mum ... well, she couldn't bear to look at me. After a few months I knew I was best away from home so they could forget about me and what I'd done completely. I packed a bag and left in the middle of the night and headed towards Kent. I'd thought about going to the hop fields, as I'd heard so much about them, but as it was, I only got as far as Woolwich and picked up a job serving in a greasy spoon. After a year or so I got a job as a live-in barmaid and got on with me life. I was popular, got on well with the punters and went out with a few blokes, who didn't ask any questions about me previous life. Our Sheila's death had been reported in the papers, and stuff like that sticks. Most people don't want to know a woman who as good as killed a kid. That's the way it was until Joe walked into the pub and I fell 'ead over heels for 'im. I think you know the rest.'

Sarah didn't know what to say. Her own life seemed so easy compared to what Maisie had put up with.

'Oi! What the bloody hell do you think you're doing in my 'ouse?'

Ruby jumped as Doreen Taylor woke from her drunken slumber. When she'd first stepped into the house, Ruby had thought Doreen was dead. Framed photographs had been wrenched from a picture rail, and ornaments had been knocked from the sideboard and mantelpiece. An empty bottle of gin lay broken on the floor. Ruby had never before seen such destruction.

'I came to see you. We need to talk. There was no need to shout yet mouth off like that in Woolworths. You know Maisie lives at my place. Why couldn't you knock on my door and break the news to the girl in a more sensitive way, eh?'

'What's it got to do with you? That girl ruined my son's life and now he's dead. How am I supposed to manage without him? It was bad enough he had his pay sent to her, let alone that I lost her housekeeping money when you lured her to live with you. Blimey, you must be coining it in with the amount of money coming into your house. You lot in Alexandra Road have always thought yerself a bit above the rest of us with yer bay windows and net curtains.'

'Now we're coming to the point. You don't give a damn about that girl or your son. It's losing the money that you're concerned with.'

'Well, she ain't gonna put any money through me letter box each week now she's not got a man to support her, is she? I've got ter look out for meself.'

Ruby looked at the woman sprawled in front of her. She had no respect for a person who would do what she'd done to Maisie. Greed and self-preservation had outweighed any grief the woman may have felt.

Doreen Taylor reached out for the gin bottle on the floor before realizing it had smashed. She pulled herself to her feet with some difficulty and headed to the small kitchen. Ruby could hear her rummaging in a cupboard and swearing to herself as she searched for more alcohol. Ruby enjoyed a social tipple, but God forbid that the taste of drink ever turned her into the drunk, sodden hag that Maisie's mother-in-law had become. No wonder the girl was desperate to move away from Manor Road. Maisie was a good girl to keep sending money to the woman, even though most of it would have been spent on booze.

She looked on the table that stood in the middle of the untidy room. It looked as though Doreen had turned the contents of the sideboard drawer out searching for something. Ruby spied a crumpled telegram. This must have been what she took to Woolies when she confronted Maisie. She picked it up and scanned the few words as quickly as she could in case the woman came back into the room and noticed Ruby was poking around in her property. She tried not to gasp aloud when she spotted the telegram was addressed to Maisie and not Doreen. The old bag had opened her daughter-in-law's correspondence. Nearby, an envelope confirmed that it was addressed to Maisie, and alongside that were an insurance policy and Maisie and Joe's marriage certificate. What was the old cow up to? Was she going to fleece Maisie out of any inheritance she was entitled to from the death of her husband? Well, she'd soon put a stop to that. Ruby stuffed the paperwork into her pocket. By rights it all belonged to Maisie anyway. She was only returning it to its rightful owner. She turned and left Doreen Taylor's home. She had nothing more to say to her.

'Phew, what a day, Nelson. I'm glad to have a sit-down and put my feet up.' Ruby stroked the dog's head as he leant against her knee. She had taken to allowing the dog into the house when she was alone or the girls had gone to bed. He was a comfort and demanded nothing from her apart from the occasional meal and a bowl of fresh water.

'I wonder who your owner is. I should make some enquiries, I suppose, but if truth be known, I'd miss you, lad, if you were taken away now.' The dog placed his paw on Ruby's knee and gazed up at her with his large brown eyes. 'I'll put a card up in the corner shop when I get around to it. There's no great rush. Let's listen to the wireless while we wait for Freda to come home from her late shift, shall we? It's about time for the news. No doubt it's not gonna be good.'

Ruby turned the large knob on the Bakelite wireless and waited for it to warm up, wondering what the news would be this evening.

'Nan, any chance of a cuppa? I'm gasping. I think it's all that talking we've done today.' Sarah yawned and stretched her arms as she entered the room.

'Sit yourself down, love. I was just thinking of making some cocoa. Would you fancy that?'

'Lovely. I see you've let Nelson indoors again.'

'He's no trouble at all. He's good company for me.'

Sarah laughed. She knew her nan had a soft spot for the stray dog. 'I'm sure he is, as long as you can manage to feed him.'

'There's always a few scraps going, and I reckon he would guard the house a treat when we aren't here. The wireless is just warming up. I thought I'd listen to a bit of news. See if anything is happening. Make yourself comfortable and I'll get that cocoa.'

Sarah sat on the sofa and tucked her feet underneath her. She was feeling more tired every day and relished the time she could sit and just relax. Everyone was telling her to stop work and rest at home, but she still wanted to walk to Woolworths each day and be able to focus on her job to keep her mind off Alan and the dangers he must be facing. 'The news is starting, Nan.'

Ruby handed Sarah her cocoa and made herself comfortable in her armchair. 'Right, let's have a listen and see what's been happening in the world today.'

'Oh my God, Nan! Something's happened.' Sarah turned the volume on the wireless as high as it would go. They listened intently as broadcaster Bernard Stubbs gave the grave news from Dover.

'For days and nights ships of all kinds have plied to and fro across the Channel under the fierce onslaught of the enemy's bombers, utterly regardless of the perils, to bring out as many as possible of the trapped BEF. There was every kind of ship that I saw coming in this morning, and every one of them was crammed full of tired, battle-stained and bloodstained British soldiers...'

'What does "BEF" mean?'

'Nan, it means "British Expeditionary Forces". I wonder if all those ships I saw from the riverfront the other day were heading over to save our boys.'

'They may well have been. Ssh, listen. It's just too awful.'

'...Soon after dawn this morning I watched two warships steaming in, one listing heavily to port under the enormous load of men she carried on her decks. In a few minutes her tired commander had her alongside and a gangway was thrown from her decks to the quay. Transport officers counted the men as they came ashore. No question of units. No question of regiments. No question even of nationality, for there were French and Belgian soldiers who had fought, side by side, with the British at the battle of Flanders...'

Ruby pulled her handkerchief from the sleeve of her blouse and dabbed at her eyes. 'Those poor lads.'

'...All of them were tired, some were completely

exhausted, but the most amazing thing was that practically every man was reasonably cheerful and most of them managed a smile. Even when a man was obviously on the verge of collapse from sheer fatigue, you could still tell by his eyes that his spirit was irrepressible. And that is a thing that all the bombs in Germany will never crush...'

Ruby and Sarah remained silent, listening intently and not believing what they heard.

'...Another man told me how he'd been on the beach at Dunkirk for three days with hundreds of his comrades waiting for a boat. Embarkation was often difficult because the pier had been bombed and the ships could not get close enough in. So they joined the ships in boats and paddled in the water some of the way. All the time the gallant German airmen were bombing and machine-gunning with no discrimination between the fit and the wounded, and with no discrimination between the warships and the hospital ships...'

'How can they continue to fire at wounded men, Nan?' Sarah asked as she listened to the horrifying news.

'I don't know, love. War is a mystery to me.'

'...The organization at the port was excellent: the ships were being unloaded at an astonishing speed. No sooner were they emptied they were disappearing through the harbour entrance back to France to fetch more men home...'

'God bless 'em all,' Ruby murmured.

Sarah could only nod in agreement.

'...On the station, I watched the men climb into the long waiting trains, where it was astounding to walk from carriage to carriage full of soldiers to find silence, for most of them were fast asleep where they sat...'

'Those poor men must be completely shattered. I can't imagine having to endure such torture. Fancy not knowing what was going to happen while on the beach.' Ruby held her handkerchief to her face, not wanting to hear what came next.

'...*Train after train puffed out of the station, all full of sleeping men. All the way along the line, the people of England stood at the level crossings and the back gardens to wave at them. And so the men of the BEF came home.*'

'We are losing this war, aren't we, Nan?'

'It's certainly a setback, Sarah, but we won't say we've lost until Hitler's walking up Erith High Street. Then he'll 'ave me to face,' Ruby declared defiantly.

Sarah was pretty sure her nan meant what she said.

They both sat in silence contemplating what the broadcaster had reported.

'What the hell does that dog want?' Ruby asked as Nelson started to scratch at the back door, barking and jumping to be let into the garden.

'For heaven's sake, lad, you'd better not be chasing next door's cat again. I don't want to have to face them if you ever catch him. Mind you, it would stop the bugger digging up my carrots and leaving his little parcels everywhere.' Ruby eased herself out of her armchair and opened the door, whereupon Nelson raced to the Anderson shelter, barking furiously at the entrance. 'Don't say we have a rat in there. Vera reckons she's seen them in her shelter.'

Sarah shuddered. 'One of us is going to have to

look, otherwise the neighbours will be complaining.'

Ruby armed herself with a broom. 'If our lads can face the Germans, we can face one rat. Stay behind me in case it bites. Nelson, shut up and come here.'

The dog obeyed his new mistress and stopped his barking, although he stayed alert and bright-eyed. Sarah picked up a torch from where it had been left by the door in case of an air raid and reached for the poker beside the fire before following Ruby out into the dark garden. Nelson lay by the entrance to the Anderson shelter and growled quietly, his attention focused on whatever lay within.

Ruby leant closer to Sarah and whispered in her ear, 'I'm going to throw the door back and holler as loud as I can. If anything gets too close to you, wallop it with your poker. That'll scare off any rodents in there.'

Sarah nodded and raised the poker over her shoulder ready to take aim.

Ruby reached forward slowly and, using the broom, pushed open the door that George had built to protect anyone inside the shelter and bellowed, 'Get out of there now, yer bugger.'

For a moment there was silence; then a plaintive voice called out, 'Don't hurt me, missus. I didn't mean no harm.'

A face appeared at the door. In the dim light from her torch Sarah could see a young man. She felt that perhaps she'd seen him somewhere before, as there was something familiar about his features. She lowered the poker. 'Come out slowly and don't try anything stupid.'

The man climbed out of the shelter and walked towards the back door as Nelson followed close behind, keen to snap at his heels if he tried to run away.

'Inside and sit yourself in that chair.' Ruby indicated it with a nod as she closed the back door and pulled the blackout curtain across. Both women stood in front of him as he cowered slightly.

'Now, where have you come from, and what were you doing in our shelter?' Ruby asked, still holding the broom firmly and ready to bash him on the head if he dared to do anything wrong.

At that moment, they heard a key in the front door and a familiar voice. 'It's only me. I got off on time for once.' Freda entered the room, her eyes widening in amazement at the scene in front of her. 'Lenny? What are you doing here?'

A sob caught in the young man's voice. 'Sorry, sis. I had nowhere else to go. It's that Tommy Whiffen. He found out where I was and came after me.'

21

'I think the pair of you ought to sit yourselves down and do some explaining,' Ruby said as Freda hugged the young man. They looked like two peas in a pod.

'Aw, Lenny, where have you been? I've been that worried about you,' Freda said.

'I had a job on the docks for a good while and some digs, so things weren't so bad. There's always someone wants a job doing for cash and no questions asked. Then I bumped into a bloke who recognized me and I had to leg it a bit quick. I headed towards Erith, as I knew you were here, but then you'd moved and I had to sleep rough for a couple of nights.'

Ruby frowned. 'I don't understand.'

'I'll explain as much as I can,' Freda said. 'You look fit to drop, Lenny.'

The lad nodded and leant back in the armchair.

'Lenny got in with a bit of a bad crowd when we lived at home.'

'But I didn't mean to, sis.'

'It's all right, Len – I'll tell Ruby and Sarah.' She glanced at Ruby, who nodded for her to continue with her story. 'After Dad died, Mum started courting another bloke. She said it was because we needed a father, but once he had his feet under the table, he changed overnight. He spent most of the time down the pub and we know he was carrying on with other women. Mum wouldn't have any of it. She was smitten with him. Well, that's when our Lenny started bunking off school and hanging around with Tommy Whiffen and his gang. I begged him to help me on the market and keep away from Tommy, but would he listen?'

Lenny bowed his head and looked ashamed. 'I only did a bit of fetching and carrying for him until that time we got caught.'

Ruby's face turned red and she glared at Lenny. 'There's no excuse for nicking stuff.'

'I know that now, and I wish I hadn't done it. It

was just a bit of fun.'

Ruby's heart softened. He did look contrite. Without a father figure around, any lad could go off the rails. 'Carry on, Freda. What happened next?'

'Tommy started moving into the big time. He wasn't content with a bit of nicking. He broke into a warehouse and pinched some money.'

'It was a lot of money, sis. Hundreds of pounds, which were wages for the workers.'

Ruby tutted. 'Stealing the bread from people's mouths. Terrible. Did you help him take the money, Lenny?'

Lenny was quick to respond. 'No, I was the lookout. Bob, Tommy's brother, was driving the getaway car, and his cousin Ned picked the locks so they could get in. All I had to do was stand by the gates of the warehouse and look out for the night watchman. If I saw him coming, I had to whistle like mad and jump on the running board as we made a getaway.'

'Sounds just like one of those American movies,' Sarah said, bringing in a tray holding cups of cocoa and a plate piled high with slices of bread covered in dripping. Lenny took the plate gratefully and tucked in as if he hadn't eaten for days. 'What happened next?'

'I didn't see the night watchman until he'd walked past me and had gone into the warehouse.'

'He was reading a newspaper. He couldn't even get that right,' Freda sighed.

Lenny ignored his sister. 'By the time I ran to the car, Bob was revving the engine, Ned and Tommy climbed in, and they took off with the loot. I tried to jump onto the running board, but they were going too fast and I fell and twisted my ankle.'

Ruby tried not to smile. 'It don't sound like you was made out for a life of crime, lad.'

Freda looked sad. 'But that was only the start of it. Our Lenny was nicked and the others got away with it.'

'What could they nick him for? It's not a crime to read a newspaper, is it?' Sarah asked as she sipped her cocoa.

'It is when the night watchman is coshed over the head, the wages are gone, and all he can remember is our Lenny's face,' Freda declared.

'Oh bugger,' was all Ruby could think to say.

'They sent me to prison for eight years.'

'Eight years? But you're no more than a kid. When did this happen?'

'Two years ago.'

Ruby scratched her head in confusion. 'I don't understand. Why didn't you tell them about this Tommy bloke, and why did they let you out of prison so soon?'

Lenny looked to Freda for help, but she nodded for him to explain. 'Tommy got word to me that if I spilt the beans and told the coppers about his gang, he'd hurt our Freda, but if I kept quiet and served me sentence, he'd see me all right afterwards and Freda wouldn't be hurt.'

Sarah gasped. 'Was that chap that was hanging about your old digs the Christmas before last one of Tommy's gang, do you think, Freda?'

'I think it might have been. I'd sent Mum a Christmas card with a postal order inside for her

Christmas box. I'd just written that I was all right, but the envelope may have given a clue to where I was.'

Sarah briefly explained to Ruby the reason why Freda had moved away from her first lodging house so quickly that Christmas.

'Well, I never,' Ruby declared. 'I still don't understand why Freda came to Erith. Not that you aren't welcome,' she added hastily. 'And why did that bloke follow you?'

'I decided to move down to Erith after I received a letter from Lenny warning me to stay away and saying that he had escaped from a prison down near Maidstone. The envelope had Erith on the postmark. He'd had to have posted it somewhere around here, so if I hung around long enough, I thought I might just find him before he got himself in any more trouble. I think when I sent my card to Mum, before that Christmas, my stepfather would have seen it and guessed by the postmark where I was. No doubt Tommy Whiffen was sniffing around asking where we were. Our stepfather will do anything for a few bob in his pocket to spend at the pub or down the dogs. He would have shown Tommy. I'm such a fool.'

'You're no fool, Freda,' said Sarah. 'You just wanted to protect your family. Anyone would have done the same. Lenny, why did you escape from prison? Wouldn't it have been best to tell the governor what you knew?'

'It was horrid in prison, and when I told someone I was innocent, they started knocking me about and calling me names and everything. I didn't have anyone to talk to in there and knew I

301

couldn't face another six years behind bars. I did plan to go back to the Midlands eventually and tell the coppers what arrested me, but I was worried about Freda down here on her own. Then I was frightened in case they sent me back to prison.' He looked so tired and close to tears. 'I ended up not knowing what to do, and then I thought that I'd left it too long to tell them I was innocent. When the war started, I didn't think anyone would be bothered with me, so I carried on doing odd jobs and that. Freda, I don't know what to do.' He looked at his sister beseechingly and Freda turned to look at Sarah and Ruby. What were they to do?

'I think before we make any decision, we should let this lad have a wash and some shut-eye. You need your sleep as well, Sarah. It can't be doing that great-grandchild of mine any good you being up so late. Get yourself up to bed. Freda, take your brother out to the scullery and show him where the soap and water are. There's a few bits of clothes that were my Eddie's you can put on while your own clothes are washed. No doubt they'll drown you, but needs must. I'll get you a blanket and pillow. You can sleep on the settee for tonight and Nelson will keep you company. I'll make sure the house is locked and bolted. No one will come to any harm tonight. They'll have me to answer to if they want to come in here and cause any trouble.'

Lenny gave Nelson a wary glance but nodded in agreement.

Ruby pulled a thick woollen blanket from the top

of a wardrobe in the spare room as Sarah slipped into bed. 'Can I get you a hot-water bottle?'

'I'm fine, thanks, Nan. It's summer, so I'm not really cold.'

'I know, love, but in your condition you have to take care,' Ruby said as she sat down on the end of the bed, the blanket on her lap.

Sarah laughed. 'What's happened to all that talk about women being able to work and have a baby as well as keeping the family home in order?'

'I stand by that, but I can spoil my grand-daughter, can't I? By the way, how does Maureen feel about you staying here? Is she all right on her own?'

'She's fine, Nan. It was Maureen who was pumping tea down us when Maisie collapsed at Woolies. She told me to stay and be with Maisie for as long as it takes.'

'That's good of her. It's been a rum old day. Who would have thought Maisie would find out about her Joe like that? Bad enough to hear your husband's dead, let alone in the middle of a busy shop and from that awful woman Doreen Taylor too.'

'It was good of you to go and sort her out, Nan, and pick up what belonged to Maisie. When I looked in just now, she had fallen asleep holding her wedding licence. The poor girl's got a lot to face in the coming days.'

Ruby nodded. 'She's strong and she's got us to help her through it.'

'Nan, I was wondering... Do you think that Joe was caught up in the evacuation at Dunkirk? The bit we heard on the wireless sounded awful. So many men injured and killed. We are definitely losing this war.'

Ruby thought for a while. 'We won't lose this war, Sarah. Don't think it for a moment. It may take months, years even, but we will win. The British have a spirit that no German can break.'

'You're right there, Nan.'

'As for Joe, I don't think we'll know for sure, but it may have been a while ago that he died. We know he was on foreign shores, and most likely he was over there, but news takes a while to travel, especially in wartime. Maisie will know more one day, but she may have to face the fact she won't have a body to bury. It happened in the last war. However sad it is to stand at a graveside, it helps no end when a woman is grieving for her man.'

Sarah fell silent.

'Are you thinking of your Alan?'

'Yes. He could have been there, Nan. The man on the wireless said our planes were flying over the Channel trying to protect the ships.'

'He'll be fine, love. Have you heard from him lately, since he told you how pleased he was about the baby?'

Sarah burst into heartrending sobs, covering her face with her hands. 'Oh, Nan, I don't know what to do.'

Ruby dropped the blanket to the floor and reached over to put her arms around her grand-daughter. 'There, there, love. Whatever is wrong?' She rocked her in her arms until the tears subsided.

Sarah gulped and rubbed away the tears with the corner of the bed sheet. 'I haven't heard from Alan. Not since I wrote about the baby. I just said he'd written and was happy as I didn't want Maureen to worry. Now, with all this news from Dunkirk, I don't know what to think.'

'You silly girl. You shouldn't have kept this all to yourself,' Ruby soothed her granddaughter. 'Why, he's probably training and working all hours, God knows where, and his letters just haven't arrived yet. Now, you settle yourself down and try to get some sleep. No more secrets. I think we've had enough of them for one day, don't you?' Ruby pulled the covers up over her granddaughter's shoulders and tucked her in. Turning out the light and pulling the door to, she wondered why Alan hadn't been in touch and prayed he was safe.

Alone in the dark, Sarah's fears multiplied. How could she tell her nan that she thought that Alan didn't love her anymore? No one else seemed to notice how much he had changed at Christmas. He'd met new people who came from a different world from his new wife and family. The news of the baby must have been too much. Would she ever hear from him again? Did he still love her?

'Tuck in, and then you can listen to what I have to say.' The faces round Ruby's table looked apprehensive as they watched her dish out portions of porridge from a large saucepan. 'This'll stick to your ribs and keep you going until dinnertime.'

Maisie placed a hand over her bowl and re-moved a cigarette from her mouth with the other hand, blowing smoke away from the pan. She'd been chain-smoking since appearing downstairs still in her dressing gown and unwashed. If she was surprised to see Lenny at the table, she didn't say so and hardly acknowledged him when Freda made the introductions. 'Not for me, ta. I'm off out as soon as I've got meself ready. I'll get something then.'

'But, Maisie, you didn't eat anything yesterday. Why not take yourself back to bed? I managed to get a nice bit of brisket yesterday, and I'm going to make it into a pie so it'll stretch a bit further. You'll be ready for that by dinnertime. They don't expect you at Woolworths today, so you can take it easy.'

Maisie glared at Ruby. 'I said I'm going out. I've got things to do.'

'If you want to wait until tomorrow, Maisie, I can come with you if you like? It's my day off, so we can go wherever you want.' Sarah tried to pacify her friend. 'You've had an awful shock. Perhaps you should rest a little more today.'

'I said I'm going out. Why can't you all just leave me alone?' Maisie rose to her feet. 'I'm off to get meself dressed.'

Ruby raised her eyebrows at Sarah. It was better to let the girl alone. She wasn't herself at the moment. 'As you please, love. Just remember we're here if you need us.'

Maisie stubbed out the remains of her cigarette and lit another. She nodded to Ruby and left the room.

'Right, you lot, stop your gawping and finish your porridge. We've got things to do. As soon as we've cleared the table, we are going to write down everything you know about this chap Trevor Whiffen.'

'His name is Tommy Whiffen, Mrs Caselton,

306

but I don't know what good it'll do. I'll be off out of your hair this morning. I shouldn't have come here in case I was followed.'

'Trevor, Tommy, it doesn't matter to me what his name is as long as he pays his dues and you two young ones aren't in fear of your lives. As for you heading off, Lenny, you can just stay where you are. I have plans for you, young man.'

Freda and Lenny spent an age at the table writing down anything they could think of about Tommy Whiffen and his gang. From time to time Ruby would stop to ask a question. How did Lenny first know of their crimes? Did they force Lenny to do wrong? Did he try to escape their clutches? What really happened on the night of the warehouse robbery?

By the time the midday meal was ready, Ruby had read through every word that Lenny and Freda had written and decided there was nothing more to add. Against his wishes Ruby had even insisted he wrote down why and how he'd escaped from prison and what he'd been doing in the time he'd been on the run. 'Be as honest as you can, Lenny, and the authorities will do their best to listen to you,' she advised as she put a plate on top of Sarah's dinner ready for her to heat over a pan of boiling water when she returned home from work.

Ruby had invited Maureen as well, as she was worried the woman would feel lonely with Sarah staying at number thirteen to care for Maisie, but Maureen assured them she understood and was taking herself off to the pictures with her neighbour, so they weren't to worry. All the same, Ruby did worry, as Maureen was family now, even though Sarah had not heard from Alan since Christmas. Whatever was that lad playing at? There was so much going on in their lives that Ruby's head was in a spin. She didn't know what to think.

'Authorities, Mrs Caselton? I don't want anything to do with no authorities. It's them what put me behind bars to begin with,' Lenny said as he piled his fork with cabbage, which his own sister had grown in Ruby's garden.

'What put you behind bars, young Lenny, was that Tommy Whiffen forcing you to tell lies on his behalf. Now, you can stay here tonight and then tomorrow we will walk down to the police station and you can hand yourself in. We can show them what you've written and let the police look into this sorry mess and sort it out once and for all.'

Lenny dropped his knife and fork onto his plate with a clatter. 'What? Me go back to prison? No, I'm sorry, Mrs Caselton, but I ain't going back there – not for a million pounds.'

'No one is offering you money, Lenny. If you go back to prison for now, then this Tommy Whiffen won't be wanting to harm Freda. You will be safe as well. Once the police know the truth, the right person will be locked up and then you will be set free. Now, eat your dinner up before it gets cold. We need to get you a haircut so you look presentable for tomorrow. Your clothes are washed and ironed, and you can keep the bits you're wearing now.'

Lenny bent his head over his dinner and muttered, 'Yes, Mrs Caselton.'

Freda looked at her brother and wondered. What was Lenny thinking right now?

'Sit yourself down, Sarah. You look all in. Your dinner will be warm before too long.'

Sarah kicked her shoes off and rubbed her ankles. 'Thanks, Nan. I worked through my lunch hour. What with Maisie off and us being short-staffed, I just had a sandwich with Betty in the office. How is Maisie?'

'Your guess is as good as mine, love. She hasn't come home since this morning. It's nearly seven o'clock. I hope she's all right.'

'Do you think we should go out and look for her, Nan?'

'How would we know where to start?'

Sarah shook her head. 'I have no idea. Whenever she wasn't going to work, she went out with me and Freda, unless she went to Woolwich to buy fabric at the market. I don't think dress-making is on her mind today. Do you think she's done something silly?'

Ruby shook her head. 'I wouldn't think so, love. She's made of stern stuff is our Maisie.'

'But she's been so down since Joe joined up, and it was only yesterday that she collapsed in Woolworths. We shouldn't have let her go out on her own.'

'We had no choice in the matter, Sarah. She made it quite clear she didn't want our help. We couldn't very well follow her, could we? We will just have to wait for her to come home. I only hope she isn't too late. I'm fair exhausted after last night and Lenny turning up like that. Young Freda's

309

been right embarrassed about what happened. I told her not to be so daft. She really should have told us everything sooner. We may have been able to help her. She's not got a shift tonight, so I suggested she take Lenny to the pictures. It'll cheer him up before he goes back to prison. It's a shame, though, as Nelson has really taken to the lad.'

Sarah almost choked on her cup of tea. 'What? He's going back to prison? How did you manage that, Nan?'

Ruby went to the sideboard and pulled out pages of paper covered with Lenny and Freda's handwriting. 'Read that while I get your dinner. I've explained to Lenny that if he goes back to prison, we can get the police to sort the mess out and I think they might let him out. It's obvious the lad was set up, and there's enough on that paper to lock Tommy Whiffen up for a very long time.'

Sarah scanned the sheets of paper, and although she was surprised at what was written there, she couldn't help think that Nan was rather optimistic that Lenny would be let out of prison so quickly.

Sarah was just finishing off a knitted bootee when there was a sharp knock at the door. Ruby, who had been dozing in her armchair, jumped and dropped the newspaper she'd still been holding. 'It must be Freda and Lenny. Why didn't they use the key that's hanging inside the front door?' she said as she pulled herself to her feet and headed towards the hall.

'We took the key off the string, Nan, in case Mr Hitler broke in. Remember?' Sarah grinned to herself. They'd pulled Nan's leg for ages about that. 'Don't forget the blackout.'

'Goodness, Vera, whatever are you doing banging on my door at this time of night? It's nearly ten o'clock.'

Vera hurried into the room gasping for breath. 'I thought you ought to know. It's Maisie. I ran all the way here.'

'My goodness, Vera. Calm yourself down and take a few deep breaths. Now, what about Maisie? Has there been an accident?'

'No, much worse.'

Sarah felt her head, spin as she rose to her feet. Whatever had happened, she had to get to her friend as soon as possible. 'Where is she, Mrs Munro?' Sarah wanted to scream with impatience as Vera eked out the dramatic moment, putting her hand to her heart and breathing deeply.

'Maisie Taylor is at the Prince of Wales with a couple of soldiers and she's the worse for drink.' Vera looked from Sarah to Ruby to make sure they had both absorbed her scandalous news.

'When you say she's the worse for drink, exactly what do you mean, Vera?' Ruby demanded.

'What I mean is that if someone doesn't sort her out, I think she will be in a sorry state tomorrow and may not know whose bed she wakes up in.' Vera looked like the cat who'd got the cream.

'Now's not the time to gloat, Vera. Maisie doesn't know if she's coming or going at the moment. She needs friends, not people who are going to question her morals.'

'Hear, hear, Nan. I know what I'm going to do. I'm going to find my friend and bring her home where she is welcome.' Sarah headed for the front door, only stopping to slip her feet into her shoes.

'I'm right behind you, love. Vera, I'll thank you not to come gloating at my front door, thank you very much.'

'I came to tell you she was in trouble,' Vera moaned as she followed them out of the front door.

Sarah and Ruby could hear a piano playing loudly as they crossed the road to the Prince of Wales public house. Sarah was reminded of the night of the Woolworths Christmas party, when she first danced with Alan, how he'd held her in his arms and sung softly in her ear. They'd been back to the pub a few times while they were courting, and each time Sarah felt the pub held a special place in her heart. Somewhere she would visit when she was a grandmother and could tell her grandchildren about the day she fell in love with their granddad.

Stepping over the threshold of the busy pub, Sarah expected to be shocked by whatever it was that Vera had seen Maisie doing. Instead, she found her by the piano swaying in time to the music. Granted, alongside her were a couple of soldiers, but there was nothing untoward happening. Trust Vera to make a mountain out of a molehill.

Maisie spotted her friend by the door and called her over: 'Come and 'ave a drink and meet me friends Henry and Ollie. They used to work with my Joe. They all enlisted at the same time. Small world, innit?'

Sarah pushed through the crowd, and as she approached Maisie, she could see that her friend had indeed enjoyed a few drinks but was still in control of her faculties. Henry and Ollie shook her hand politely and offered her a drink. Sarah declined. The pub was too smoky and noisy for her liking. Henry found a chair, which she gratefully accepted.

'We were sorry to hear about Joe,' he told Sarah. 'He was a nice bloke, salt of the earth so to speak. When we met his missus in here, we didn't like to leave her alone in case she felt poorly, like. We didn't know where she lived, and she made it clear she didn't get on with her mother-in-law. Not that many of us liked her much either.'

Sarah warmed to Henry straight away. What a gentleman he was. 'Maisie lives with my nan now.' She indicated to where Ruby was sipping a glass of port and talking with Ollie. 'I think we need to get her home to her bed. The poor love is still in shock. She only heard about Joe yesterday. We have no details of what happened. Would you know?'

Henry shook his head. 'Sorry, love, I wish I could help you. We haven't seen Joe since we enlisted. I reckon he went off to France and probably copped it over there. Ollie and me was sent off to be drivers up north. We drew the lucky straws.' He looked sad. 'A bloody shame about Joe. I 'ope my missus never has to go through what his wife is going through right now.'

Sarah nodded. Perhaps her Alan was consoling another man's wife just like Henry and Ollie were.

'Would you like me and Ollie to walk you ladies home? She's a bit maudlin and I can see that you ain't in any position to steer her in the right direction much.'

'That is very kind of you. Thank you, Henry.'

Henry turned to where Maisie was leaning against the piano and humming to the music. 'Come on, my dear, time we were getting you home.' He reached out to take her arm.

Maisie pulled away. 'I want to sing a song,' she said in a slightly slurred voice. 'You've all gotta sing along with me.' She leant over and whispered into the pianist's ear. He nodded and changed the tune to something Sarah recognized. It was a sad song of lost love. 'I'll See You in My Dreams'.

Maisie stepped in front of the piano and made lots of shushing noises until all fell quiet. After a few bars everyone started to sing, but above them all Sarah could hear Maisie's plaintive voice. She could see the haunted fear in her friend's eyes as Maisie realized she would never again see her Joe.

Maisie started to sob and sank to her knees, but still she sang clear and loud of the man who had gone from her life forever.

'...*I'll see you in my dreams...*'

Henry and Ollie helped Maisie to her feet, and Sarah picked up her bag and coat. More than ever she prayed that she would not have to endure the heartache that her friend was experiencing at this moment 'Wherever you are, Alan, and whether you want to come home to me or not, please stay safe,' Sarah prayed.

'Where is he? Where's that lad got to?' A red-faced Ruby rushed to the bottom of the stairs. 'Freda? Get yourself down here now.'

Freda appeared in the doorway to the kitchen, rubbing her eyes, as Ruby slammed a blackened kettle on the stove. 'Is there anything wrong, Mrs Caselton?'

'Get yourself into the front room and tell me if you can see that brother of yours.'

Ruby followed Freda and watched as she pulled back the heavy blackout curtains, allowing early morning sunshine to flood the room. 'Oh my God! But he was here last night. I saw him go to bed.'

They both stared at the settee, where Lenny's blanket had been neatly folded on top of a pillow. Apart from that there was no evidence that he had been staying at number thirteen.

'The few bits and bobs that he had have all gone. He's scarpered,' Ruby said sadly. Her initial anger had gone and was replaced with sadness that Lenny hadn't hung around long enough to clear his name.

Freda shook her head. 'I'm so sorry. He never gave me any idea he would do this. He seemed happy enough at the pictures last night, and even when we went for a bag of chips afterwards, he chatted away like he usually does. What an idiot.'

'Fear's a strange thing, Freda. No doubt alone down here in the middle of the night, he had second thoughts. Fear can do funny things to the mind. Perhaps we were expecting too much of him to face the police and most likely go back to prison.'

'I'm embarrassed that Lenny has caused so many problems. He has left me in the same state as before he appeared and inconvenienced people that I think of as my family. I love him dearly, but right now I could ring his blooming neck.'

Ruby thought for a moment. 'But Lenny hasn't left us in the same situation.' She pulled open the drawer of the sideboard and removed the sheets of paper upon which the brother and sister had so patiently noted everything of importance about Tommy Whiffen and his gang. 'With this we can still have the bugger locked up and then you and your Lenny will be safe to go home.'

Freda took the papers from Ruby's hand and placed them back into the sideboard, firmly closing the drawer. 'I know you mean well, Mrs Caselton, but I think it's too late for that. The police will want to know why we entertained an escaped prisoner under your roof. They won't care that you think he is innocent. They may not even be interested in what Lenny wrote. Then where will we be? They could charge you and me for hiding a criminal, and perhaps Sarah as well, and that isn't a good thing in her condition, is it?'

'Blimey, I hadn't thought of it that way,' Ruby said, and sat down to think about the situation. She'd only come downstairs to let Nelson into the garden and wake the boy. She was still in her old dressing gown, and her hair hadn't seen a comb or her face a lick of soap and water.

'Well, I did, and what's worse is I fear Tommy and his gang may know that Lenny has been in the area and come looking here. Think what they would do if they found the statement. We should burn it. It will be safer for all concerned.'

'No, I'll put it somewhere safe for now. You never know – it may just come in handy one day. Let's get some breakfast on the go. Sarah will be up soon and wanting to go into work. They are so overstretched there she has cancelled her day off and offered to go in for the morning. In her condition!'

'I don't think Betty will have her come to harm. What about Maisie? Will she be down?'

Ruby sighed and thought of how they'd managed to get her home last night with the help of the two soldiers. If she woke up early, chances are she'd have such a heavy head that breakfast would be the last thing on her mind. 'Come on, let's get into the kitchen and I'll tell you all about last night.'

Ruby reached for a large cast-iron frying pan that sat on a shelf behind the stove. Striking a match, the gas came alive with a loud pop. 'We can have an egg and some toast for our breakfast, if you want? Can you fetch the bowl of eggs from the pantry?'

Freda opened the door to the pantry and stepped into the large, cool cupboard. Reaching for the bowl of eggs on one of the stone shelves, she called out to Ruby, 'There's just one thing I'd like to make clear.'

'What's that, love?'

'I'll never go back home,' Freda admitted. 'There's nothing for me in the Midlands anymore. Mum made it clear she would always side with her new husband if anything went wrong, and she reminded me of that when Lenny went to prison. I'll send her a card on her birthday and Christmas, but that's as far as it goes. Erith is my home now.'

Ruby took the bowl of eggs from Freda and put her arms around her. 'No need to get yourself upset, love. You're as welcome here as my own family, whatever happens in the future. Now, let's have our breakfast.'

22

'We have another consignment of canned snoek due in today.' Betty checked the list in front of her. 'It may be advisable to put another member of staff on the counter. It is rather popular.'

Sarah wrinkled her nose. 'Who'd have thought the war's a year old and we're eating this awful fish?' She'd only popped into Woolworths to see her friend. Being confined to home, waiting for the birth of the baby – who was due in just over a week – was driving her to distraction. She relished being talked to as a colleague by Betty rather than a delicate flower. Her mum had written from Devon almost every day telling Sarah to stop working, as it wasn't dignified for a woman in her condition to be seen at work. Only the threat that Irene would get George to collect Sarah and take her back to the West Country had made Sarah stop working the few hours each day at Woolworths that she so enjoyed. Even Ruby kept reminding her to 'think of the baby' when she was caught planting a few vegetables in Maureen's small garden. Sarah would be glad when the next few weeks had passed and she had her baby in her arms.

The one chore she had been allowed to continue with was feeding Nan's chickens, who had recently become the latest residents at number thirteen and were most amusing. The girls had given them names, despite Ruby reminding them that their new pets would be destined for the pot if they stopped laying. However, discussing the sale of the horrid canned fish called snoek was beginning to make her feel slightly nauseous. 'Ugh, it's disgusting. It tastes like burnt rubber and is only popular because it isn't rationed.'

'We must make the most of this product. With rationing starting to make supplies of some goods almost impossible to obtain, we need to make sure our counters and shelves look full. If that means stocking previously unheard of items like canned snoek, so be it. How we make it sound appealing to our customers I do not know.'

Sarah thought that with food now becoming scarce, customers would be happy just to be able to fill the bellies of their families. However, Betty had a point and they should try to help them as much as possible. She thought hard. 'We could advise customers how to turn it into a meal, I suppose. We could learn a few recipes and share them. That would encourage them to try something new.'

Betty nodded. 'Yes, that's an excellent idea. In which case, we should have the married women work that counter, as they would know more about preparing food.'

Sarah tried not to giggle. Betty could be a bit of a stuffed shirt sometimes. 'I think you'll find that most women know how to cook, Betty. It's something we learn at our mother's knee.'

'Oh dear, I feel a bit of a ninny. I'm one of those

rare females who never knew what to do in a kitchen. I have to admit I had a lot to learn when I first lived alone.'

Sarah was amazed at what her friend told her. Surely every woman knew her way around a kitchen? 'Did your servants do all the cooking?' she joked.

Betty nodded and looked embarrassed. 'We had live-in help and someone who came in once a week to deal with the laundry. I'm afraid I was not prepared for life. My mother didn't think it right for a young lady to learn such things. If my Charlie had come home from the last war, my life would have been so different to what it is now.'

'You mean you'd have had servants?' Sarah couldn't imagine that someone working at Woolworths would have had servants. Betty was the first person she had ever met who had been in that situation.

'No doubt I would have had some help in the house. That was the way my family lived in those times. That war changed a lot of things, Sarah.'

'Does your family mind that you work?'

Betty sighed. 'Sadly I was an only child. My arrival was... Let us say I was a pleasant surprise after they had been married many years. My elderly relatives are now long gone. I kept in touch with Charlie's sisters, but time has moved on and we now just exchange a card at Christmas and occasional pleasantries. When I lost Charlie, I also lost any chance of having a family.'

Sarah's heart ached for her friend. 'But you have a family now. You're part of my family. You were a bridesmaid, and you will be an honorary aunty to my baby along with Freda and Maisie.'

Betty smiled. 'I'm so thankful that you decided to work for Woolworths when you came to live with your nan. My life has changed so much since I met you. Considering we are at war, I had so much fun going to the cinema to celebrate your birthday last week and just being able to share confidences. What am I saying? Why, your life has changed too. You would never have met Alan if it were not for Woolworths.' Betty noticed the smile fade from Sarah's face. 'Have you still not heard from him?'

'No. Not a word. Maureen is being very brave. She has decided that no news is good news and until we hear otherwise, we are to assume he is very busy protecting our country.'

Betty considered what Sarah had said. She admired the girl greatly, and when Sarah had confided in her that she feared Alan no longer loved her, as he'd made no attempt to get in touch for the past eight months, she had done her best to comfort the girl and give reasons as to why Alan had remained silent. They'd grown accustomed to planes overhead. Not just the squadrons flying towards the coast, but also enemy fighter planes in dog fights over the Kent countryside. Each time she spotted a Spitfire in the sky, she thought of Alan. Goodness knows what Sarah thought. The girl had adopted a calm exterior and thought only of the child she was carrying.

Erith had yet to experience the war directly. Staff at Woolworths religiously carried out fire-watch duties and knew exactly how to help customers and direct them to the basement if an air-raid warning was to sound. There were now few male staff, apart from the much younger men and older retired staff who had returned to work when contacted by Betty. Several staff members had already lost family, including Maisie, and there were many reports of injuries, but the little town by the Thames carried on day by day, preparing for whatever would be thrown its way. Woolworths was ready and waiting should Hitler attempt to do his worst.

'Have you thought about writing to someone in authority and enquiring about Alan? They may be able to give you some news.' Betty still wore her tweed suits at work and took her role as temporary store manager seriously. However, her friendship with the younger women had influenced her slightly and she had taken to wearing a dab of powder and a little lipstick. The blouses beneath her suit jacket were not so severe, thanks to Maisie and her dressmaking skills.

A look of horror spread across Sarah's face. 'I couldn't. Either way it would be bad news.' She lay a protective hand across her stomach. 'Either my baby's father is dead or he just doesn't care about us anymore. I'd rather not know at the moment. When the baby comes, we can face the future together.' She rose to her feet. Apart from swollen ankles after a day spent at Woolies, Sarah had sailed through her pregnancy. The only sign she was expecting a child was the swell of her stomach under the colourful smocks made by Maisie in the days before she'd heard of Joe's death. 'It's time I headed back to Nan's. She insists I stay there during the day while Maureen's at work. She's convinced the baby will be early and I'll give birth alone in Maureen's front room.' Sarah started to laugh at her own joke until a sharp pain made her wince.

'My goodness, Sarah. Are you in pain? Is it the baby?' Betty jumped to her feet and rushed to take her friend's arm. 'Perhaps we should get you home. I'm sure you wouldn't be the first woman to give birth in a Woolworths store, but there are better places. I'll walk you back to Alexandra Road myself. That's if you think you can walk?'

'Don't fuss, Betty. I'm fine. I've had a few pains like this. Nan said it's to be expected. I have over a week before my due date and first babies are notoriously late. Maisie said she would walk back with me when she takes her lunch break.' Looking at the clock on the wall of Betty's office, Sarah started to pull on her coat. 'She'll be looking for me very soon, so I'll start my way downstairs. Now, you will come round for your tea this evening? Nan told me to remind you. Dad's working up here and will be home this evening. It seems an age since we've all had a family evening at home.'

'Yes, I'm looking forward to it. Thank you again for thinking of me. Now, let me help you downstairs and I'll hurry Maisie up. She tends to dawdle rather a lot.'

'Her heart isn't in anything much anymore. It's like the light's been taken out of her life since Joe's death I wonder if she will ever be the same again.'

'I miss the old Maisie,' Betty said. 'She could be brash and loud at times, but the customers liked her. I've tried to give her more responsibility –

God knows I could do with the help – but she just drifts through the day without taking much notice of the world around her. She arrives for work as tired as she was when she left the night before.'

Sarah nodded. She didn't like to say that Maisie was never at home much of an evening, and when she did arrive, at some unholy hour, there was alcohol on her breath and a different member of the armed forces waving her goodbye at the gate. Something had to change before Maisie gained the reputation of being a good-time girl. 'We need to give her time, Betty. She has friends that care for her. Together we can see her through this.'

Betty linked arms with Sarah as they headed to the stairs that led to the shop floor. 'Don't forget that we are here for you as well, Sarah.'

'I know, Betty, but I'm fine, really.' She kissed her friend on the cheek. 'I'll see you this evening.'

Sarah and Maisie walked in silence back to number thirteen. Sarah's thoughts returned to a year ago. She'd not long been home from her honeymoon and was full of hope for the future with Alan. The war was only days old, and the town was ready to face Hitler and his army. Alan was preparing to join the RAF, and although the country was at war, they still looked forward to a life together. Now, Alan had all but vanished, Joe was dead, and Maisie had turned into a stranger and was no longer the happy woman Sarah had met the day she stepped over the threshold of Woolworths.

They walked on deep in thought. Not once did Maisie mention something funny that had happened at work or tell a joke, as she would have done in the days before Joe died. The only time a smile crossed her face was when a lorry with soldiers on board drove past. Whistles and cheers were heard from the cab as the driver tooted the horn. Maisie burst into her usual smile and waved back. 'See you down the boozer later, lads.'

'Do you know those soldiers, Maisie?'

Maisie shrugged. Her smile vanished. 'I've met 'em down the Running Horses a few times. They're a bit of a laugh.'

Sarah nodded her head thoughtfully.

'What's wrong with that? You look as though you don't approve of a girl 'aving the odd drink to cheer herself up.' Maisie pouted. 'With what I've been through, no one would begrudge me the odd drink with me mates, would they?'

'Of course not, Maisie. It's just that...'

'What?'

'It's not the odd drink, though, is it? You're out every night and the worse for wear the next morning.'

'Oh, so that's it, is it? You're pulling rank on me, what with being me supervisor at work. Well, you ain't in charge of me anymore, as you've got a baby on the way and you're going to be a mother now, not a boss at Woolies anymore.'

Sarah sighed. She didn't wish to argue with Maisie. Not today. Her back ached and she felt uncomfortable. She just wanted to get home and put her feet up for a while. With Dad staying at number thirteen tonight, he might be able to put a smile on Maisie's face. Perhaps he could even have a word with her. Yes, she'd ask Dad to sort things out. She could rely on him to put the world to rights.

'I've not packed up my job. I plan to go back after the baby is born. It'll only be for a few hours a day and Nan is going to help out. Freda said she'd be only too pleased to take a turn as well when she isn't on one of her shifts.'

'What about me?'

'Pardon?'

'What about me? Why haven't you asked me to 'elp out? I thought I was yer friend.' Maisie sounded hurt.

Sarah sighed. Her friend had changed since the loss of her husband. Although someone meeting Maisie for the first time would think she was well turned out, people who knew her could see that her hairstyle was not as perfect and her make-up was a little too heavy. There were also grey shadows around her eyes, and Maisie didn't smile as much as she used to. 'Of course you are, Maisie. I only suggested it to Nan and Freda the other night. You were down the pub at the time. How could we have discussed it with you?'

A tiny flicker of annoyance crept across Maisie's face as she thought of what Sarah had said. 'All right, I s'pose I ought to think about not being out late so often. Then I'll be up to doing the odd shift looking after the baby when I'm not at Woolies.'

They'd reached the gate of number thirteen and Sarah fished around in the pocket of her coat for the door key. Ruby had stopped leaving the key on a string inside the letter box since war had broken out. It was part of her plan to stop Hitler's army invading their home. 'That would be nice, Maisie. I want the baby to spend as much time as possible with its aunties as it grows up.'

Maisie grinned. 'I forgot that I'll be an honorary aunty. That'll be fun.'

Sarah nodded in agreement. Perhaps the old Maisie wasn't far away after all.

Sarah had not long slipped into her comfortable slippers and put her feet up when a familiar eerie sound could be heard. It continued to rise to an ear-splitting wail. Ruby, half into the room with a cup of tea in her hand, was annoyed. 'It's always the bloody same. I swear the whole of the German Air Force know when I've put the kettle on. Well, they ain't going to spoil my cuppa. I'll tip it into the Thermos flask and we can take it into the shelter with us. Maisie, you get Sarah onto her feet and into the shelter. Freda, you grab the bread so we can make a few sandwiches. God knows how long we'll be there or whether it's another false alarm. I know I shouldn't wish the bombs land somewhere else, as it means some other poor bugger has been hit, but fingers crossed we'll be safe.'

Freda followed Ruby from the room, saluting behind her back, which made Maisie and Sarah laugh. A regimental sergeant major had nothing on Ruby Caselton when she organized her troops. The women were used to working quickly together once the siren went. The cooker was turned off, and tea-making provisions were quickly grabbed. Ruby had taken to leaving cushions and blankets on a chair by the back door, as she found they grew damp if left in the shelter. A little attaché case held her insurance policy and the few items of jewellery that Eddie had bought her. One of the girls made sure it went with them.

Sarah winced as Maisie pulled her from the settee.

Maisie frowned. 'Are you in pain?'

'No, it's just a twinge and a bit of backache. Being the size of an elephant doesn't help!' Sarah didn't want her family to fuss. She was just over a week away from when she'd been told the baby would arrive, although Nan had told her more than once that Caselton babies didn't hang about for due dates.

Maisie wasn't so sure it was just a twinge, but decided it was better to get Sarah into the shelter rather than keep asking questions. 'Do you want help putting yer shoes on?'

'No, thanks. I'm more comfy in my slippers. It's not so damp on the floor of the shelter since Dad put down those old wooden pallets. It hasn't rained for over a week, so I shouldn't get my feet wet. It's like home from home in there now, what with the seats and bed that Dad built, plus the cushions you made.'

'I wouldn't call it a home from home, but it's nice enough. Needs must when the devil dictates, as the saying goes,' Maisie said as she pulled on her siren suit. 'Are you fit?'

'Oh, you and your sayings,' Sarah said as she picked up her knitting bag and they headed out to the back garden. Both stopped to look skywards as they heard ack-ack guns in the distance and saw plumes of smoke in the sky. 'I don't think this is a false alarm.'

'Best we get down the shelter a bit nippy like,' Maisie said. In normal circumstances she'd have given her friend a mighty push but was considerate of her condition.

'I don't feel exactly elegant climbing down into this shelter,' Sarah said as Freda offered her a helping hand down the wooden steps. 'As soon as this baby arrives, I want one of those siren suits. It's as draughty as hell in this frock.'

'I'll make you one, and one for the baby as well, but for heaven's sake, get a move on, otherwise you'll be wearing a bloody bomb on yer 'ead,' Maisie said, flinching as they heard a mighty explosion from the river.

Freda shoved the wooden door shut behind them and pulled down a curtain that would protect the inside of the shelter from dust if there should be an explosion outside. George had built a bench along one side that could double as a bed, and opposite there was a narrow bunk bed too. 'Shall I light a candle?'

'Save them for now. I'm going to knit. I've made that many balaclava helmets I can knit them in the dark. I've got my torch if I need to pick up a dropped stitch,' Ruby said.

'Knitting in the dark it is, then,' Maisie declared. 'I'm knitting a scarf, so a few odd stitches gained or lost won't make much odds. How about you, Sarah?'

Sarah laughed. 'Perhaps by the end of this war your knitting might have improved, Maisie.'

'At the end of this war I'm going to throw away me knitting needles and never cast on or cast off again,' Maisie said. 'I'll stick to me sewing machine, thank you very much.'

'George said he's going to fix up an electric

light when he has a minute. Vera's got one in her shelter and she said it comes in very handy,' Ruby announced from the darkness.

They fell silent listening to the telltale signs from outside that showed the enemy were approaching. Each woman continued to knit, then stopped as they heard another explosion from the nearby docks.

Suddenly Sarah's groans shattered the silence.

'Oh my God, Sarah. Are you in pain? Is it the baby?' Freda shone her torch onto Sarah's face, causing her to flinch in the bright light.

'No. It's just a stitch. This bunk bed isn't the most comfortable thing to relax on.' She held her breath as another pain gripped her body. She wasn't going to worry Nan or her friends while they were in the shelter. There would be time enough later to tell them she thought that baby Gilbert was on its way; she'd try to wait for the all-clear to sound.

Maisie shuddered as the ground shook, causing a dust cloud to form in the shelter, and checked her watch by the light of the candle. They'd long ago stopped knitting. Sandwiches had been made by candlelight and consumed with relish, as it was long past their midday meal and fast approaching teatime. They now sat silently listening and praying for the all-clear.

'That was a close one. They seem to have moved away from the London docks.'

'Perhaps they're heading for home. Someone at work said the enemy planes use the Thames to guide them back to the sea and then home,'

Freda said.

'What 'appens to the bombs they have left?' Maisie wanted to know. 'I doubt they take 'em home to Hitler.'

'I heard they dump them,' Ruby said.

'What, in the river or out at sea, do you mean?' Freda asked.

'Don't be daft,' Ruby laughed. 'They dump them on the poor buggers that live between London and the coast. Old George up the Co-op's son-in-law is in the RAF and he told him that they will look for a likely site and get rid of them. London isn't the only place that has docks and the like, and the Luftwaffe aren't daft. They'll find out where our big factories are and they'll drop their bombs where they will do the most damage.'

'Like Burndept's, where I work, do you mean?' Freda asked fearfully.

'And Vickers where George works,' Ruby added. 'So think on when you're chatting to your new mates in the pub, Maisie, and mention where your friends work. Who knows who is listening? And as the posters say, careless talk costs lives.'

'Blimey. It's bloody frightening when you think about it,' Maisie said. 'Don't you think so, Sarah?'

There was silence apart from a groan where Sarah lay on the lower bunk bed.

'Sarah?' Maisie fumbled for her torch. 'Goodness, Sarah. Is the baby on its way? Why the 'eck didn't you say something earlier?'

'I ... I didn't want to worry you. I ... I thought we'd be out of the shelter and indoors by now.'

Ruby knelt beside the bunk and checked her

granddaughter. 'I think this little one is going to be born right here – and very soon.'

'No, no, this isn't how it's supposed to be...' Sarah sobbed as another pain gripped her. 'I want Alan. I want my dad.' She began to sob uncontrollably.

Maisie leant over and took her by the shoulders. Leaning into her face, she spoke clearly and loudly. 'Now look here. This baby is going to be born, and whether you like it or not, it's gonna be born in this Anderson shelter. You can yell all you want for Alan and yer dad. You can even yell for yer mum too, although I couldn't see her down here in a muddy hole in the ground delivering a baby. Even if they was here, there isn't room in this shelter for them. There's no room to swing a cat, let alone a baby.'

Sarah stopped sobbing and went quiet for a moment. 'I'm sorry. I'm all right now... Thank you, Maisie.'

'Well, I don't know why you're thanking me, I'm sure. I have no idea how to give birth, and the most Freda's ever taught at her Girl Guide meetings is how to use her tie to make a knee bandage or a sling for a broken arm. Just be thankful yer nan's here, as without her we'd all be up the creek without a paddle.'

Maisie's humour broke the tension and for a few minutes the women laughed as they prepared for the arrival of the baby, making do with what they had at their disposal in the shelter.

Ruby gave Freda the task of sorting out the bedding. She prided herself on the blankets being fresh, and the beds had sheets on them, which meant there would be something to clean and wrap the baby in. Ruby didn't feel it was right that young Freda should witness a birth, but there wasn't much she could do about that at the moment.

Maisie tipped some fresh water from a stone bottle that Ruby kept in the shelter onto a piece of torn sheet and wiped the sweat from Sarah's brow and spoke soothing words to her as contraction after contraction swept through her tired body.

'I can see the baby's head,' Ruby called out as an explosion almost shook Sarah from her bed. Ruby flung herself across Sarah, fearing the worst, as Maisie and Freda righted the candles before a fire started. From outside the shelter, there was an almighty crash and again the ground shook, followed by a groaning noise as something heavy landed close by.

'My God! The house must 'ave been hit,' Maisie shouted, while from the bunk there could be heard the sound of a baby crying.

'Well, you certainly chose a good time to enter the world, Miss Gilbert,' declared her great-grandmother.

The women worked together quickly to help tidy Sarah up and check that the baby was all right. With dust still settling around them in the shelter, Ruby wrapped the baby in a clean sheet. 'I'm going to give the little 'un to Maisie to hold while I wipe some of the dust off your face and give you a sip of cold tea. Fortunately, there's a bit of sugar in it, so you'll get some energy. God knows you need it after giving birth in this hellhole.'

Freda tugged a blanket from the other bunk,

ready to hand it to Ruby as she pulled the soiled ones away. 'I reckon we'll have to boil these in the copper on laundry day.'

'We're probably best to just burn them, Freda. There's a few more where they come from and I wouldn't begrudge a blanket for my beautiful little great-granddaughter, or my granddaughter, come to that,' she said as she gave Sarah a hug. 'Now, let's sort that cup of tea out. It's not much, but I suppose it'll be welcome.'

'You can say that again,' Sarah said with a weak smile. 'Thank you, Nan. You too, Freda and Maisie. I don't know what I'd have done without you.'

'I wasn't much help at all. If we wasn't shut in down here because of the air raid, I'd have more likely run a mile,' Freda laughed. 'What about you, Maisie?'

The women looked to where Maisie was cuddling the baby, rocking her back and forth. She looked up at them with tears in her eyes. 'I've just been telling her what a lucky little girl she is to have so many people to look out for her and how we will never stop reminding her of how she came into the world.'

As Maisie spoke, the all-clear began to sound. 'Thank goodness for that,' Freda declared. 'I'll get the door open. We could do with some fresh air in here after all this dust.'

'Be careful, Freda. We've got no idea what came down after that last explosion.'

Maisie handed the baby to Sarah so carefully she could have been made of china. 'Here you go, Mum. You hold yer daughter while I give Aunty

Freda a hand.'

Ruby roared with laughter and relief. 'Why, you're all not much more than kids yourself and here you are calling each other "Mum" and "Aunty".'

Maisie nudged Ruby in the ribs. 'Get away with you. You're only calling us kids 'cos it'll make you sound younger now you're a great-granny.'

Even Sarah joined in the laughter, although she felt as though she was in a dream. Looking down at her daughter's face was like looking at Alan. There was such a likeness. She tried to fight the tears that threatened to fall as she kissed the baby's forehead. 'It's just you and me, my little treasure, until your daddy comes home. Won't he be surprised to meet you?'

'I think we've got a problem,' Freda said. 'The door won't budge.'

Maisie came alongside her. 'Let's both try together. One, two, three, push!' They both shoved the door and it moved a couple of inches, but try as they might, they couldn't move it another inch.

Freda squinted through the small gap. 'I think I know what came down in that last crash.'

'Please don't say it was the back wall of the house,' Ruby cried.

'I think we'd all be as flat as a pancake if it was,' Maisie snorted. 'What can you see, Freda?'

'I can see leaves and some branches. It must be next door's apple tree.'

'Oh bugger. Bang go the cooking apples,' Ruby sighed.

23

'What's that noise? I hope it isn't a rat. There's no knowing what can get in here, being below ground.' Ruby started to stamp on the wooden floor to frighten off whatever was making the scraping, scratching noise.

Sarah held her baby close. It was over an hour since the all-clear had sounded and it was getting increasingly chilly in the Anderson shelter. Would anyone realize they were trapped? Her dad would be home later that evening, and Betty was due round for her tea. Surely one of them would find them in the shelter.

'Ssh. The noise is coming from outside,' Maisie hissed. 'Hello? We are trapped in here. Can you help us? It's Mrs Caselton and her family. Help!'

They all held their breath and listened. Sure enough they could hear something close to the small opening in the door.

Freda crept forward. 'Hello. Can you hear me? It's Freda.'

An excited yelp, followed by loud barking.

'It's Nelson. Thank goodness he's safe,' Ruby said. 'I was a bit worried when he didn't come into the shelter with us.'

'He won't be much use. I can't see him digging us out, and he's not likely to go get help, is he?' Maisie sniffed.

'No, but his barking might alert someone. Vera

from up the road reckons she can hear him a mile off and he wakes her up at night,' Freda said.

Ruby snorted. 'She'd say black was white if it meant she got some attention.'

'I have an idea. Maisie, can you tear off a strip of that blanket and tie some knots in it?'

Maisie did as Freda asked, although the look on her face showed that she thought Freda was bonkers.

Freda poked the end of the rag through the gap in the door and teased Nelson, who was soon playing tug with the girl. Freda pulled the rag inside the door and encouraged Nelson to bark. 'That's it, boy, ask for it. Good boy!'

'Gawd, it's been ten minutes. I'm not sure I can stand that dog barking much more. He'll have the neighbours complaining that I've got a wild dog in the garden. Look, he's woken the baby now,' Ruby sighed.

Suddenly Nelson stopped barking and ran off. Freda could hear him excitedly yapping and a human voice talking to him. 'Help, help! We're trapped in the Anderson shelter. Can you hear me?'

'Well, blow me down. Thank goodness I came round the back way when I couldn't get a reply at the front door. I thought you girls was playing with that mutt in the garden. I told you he was a bit on the noisy side, Ruby,' Vera called loudly.

'Do you think you can get us out, Vera?' Ruby shouted. 'Only, the baby will freeze to death in here if we aren't careful.'

'Baby? Oh my! I'll go get some help. It's only next door's tree blocking the doorway. It's too heavy for me.'

'Vera, is the house still standing?' Ruby called.

'Some slates off the roof and a few broken windows. Nothing to write home about. A landmine dropped on the sidings up the road a bit. No one's been hurt.'

'That's not so bad, then. Hurry up, Vera. I could do with me dinner.'

Two hours later they were sat round the wireless listening to the evening news. The East End had taken another battering and many lives were lost.

'It seems strange to think that while so many people were being killed, we welcomed a new life into the world,' Freda said.

While Maisie and Ruby had set to covering the broken windowpanes and arranging for someone to come in and look at the hole in the roof where some slates had been smashed, Freda had helped Sarah wash herself and climb into bed. The baby's cradle was at Maureen's house, so they'd made a bed up in a deep drawer, where she had fallen into a contented sleep wearing one of the nightdresses that Maisie had sewn by hand.

'She's so beautiful,' Freda sighed as she watched over the new arrival.

'I think we are a little biased, but I must agree with you,' Sarah smiled as she stroked her daughter's cheek.

'Won't Maureen be surprised when she finds out she has a granddaughter?'

Sarah agreed. 'I thought she would have been round here by now to find out what happened.'

'We don't know what's been going on at Woolworths this afternoon. Perhaps they are staying late to clear up. If we were affected by the land-mine, they must have been as well. If you like, I'll jump on my bike and pedal round to let her know the news.'

'Have your dinner first, Freda. It's been a long day for all of us.'

'If you're sure. I'll go and help your nan and bring you something up.'

'That would be lovely, thank you, Freda.'

'It's no trouble to run upstairs with a tray. I'll get to see little Miss Gilbert again.'

'No, I mean thank you for everything today. It must have been scary for you.'

Freda bent over and kissed the baby's head. 'I wouldn't have missed it for the world.'

Sarah snuggled down in the bed. It would have been perfect if Alan had been there to greet his daughter. She didn't know how she felt about him anymore. What man doesn't keep in touch with his wife? Perhaps once she was back on her feet, she would do what Betty suggested and see if someone in authority in the RAF could tell her where Alan was. If he didn't want to see her, he could at least know about his daughter.

The women had just finished a scratch meal of sardines on toast when there was a knock at the door. Maisie let Betty and Maureen in.

Ruby jumped up. 'You must be famished work-ing this late. Let me get you both something to eat. We have such a surprise for you.'

Betty raised her hand, indicating for Ruby to stay where she was. 'Ruby, we have some bad news. Where's Sarah?'

'We packed her off to bed. She had the baby this afternoon while we were in the shelter.'

Rather than look happy, Maureen started to cry into her handkerchief.

Maisie took the woman in her arms to comfort her. 'She's fine, Maureen, and so is the baby. Why don't we take you up to see them both?'

Maureen shook her head. 'No, not at the moment. We have something to tell you.'

They all turned to see Sarah standing in the doorway.

'I heard the front door. What is it?' She looked from Maureen's tear-stained face to Betty, who stood there looking so helpless. 'It's Alan. He's dead, isn't he?'

Betty took her hand. 'No, my love, it isn't Alan. We were still clearing up at the store after this afternoon's raid and there was a phone call. The nurse knew that you worked at Woolworths and hoped that we could contact you.'

Sarah looked puzzled. 'I don't understand. If it's not Alan...?'

'It's your dad, Sarah. George was driving home in the blackout and a lorry pulled out in front of him. He's very poorly. They're operating at this very moment.' She turned to look at a now ghostly white Ruby. Freda went to her as Ruby crumpled into her armchair. 'Things don't look good, Mrs Caselton,' Betty added sadly.

'Dad,' was all that Sarah could say before falling to the ground in a deep faint.

'The poor love. It's been a long day and one she

won't forget for many a year. I'm so glad that Maureen stayed with her while she slept,' Ruby said to no one in particular as she stared at the wall of the hospital corridor. Either side of her, Betty and Maisie sat and let her talk. They'd been at Erith Cottage Hospital for two hours and had yet to see George. The sterile corridor with cream walls and a simple bench echoed with the brisk footsteps of nursing staff as they hurried between the ward and a door with the ominous words 'No entry'.

They'd been informed upon arrival that there would be no news until George had been to the operating theatre, but he was very poorly.

'I don't understand what happened,' Ruby said sadly. 'George is such a good driver.'

'I was told little more than his car swerved to avoid something in the road and he crashed into an army lorry driving in the opposite direction. It is through the care of the soldiers that he even made it to hospital.'

Ruby nodded thoughtfully. After hearing the news and seeing her granddaughter faint, she had started to organize things so they could get to the hospital as soon as possible. It was decided that Maureen and Freda should stay with Sarah and one of them would run for the doctor if she remained in a distressed state. Ruby was of a mind that a strong cup of tea and a cuddle with her baby would be all that was needed to calm the girl.

Maisie and Betty made it clear they would accompany Ruby to the hospital, which was a twenty-minute walk on the other side of Erith.

A nurse dressed from head to foot in a white

341

gown, her hair pulled back behind a starched cap, appeared from the door marked, 'No entry'. 'Mrs Irene Caselton?'

'I'm George's mother, Mrs Ruby Caselton. His wife is in Devon. How is my son?'

'The surgeon will be out to speak to you shortly. I've organized some tea. You've been here for a while now.'

'That's very good of you, love. Can you tell me anything at all about George's injuries?'

'I'm afraid I can't, but the surgeon will not be long.' Ruby nodded and watched as the nurse disappeared through the swing doors.

'They do a marvellous job,' Betty said.

Maisie wrinkled her nose. 'It's not something I could do. Think of all that blood.'

Betty raised her eyebrows at Maisie, but Ruby didn't acknowledge the words. 'It's certainly a calling.'

'They're nothing short of angels. Every single one of them.'

They'd just finished their tea when the surgeon appeared. He introduced himself to Ruby and pulled a chair forward to sit in front of the women. All three watched the man's face for clues of what he was about to say.

Ruby cut straight to the chase. 'How is my son, Doctor?'

'He's a very lucky man, Mrs Caselton. If there hadn't been an army first-aider on that lorry, your son would have been in the morgue by now.'

Ruby flinched. He didn't mince his words. 'Does that mean he's going to be all right, Doctor?'

'It's still touch and go. I've done my best to save

his leg, but we won't know for a few days yet if I've been successful. We've stitched up a few gashes, and he will have a scar on his forehead, but all in all he has been very lucky. They have just taken him back to the ward, so if you would like to visit him for a few minutes to see him, that will be in order. He is still sedated, so don't expect him to respond.'

'He's a fighter, Doctor. I know he'll do his utmost to get well again. He may not hear me, but I want to tell him that his granddaughter was born today. He'd be chuffed to know that.'

The doctor patted Ruby's hand and returned to his duties.

'So you see, your dad is very poorly, Sarah. We need to let your mother know and bring her to Erith as soon as possible.' Betty sat watching Sarah as she explained what had happened at the cottage hospital the night before. Sarah had declared herself recovered from her faint and wanted to be out of bed and visiting her dad. However, both Ruby and Maureen had put their foot down and she was to remain in bed until they said otherwise.

'We could telephone the golf club and ask them to tell Mum, but it may be rather a shock to hear news like that. I'm not sure what we should do, Betty.'

'I think I have the answer, but I wanted to speak to you first.'

Sarah nodded her head and listened quietly as Betty explained her plan.

'As you know, my car's locked away in a garage due to petrol rationing. However, I do have a little petrol stored away for emergencies.'

Sarah raised her eyebrows at her boss. She'd never known her do anything even slightly wrong before.

Betty smiled. 'As I said, it was for emergencies. I contacted your father's employers this morning from my office, as they would need to know about his accident. They were most sympathetic and immediately offered to help. I explained that Irene is in Devon and, at the moment, oblivious to George's predicament. I indicated that I would be prepared to drive to Devon and break the news to Irene.' She raised her hand to silence Sarah as the young woman opened her mouth to protest. 'I said that petrol for the journey was a problem and at once they promised to assist me in any way they could. It was all I could do not to cry at their generosity.'

'Betty, I can't let you do this. It is not your responsibility. We have no way of knowing how Mum will take the news.'

'I'm aware of that, Sarah, but there is no other option. It would not be right to give your mother such devastating news over the telephone even if we could contact her. You are not fit to make a long journey at the moment, and your grand-mother needs to be at George's bedside at this time. Maureen and Maisie are at Woolworths, and I am promoting Maisie up to supervisor to help cover for the few days I'll be away. I'm sure she is up to the task, don't you?'

'It could be the making of her,' Sarah agreed.

'Freda is needed here, as she has essential war work to do. So that just leaves me, and though I say it myself, I do get on rather well with your mother. We struck up quite a rapport at your wedding.'

'Only because she knows you are not exactly working class, and also because you wouldn't do the hokey-cokey in the middle of the street with the rest of us.'

Betty smiled at the memory. 'To be honest, I was dying to join in, but I had no idea what to put in and what to pull out and I didn't wish to make a fool of myself.'

Sarah burst out laughing. 'Oh, Betty, you are a treasure. Whatever would we do without you?'

'You said yourself I was part of your family, so I intend to pull my weight and share your family responsibilities. Whatever are you doing? You shouldn't even consider getting out of bed.'

Sarah held on to Betty's arm. 'I'm just a little wobbly. I can't stay in bed all day. I have things to do.'

'Nothing that can't wait. You get yourself back into bed this minute.'

'No, Betty. I need to see my dad.'

'It can wait a day or two, Sarah.'

'No, you don't understand. He's very ill. I need to see him and show him he has a granddaughter. If I wait, it may be too late. I'd never forgive myself.'

Betty thought for a moment. 'Right. If you pro-mise to rest for a couple of hours, I will collect my car from the garage and then I'll drive you to see George this afternoon, but it will only be for half an hour. Then I'm going straight to collect Irene.'

Sarah hugged Betty and allowed her to help her

back into bed. 'Thank you, Betty. You don't know how much this means to me.'

Betty pulled the covers up over Sarah's shoulders and tucked her in. 'Believe me, I do.'

Sarah closed her eyes and drifted off to sleep, content that she would soon see her dad and introduce him to his granddaughter.

'Now, your dad is still groggy from his operation, so be patient if he seems confused.' The nurse drew a seat up close to the bed and left Sarah alone with George. Apart from a bandage round his head and a cradle keeping the bed covers from touching his damaged leg, George looked his normal self.

Sarah rocked the baby in her arms, soothing her softly as she started to cry. 'Ssh, there's no need to cry. This is your granddad. He's been waiting a long time to meet you.'

George's eyelids fluttered before opening. 'Sarah, is that you?'

Sarah reached over and took her dad's hand. 'Yes, it's me, Dad. I have a little visitor for you.' She pulled back the white knitted shawl that had been lovingly made by Freda and held the baby close so George could touch her. 'Georgina, meet your granddad George.'

A smile crossed George's face. 'Well, well. When did you make an appearance, young lady?'

'Yesterday, during an air raid. It was quite frightening. None of us will ever forget what happened.'

George stroked his granddaughter's face. 'She is beautiful and looks just like you did as a baby, apart from her hair. Yours was very dark.'

'I think she has her dad's hair colouring, but it could change, from what Maureen told me.'

'Does Alan know?'

A shadow crossed Sarah's face. 'No. I posted a letter as we drove here to give him the good news. I have no idea if he will receive it.' She didn't add that she'd also written to the authorities, as she was worried about the lack of communication from her husband.

George squeezed her hand. 'I know he would be in touch if he could, love. He's doing a dangerous job. We should be proud of him.'

'I'm immensely proud of Alan, Dad.' But I don't think he cares for me anymore, she thought to herself.

They sat in silence for a while as George watched his granddaughter and a smile crept across his face. 'Your mum is going to spoil this little one.'

'Oh crikey. I forgot to tell you. Betty is going to drive down to Devon to give Mum the news about your accident. Then she is going to bring her back to Nan's. Freda and Maisie are going to stay at Maureen's for a while so we can all be together at number thirteen.'

'You have good friends, Sarah. Your mum has taken to Betty. I hope she isn't too upset when she hears the news.'

'Mum's made of stern stuff, Dad. She won't buckle.'

George started to doze off. 'You are both strong women, Sarah...'

Sarah sat quietly watching him sleep. Dad thought she was strong? Then she would have to be. She would cope with Alan or without him. She could do this.

'So this is my granddaughter.' Irene peered into the cot where Georgina slept.

In the few days since the baby had been born, the women of number thirteen had become her devoted slaves. Sarah felt she could have walked out of the front door and never returned and little Georgina would still have thrived. But would her mum feel the same as the rest of her family and friends?

Irene had just walked into the house after breaking the long journey back from Devon to see George at the hospital. Betty had managed to telephone Woolworths and update Maisie on how Irene had taken the news. From the way Maisie relayed the message, Irene had gone straight to pack her bag after enquiring if George's car had survived the accident. Ruby had not been impressed with this, but Sarah knew it was her mum's way of coping.

Scooping the baby into her arms and holding her close, Irene started to sob. 'She's adorable. To think she may lose her granddad is just too much to bear. Whatever will we do?'

Sarah's emotion jumped from happiness at seeing Irene's reaction upon meeting her granddaughter to shock at her words. 'Mum, Dad will be fine. It may take time for him to get over this, but he will be out of hospital and home with you before too long.'

Irene handed the baby back to Sarah and wiped her eyes with a dainty handkerchief she pulled from her sleeve. 'He took a turn for the worse early this morning. The ward sister told us that he will have to go back into the operating theatre today. He may lose his leg.'

Sarah couldn't believe what she was being told. Granted, the surgeon had said the next few days would be critical, but to hear this awful news...

Ruby took control of the situation. Her heart was breaking for her only son, but she knew that weeping and wailing would not solve anything. 'I've made up the bed in the front bedroom for you, Irene, and here is a front-door key so you can come and go as you please. I think we should show you the Anderson shelter and what we do when there's a raid; then perhaps we can all have a bite to eat before you head back to the hospital. Betty, will you stay to eat with us?'

Betty wanted nothing more than to fall into her bed, as the journey to and from Devon had taken its toll. However, she had to go into Woolworths and see that everything was as it should be before she even thought about her bed. 'That would be delightful, Mrs Caselton. Thank you.'

'That reminds me,' Ruby said as she reached for a large parcel that was on the sideboard. 'Maisie left this for you, Irene. We all have one and they are most comfortable.'

Irene frowned as she unpicked the string and opened the brown paper wrapping and pulled out a dark green woollen siren suit. 'Oh my! Is this what I think it is? Josephine Hopkins at the golf club has been boasting about her siren suit and I must admit to being a little green with envy.' She held the outfit up against herself. 'I shall go and put it on right now. Anything that's good enough for Mr Churchill is good enough for me.' Irene picked up her suitcase and headed upstairs.

Ruby turned to Betty and Sarah with a grin on her face. 'Are you sure that's my daughter-in-law and not an imposter?'

After a filling meal of corned beef hash with vegetables from the garden, Betty set off for Woolworths, dropping Irene at the hospital on the way. She was given strict instructions to telephone Betty if George should get any worse. Betty had promised Ruby that she would get a message to them if anything should happen.

Ruby picked up her knitting. 'It's a treat to put my feet up for a few hours, I must say. I've been itching to make this pink matinee jacket ever since young madam there made her appearance. I just hope we don't have an air raid tonight. I don't think I can face that shelter after the other day.'

Sarah yawned. 'We can always sit in the cupboard under the stairs. It's as safe as anywhere. I'm going to read my book until Georgina wakes for her next feed.'

'If you can keep your eyes open. It was good of your mum to bring us the box of food. That tin of salmon will go down a treat with the salad stuff from the garden.'

'Once I'm on my feet properly, I can walk Georgina down to the allotment and do a few hours.'

'You'll do no such thing. You take it easy for a few months, my girl. Besides, you'll be wanting to see your dad in hospital and pop into Woolies to help Betty. You can't burn your candle at both ends or you'll be heading for trouble.'

Sarah sighed. 'I suppose you're right, but I don't like not helping out.'

'Not helping out? Why, we'd be lost without you, love. Give it a couple of weeks and things around here will be a little more organized. Your dad will be on the mend and you will have your strength back to do a few hours with Betty while I take care of the little 'un.'

'Do you think Dad will be on the mend?'

'Let's just hope so, eh? Besides, we haven't been sent a message to say otherwise. Betty will have someone banging on our door minutes after she hears anything.'

At that moment there was a loud knock on the door.

Sarah's face turned white. 'Oh no.'

Ruby pulled herself to her feet. 'Don't you worry none – it's probably Vera knocking to see if I want to go to the whist drive. Any excuse to check what's going on,' she chuckled.

Sarah held her breath as Ruby opened the front door and invited someone in. Surely it wasn't Vera, as she'd have heard her chatter. It must be someone from Woolworths with a message from the hospital.

Sarah's world stood still as the front-room door opened. It wasn't a Woolworths staff member. It wasn't Vera wanting to know what the Caselton family were up to. Instead, two uniformed members of the Royal Air Force stepped into the room.

Sarah's heart thudded loudly in her breast as the men refused the offer of a seat.

The older officer cleared his throat. 'Mrs Alan Gilbert?'

'That's my married name. Is it Alan ...?'

'Yes. I have some bad news, Mrs Gilbert. Your husband is missing, presumed killed.'

The tall, distinguished man continued to speak, but Sarah could only hear the blood pumping through her head and her stomach started to churn. Placing her hand over her mouth, she dashed from the room.

Not having made it to the outside lavatory, Ruby found her granddaughter bent double outside the back door. Ruby rubbed her back until the convulsing stopped and led her inside to a seat, where she carefully wiped her face with a damp flannel and encouraged her to drink a cup of cold water. Wrapping her arms around the girl, she rocked her gently, making soothing noises until the tears subsided. 'There, there, my love,' she whispered.

When Sarah had composed herself, they returned to the front room, where they found the officers sitting on the sofa with the younger one holding Georgina in his arms. He smiled shyly. 'Your daughter was crying. I hope you don't mind that I picked her up? I have a son. He's six months old now.'

'She looks like your husband, Mrs Gilbert.'

'You knew Alan?' Sarah thought it felt strange to speak in the past tense. 'Please, I need to know what happened.'

'I'm going to put the kettle on. I don't know about you, but I think we could do with a cup of tea and a spoonful of sugar to help with the shock.

Are you all right holding our Georgina?'

The officer nodded. He seemed quite at home with the baby in his arms.

Sarah stared at the older officer. 'Please?'

'His plane was shot down over the French side of the Channel. There was a sighting of a parachute but nothing more.'

Sarah thought hard before speaking. 'Was this during the Dunkirk evacuation we heard about on the wireless?'

The two officers looked at each other before the younger one spoke. 'No, it was a little earlier, but we can't really say much more.'

'Even if we knew,' his companion added quickly.

They all sat in silence until Ruby appeared with the tea, at which point they made polite small talk, avoiding mentioning the war or the fact that Sarah was most likely now a young widow, like so many other women.

'How did you know to come here?' Ruby asked, as she knew that they had Maureen's address in nearby Crayford Road as where Sarah and Alan resided.

'We knocked and a neighbour said we would most likely find Mrs Gilbert here.'

Ruby was just grateful that Maureen hadn't been home when they called.

The two men left after promising they would be in touch about Alan's property or if they had any more news.

Ruby returned to the front room to collect the teacups and tidy up. 'You wanted news, love, but not news like that. But hold on to the thought that he is only missing.'

Sarah turned to her grandmother. Her face filled with anger. 'Only missing? Alan has been missing to me since last Christmas. You heard the men. He went missing just before the Dunkirk evacuation. That was the end of May. Where was he for the other months, and why didn't he get in touch? No. Alan has been missing to me for much longer. He had moved on with his life and now so shall I.'

Ruby struggled to know what to say to Sarah. How could she advise a young woman whose husband was most likely dead, when she'd had a long and happy marriage until her Eddie passed two years before? 'You're in shock, Sarah. Give it time and don't do anything you'll later regret.'

Sarah shook her head. 'No! Even if Alan walked through this door right now, he wouldn't be the man I married. The only good thing we had between us is Georgina. For that I am thankful. The rest can go to hell. Now, I'm going to put Georgina into her pram and walk round to Maureen's house and break the news to her before someone else lets her know that the RAF have been knocking on her door. Of course I'll be gentle with her. I'll always think of Maureen with fondness, but life moves on. I'd like you to come with me, Nan, but will understand if you don't wish to.'

Ruby picked up her coat and helped Sarah put baby Georgina into her pram. She'd keep quiet for now, as she knew Sarah wasn't thinking straight, but she couldn't help wonder what else was in store for her extended family. Maisie was all at sixes and sevens since her husband was killed;

Freda still didn't know what was happening with that rascal of a brother; Alan, for whom she had more than a soft spot, was possibly lying dead somewhere in France; and her own son was facing goodness knows what at the cottage hospital. This war had a lot to answer for.

24

'No! I am putting my foot down over this once and for all. You are not going on fire duty. If I see your name on the rota one more time, I will have no choice but to give you your cards.'

Sarah had never seen Betty so angry before. Everyone agreed that the month had been one of highs and lows, what with George's accident, baby Georgina's sudden arrival and Alan now officially presumed dead. At least George was now out of hospital and being cared for by his family.

'But, Betty, we are short-staffed. We don't even have someone full-time to cover the staff canteen since Maureen moved away to live with her sister.' Sarah had been relieved when her mother-in-law decided to leave Erith. As much as she loved her, Maureen was a reminder of Alan and what might have been if the war hadn't started and he had remained a trainee manager at Woolworths with prospects.

'I know, but you are a mother now and you have to think about Georgina. I'm truly grateful to your grandmother for stepping in to make the staff lunches.'

Sarah smiled. 'She is more than happy to help out, and everyone gets to see the baby.' Sarah knew that under normal circumstances a baby would not be allowed in the staffroom, but Ruby was able to check on her granddaughter while she cooked and served and there was no shortage of people wanting to coo over her daughter. It also meant that Sarah could help Betty for a few hours more. 'Nan says it is no different to being at home and caring for Georgina, and she loves to push the pram through the town.'

'That's all well and good, but as for fire-watch duties ... what if something were to happen to you?' Betty held her breath, not knowing how Sarah would take her next words. 'With Alan no longer here, Georgina wouldn't have a parent if you were killed.'

'Betty, any one of us could be killed at any time. There is a war on. If a bomb has my name on it, then I know I will leave Georgina well provided for with her godmothers and family.'

'The christening was such a lovely day, wasn't it?' Betty became thoughtful as she recalled the previous Sunday, when the family had returned to St Paulinus Church for Georgina's christening. There had been prayers for Alan, as well as other friends and family not able to be there. Ruby had begged and borrowed ingredients for a small cake, and Maisie had used fabric from Sarah's bridal gown to make a beautiful christening dress, while Freda's white knitted shawl kept the baby warm. Betty's present to her goddaughter had been a generous gift of money that was to be invested for her future.

'I was so pleased that Dad was finally out of hospital and able to attend. Mum's a dab hand at manoeuvring his wheelchair now and is learning to drive so that Dad can get around as much as possible.'

'Will he ever walk again?' Betty missed seeing George at number thirteen.

'If Mum has anything to do with it, he will. She plans to supervise his exercise programme, and he has already stood for a few minutes with the aid of crutches.'

'Your mother is a changed woman since she became a grandmother. Who'd have thought the day would come when she would be seen out in broad daylight in her siren suit?'

Sarah giggled. 'She's seen Mr Churchill wearing his and has adopted his style as if it was a uniform. Maisie has received orders for two more in red and blue, and reckons she will be taking orders from Mum's friends at the golf club before too long.'

'Oh my,' was all Betty could think to say.

'So what work would you like me to tackle today?' Sarah asked. She wanted to steer Betty away from talk about fire-watch duties. She liked to do her bit to keep her place of employment safe and secure from enemy attack. After all, if she was to be the sole provider for her daughter, she needed to have an income. These days, she never thought of Alan as her husband, as in her heart she was sure that if he had never perished in action, they would have drifted apart. He had changed too much for them ever to be a couple again. She was sad when she thought back to the days when she had first fallen in love with Alan and how they planned to be together forever. She grieved for what might have been if there had never been a war.

'Well, I have to drive up to the Bexleyheath store to deliver some paperwork and to see if the new manager has settled in. It will only take an hour. Why not come with me and meet the staff?'

'I'd love to. Nan is on baby duty and she knows not to expect me back until late afternoon. Even though the Bexleyheath Woolies is just a couple of miles away, I've never visited.'

For the rest of her life Sarah would remember the silence before the screaming and cries for help started. The silence could only have lasted for a few seconds, but it felt like a lifetime as she lay in the rubble that was once a thriving store. One minute she'd been walking beside Betty as they headed towards the side entrance of the Bexley-heath shop, chatting excitedly about how they could copy the patriotic window display in the store, which showed local shoppers how to save money and make ends meet. Then nothing. Just the silence. There had been no warning at all that the store would be hit by whatever had caused the explosion.

Sarah licked her lips. They were thick with the dust that was still settling around her. She tried to swallow. The exertion made her cough. Slowly she stretched her arms and then her legs. Everything seemed to work without too much pain, but where was Betty?

Sarah tried to call, but however hard she tried,

her words weren't loud enough. 'Betty, are you hurt? Can you hear me?' she managed to croak. With no response from her friend, she started to feel around, catching her fingers on rubble and pieces of wood until they were sore and stinging, but still she continued. A wave of fear washed through her as she realized her dear friend could be lying dead beneath the walls of the company she loved so dearly, a place where she had found solace in work since losing her beloved fiancé after the last war. It wasn't fair, she thought to herself as she grabbed desperately at the rubble. Rubbing at her eyes and clearing her throat as best she could, she shouted, 'Betty, where are you? It's Sarah, I'm trying to help you. Please, please speak to me.'

Sarah coughed. This time it wasn't brick dust but smoke that she was inhaling. The building was on fire. She continued frantically to feel for Betty's body, crawling on her knees into the small spaces around her, fearful now that they would both be consumed by flames. Betty couldn't be far away, as they were together when what she presumed was a bomb had hit the building.

'Betty, please, where are you?' Sarah begged.

Sarah heard a small groan to the left of where she was crawling in the debris. 'Betty, is that you?' In the darkness, she pulled away part of a door frame and found her friend propped against the remains of a wall. She shook Betty's arm. 'It's me. Betty, are you hurt?'

Betty could only groan in reply.

Sarah knew she had to get her friend to safety, as the smoke was getting thicker by the minute.

But try as she might, she couldn't budge Betty from where she was trapped. There was only one thing to do. Reluctantly she backed away to where she had started her search and called out as loudly as she could, 'Help! There are two people trapped in here.' She shouted and shouted until she felt faint. As she lay gasping for breath, she was beginning to think she would never see the outside world again or hold her baby in her arms until finally she heard the shrill tones of a whistle and then men's voices.

'There's one alive in here. Give us a hand, Charlie!'

Sarah blinked as she was helped to her feet by two men as others pulled back the debris that had once been a thriving Woolworths store in a busy market town. 'Please, you have to help my friend, Miss Billington. She's one of our store managers. She's trapped over there.' She pointed to show where she had left Betty.

The men stepped carefully through the rubble that had once been the side wall of the Bexley-heath store. Within minutes Betty was being pulled from the building and gently carried to the other side of the road away from the smoke and dust. Shopkeepers were helping, bringing out chairs and water as well as soothing those who were distressed at what had happened.

Sarah helped the men carry Betty across the road to a chair and held her as her friend's face was wiped clean and a nasty gash on her cheek covered with a bandage.

Betty's eyes fluttered. 'Charlie, is that you?' she mumbled.

360

'Is that her husband?' the first-aider asked as she checked the bandage was secure. 'It's all right, love. You'll see your Charlie soon,' the woman soothed, not knowing that Betty would never again see her intended. 'You've had a nasty bump on the head, but you're one of the lucky ones. We'll soon get you sorted out.'

It was then that Sarah looked across the road to what had been a busy Woolworths store only hours before.

Sarah put her hand to her mouth in horror. The large building did not have one window remaining, and from the gaping holes smoke and flames billowed out. Already a fire engine was positioned in front of a first-floor window with water from hoses aimed into the burning building. That was shocking enough, but what really distressed her was the row of bodies that were laid out on the pavement, each with a blanket covering the unfortunate staff and shoppers. What was she to do? Head office needed to be notified, and as Betty was out of action, it meant that Sarah, her second-in-command, was not only in charge of the Erith branch but would have to get in touch with head office and let them know of the devastation of the Bexleyheath store caused by enemy action.

She leant close to Betty, trying to make her understand. 'Betty, I need to get back to Erith and organize help for the staff here. I'm going to find someone to sit with you. I'll be back as soon as possible.'

Betty looked at Sarah's face and mumbled a few words.

'Sorry – I didn't catch what you said, Betty.'

'Charlie. I heard my Charlie…'

Sarah didn't like to leave her friend while she was so confused, but she knew her duty lay with Woolworths. She grabbed hold of the first-aider's hand. 'I need to get back to Erith Woolworths and let everyone know what has happened here. Can someone sit with Miss Billington? She seems to be rather confused at the moment.'

'Don't you worry, my love – there's plenty of people here to give a hand. I would think we'll be taking her to the cottage hospital shortly, once we've helped those poor souls.' Both women looked to the row of bodies. 'You and your mate can count yourselves lucky.'

Sarah had never felt so helpless. The Erith branch of Woolworths may only have been a couple of miles away, but at that moment it felt like it was on the other side of the world. If she could drive, she would have been able to take Betty's little car back to Erith. However, that too could be a victim of the explosion, as Betty had left it in a road just behind Woolies. No doubt it would be out of action. Sarah swore she would learn how to drive as soon as possible. If her mother could do it, then so could she.

'Excuse me, miss?'

Sarah, deep in thought, had not seen the policeman in front of her and jumped as he spoke.

'I didn't mean to startle you, miss.'

'Please don't worry about me, Officer. I think we are all a little jumpy after what has happened.'

'You can say that again, miss. I understand you want to get back to Woolworths at Erith?'

Sarah nodded and then explained about Betty

being manager and needing to alert head office.

'I thought that was the case, miss. I wondered if I could drive you back to Erith. Under circumstances like this' – he nodded towards the burning building – 'we have to follow certain procedures.'

As Sarah travelled back to Erith, she was told how news of the tragedy at the Bexleyheath store could not be made common knowledge. The kind officer explained that if the enemy knew they'd caused so much destruction, it would not be good. The news should also be kept quiet to keep public morale high. It all made sense to Sarah.

At Woolies, Sarah took the policeman to Betty's office and soon had him talking to head office on the telephone. She was relieved to be able to hand over responsibility to others, as she was still reeling from the shock herself.

Maisie and Ruby were shocked to hear the news and were soon fussing around Sarah. Ruby found a clean overall and helped Sarah wash and change, as she'd refused to go home until she'd done all she could for the colleagues from the Bexleyheath branch.

'You certainly had someone looking out for you today, love,' Maisie said as they sat in the staff canteen fussing over baby Georgina. 'This little one was almost an orphan! I didn't expect to almost 'ave to take on my godmother duties so quickly.'

'Thank goodness she has so many people to care for her if anything should happen to me.' Sarah held her baby close, thinking what might have been if she had perished that afternoon.

'Right, so what shall we do about Betty?' Ruby

sat down, wiping her hands on her pinny.

'She will be at the cottage hospital by now. I'd really like to go and see how she is, but how can I with head office due to ring back with instructions?'

'I'll go,' Maisie said with a determined look on her face. She stood up and started to unbutton her Woolworths overall. 'She's been bloody good to me since I lost my Joe and it's time I started paying her back. I'll borrow a bike and cycle up there right now.'

'No, I need you to take charge downstairs and make sure everything ticks over while I'm in the office. The police will be back soon, as head office are sorting them a list of staff members so their next-of-kin can be contacted.'

'The poor blighters. Them bloody Jerries have got a lot to answer for, killing so many innocent people,' Ruby said indignantly.

'That's something else, Nan. We are not to talk about this. If the Germans knew they'd caused such destruction, they would think they were winning the war and would gloat. That's what the policeman told me. We are not to talk about it.'

Ruby nodded wisely. 'That makes sense, love. Careless talk costs lives, as they say.'

'Seems to me there's already enough lives lost before anyone has done any talking,' Maisie said angrily. 'So what's to 'appen with Betty? If she's still rambling about her Charlie, like you say, then she could 'ave a bad 'ead injury.'

'Well, we ain't gonna know sitting here,' Ruby said resolutely. 'The afternoon tea break's done and dusted, so I'll walk up to the hospital and see to Betty. She was a godsend to me when your dad had his accident, so the least I can do is be there for her now. If needs be, she can come back to number thirteen for a while until she feels better. We can't have her alone at her place when she's poorly.'

'Blimey, Mrs C. You'll need a shoehorn to fit everyone into your house at this rate.'

'Maisie, I'll always find room for family and friends, don't you fear.'

In the weeks that followed, number thirteen was a hive of activity. The girls all mucked in with caring for Georgina so that Sarah could work as many hours as were needed in Woolworths. Every one of them was a dab hand at changing a nappy or preparing a bottle to feed the growing baby. Ruby would push the baby's pram to the store to do a few shifts in the staffroom kitchen to help out, safe in the knowledge that Georgina was doted on by the staff.

Head office had promoted Sarah to store manager, on the understanding that it was a temporary position until such time that Betty was back on form or they had found a male manager to take over. While the Bexleyheath store was being rebuilt, the able-bodied staff cycled to the Erith store to work, so there were extra staff under Sarah's control as well.

Sarah's main concern was Betty, whose recovery was slow. Her cuts and bruises healed, but she was often in low spirits and talked of her Charlie often. The many nights spent in the Anderson shelter in the garden of number thirteen were fraught, as

Betty found it hard to be confined in the small space after her recent experience.

Ruby was concerned that there was no improvement in the pleasant, well-spoken woman who had come to mean so much to the family.

'They'll have her locked up in the nut house before too long if she carries on like that,' Vera pointed out, after observing Betty clutching her arms around her body and jumping at a sudden noise from the road outside the house.

'That's uncharitable, Vera. Betty has been kind to this family and is a good friend. I doubt you'd have coped so well if you'd been trapped like she was.'

Vera shrugged. 'You'd take in any lame duck. Time you thought about yourself for a change, Ruby Caselton.'

Ruby sighed. Vera was right, but she wasn't going to give her the satisfaction by saying so. She felt like a coiled spring at times, as she worried about the girls. If they were home late from work and there was an air raid, she fretted that they were caught somewhere. She worried that Georgina would not thrive while there was a war on. Although, she had to admit that when she mentioned this, the girls had taken her to the garden and pointed out the amount of vegetables growing, as well as the nearby allotment they did their best to maintain. When the time came to wean the baby, she would not want for fresh vegetables. They were right: Georgina would be the healthiest toddler in town.

However, there was Betty. Her health was not improving and something had to be done. Irene was driving George up from Devon the next day. Perhaps having visitors would perk Betty up a little. At least Ruby didn't have to worry about George and his health. He had improved in leaps and bounds since his car accident. They managed to save his leg, although George would always have some mobility problems. What had amazed Ruby was the way that her daughter-in-law, Irene, had taken control of the situation. In the few short months since the accident she had learnt to drive and now ferried George back and forth to see his specialist, and even found time to visit their granddaughter. Irene was truly a changed woman, and as far as Ruby was concerned, it was for the better.

George and Irene didn't arrive until the early evening, having to stop twice on their journey, once because of an air raid and the second time to pull over to the side of the road as the gallant RAF fought off the enemy overhead. Irene was full of it when she arrived, but stopped talking about the RAF when Sarah entered the room with Georgina, as by then the whole family knew that it was a taboo subject. Alan was not to be spoken about ever again. However, all thoughts of her missing son-in-law went out of her mind when Irene spotted Betty.

'Oh, my poor woman. You look a shadow of your former self. Come and sit with me and tell me all about it.' Irene picked up their teacups and carried them into the front room for some privacy. 'Now, sit down here and take your tea.'

An hour later the two women rejoined the family. Betty's face was tear-stained, but to Ruby she looked calmer than she had done for weeks.

Irene clapped her hands for attention and the family listened intently. 'I've had a long chat with Betty and we've decided that it would be a good idea for her to come back with us to Devon for a while. The fresh air will do her good and she will be able to return to her job with renewed vigour.'

George kissed Betty on the cheek. 'You don't happen to play golf, do you?'

Sarah laughed out loud. Her dad would do anything not to accompany her mum to the golf club.

Irene frowned at her husband, but then joined in with the laughter. 'It will be good to have female company again, since my own daughter won't return to her home. Now, who mentioned fish and chips for tea? This is our treat.' She had no sooner asked her question than the air-raid siren started to wail. 'Oh well, food will have to wait. Time to visit Georgina's birthplace. Come along, everyone.'

Two hours later they were back in the house and Sarah had started to make a list of who wanted fish and chips when the front door burst open and Freda rushed in. 'They've got the Running Horses,' she gasped.

'Was anyone hurt?' George asked.

Freda nodded. 'A few, from what I heard. We took shelter at work, and when I was coming home, I could see people tending to the injured. Sarah, wasn't Maisie going there this evening for a drink?'

Sarah breathed a sigh of relief. 'No. She said she was meeting someone special at the Crown instead.'

Freda looked horrified. 'But that pub was damaged as well. It's only across the road from the Running Horses.'

Ruby sat down, her face a ghostly white. 'No, she changed her plans at the last moment. She decided on the Running Horses. Why is it that everyone who has slept under my roof has been put in so much danger?' she moaned, a stricken look on her face. 'That girl's already lost her old man, and now she could be injured or, worse, dead herself...' She got up and headed to the cupboard under the stairs where she kept her coat. 'I won't be able to sleep until I know the girl is safe.'

Sarah got up to follow Ruby. 'No, you stay here,' Irene said. 'I'll go with your nan. I'm just glad you weren't on fire duty tonight. We don't want any more sadness in our lives.'

Sarah tried to keep herself occupied while she waited for news of Maisie. She busied herself rinsing out a few baby clothes, while Freda kept her company in the kitchen deciding whether to make everyone a bite to eat. They'd all gone off the idea of fish and chips. 'Do you have any idea who Maisie was meeting, Freda?' she asked as she added some soap flakes to the warm water and gently squeezed the suds through a pink matinee coat.

'I've no idea at all. She was polishing her shoes and getting her best frock out of the wardrobe before I left for work, so it must have been someone special.'

'Do you think it could be her brother? She's not seen him in years from all accounts.'

Freda thought for a moment 'No, I don't think

so, otherwise she'd have said. No, I think it's a bloke. She had quite a sparkle in her eyes.'

'It would be good to see Maisie happy again. She'd make someone a good wife,' Sarah added, trying not to think that her friend could be lying dead in a bombed-out pub at this very moment. 'How about your Lenny? Where do you think he's got to? I thought you'd have heard from him by now.'

Freda looked sad. 'I've not heard hide nor hair of him since he legged it from here. We are no nearer to clearing his name. I'll get my hands on the little toe rag, I'll wring his neck.'

'I liked Lenny. He's just a kid who got in with the wrong gang. I'm sure it'll work out all right. Once he turns up, we can make sure that he tells his story to the authorities and all will be well.'

'I just hope he's all right out there. Being on the run in wartime ain't no picnic,' Freda said sadly.

Both girls continued pottering around in the scullery deep in thought about their loved ones.

Time slowly ticked by as the family waited for Ruby and Irene to return. George suggested they play a game of cards to while away the time, but no one could concentrate. When a key was heard turning in the lock just before eleven o'clock, they all jumped and turned as one to see who would walk into the front room.

Everyone gasped as Maisie entered. Her usually perfect hair was askew and her make-up smeared. Her clothes seemed to be covered in dust. She flopped into the nearest armchair before Ruby and Irene entered, followed by a tall, broad-shouldered man in RAF uniform who was introduced as David Carlisle.

'Take a seat, David. I'll get us all a drink. I think we can do with it after what we've seen,' Ruby said. 'There's a drop of whisky in the sideboard. Let's see it off, shall we?'

Freda found the bottle and the small glasses Ruby used when they drank sherry. No one seemed to mind as they sat silently sipping the strong alcohol. Freda considered putting on the kettle – she wasn't one for strong drink – but she didn't want to miss out on anything that was said.

George was the first to speak. 'So what happened?'

'Thankfully Maisie and David changed their plans and met at the Prince of Wales, otherwise they'd have been at the Running Horses when it was hit by the blast from the landmine,' Irene said.

'Was it a direct hit?'

'No, George, and possibly if it had been, the people in the pub across the road would have survived. From what we were told, the landmine struck the concrete by the riverfront and it was the blast that hit the two pubs.'

Maisie spoke for the first time. 'We were walking down the road from the Prince of Wales when it went off.' She glanced at Ruby. 'I know we should have been in the shelter, but we thought the all-clear would go soon and wanted to get to the front of the queue for a drink.'

Ruby didn't answer. Now wasn't the time and the girl had learnt her lesson from what she'd seen this night. However, Ruby had always lived by the rule that it was better to be late in this

371

world than early in the next. She'd have a word with Maisie later.

Maisie continued. 'We were the first to get there. There were a couple of blokes lying in the road, so David went to check, but there was nothing he could do. I could see through what was left of the windows of the Running Horses. People were still sitting at a table and they seemed to be all right. I went to look, but ... they were all dead. Not a mark on them and they was all as dead as doornails.' She chewed her painted nails, her hands still shaking as she told of what she'd seen.

'I've heard it can happen like that,' George said. 'If it's any consolation, it would have been so quick they wouldn't have known a thing about it.'

'It was a shock, sir. I've seen some things since the war began, but this was truly awful,' David said to George.

Freda felt sick. 'Those poor, poor people. Where did you find Maisie?' she asked Ruby.

'By the time we got down the road, they weren't letting people past, but I knew the ARP warden who had taken charge and told him we was looking for Maisie. When he said he'd seen her, my heart near leapt out of my chest, I can tell you. When we saw her and David, I'd never been so happy in all my life.'

'I know the whisky went down well, but I think we still need a cuppa,' Sarah announced.

'I'll give you a hand,' David said, getting to his feet and following her from the room.

After putting the kettle onto the stove, Sarah reached into a cupboard and handed the cups and saucers to David, who laid them on a tray.

'So you're a friend of Maisie's?' Sarah asked.

'You could say that.' He smiled down at her. David was taller than Alan and as dark as Alan had been fair.

Sarah thought his smile was wonderful. It lit up his face. 'Have you known her long?' She was still worried that Maisie would return to her wild ways, as she had done after Joe's death.

'Oh, we go way back. You could say we're almost family.'

'Really?' Sarah didn't wish to appear to be prying, however much his words intrigued her. She poured the boiling water into a large teapot and covered it with the brown knitted cosy before placing it onto the prepared tea tray.

'Shall I take that?' David said as Sarah also reached for the tray. David's strong hands covered hers and for a moment Sarah felt as though time stood still. She looked up into his deep brown eyes and felt an immediate connection. She hadn't had feelings like this since she first met Alan. A thrill of excitement ran through Sarah and reminded her of how she'd felt when she fell in love, but at the same time it terrified her. She felt so confused.

25

'You are still coming to us for Christmas Day, aren't you, David?' Ruby asked. She'd taken to the RAF officer, even though she felt her granddaughter was getting far too fond of him. It wasn't quite a year since Alan had been with them for Christmas dinner, and only months since they'd heard he was missing and presumed dead, but David had become a regular visitor to number thirteen since the night Maisie first brought him home. Being based at Biggin Hill, he would often jump into his car when off duty and call in to invite the girls to the cinema or a drink down the pub.

'I certainly am, Mrs Caselton, and thank you again. In fact, I have something for you in the boot of my car.'

'But, David, you've already treated us all to a trip to the cinema.' Ruby was still humming the tune to *Strike Up the Band* the day after the trip to Erith Odeon, while young Freda was more than a little in love with the American movie star Mickey Rooney. Even with the worry that the Luftwaffe could have spoilt the evening with another bombing raid, they had enjoyed themselves. As it was, the film wasn't broken by an announcement to head for the public shelter, so there was even more cause to celebrate.

All in all, Ruby thought, the lead-up to Christmas 1940 had been a festive affair, considering that it was the second since the country had gone to war with Germany. She was still enjoying her part-time job in the staff kitchen at Woolworths. Her Eddie would have chuckled to see her working at her age, but she knew he would have approved. He'd never been one of those men who thought a woman's place was just to be at the beck and call of her husband. No doubt if he had still been with them, he'd have been helping out as an air-raid warden or doing his bit defending the town as a home guard. No, the Caseltons were not a family to shirk their responsibilities. He'd also have been proud of their Sarah getting back to work so soon after giving birth to Georgina, and of everyone who'd mucked in to help care for the baby. Why, even Georgina played her part in the war effort by being the most delightful child that ever had the grace to be placed on this earth. Vera from up the road agreed the child was a little angel, and she never usually voiced such positive opinions. She'd even looked after the baby when they all went to the cinema with David.

Ruby snapped out of her thoughts as David staggered back into the house carrying a large wicker hamper.

'My goodness, David. Whatever have you got there?'

'Just a few things from my mother, Mrs Caselton. She doesn't like to think of me eating you out of house and home when so much is rationed.'

'But where would she get all this when we have so much rationing?' Ruby asked. 'So sorry if I sound nosy, but I wouldn't like to think anyone was going without, like.'

'You're all right there, Mrs C. David's family won't go short – they've got acres of land,' Maisie announced, diving into the hamper and pulling out a large pork pie with a whoop. 'I haven't seen one of these for a while. A slice of pie and some of the pickle you put by before the war will go down a treat for Christmas night tea.'

'Oh my,' Ruby said as she spotted a goose wrapped in muslin nestling in straw at the bottom, surrounded by what looked like a plum pudding, a bottle of port and an iced cake. Apart from being overwhelmed by the thought of such a wonderful gift from people she'd never met, she was already worrying about how to cook the goose. It was a bird she'd never encountered before, apart from the gaggle that wandered in the yard of the farm where her daughter, Pat, lived with her farmhand husband. That's it, she thought with relief, I'll ask Pat when I pop down with the kids' Christmas boxes later. She must have cooked a few of the vicious buggers since she's lived there. 'Remind me, how are the pair of you related?' she asked Maisie and David.

'We're not blood relatives as such,' Maisie explained. 'David's mum and my Joe's dad were cousins.'

'Joe used to come to stay with us when we were kids and we kept in touch over the years. I looked him up again when I was based over this way and met Maisie just after they were married. When I heard about Joe, I searched out Maisie to offer my condolences. You could say the rest was history.' He glanced at Sarah and gave her a warm smile.

Ruby raised her eyebrows at what was explained

to her and Maisie noticed. 'David and my Joe were like chalk and cheese. However, David's family are the cream of the crop,' she said.

And Joe's mother, Doreen, was three-day-old sour milk, Ruby thought to herself.

Sarah and Maisie packed away the food and bottles, and tried to insist that David return the wicker hamper to his mother. He refused, saying that she had plenty and Sarah was delighted to be given it to store away some of Georgina's baby clothes. Space was at a premium at number thirteen with so many under the roof. Maureen, Sarah's mother-in-law, had insisted that Sarah use her house in nearby Crayford Road while she stayed with her sister, but Sarah preferred to live in Alexandra Road with her nan, so it had been rented to a local family whose own home was uninhabitable after the bombings.

David had to return to Biggin Hill. Sarah knew that his job didn't involve flying anymore, but as Ruby kept reminding them all that 'careless talk costs lives', she thought better than to ask him too much, even though she would have loved to know more about an RAF pilot's life so she could tell Georgina when she was older.

When Ruby went to visit her daughter, Pat, in nearby Slade Green, Sarah took the opportunity to speak to Maisie about something that had been playing on her mind since she'd met David. 'Maisie, do you mind awfully if I ask you something personal?'

Maisie could see that Sarah looked serious and sat down on the sofa, tucking her long legs beneath her. 'Ask away.'

'It's David. I feel such a fool for wondering but think it best we clear the air. I'd hate to fall out with you.'

'Blimey, this sounds serious. What do you want to know? I couldn't tell you exactly how much they've got in the coffers, but it's a fair amount,' Maisie laughed.

Sarah blushed. 'Goodness, no. It's nothing like that I wouldn't dream of asking such a thing,' she stammered.

Maisie hooted with laughter. 'Don't look so worried, you daft thing. I was 'aving a laugh with you.'

'Thank goodness for that.' Sarah smiled and took a deep breath before spilling out her thoughts. 'I've got myself so worked up about this I didn't realize you were joshing. The thing is ... well, I wondered if there was a chance that you and David would ever get together. I know you are good friends and I didn't want to tread on your toes.' At last she had said what had been on her mind for the past few weeks since she'd met David. There had been some warmth between them, and although he had yet to kiss her, she knew she wouldn't mind at all if he did. He'd reached for her hand in the cinema and his touch had thrilled her so much. However, if there was any chance at all that Maisie had designs on David, then she would back off and try not to feel disappointed. Her friendship with Maisie was worth too much to fall out over a man.

The smile had left Maisie's face as she listened to Sarah's question. 'David is a friend. Nothing more. I'm surprised you even felt the need to ask.

It's not a year since I lost Joe. I'm not sure I'll ever love another person like I loved my Joe. Perhaps you should be asking yourself the same question, Sarah. Your Alan may not even be dead and you seem to have erased any memories you 'ave of him.' She gave Sarah a withering look. 'Don't play games with David just because you're unhappy. He means a lot to me and I don't want to see him hurt.'

'But it's different for me. Your Joe loved you. Alan didn't love me. Not in the end.' Sarah was saddened that Maisie had been so sharp with her. Surely her friend knew how upset she had been that Alan had changed so much on his last visit home. It was still painful for her to think about last Christmas. Did Maisie expect her to be alone and never love again, just like Betty?

Maisie picked up a magazine and opened it. 'If you think that, then you're a fool, Sarah Gilbert.' She started to read her magazine. The conversation was at an end.

'It's lovely to see you back at work, Betty, even if it is for just a few days.' Sarah beamed at her boss as she leant against the door frame of Betty's old office. 'You'll see I've kept everything as it was before the accident.'

'It wasn't an accident, Sarah; it was enemy action that ended with many civilian deaths.'

Sarah closed the door quickly, looking behind her to make sure no one was in the corridor and had heard Betty's words. What happened at the Woolworths store was still shrouded in secrecy. No one spoke about it due to national security. 'I know that, Betty, but don't forget we have to be careful what we say,' she said kindly.

Two months on from the incident, Betty was still quite frail and having nightmares about what happened. Irene was taking good care of their friend, which had speeded up her recovery, but it would be a long time before she was the efficient Woolworths manager they all knew and loved. George and Irene had travelled up to Erith to join the family for Christmas and brought Betty with them. However much Betty insisted that she would prefer to move back into her own home, Irene intended to take her back to the West Country for another month of recovery. 'You're right, Sarah – I didn't think about the consequences. I must really get myself back to work before I forget everything.' She looked at the paperwork in front of her and ran her fingers through her hair distractedly. 'I just don't know where to start.'

Sarah, who'd had her own nightmares about her boss turning up and finding her staff had been slacking, had made sure that everything that needed doing in Betty's office was up to date and rubber-stamped. She realized that Betty was not yet ready to return to her full-time job but would humour her for now.

Sarah looked at her watch. 'Why don't you come down to the shop floor for a while? There are bound to be customers who want to say hello, and we still have staff from the Bexleyheath branch working here. I'm sure they'd like a word with you. We are closing on time tonight, as it's the tea party for the old soldiers. You know how much you enjoy playing the piano when we have a sing-song.'

Betty visibly brightened. 'I'd forgotten about the party. How strange it will be not to have Mr Benfield and so many of the old staff with us. Will Maureen Gilbert be joining us?'

Sarah shook her head. 'No, she's staying with her sister for now. She can't face Erith at the moment.' Sarah didn't add that she was relieved Maureen would be absent, as it reminded her so much of Alan and that was a part of her life she wished to forget. 'Let's get down to the shop floor, shall we? I'd also like your opinion on the window display.' Sarah led Betty from the office and towards the stairs. 'Do you recall the tinned snoek from last Christmas and how it tasted like rubber?'

Betty laughed. 'That wasn't one of our best window displays, but it sold well. I didn't stop to look when I came in, as the fog is starting to thicken.'

'Let's take a quick look now before it gets any worse. I hope we aren't in for a pea-souper.'

'At least it will keep the Luftwaffe away,' Betty shuddered.

'I don't know about that. Vera from up the road was saying how sometimes the crane drivers at the docks work above the fog. Seems it sits like a blanket and above it the skies are clear.'

'That's as may be, but the pilots still need to know where they are going, and if they can only see fog, they could be heading in the wrong direction,' Betty pointed out.

Sarah wasn't so sure it was as simple as that, but wasn't prepared to argue. Besides, she liked to think of the Luftwaffe heading in the wrong direction and not being able to drop their bombs. This would at least allow them to sleep in their own beds over Christmas, rather than spend the festivities in the Anderson shelter. The Caseltons would need a second shelter to accommodate everyone at number thirteen.

'This is delightful, Sarah. Well done. I particularly like the patriotic theme of red, white and blue on the little Christmas tree. Is it real?'

'Yes. It's Maureen's, and as she wasn't using it this year, we dug it up and planted it in a pot for the window;' Sarah replied, delighted that her boss liked their Christmas display. 'Can you see the chestnuts in the basket by the pretend open fire? We collected them from Frank's Park in the autumn. Freda made the cardboard fireplace with help from the Girl Guide troop.'

'It's magical,' Betty declared. 'The stockings hanging above the fire – are they Maisie's handiwork?'

'Yes. We are going to donate them to the cottage hospital on Christmas Eve for the children who can't go home for Christmas Day.'

'Magnificent. I shall write to head office and let them know how creative the staff of the Erith branch have been. Now, tell me, is there any chance that Freda will be returning to work for us anytime soon?'

Sarah opened the door for Betty and they returned inside the store. 'I don't think so. She sees it as her duty to the war effort.'

'My goodness. That girl never stops doing war work. She's an inspiration, what with the Girl Guides and the knitting she does to send out to the services. Look how she has shared her skills with all of us as well.'

'Freda still pops in to help when I'm on fire-watch duty, and she will be with us tonight for the old soldiers' party,' Sarah added. She too was constantly amazed at her young friend's stamina. She wasn't even fazed recently when a Christmas card had arrived from her brother, Lenny. Although Lenny didn't say where he was, both girls felt in their bones that he wasn't far away, and Freda at least knew he was safe, even though he was still hiding from the gang he had lied for.

Betty beamed as a customer recognized her and waved back across the store before adding, 'Freda is truly a Woolworths girl.'

The evening turned out to be a wonderful event. Even with the constant fear of bombing and thoughts of loved ones overseas, everyone pulled out all the stops to make it a memorable evening for the retired old soldiers. Sarah recognized many faces from the previous Woolies parties, and the men recognized her too. Some asked whether she was enjoying married life and she found a smile was easier than explaining about Alan. Irene and George were on babysitting duties and Ruby arrived accompanied by Maisie and David. All three rolled up their sleeves and joined in as a fish and chip supper was distributed. It had been Sarah's idea not to have the usual sandwiches and cakes. Due to rationing, they would not have been able to put on the usual grand spread, but fish and chips were not only plentiful but easier to prepare by staff members, leaving others to continue with fire watch and entertaining the guests.

Betty was soon seated behind the piano, accompanying Maisie as she belted out a rousing rendition of 'Bless 'Em All'.

As she finished her song, she grabbed Sarah by the hand and nodded to Betty, who started to play. After a faltering start Sarah soon lost her nervousness and sang. Around the room, the men put down their beer glasses and listened. Some were glassy-eyed and lost in memories as her sweet voice soared.

'...*and a nightingale sang in Berkeley Square.*'

The men cheered, and those who were able to got to their feet and applauded Sarah. She felt her cheeks start to glow with embarrassment and was grateful to David when he swept her into his arms as Betty started to play a waltz. Around them, others joined in and the party continued.

'I didn't know you could sing like that,' David said as he held her close.

'I don't often sing in public, but we have so few staff available to entertain the guests this year that it would have been churlish of me not to volunteer. We've had some lovely parties in years gone by.'

'This one seems perfect to me,' he said as he pulled her closer.

It felt good to be in the arms of a handsome man. She closed her eyes and enjoyed the feeling of being held and desired once more. She was oblivious to what was going on around her until the song finished and another started. Sarah froze, then pulled away from David.

'Is there something wrong, Sarah?' David

asked, showing concern.

Sarah could feel the blood pulsing through her body. If she wasn't careful, she would faint.

Around her, the old soldiers joined in with the song. *'If you were the only girl in the world...'*

It felt like only yesterday that Alan had pulled her onto his knee and serenaded her with the same song, when in fact it had been two years ago – Christmas 1938, when the country was not yet at war and she was falling in love with Alan.

'I'll be all right. I just need some water. I feel rather hot.' All Sarah wanted to do was run away from her memories. She needed to move on and forget that her dreams of living happily ever after with a man who loved her were not to be. She may have been in love, but she knew better now. Alan didn't feel the same. He showed that only too well last Christmas. She would always be saddened that Georgina would not know her daddy, but perhaps one day there would be a man she could look to as her second parent. Forget Alan, she told herself start a new life with Georgina. However, as much as she told herself to move on, the memories of her short, happy life with Alan just wouldn't stop haunting her.

David helped Sarah to a seat and returned with the drink she so desperately needed. 'How are you feeling?' he asked, after watching her sip the cool water.

'I'll be fine,' she assured him. 'Why don't you rescue Maisie from the old folk? I'm sure she would rather be dancing with you.'

David didn't need a second bidding and went to seek out Maisie, who was only too pleased to join him in a foxtrot round the staffroom floor.

All too soon the evening came to an end. Maisie and David accompanied Woolies staff as they took their guests home. By this time the fog was thick, and aided by the blackout, it was almost impossible to see a hand in front of their faces. The staff intended to see every last man to his front door. Sarah stayed behind to help Ruby and Betty clear up the remains of the party. It was as she was sweeping the floor around the piano that Betty put down the sheet music and faced Sarah.

'Sarah, I do hope you don't mind me asking you a question.'

'By all means, Betty. I don't have any secrets.'

Betty had a slight frown on her face and wouldn't make eye contact with Sarah. She seemed worried. 'Who is the man in the RAF uniform that you were dancing with?'

Sarah smiled. 'That's David Carlisle. He was a cousin of Maisie's husband, Joe. He will be joining us for dinner on Christmas Day. You'll like him.'

'I gather you like him, Sarah?'

'Oh yes, he's very nice. Nan likes him too. Even more since he delivered a hamper from his mother for us to celebrate Christmas in style.'

'I'm sure he is a very pleasant young man. What I mean is, do you like him in a specific way?'

Sarah felt her face grow warm. 'If you mean, am I stepping out with him, then the answer is no. However, if he should ask me, my answer will be that I'd be only too happy to.' She noticed Betty purse her lips into a thin line of disapproval. 'I no longer have a husband and can do as I wish. David would make a very suitable daddy for Georgina and she is now my only concern.'

Sarah flounced off to the cloakroom to find her coat, not allowing Betty to finish the conversation. From across the room Ruby raised her eyebrows in sympathy as she observed Betty Billington's discomfort. Betty had asked the very question that was playing on her own mind. Sarah's answer was not what she had wished to overhear.

'I haven't had a feed like that in a long while. You must have some good contacts, if you know what I mean?' Vera winked at Ruby.

Ruby bristled. 'I'll have you know that every morsel of food on my table was come by completely legit. If you thought that way, Vera, I'm surprised you even put one forkful of that goose in your mouth. David's mother very kindly sent me a hamper and I for one am very grateful. Now, who wants custard on their pudding?'

Vera slid her bowl forward. 'So, David, are you and Maisie courting?'

Maisie spluttered with laughter and grinned at David. 'Gawd love you, Vera. David's an old family friend. I'm sure he ain't interested in someone like me. No, it's our Sarah he's taken a shine to.'

A silence spread round the dining table. The only sound was Ruby spooning dollops of thick custard onto the bowls of plum pudding. 'Look out for the silver thruppenny bits,' she said, trying to break the ominous silence. 'I don't want anyone choking on 'em.'

'Did you hear the announcement on the radio that we were not to use them nickel thruppenny bits, as they can kill us?' Vera asked, her eyes like hawks as she surveyed those present. Something interesting was occurring and it was more important than any plum pudding or another slice of the tasty goose.

'More likely to choke someone than poison them, Vera,' George answered as he watched his daughter, who was looking down into her lap. 'They are a fair chunk of metal. Now, Vera, did you go to church this morning?'

'No, I didn't. I told the vicar that it didn't seem right not having any church bells ringing on Christmas Day. I bet that Hitler allowed bells to ring in Germany.' She snorted with disgust.

Freda smiled at the older woman. 'But, Vera, think how it would have frightened so many people if they'd heard the bells ringing out. They may have thought we were being invaded.'

'I'm sure even Hitler observes Christmas and won't send any planes over today,' Vera said.

'Even if he does, we can still enjoy Christmas in the Anderson shelter. Maisie helped me put up a few old decorations in there to make it look a bit more festive.'

Irene, who had seated herself next to the handsome airman and was oblivious to the rising tension round the table, patted his arm possessively. 'I know that if the opportunity was to arise, I would be more than proud to accept David into the family. Now, George, are you going to pour us all a drink so we can toast the King? It must be almost time for his speech.'

Sarah watched as her dad filled glasses and instructed Maisie on how to tune in the wireless.

She could feel Vera's eyes burning into her and knew that more than one person seated round the table was wondering what was going on in her life. She would not be ashamed of her growing friendship with David, whatever anyone thought.

'...*The future will be hard, but our feet are planted on the path of victory, and with the help of God we shall make our way to justice and to peace.*'

They all stood as the national anthem was played at the end of the King's speech.

George raised his glass as the last notes faded away. 'To absent friends.'

Ruby dabbed at her eyes and joined in the toast along with her family and friends. 'That was a lovely speech.'

'It's all right for them up there in London in their posh palace. I bet they aren't going short. They might have allowed us a few more ounces of tea and sugar for Christmas, but what they give with one hand they'll be taking away with the other when they cut the meat ration in a couple of weeks' time.'

'But, Vera, that is the government, not the Royal Family, and besides, we can all manage if we try really hard.'

Vera snorted. 'You'll believe anything they tell you, Ruby Caselton.'

Sarah felt stifled. She needed some fresh air, not that the patchy fog outside was very fresh. 'I think I'll go for a walk, if that's all right? I'll help with the washing-up when I get back.' Although she didn't wish for company, she would feel bad if she didn't at least ask if anyone wished to join her. 'Who else feels like stretching their legs?'

'I'll get started on the clearing up,' George replied. His leg wasn't up for a long walk yet, but he could manage standing at the sink in the scullery. Ruby started to rise to her feet. 'Sit yourself down, Mother, and have a rest. You've worked hard today to provide us with a feast. Why not open that bottle of port and have a glass or two with Vera and Irene?'

'I won't join you, if you don't mind?' Maisie said. 'My feet still ache from working late yesterday. I know it was festive and fun, but I'm fair whacked still, and Betty is almost asleep in her chair as well.'

'I must admit I am a little tired,' Betty said. 'I'll stay here and take care of Georgina. She has been a little star.'

'It'll be different next year. She'll be toddling and into everything, I've no doubt,' Ruby added, clucking over her great-granddaughter, who was gurgling happily in her pram.

'That's if we aren't all murdered in our beds by the Luftwaffe,' Vera chipped in somewhat gleefully.

Sarah pulled on her coat and gloves, and headed to the front door as the room erupted into laughter at Vera's comment. 'Trust you to cheer us all up,' she heard Maisie retort.

'Wait up.' Sarah turned at the gate to see David following her, pulling on his overcoat at the same time. 'You don't want to be out alone. It's getting dark, and this fog might be shifting, but visibility's not so good. Besides, I want to give you something.' He tucked Sarah's arm through his and they strode out at a brisk pace towards the river.

Sarah shuddered. 'It's rather spooky in the gloom, isn't it?' Out on the river, they could hear the mournful sound of ships' horns in the fog, as well as a bell ringing dolefully on a nearby buoy as it bobbed on the waves. Sarah leant on a wall and watched the waves lap against the small pier. 'I've always loved the Thames. When Dad brought me to see Nan and Granddad when I was a kid, we always came to the river. Sometimes we walked downstream to the marshes. It's lovely there in the summertime.'

'I'm sure it is,' David said, reaching into the pocket of his coat. 'I have a present for you. I wanted us to be alone when I gave it to you.' He handed her a small, square box.

Sarah pulled off her warm gloves and took the box from him. 'Thank you, David, but you shouldn't have done. The silk scarf you gave me was more than enough.'

David shrugged off her comment and encouraged her to open the box. 'It belonged to my grandmama. She told me I would know the right time to give it to someone special.'

Sarah lifted the lid and pulled back the small wad of cotton wool that lay underneath and gasped. 'David, I can't accept this. It's beautiful and must be so valuable.'

She ran her fingers over the small silver brooch in the shape of a bow that lay in the box. A row of pearls edged the delicate piece of jewellery. 'It's lovely,' she sighed.

David reached for the lapel of her coat and removed the brooch she'd pinned there to brighten it up for the festivities. 'As soon as I saw this, I knew that Grandmama's brooch would be the perfect replacement. No cheap glass jewellery for you, my love.' He pinned the silver-and-pearl bow to her coat.

Sarah could only gaze to where David had placed the other brooch on the wall beside them. She recalled so well the day she'd first seen the piece of jewellery when she opened a similar box and discovered with joy the brooch from Alan nestled inside. She slipped it into the pocket of her coat, suddenly feeling sad. She would share the memory with Georgina when she was older.

26

'Who'd have thought Woolies staff could have bought two Spitfires for the RAF?' Sarah said as she pinned the announcement to the wall of the staff canteen.

'What? Where will we put them?' Maisie snorted with laughter. 'I can't see them landing in the High Street.'

Sarah giggled. 'Don't be silly. Look, it says here that the donations we made from our pay packets each week have not only amounted to enough to buy one plane but that head office have matched the money and bought another one. It makes me proud to think that up in the sky somewhere are our planes fighting the enemy.' A faraway look appeared in her eyes.

Maisie stopped laughing as she saw the change

in her friend's expression. 'You still miss him, don't you?' she asked softly, placing her hand on Sarah's arm.

Sarah nodded. 'There will always be a place for Alan in my heart, but we married too quickly. We should have enjoyed falling in love with each other, rather than rushing into marriage. I know that now. "Marry in haste and repent at leisure" is what Nan would say. We should have waited and had a long courtship instead. That would have been best.' Then I'd have learnt that he didn't really love me, she thought to herself.

'But then you wouldn't have Georgina. Think how bleak our lives would be without yer beautiful daughter and how happy she has made Maureen.'

Sarah had to agree. 'It's lovely to see Maureen home again, even if it is only for a few weeks until someone else rents her house. She was almost back to her old self. Did you know that Betty asked her to consider moving back to Erith and working at Woolworths again?'

'Good for Betty. It would be great to have the old gang back together again.'

'I fear it is still too soon for Maureen. There are too many reminders of Alan in Erith. I'm sure she wouldn't be able to cope with that,' Sarah said.

'How about you? Doesn't Erith and Woolworths remind you of Alan?'

Sarah thought for a moment. 'I can live with it, but Maureen was his mum and that's a completely different kettle of fish. I've come to terms with what happened, but I doubt she ever will.'

Maisie frowned as she stepped aside to let fellow staff members read the poster. 'Does your "coming to terms" include David?'

Sarah tried to find the right words before she spoke. Since Maisie had made her feelings clear about Sarah and David courting, the subject had not been mentioned. 'I'm extremely fond of David. He dotes on Georgina, and I'm happy in his company.'

Maisie shrugged her shoulders and walked away to the counter to collect her tea.

Perhaps Maisie does have feelings for David, after all, Sarah thought as she collected her files from the table and headed back to the office.

'You look tired, Betty.'

Betty Billington looked up from where she was studying a staff rota. 'I'm just trying to rearrange the part-time rota now that the Bexleyheath store has reopened. I must say I'm pleased not to have to travel back and forth to the town now we've got the store up and running again.'

Sarah thought that Betty was still not completely well since the previous October when she was injured. 'A few nights when we can sleep right through without a raid would be handy.'

Betty nodded. 'I agree, but we must think of those who have lost loved ones and their homes.' She straightened herself in her chair. 'We shall carry on valiantly. After all, what is sleep?'

They both laughed.

'Now, Sarah, I was wondering if you would be able to work a few extra hours until I find more staff? Young Simon in the warehouse joined up last week, and I lost two girls who have gone off to join the Land Army. At times Woolworths seems to be like a sink, with so many of our staff vanishing down the plughole.'

Sarah thought for a moment. Of late she felt as though she was being pulled in so many different directions. As a mother, her duties lay with her young daughter, but then she needed to work and Betty relied on her support. She also liked to help out at number thirteen, as Nan was on her feet all day, not only caring for Georgina but also putting in a few hours at Woolies working in the staff canteen. Nan was doing too much and the strain was starting to show. Then there was David. He'd been a constant visitor to the house and wanted to take her out and have some time together. He had grumbled on more than one occasion that they never had enough time alone. He was good with Georgina, and when the weather was fine, they would tuck her up warmly in her pram and head out for long walks, though Sarah was always aware that there could be an air raid at any time and worried they wouldn't reach a shelter.

Their few outings together had been to the cinema, where David would hold her hand as they sat watching the film. She enjoyed his kisses at the front door as he said goodnight, but was aware he was growing more demanding. Why was she holding back when she admired David and thought of him as a suitable replacement father for her daughter? Was she waiting for the heady magic she had felt when she was with Alan, or was that too much to wish for? Her duty to Georgina came first. She felt so muddled.

'I'm not sure, Betty. It would mean Nan having Georgina for more hours and I don't like to put on her too much. She's no spring chicken, as Maisie would say.'

'I appreciate that, Sarah. Ruby has been a saint these past months. I mustn't take advantage of her generosity.'

'If it's only for a while until you find more staff, we may be able to call on Maureen Gilbert, but it would depend on how she feels, what with Alan no longer being here. I fear she wouldn't be strong enough to cope at the moment.'

'I know you mean well, but I don't feel that it would be fair for her to see you walking out with David Carlisle. I've seen him meet you at the staff door on a few occasions and it could be upsetting for her. After all, you are still married to her son.'

Sarah took a deep breath. She was fed up with people poking their noses into her business. 'Betty, it's none of Maureen's business who I am seen with. As for David, I like him and I have to think of the future. I don't want to end up a dried-up old maid living alone after my daughter has grown up.'

As the words left her mouth, Sarah knew she had said the wrong thing. She could see the hurt on Betty's face. 'Betty, I'm so sorry. I didn't mean what I said. It's just that I don't know what to do anymore.' Sarah sat on the chair opposite Betty and lay her head in her hands. 'It's all such a mess,' she sobbed.

Betty reached into the top drawer of her desk and pulled out a clean white cotton handkerchief. She left her seat and knelt beside her friend. 'There now, cry as much as you like. I'm not a fool. I've been watching you and know that you are deeply unhappy and have been since Alan last came home. Even then you seemed unsettled.'

Sarah took the handkerchief and sniffed into it but couldn't bring herself to speak. She was deeply ashamed of what she'd said. Betty was a good friend and didn't deserve her unkind words.

'Sarah, did something happen for you to feel this way? I don't mean Alan going missing, but before that?'

Sarah nodded. Taking a deep breath, she explained about the way Alan spoke to her and how she feared that being a Spitfire pilot had changed him, as he was so distant when he last came home.

'He couldn't have been distant all the time,' Betty added, raising her eyebrows.

Sarah blushed before continuing. 'But then he never replied to my letters when I wrote about the baby, so he must have hated the idea.'

Betty was silent for a while. 'I thought you'd heard from Alan. I swear I heard Maureen talking about it when she was working in the staff canteen.'

Sarah looked shame-faced. 'I'm sorry. I lied. I didn't want Maureen to worry.'

Betty patted her shoulder. 'This war has a lot to answer for. If it's any consolation, I'd have most likely done the same thing. We never want to see our loved ones suffer.' She rose to her feet. 'What a pickle.'

Sarah nodded. It felt good to have shared her problems with someone. 'I'm sorry, Betty. I always seem to be crying in your office.'

'And think back to why you were crying and what happened afterwards?'

Sarah smiled. 'I was crying because of Alan. He used to call me "Sixpenny" because we met in Woolies.'

Betty smiled. 'And where was Alan...?'

'Outside in the corridor, and you sent him in to me.'

'Yes, and shortly after we had a lovely wedding. Sarah, that man loved you to distraction. It warmed my heart to see you together, and that doesn't happen often to this dried-up old maid.' She laughed. She raised her hand as Sarah went to apologize. 'Now, does anyone else know of this?'

'Only Nan.'

'Let's leave it like that, shall we? But I need to know how you feel about David Carlisle. He is a very nice man and doesn't need to be led along by a young woman who doesn't know her own feelings. It would be unfair of you to be with someone you didn't love. I'm assuming this would have been the end result of this liaison?'

'Nothing's happened, if that's what you meant.'

'I really don't wish to know, Sarah, but knowing your parents and grandmother so well, I know that you have been brought up to respect yourself enough not to do anything that would bring shame to yourself and your family.'

'I would never do that, Betty.' Her friend could be old-fashioned in her words sometimes, but she was right.

'I have also noticed that someone else is an admirer of Mr Carlisle.'

'You mean Maisie? I thought so too, but she denied it.'

Betty nodded wisely. 'Time will tell. Now, the way I see it, you need to tell this young man how you truly feel; then perhaps you can carry on with your life without failing those you love.'

'I'll do that, Betty.' Sarah rose to her feet. 'He's meeting me after work and taking me for a drink. I'll do my best to tell him how I feel. I'll speak to Maureen as well and ask her if she feels up to coming back to work for a while. You never know, I may just have got that wrong as well. I'll be back later tonight, as I'm on fire-watch duty.'

Sarah spent the afternoon helping out on the household goods counter. She loved to serve the customers, and although her promotion to assistant manager brought with it added responsibility and a welcome pay rise, she knew that if it was her choice, she would sooner work on a counter all day long. It was while wrapping up a saucepan that she recalled Alan proposing to her on the spot where she was standing. Oh, Alan, I do miss you, she thought to herself. Perhaps Betty was right, but still, deep down, she was fearful that Alan had changed too much on his last home leave to be the man she thought of as her husband. Whatever had happened to him, perhaps she should forget Alan the Spitfire pilot and remember Alan the assistant manager from Woolworths. She would always be his Sixpenny Sarah.

David was in high spirits as they walked the short distance to the Prince of Wales. After leading Sarah to a table in a quiet part of the pub, he went to collect their drinks. 'No gin, I'm afraid, so I got you a pale ale.'

Sarah nodded. She didn't like strong drink at the best of times and one could last her all evening. 'David, I have something to tell you.'

'Me first. I have some news.'

'But–'

He raised his hand to stop her speaking. 'No buts – this is important. I'm going away for a while and want to put my cards on the table before I leave. You must know that I'm extremely fond of you, Sarah.'

Sarah's heart skipped a beat. It was time she explained her feelings to David. 'David, please–'

'Let me finish, Sarah.' David reached across the table and took her hand. 'When I return, I thought we could put our friendship on a more formal footing. I would like to court you properly, if I may?'

Sarah pulled away. 'David, please listen to me. I discovered something today. I still love Alan.' She suddenly recalled the happiness in Woolworths when he proposed and then her twenty-first birthday, when, despite the start of war, they had been married. 'I know that Alan is most likely dead, but I will love him until the day I die whatever he thought of me. I want to be able to think of our few months together with joy, and that would not be fair to you or any other man I married. However, I do feel there is another woman for you. Whatever our Maisie says, she does care for you, David, and would make a much better wife for you than I ever could.'

David looked sad. 'I do care for you Sarah, but I understand. You must be sure, though. You do realize it will be a long time to live with just a memory?'

Sarah squeezed his hand. 'I'll always think of you fondly, David, but for me there will only ever be Alan. Whatever happened to him, I do hope his thoughts were of his family and what might have been. Our last days together were not as good as they could have been, but a good friend told me not to dwell on that.'

David showed interest. 'You never did tell me about Alan's last days. I only knew he was missing, presumed dead. It didn't seem right to pry when I was almost walking out with his wife.'

For the next half-hour Sarah explained to David how distant Alan had been on his last trip home and then what had happened when the RAF officers had arrived with the news that her husband was missing. 'By then I was sure that he didn't love me, as he had never even answered my letters about our baby.'

David frowned. 'It doesn't sound right. I'm not at liberty to tell you about my duties in the RAF, but I may be able to make some enquiries. Do you trust me to do this?'

'Oh, David, that would be wonderful. I don't know how to thank you. I know that Alan has gone from me, but to know something more would bring some peace to us all.'

'Then leave it with me. It may take time, but be assured that I'll do my best for you.'

Sarah felt a heavy weight lift from her heart. 'There's something else I want you to do for me.'

'By all means. What is it?'

'Keep in touch with Maisie. Please don't give

401

up with her. I know she cares for you.'

'Do you really think so? She said–' He stopped mid-speech realizing what he had said. 'That is so ungallant of me. Please don't think that I was attracted to you because Maisie had rejected me.'

Sarah laughed at his discomfort. 'Oh, David, I do love you – but only as a kind of brother. Maisie loved her Joe, but I know my friend well. She is a different person when you are around. I'm not sure yet if she knows of her own feelings for you, but I'd lay money on her realizing one day soon.'

He leant across the table and kissed her cheek. 'Then I'll hang around.'

'Please do, and think of number thirteen as your home whenever you are in this part of the country. There will always be a place for you at our table. Now, I must get home and see my young daughter before she forgets what her mummy looks like. I'm on fire watch later tonight, along with Maisie, so perhaps you'd like to escort two ladies home afterwards?'

'It would be my pleasure. I'll come along early and help you man the stirrup pumps if things get hairy.'

Sarah shuddered. 'Please don't tempt fate.'

'Quick, over here!' Sarah shouted out to Maisie. 'We need more water if we don't want the store to go up in flames.'

Maisie struggled over to a flat part of the roof, balancing two buckets of water, to where Sarah and another staff member were valiantly working the stirrup pumps to dampen down burning debris as it landed on the roof. 'Blooming 'eck, this is the worst it's ever been. It looks as though half the town has copped it. Where's a fire-tender when you need one?'

Sarah stretched her aching back, using the back of her hand to wipe the sweat and smoke stains from her forehead beneath the tin helmet that Woolies provided for staff to wear when undertaking firefighting duties. 'It looks as though the worst of the fire is in the direction of Burndept's. I would think that's where the fire service is right now. We'll just have to make the best of a bad situation.'

Maisie ducked as a flurry of orange sparks flew overhead. 'Are you sure there aren't any incendiary bombs being dropped?'

'Not that many. The enemy seem to have gone straight for the factories down the road, but that's just as bad for us. The wind's blowing the embers and smoke in this direction. What's happening downstairs?'

'I've got four people filling buckets in the staffroom kitchen and running them to the bottom of the ladder. We're taking turns carrying them up here to the roof. I'll 'ave muscles bigger than a navvy's by the time the fire's out.'

If we put the fire out, Sarah thought to herself. It was fortunate that staff were still in the building when the bombing raid started. Thank goodness for Betty, who, realizing that factories had been hit nearby, decided to ask for volunteers to check the store. Every person had left the safety of the cellar and started to put out the small fires on the roof and in the surrounding street.

'It's going to be a long night, Maisie. I just hope

everyone is safe in the shelter at home... Can you remember what shift Freda was on at Burndept's?'

'Oh my God, I think she was on the two-to-ten shift. That means she could be caught up in that.' Maisie pointed to where a glow in the night sky was all that could be seen of the large factory.

Sarah handed her the stirrup pump. 'Take over here and I'll see what's happening in the store. David said he would walk us home, so he may just be downstairs with some news. I'll send up a couple more people to help. It looks as though it's going to take a while before everything subsides.' In the distance, they could see searchlights piercing the black sky, while further down river, the sound of ack-ack guns could be heard.

Climbing down the ladder and in through the staffroom window, she bumped into David. 'I was just on my way up to give you a hand. It looks like a busy night out there. How are you coping?'

'We're just about on top of things, but it's Freda we're worried about. She would have been working a shift this evening and may be caught up in the fire. Do you know if she made it back to number thirteen?'

'I was there not half an hour ago. Everyone is safe, but Freda isn't home. I should go and look for her.' He peered through the open window to where the glow of the burning building lit up the night sky.

'Wait. I don't think you should go alone.'

'I'm not taking you. It's too dangerous and you have a child to think about.'

Sarah wanted to stay and help Betty. It was her duty as assistant manager to look after the staff.

'I can't leave Woolworths while it's at risk. I'll get someone to help you.' She quickly climbed back through the window and up the ladder to where Maisie was supervising the stirrup-pump operation. 'Maisie, I need your help,' she called as she beckoned to her friend to follow her.

Maisie was behind Sarah by the time she climbed back through the window. 'Blimey, this going up and down ladders isn't much of a lark.'

David took her arm as she staggered into the room. 'I need your help, Maisie.'

Maisie blushed bright red, pulling off her tin helmet and trying to straighten her hair, oblivious to a large black smut on her nose. 'Hello, David. What's the problem?'

'I'm going to find Freda and I need your help. Sarah won't let me go on my own.' He grinned.

'Right, I'm your woman. Just wait while I grab me coat and we'll get cracking,' Maisie said.

Sarah reached for David's arm. 'Take care of her, David. She's not as tough as she pretends to be.'

David squeezed her hand. 'She will be safe with me, Sarah. I'll treat her like a precious jewel.'

It was past midnight when Sarah reached number thirteen. She'd convinced Betty to come back with her, as Alexandra Road was closer than Betty's home. They were tired, hungry and extremely dirty, but more than anything else they were worried about Freda. 'No news is good news,' Betty had told Sarah as they stumbled along the dark street by only the light of a torch.

'I just wish someone had thought to tell us what

has happened,' Sarah muttered. She was annoyed with David and Maisie that they'd not thought to stop off at Woolworths and give them an update on Freda. For all they knew, she could have died in the fire. She tried to keep her dark thoughts from surfacing as they closed the door and made sure the blackout curtain was in place before switching on the light. They could hear voices in the front room but thought it best to go through to the scullery and wash off the worst of the grime first.

Sarah scrubbed her face and arms as well as she could, with Betty pointing out any bits she'd missed. They'd done their best at Woolworths to clean themselves, but with the water pressure low and other staff wishing to clean their smoke-stained faces and hands, they'd decided to finish cleaning themselves up at number thirteen.

Sarah put on the kettle as Betty dried herself. 'That's a grand idea. I could kill for a hot drink,' Betty said.

'It's only cocoa. We're a bit short on tea at the moment,' Sarah apologized.

'That suits me down to the ground. There's nothing better before bed than a cup of cocoa. Shall I go see if anyone else would like one?'

'That's a good idea, Betty. I'm surprised Nan hasn't been out to see us yet.'

Sarah placed cups and saucers onto a tray. She followed behind Betty into the front room, almost crashing into her back when Betty stopped suddenly with an 'Oh my gosh!' Betty then tried to stop Sarah entering the room.

'Whatever is wrong, Betty? Let me in – this

tray's heavy.'

'Come in, the pair of you, and don't be so daft,' Maisie called out.

'Well, if you're sure,' Betty said in a surprised voice.

They both entered the room to find Maisie sitting on David's lap. Her usually perfectly applied lipstick was smeared, and David had loosened his tie. Betty looked between Sarah and the couple with trepidation.

'Is this what I think it is?' Sarah grinned.

'I thought you'd be angry, Sarah. That's why I tried to stop you coming into the room.' Betty sat down on the sofa. 'I'm somewhat confused.'

Sarah placed the tray onto a side table. 'There's no need to be confused, Betty. David and I had a little chat earlier today. You could say I made him see sense, although I never expected this. Let me get the cocoa and you can tell us everything that happened since you set off to find Freda.'

'So no one was killed at Burndept's? I find that amazing,' Betty said as they sipped the last of the cocoa.

By now they knew that Freda was tucked up in bed none the worse for her experience, although it seemed her hair got singed when she dashed back into the building to help an elderly colleague. Maisie had promised to give her a trim the next morning. 'The poor kid was more distressed that she didn't have a job anymore.'

'But she has. I've already said I'd have her back at Woolworths in a shot, so if she is willing, and when she is over the shock, she can have her old job back,' Betty said.

'Is tomorrow too soon?' a quiet voice said from the doorway. 'I heard voices and wanted to check that you were all in one piece. We heard that people were trying to put out fires in the town as we walked home.'

'That's where we found Freda,' Maisie added. 'She was at the top end of the High Street 'elping her workmates get home. We went with her to make sure they were all safe, then got her home to her bed. It's been a long day.'

Betty patted the seat next to her on the sofa. 'Come and sit down, Freda.'

Freda sat down, refusing the cocoa that Sarah offered to make for her. Nelson trotted along behind her. The dog had taken to creeping onto her bed at night and had been woken by the people talking downstairs. 'I just want to know what you've all been talking about. Have I missed anything?'

'For a start, David has asked me to marry him,' Maisie declared to her stunned friends. She gazed at their dumb-struck faces. 'There's no need to look like that. Seeing the destruction in the town this evening made us realize that life could be cut short at any moment. David had already told me about yer little chat, Sarah. He'd said how he felt about me, but as there was no chance of us getting together, he had buried his feelings. Tonight those feeling came tumbling out.'

David, who had kept quiet and let Maisie talk, said, 'It seems that when Maisie saw us together, Sarah, it made her aware of how she felt about me.'

'Please don't think that I'll ever forget my Joe. He was a big part of my life. With David and Joe growing up together, it seems natural for us to become close. We have shared memories.'

'I'm so pleased for you both,' Sarah said, and rushed over to hug them. 'So when is the wedding to be?'

'Soon. We thought the end of June would be lovely.'

'That is only two months away,' Betty said. 'Does it have to be so soon?'

'There is a war on,' the three girls said together, and burst out laughing.

'Well, that was a day and a half and no mistake,' Vera said as she followed Ruby up the path of number thirteen and waited for her friend to unlock the door. 'I've not tasted ice cream in a while. How did they come by it?'

'I've no idea, Vera. I thought it was very good of Woolworths to treat their staff and customers to ice cream after they all worked together to put out the fire the night that Burndept's burnt down. All I want now is to put me feet up for a while. I'm fair shattered. Spending half the night in the shelter hasn't helped none.'

'It's time you gave up that job at Woolworths. You're far too old to be doing things like that. Your Eddie would turn in his grave if he was here.'

Ruby tried not to laugh at Vera's words, but in a way she knew the woman was right. She was finding it tiring to care for baby Georgina, who was now a lively eight months old, and also do her shifts at the shop. The girls mucked in when they could, but with Freda back working at Woolies, it meant Ruby no longer had her around in the daytime to help in between her shifts. There was talk of Maureen moving back to Erith, so perhaps she would resume her job in the Woolworths staff canteen? Ruby decided to have a word with her next time she came to visit her granddaughter. Yes, she'd do just that.

Ruby sat down to take of her shoes. 'Stick the kettle on, Vera. I'll find us something to eat in a minute.' She rubbed her feet and yawned. Hopefully it would be quiet tonight and she could catch up on her sleep. Her eyelids started to droop. Perhaps just five minutes...

'Ruby!'

Ruby woke with a start. Whatever was wrong with Vera? She stepped into her slippers and hurried to the kitchen, where hopefully Vera had a brew on the go. She pulled up sharp as she saw that Vera was not alone. 'Lenny, whatever are you doing here?'

They hadn't seen Freda's brother since he'd run away the previous summer. Ruby had hoped the lad would take himself back to prison, but it wasn't to be. He looked the worse for wear, his face dirty and his clothes torn. Lenny kept looking over his shoulder towards the door.

'Sorry, Ruby. I heard a noise at the back door and thought it was Nelson wanting to come back in. The lad rushed in as if the devil was after him. He smells a bit.'

'Have you been living rough, lad?' Ruby asked.

'The boy's fine. I've been taking good care of

him. Haven't I, Lenny?'

A tall man with dark hair slicked back from his face and wearing a grey striped suit stepped in through the open door. He was wrapping a silk handkerchief round his left hand, which was dripping with blood. 'You'll find your dog shut in the Anderson shelter, Mrs Caselton. He's not a friendly chap, is he?' he said in a broad Birmingham accent.

'He's good to his friends. You must be Tommy Whiffen. What are you doing here where you ain't wanted?' Ruby asked, wondering if his two sidekicks were about.

Tommy kicked the door closed and turned the key in the lock. That answered her question. He was alone. 'You could say you have something that I want, Ruby.'

'Mrs Caselton to you, sonny.'

'Now, now, Ruby. There's no need to be un-friendly. The lad here told me as how you have some information about my business dealings. I'll be taking it off you and be going on my way.'

'There's nothing here that concerns you. Now, be off before the rest of my family get home.' She looked at the clock on the mantelpiece in the living room behind her, praying that Maisie and Freda clocked off on time at Woolworths and would be home soon to help. Thank goodness Sarah had baby Georgina and had gone to queue at the butcher's for something for their tea. She didn't want the baby hurt, and there was no knowing what this bloke could get up to.

'I'll go when you give me the papers,' Tommy sneered, gazing around the room.

411

'Ruby, who is this man?' Vera asked fearfully.

'This, Vera, is Tommy Whiffen, a small-time crook who got Freda's brother here to carry the can for him when the lad had done no wrong.' She turned to face Tommy. 'I said I ain't got nothing for yer, so get out of my house.'

'That's not strictly true, now, Ruby, is it? Lenny told me what he had written down for you.'

Ruby gasped. How could the lad have been so stupid?

'I'm sorry, Mrs Caselton. Tommy found out where I was and wanted to take me back 'ome to help him with some more of his work. He said if I didn't, he knew where Freda lived and would come and hurt her.'

Ruby sneered at the tall man. 'By "work" I assume you mean more robbing, or perhaps killing another night watchman?'

Vera gasped as Tommy raised a hand to hit Ruby. Lenny stepped between them. 'I thought that if I told Tommy how we had everything in writing, and we'd give it to the coppers if he hurt Freda, he would go away and leave us alone.'

Ruby thought the lad was foolish to have said what he had, but at the end of the day he was only thinking of his sister's safety. 'There's nothing here for you. I got rid of it all.'

'I don't believe you, old woman.' Tommy pushed Ruby to one side. She staggered against the cooker.

He headed towards the sideboard in the living room, where he pulled open drawers and tipped the contents onto the floor as he looked for anything that resembled handwritten notes. In anger he swept his arm across the top of the sideboard, sending Ruby's treasured photo of her Eddie crashing to the floor. Ruby felt anger swell up inside her. No one came into her home uninvited and destroyed her property. She looked around her and spied the large iron frying pan on the hob. Grasping the handle, she crept up behind the man, then roared like a lion as she swung the pan into the air and down onto his head. Tommy crumpled to the floor just as she heard a key turn in the front door.

'What the hell is going on here?' Maisie exclaimed as she entered the room, followed by Freda and David.

'Let me introduce you to Tommy Whiffen,' Ruby said as she examined the dent in her best pan. 'Maisie, you'll find some washing line in the cupboard under the stairs. I think we'd best tie this chap up before he comes to. Freda, would you run down to the police station and leave a message for Sergeant Jackson? Tell him that the man I told him about is at this moment being trussed up like a turkey in my living room.'

Freda looked puzzled. 'But we didn't go to the police. Lenny ran away, so we didn't bother.'

'Aw, you told the coppers, Mrs Caselton,' Lenny said, looking miserable.

'Yes, Lenny, I told the coppers. Something you won't understand yet, because you are too young, is that we collect good friends as we go through life. Sergeant Jackson has known my family since he was a nipper. I knew I could trust him, so after you ran away I went to ask his advice and I showed him what you and your sister had written down about this nasty so-and-so.' She tapped Tommy Whiffen with her foot. 'So pin a smile on your face, because I reckon before too long you can stop looking over your shoulder. I reckon you've learnt your lesson. Vera, close your mouth – you look like a goldfish. Is there any chance of that cuppa we promised ourselves a while ago?'

Freda burst into tears and hugged her brother.

'David, you might want to let Nelson out of the Anderson shelter before he howls his head off then I'll tell you all about it.'

Sarah arrived as Tommy Whiffen was being taken away, protesting loudly that Ruby had tried to kill him. She pushed the pram into the hall and picked up her daughter. 'It looks as though you've all been busy while I was out.'

Sergeant Jackson nodded to Sarah. He'd known her since she was a baby, having gone to school with her dad. 'I'm just going to take Lenny down to the station to tie up some loose ends, Mrs Caselton,' he called up the stairs to Ruby.

David saw them to the door and came back to where Sarah was standing in confusion. 'It's been a little hectic here this past hour. We've made your nan have a lie-down for a little while. She's exhausted.' Sarah went to go upstairs, but he held her back. 'Let her be for now, Sarah. Vera and the girls are tidying up. Would you like to come into the front room with me for some privacy?'

Sarah frowned. 'Privacy?'

'I have some news about Alan.'

Sarah knew the day had to come when Alan's death would be confirmed. She followed David into the front room, clutching Georgina close to her chest. She allowed David to help her to a seat and soothed the baby as she murmured in her sleep. 'It's bad news, isn't it?' she asked fearfully.

David knelt in front of Sarah and looked into her eyes. 'It's good news, Sarah. Alan is alive.'

27

'Well, the sun certainly shines on the righteous,' Vera said, before biting into a salmon sandwich. 'I must say they've put on a good spread.'

Ruby could only agree. The bride had looked radiant in her ivory silk gown as she'd walked down the aisle towards her handsome husband in his smart RAF uniform. Beams of sunlight had shone through stained-glass windows as they'd spoken their vows. In attendance had been her granddaughter, Sarah, and Freda. Young Lenny, now a free man, dressed in a new suit, sat in the pew proudly watching his sister. The two bridesmaids looked pretty in pale pink, carrying flowers grown in Irene and George's garden, which had been carefully transported up from Devon the day before. Even little Georgina wore a matching gown, though she sat on her granny Irene's lap gurgling contentedly.

Ruby was pleased to be able to meet David's parents and thank them for the Christmas hamper. They seemed a decent lot considering their posh accents. It had been David's mother who'd insisted on taking charge of the wedding breakfast in the absence of Maisie's relatives. Even a wedding couldn't mend a broken family. It had been a proud moment when Ruby watched George walk Maisie down the aisle to give her away. He was recovering well from his injury, although there would always be a slight limp. Things could always have been worse, she thought to herself.

The wedding reception was being held in the hall of the Prince of Wales. Mrs Carlisle had suggested a local hotel, but Maisie insisted that the pub had played an important part in the lives of her and her friends, and she wanted to hold the reception in the large hall at the back of the building. Colleagues from Woolworths were there to help celebrate their friend's happiness, including Maureen, who had returned to Erith when they heard that Alan had not perished while serving his country. Even Hitler had managed not to upset the proceedings by sending his planes to the wedding.

'Fancy another sandwich?' Vera asked as she rose to her feet.

'Not for me, thank you, Vera. I'm going outside to get a bit of fresh air before the band starts playing. Maureen's going to sing a special song for Maisie and I don't want to miss that.'

She headed out into the small garden, where the landlord had placed a few benches for the guests. Although early evening, it was still warm and she fanned herself with her handbag. It would be stifling once they had to close the doors and the blackout curtains were in place. She closed her eyes and enjoyed the warmth of the sun on her face.

Ruby heard the band starting to play and then Maureen's voice as she serenaded the happy couple. '...*I found a million-dollar baby in a five-and-ten-cent store.*' She smiled to herself. The song was about a five-and-ten-cent store. In America, that was what they called the Woolworths stores. Maureen was so clever to think of that song. She hummed along to the tune as David took Maisie into his arms for their first dance as a married couple.

Through the open door, Ruby could see Sarah, with Georgina in her arms, swaying in time to the music. The happiness was catching and Ruby found herself humming along to the tune until there was a tap on her shoulder. 'Can I have the next dance, Mrs Caselton?'

Ruby turned in shock as she recognized Alan's voice. 'Oh my goodness. Alan, it's you. After all this time.' She was trembling violently with the shock and Alan led her back to the bench she had vacated to watch Maureen sing. She reached out and touched the young man to make sure he was really there. Alan kissed her cheek. 'Does your mum know you're home? What about Sarah?'

Alan laughed. 'Mum knew I'd be here. I wrote to her as I wanted her to do something for me. I swore her to secrecy.'

'No wonder she's had such a grin on her face today. Why didn't she say something?'

'I asked her to keep it a secret.'

'She's certainly done that. I'm all of a fluster. Go in and see Sarah. She's just inside the hall holding your daughter, Georgina.'

417

Alan stepped towards the door to look at the wife he hadn't seen for over a year and the daughter he'd yet to meet. He turned back to Ruby. 'Would you mind sending her out to me – and not telling anyone else?'

Ruby nodded and went into the hall. Alan watched as she whispered into Sarah's ear and took the baby from her. Sarah left the dance floor and walked into the sunshine, looking around to see why her nan had sent her out.

'Sarah?'

'Alan? Oh my God, Alan!' She rushed into his arms and he held her close, breathing in her familiar scent, scarcely believing he was home once more. He took her by the arm and walked her to the side of the building, not wanting anyone to know he was there until he had time alone with his wife.

'Why didn't you tell me you were coming home today?' Sarah asked when she had gathered herself together after the shock.

'I wasn't sure. There's been so much debriefing, people to talk to, and I've not been back in England very long.'

'I don't understand. I've not seen you in eighteen months...' She looked at his face for the first time. There were a few lines around his eyes. His cheeks were thinner. 'What happened to you, Alan? Did you know you would be going away from us when we last met?'

'I think we'd better sit down. It's a long story.' He led her to a low wall that surrounded the garden. They sat close together.

'I thought you didn't love me anymore. My

letters were never answered. You were so distant ... different, even.'

Alan gazed out across the garden, deep in thought.

'Alan, please tell me what happened.'

'I knew I was going away that last Christmas we had together. I knew it would be dangerous. I would have told you if I could, but you know the rules. It was just too much for me seeing everyone so happy and coping with the war and having to walk away from you all and return to God knows what.'

'I should have realized. I was just being selfish. I'm not a very good wife, am I?'

Alan turned to her almost in anger. 'Don't ever say that. I couldn't have done half of what you've managed in these past months and coped with what you've all been through. Then you were alone with our daughter and I should have been there for you. I didn't even see your letters through some God-awful mess-up at HQ. If only I'd seen them, I would have known we had a daughter. Can you ever forgive me?' He took both her hands in his and looked at her. She could see in his eyes that he was begging for forgiveness.

Sarah pulled her hands away. 'It is me who should be asking for forgiveness. Alan, I almost left you for another man.'

Alan looked away. 'I know. David told me.'

'You spoke to David?'

'Yes. He was instrumental in getting me back to England. He was able to pull quite a few strings. He has friends in pretty high places.'

'Back to England? Where were you?'

'In France. I was supposed to drop some people behind enemy lines, but we were shot down. If it wasn't for the French Resistance, I wouldn't be here now. They hid us for months. It was touch and go at times. I feared I would never see you again.'

'Thank goodness David could help. Wherever you were, we all wanted you back. I didn't love him, Alan. Nothing happened between us. He truly loves Maisie.'

'I wouldn't have blamed you if something had happened. This war is playing hell with so many people's lives. If I hadn't been such a bore that Christmas, then our parting would have been easier.'

'No, Alan. I think perhaps being so angry with you made me stronger.'

He stroked her cheek. 'So where do we go from here?'

She sighed. 'I want the old Alan back. Is he still there? I don't think I could stand it if I lost him again.'

Alan pulled Sarah to her feet. 'Come, let me prove it.' He led her inside the hall, only stopping to hug his daughter before heading towards the dance floor, where Maureen was still singing with the band. Her face lit up as she spotted her son. She nodded as he waved his hand.

'Ladies and gentlemen, please indulge a very happy mother as she welcomes back her son.'

To loud cheers from everyone in the hall, Alan opened his arms. 'Dance with me, Sixpenny?'

The band started to play and Maureen sang a familiar song.

'Goodnight, sweetheart...'

'My goodness, Alan, it's the song we danced to at the Woolworths Christmas party.'

Maureen sang on. *'...Goodnight, sweetheart...'*

'Did you think I'd forget?' he whispered in her ear.

The crowd on the dance floor parted as the young couple, oblivious to their surroundings, relived the night Alan had first held Sarah in his arms.

Reaching into his pocket, he pulled out a thin silver chain with a small coin attached to it and placed it round her neck.

Maureen wiped a tear from her eye. Her son was home and safe. It was hard for her to keep singing. *'...Goodnight, sweetheart...'*

'Oh, it's a sixpence. A silver sixpence.'

'... Goodnight, sweetheart, goodnight.'

'Can I walk you home, Sixpenny?'

'Yes, please, Alan.'

Acknowledgements

There are so many people to thank who helped me make the writing of *The Woolworths Girls* more than just an idea. First, I would like to thank my agent, Caroline Sheldon, who, faced with a few notes jotted on a single sheet of paper, decided to take a chance on me. To then be accepted by Pan Macmillan and have my lovely editor, Natasha Harding, and her colleagues guide me through to publication day is a dream beyond belief. Thank you all.

The London Borough of Bexley, where Erith now resides, has a marvellous archive, and staff not only share local images and stories online but contribute to Erith Facebook groups as well. I've lost count of the number of times an image or story has fired my imagination or clarified a point about the town where I was born and grew up – and where the Caselton family resides in *The Woolworths Girls*. It is a joy to belong to these cyber groups, and the number of members shows how fond people still are for the area where Sarah and her family lived during the Second World War, even though time and town planning have all but removed the area that we fondly remember.

My work was made much easier by the discovery of the Woolworths Museum (www.woolworthsmuseum.co.uk) and the information found there. I cannot thank Mr Paul Seaton, curator of the online museum, enough for the detailed information he supplied me with about Erith Woolworths and the staff who worked there during the Second World War. He helped to bring the store alive and made it a place where I could place my girls safe in the knowledge they would become true Woolworths workers.

Support and feedback are important to all writers and I'm lucky to have so many supportive friends who also write and are there to help chew over a problem when it occurs. Students and friends at The Write Place in Dartford, Kent, where I run my writing classes, are a talented bunch and always ready to help when the going gets tough. We support each other. Special thanks to Natalie Kleinman for her proofreading skills and Nats Nits!

I'm sure that my path to this day would not have happened if it were not for the Romantic Novelists' Association. Although already an established writer, I was able to join their New Writers' Scheme as my writing had been in short fiction, features and non-fiction books. The knowledge shared so generously by so many well-known authors and the friendships gained since my membership are worth more than all the tea in China.

Author's Note

If only I'd known that my first Saturday job would lead me to write this book, I'd have taken notes! Yes, I was a Woolworths girl, just like Sarah, Freda and Maisie. It was 1969, I was fifteen and three months, studying for my O-levels, and like most girls my age, I found that I was able to apply for my National Insurance card and a Saturday job.

I lived in Slade Green, Kent, at the time, which is a village between Erith and Dartford. If only I'd applied for my job in Erith, I'd have had my own 'inside information' on the Woolies branch featured in *The Woolworths Girls*, as the store where Sarah and her friends worked was still standing at that time (the original Woolworths was replaced by a more modern store in the early seventies after a fire). Instead, I followed my school chums to Dartford to a much larger store. There, I learnt what it meant to be employed by F. W. Woolworth. I learnt what each bell that resounded through the store at regular intervals meant. I yearned for the tea break and lunchtime bells, although the 'shop closed' bell was the sweetest sound of the day. I learnt we would be told off if we shortened our green overalls or wore too much lipstick. I found out that waist-length hair had to be rolled into a bun and hidden inside a net when working on the biscuit counter and not to volunteer for the vegetable counter in the dead of winter, as muddy potatoes contained worms and other creepy things.

I was moved to the electrical counter, where I had to measure out lengths of cable from rolls above my head, and to this day have a mental blank when it comes to wiring a plug. We also sold light bulbs. Each one had to be tested before being placed into a brown paper bag and handed to the customer. Testing meant inserting the bulb into a box and turning it so that it came alight. Some didn't; some shattered. I dreaded a customer asking for a light bulb and would do anything not to be the staff member who served them.

Looking back, I know I was fortunate to have my first experience of work at Woolies. Where else would I have sharpened my skills with mental arithmetic? We had to add up every item on a notepad tied to the waistband of our overalls. I learnt how to count change back into a customer's hand and help them pack the items they purchased into their shopping bags. It was all part of the service. I learnt that whatever my feelings, the customer was always right, and by pinning a smile to my face, quite often even the most annoying customer remained pleasant. I learnt that keeping busy meant that the day passed more quickly, so when not selling orange buckets and rubber plugs for the bath, I would take my feather duster and dust the rolls of toilet paper stacked on glass-fronted shelves. I learnt not to question my superiors, as they had more experience than I did and had chosen a career in Woolworths, whereas for me, it was the first step on my pathway to full-time employment elsewhere.

At the end of my working day, I would queue with fellow workers to sign for my brown paper pay packet and check the contents. One pound minus thruppence for my National Insurance stamp. I was rich!

Never, in the many years since, have I worked for a company that instilled such strict work ethics into its staff or inspired such happy memories for both employees and customers. So when writing my book about a group of friends and setting it in the memorable town of Erith, there was nowhere better than Woolworths for the girls to spend their working life, to fall in love and to experience the Second World War.

I grew up knowing Erith Woolies. It was where, as a child, I bought my mum and dad's birthday and Christmas presents. It was where I purchased pens and notebooks for school, and my first stockings and then tights when I was a teenager. Mum even bought my first bra at Woolworths. So many happy memories of times long gone.

However, my memory doesn't reach back to the Second World War. For information on this period, I went to the Woolworths Museum on-line. Contacting Mr Paul Seaton brought forth not only his own memories of the area but stories of the people working at Woolies during the war and what they did to help the war effort. Who knew that the staff at Erith helped out when the nearby Bexleyheath branch was devastated by enemy action, or that like the tragedy that occurred at Bethnal Green Underground Station, it was kept secret for the purposes of morale? The locals knew how to keep quiet back then. Careless talk could well have cost lives!

As the writing of this book continued, I was surprised how many friends and family told me they too had been Woolworths girls and had fond recollections of their time working in the UK version of the five-and-ten-cent store. We all share so many happy memories thanks to F. W. Woolworth.

The publishers hope that this book has given you enjoyable reading. Large Print Books are especially designed to be as easy to see and hold as possible. If you wish a complete list of our books please ask at your local library or write directly to:

Magna Large Print Books
Magna House, Long Preston,
Skipton, North Yorkshire.
BD23 4ND

This Large Print Book for the partially sighted, who cannot read normal print, is published under the auspices of

THE ULVERSCROFT FOUNDATION